Praise for D. Z. Church's
Perfidia

"In Church's debut thriller...Church manages, quite impressively, to maintain a sense of hidden but perpetual threat...Overpowering dread and a leery protagonist make this a suspenseful read."

—*Kirkus Reviews*

Perfidia

D. Z. Church

Bodie Blue Books
Alameda Monterey

Cover design: Bodie Blue Books

ISBN:0998329711
ISBN-13: 978-0-9983297-1-0

Dedication

To my parents:
Margaret and Lester

Contents

Late August 1974

MY FATHER, DEL LASSITER, is a handsome man in his early fifties. Dark hair shot through with gray, blue eyes coupled with a nice easy smile that makes him the darling of all his female acquaintances whom he dates prodigiously but never marries. My girlfriends all adore him, especially my best friend, Gail. When he pours his honeyed-peanut voice over them, they swoon.

A week ago on Saturday, his home office phone rang long after midnight. He padded on bare feet to answer his 1950s vintage telephone. I listened to the soft drone of his voice for ten minutes by the clock on my nightstand. He hung up and dialed again. I realized by the tenor of his voice, he was talking to a woman. I drifted off. He was gone when I woke, leaving behind only a Del like note: *Family business, see you soon.*

I was used to Del's notes. He disappeared semi-frequently. When he was gone, I missed his sunny side-up-ness. But in all those notes, he had never mentioned family. If you had asked me, I would have sworn I had none. Twenty-seven strikes me as late in life to spring family on your daughter.

I had been born, as near as I could figure, near New Orleans on a plantation with a perfectly manicured lawn surrounded by flower beds over which a gardener toiled daily. I had no memory of a mother. Whenever I'd ask, Del would repeat that he found me *'long side a Loosiana highway just pas' some four corners or somethin' with yo' li'l ol' gator.* Then, he would pat me on my curly brown-haired head.

My memories were gauzy at best. I remember running full tilt down an old gravelly path into my dad's arms when he returned from some large buildings where he worked some distance from the big old clapboard house. When he was at work, a soft lady with a funny accent who smelled like gardenias and carried handkerchiefs embroidered with little yellow roses took care of me. Later, when I asked about her, he answered that *ol' gal, she weren't no lady, she were yo' nanny, hon.*

In 1953, when I was six, my dad stuffed me in our big gray Dodge something or other, drove down the lane under the oaks then turned left then right away from the plantation. We rattled west through heat filled days; car windows cranked down, dust dropping a patina on the clothes hanging from a pole across the back seat. Beneath the clothes, the backseat brimmed with plastic encased scorpions and tarantulas purchased at reptile farms across the desert southwest. My three-foot stuffed alligator, Bontemps, took up the floor. The trip felt like it took all six of my years.

The Dodge stopped in Bakersfield, California for reasons unknown. Stopped, as in wouldn't start. Del took it as a sign. Highway 99 splits Bakersfield into two halves and Stockdale Road (Brundage on the east) into quarters. All of the street names change at that axis, so everyone knows by your street address which quadrant you call home. He bought a postwar ranch in the northeast, in an old section that backs up to the Kern River, which is an arroyo seco much of the year.

From six on, there was only the two of us. We took care of each other, always, Del holding me, blowing on my skinned knees and handing me Kleenex as I missed all of my proms.

In true Southern gentleman style, he told me frequently that he didn't understand why a little gal like me needed to be a teacher when I had a fine dowry. These words came from the same man that taught me to sail, shoot, hike miles with a heavy pack in rocky terrain, and fix my car, starting each lesson with *jus' in case*. Sometimes, he would call me Sonny,

Del took to California, particularly Hollywood. He worked his way through the motion picture industry until, with money withdrawn from his retirement savings, he became the producer of a little movie that almost won an Oscar. Now, he produces.

I downed a glass of milk as I checked the thermometer nailed to the eave outside the kitchen window. At six forty-five, the temperature was eighty and climbing. I went out in the hazy summer Saturday morning to mow the lawn in my lawn mowing armor of dark blue short shorts and bright yellow tee-shirt, no bra underneath.

The grass was still wet from an early morning sprinkling. My reel mower masticated rather than cut the blades leaving little, chewed pieces in its wake. Grass stuck to my bare ankles. I pushed my freshly sharpened reel mower through the lawn planning the fall curriculum for my third-grade class to get Del's open-ended note about the family I didn't have off my mind. It didn't work. I began to wonder if the woman he called the night he left might not be a member of the family I didn't have.

At eight, my neighbor set out a television tray table and a folding chair on her cracked cement driveway. She marched a professional looking sign to the curb to announce her annual end-of-summer garage sale held every second to last Saturday of August since she and her husband had moved in twenty years ago. This second to last Saturday was no different. We exchanged waves.

I put the handle of the mower to my hips to force the blades through a dense growth of grass. I always mowed left to right then up and down. I had ever since Del first assigned lawn-mowing duty to me. I was thirteen that summer, discovering boys at a time when I was just plump enough that they were waiting for my baby fat to disappear. Del would say in his slurry New Orleans way: *Boys gonna come runnin' when they see how you're gonna fix on up.*

Much to his disappointment fourteen years later, we still shared this house, and those boys never did come running unless you counted third-grade boys with whom I was ever so popular. No matter how delicate the neighbors were about my status, I was an old maid school teacher, though not that old.

I slapped at a red ant harvesting on my bare ankle. As I scratched, a nondescript gray sedan parked at the curb in front of my neighbor's house. Two men, one white, one black, both in gray suits climbed out of the car. They walked in step up my neighbor's driveway, looking not in the least interested in her assortment of junk.

I kneeled to wipe wet grass from the lawnmower blades keeping one eye on the men speaking to my neighbor. She pointed towards me. They waded across the lawn leaving perfect footprints in my freshly mown grass. White shirts, black ties, polished shoes, one suit coat button buttoned, they looked like the very cliché of FBI agents.

The white man pulled a slim black case from the inside breast pocket of his suit coat and flashed a badge under my nose. I craned my neck forward but missed his ID. He tucked the case back where he had found it.

"Olivia Lassiter?" he asked. "Jack Price, DEA."

My neighbor sat a little straighter in her chair, one ear cocked my way. People stopped rummaging her racks for bargains, their finds hanging limply in their hands. A woman in short shorts held a leopard-print bustier across her chest to check the fit. I stared at my sixty-year-old widowed neighbor in awe, thinking the things you don't know about the people closest to you.

"Perhaps we should talk inside." Price gestured to the house.

The men continued through the wet grass to the front door, their pant cuffs darkening from the water. I followed them wishing I had a bra on under my sleeveless yellow tee-shirt. I even considered a dash across the grass to grab the bustier.

Mr. Price held the door open for me. The house has a classic open the front door, kitchen to the right, dining room through it, living room straight ahead, four bedrooms down the hall floorplan. The master bedroom had an ensuite bathroom. My bathroom was sandwiched between two of the bedrooms. In the entry, I slipped off my black canvas skimmers. The men hesitated as if wondering whether to follow suit.

"Dirty," I said, setting my shoes on a metal tray to keep the water off of the oak planking. They didn't take the hint.

We studied each other for a moment before Mr. Price asked, "You are Del Lassiter's daughter?"

I'd like to pretend the DEA hadn't been to our front door before, but they had. The drugs wouldn't be Del's this time any more than they were the last time.

I ran my hands down the flanks of my cotton shorts, wondering which of Del's army of actor friends the DEA had hauled in for questioning about some drug related thing or another. The note Del left made more sense now. It no doubt referred to his Hollywood family, the strange people who lived on the edge of glamor, which would explain everything. I knew of at least three people for whom Del would currently provide alibi or cover.

I waved this set of agents into the dark, clutter of the living room.

The room wasn't big, yet Del had managed to stuff it with robust furniture upholstered in a chintz print that dazzled with plumeria. The same print covered Del's overstuffed swivel chair and ottoman. The heavy drapes over the picture window bore palm fronds on a deep green background. Light filtering through the drapes landed on walls painted rainforest green and on the green shag carpet.

By walking through the galley kitchen, the jungle could be avoided. I'd been avoiding the room for years. When I was about ten, I swear a cat snarled in there…a big one, like my imagination.

"Sit down?" the black agent said. He spoke with a soft, almost British accent that made me notice him. He was a warm coffee brown with, I could swear, hazel eyes. When he smiled, it unnerved me.

I shifted my gaze to Mr. Price, who was altogether very white and very ordinary despite eyebrows that ran without a break above cesspool eyes.

"Has Del gotten himself in with the wrong crowd?" I joked, sitting in the overstuffed chair.

Mr. Price cleared his throat. "We have reason to believe that your father is involved in a drug running operation."

"Can I see your identification again?" I held out my hand.

Mr. Law stepped down into the room. He was tall, a wee elegant, with movement like a Swiss clock. As he approached, he took an ID wallet identical to the one Price had shown me out of the breast pocket of his jacket. He handed it to me. I took the card wallet in both hands, flipping the black leather flap open with my right thumb. The ID was the real thing. At least the badge looked like the last one I'd seen.

"How well do you know his family?" Law loomed over me. Uncomfortable, I scrambled out of Del's chair, pulling my shorts down from where they had crept. Law watched.

Caught off guard by his hazel eyes, I stuttered, "His co-producer, well enough. I can get you his address and two others he is very close to but past that Del maintains his privacy.

"No, Miss Lassiter, his family—cousins actually." Law tapped his fingers on his ID case. He had beautiful slender fingers, more the pianist type than drug enforcement. He noticed me watching his hands and stopped tapping. A soft grin worked its way across his face.

Distracted, I stumbled over my words, "I have no family, just Del, well, I do remember a plump, soft southern woman, my nanny. No one else."

"There was never just Del," Price said curtly, clipping his words. "How long ago did you leave New Orleans?"

Price remained in the entry. He surveyed the long hall to his right, the kitchen and breakfast room to his left while I obsessed over his pronunciation of New Orleans. He wasn't American.

"I didn't say we left New Orleans; I mentioned the South. Surely how long we've lived here or there doesn't matter?"

Price was tall, perhaps six feet. Law had three inches on him.

"It's pertinent," Price said, a bit gruffly, making me feel better about their identity. The last two DEA agents had pushed their way into the house, flashed a search warrant then ransacked Del's office. Not these guys.

"How possibly?"

"Ties him to the family business," Law answered in his just off British accent.

"So, what do you want to know from me?"

"Has your father ever discussed the operation or how he fences the drugs?" Price's eyes roved over my head while images of producers, directors, and actors tramped through my mind.

"What does he drive?" Law asked.

Price began his move to the kitchen doorway. I ran to block him.

"A Jaguar, green."

"New?" Price asked trying to weasel past my block. I had one hand on each side of the door jamb, my body planted in the middle.

"Not very. Not very paid for either."

"Does he have a safe in the house?" Price pushed me out of his way. Law followed. I followed in his shadow.

"Why would I know *that* when I don't even know I have relatives? Tell me about my cousins," I said to their backs.

Price waved the comment off. "Miss Lassiter, we're talking about pirates, plain, old-fashioned pirates. There is nothing nice about these people."

I snorted. Pirates! Law narrowed his startling eyes trying to translate my snort into words. Finally, he snickered.

"Miss Lassiter, we're here because Aaron Law-Maddock, your cousin, was found like flotsam on a beach in Barbados. Last seen, your father was carrying Maddock's body ashore," Price said.

I checked the fat, round porcelain pig pitcher on the kitchen counter to cover my shock. When I did speak, I sputtered, "My father makes movies. The only thing he is guilty of is the occasional poor choice in industry friends! I want you to leave."

I skirted them then shooed them toward the front door.

"We have a search warrant." Price fumbled in his suit coat. He handed the folded document to me for my inspection.

Del was on business. Del was, well, Del. I wanted to believe he wasn't involved in drugs. I wanted to believe he wasn't a pirate, well sort of, but I'm pretty shabby at faith sometimes. I locked on his sudden trips to scout movie locations, his location shoots in far-flung parts of the world for months on end, and all that opportunity. These men had awakened thoughts I'd harbored about my father all of my life. But why had I?

"I'm calling my lawyer."

They began their search the moment I walked down the hall to my office in the spare bedroom to use my private line. I dialed my treasured black dial telephone, the kind that had weight in the receiver. The kind you could use on an intruder's head. One blow would bring a man to his knees, thump.

When the receptionist answered, I asked for Gail Kazarian. My best friend since first grade, we had been inseparable through all her boyfriends, all her breakups, and all through school right up until she went to Hastings School of Law. I went to California State University Bakersfield. She came right back home. We picked up where we left off, except that she was a lawyer, and I was a teacher.

When I heard her voice, I said, "I have a pair of DEA agents in my living room. They have a search warrant."

"You didn't let them search, did you?" When I didn't answer, she added, "Bloody hell, no! I'm on my way. Don't let them leave!"

The line went dead. I stared at the receiver until Mr. Law walked into my office. I backed him into the hallway closing my office door behind me.

They had used the time efficiently to search, one in Del's bedroom, one in Del's office. As I walked in on Price, he slid something from the surface of Del's desk into the right front pocket of his slacks.

Law held a key flat in the palm of his hand. "We found this safety deposit key in an envelope in your father's desk."

"I don't know where he banked," I lied. Law raised one artful eyebrow.

"We do," Price responded, making it clear that the bank would be their next stop.

"I called my lawyer, she's on her way. Ms. Kazarian told me not to let you leave. I don't think you should take anything with you either."

Law palmed the key. I tried to cut them off at the door, but they outflanked me through the kitchen. Next thing, they were on their way to the bank.

They had the warrant. I had opened the door. There is a special place in hell for family members that stupid.

I got to the window just as the gray sedan pulled away from the curb. I knew Gail would ask if they had taken anything. So I searched. The only thing in Del's bedroom that looked remotely disturbed was one corner of his bedspread. I lifted the mattress, wondering if, instead of finding something, they had deposited something. They had not.

I crossed through the arched opening to Del's adjoining office. Hen-scratched notes stuck to the drawers peppered the interior of Del's antique oak roll top desk. Three Mont Blanc pens rested next to bottles of ink. Paper money was crammed into the middle drawer as though he had emptied his pockets into it each night. I straightened the bills so that the amounts were in matching corners then counted. Who keeps five hundred dollars in crinkled bills in a desk drawer? Apparently, Del.

Shoved under the hanging cubby-holes, I found a black-framed picture of me in a starchy white dress in front of the huge old house from my grainy Southern childhood. By the lack of fingerprints at the corners of the glass, it hadn't been moved since it was framed.

The desk contained nothing new to me, except the crumpled money and photograph, nothing to hint at where he had gone or of any value to the DEA. I searched every corner of his office, finding no other note from Del, or anything Law or Price had added or subtracted.

Back at my desk, I hefted the receiver of my telephone and dialed information. I wrote the number provided by the operator on a little pad I kept by the phone. I called the DEA. They did have agents in Kern County given the drug trade and the number of labs in the remote areas. However, no one had been dispatched to Del's nor were there any active investigations involving anyone named Del Lassiter.

Through my bedroom window, I watched Gail park her Corvette, top-down, under a massive Raywood Ash tree filled with black-hooded juncos. Spurred to stop the juncos from raining poop onto her cherry red paint, I tore out of my shorts and into natural linen pants and an off-white tank top. I threw on my favorite multi-colored huaraches and was at the door with my cavernous, black leather hobo purse over my shoulder by the time Gail knocked.

I yelled to her that the DEA had taken the safe deposit key. She spun in her tracks racing back to her car, flapping her hands at a junco perched on her black and white leather tuck-and-roll.

By the time we arrived at the main bank, my chin length brown hair was in unrecoverable knots. We strode across the marble floor, my huaraches flapping, Gail's heels beating a tattoo, to the safe deposit officer's desk. Gail had thought far enough ahead to bring what Del called his *jus' in case* papers.

Gail is small, black-haired and blue-eyed with an hour-glass figure. She is just darling enough that most women hate her on sight. She plays up her looks with expensive haircuts, trips to the manicurist, and pricey lawyer clothes. I am taller, though never tall enough for me, athletic in an almost boyish way. I wear teacher clothes, the kind of clothes that eight-year-olds are comfortable around, mom clothes, I guess.

We navigated the safe deposit counter quickly thanks to Gail's foresight in bringing the power of attorney papers, which somehow she and Del had worked out to be good at presentation if Gail was with me. The clerk led us down a hall, through a barred door, to a private carrel then left us. He returned pushing a large stainless steel box on a cart that thumped on off-kilter wheels.

We stared at the safe deposit box for several minutes until Gail whispered, "You sure you want to do this? Del will be home soon. Maybe you don't want to know what's in there. I mean, it is in a safe deposit box for a reason."

Del rented the largest safe deposit box the bank offered, big enough to hold a pretty good stash of cocaine. I unlocked the box. It was so overstuffed that Del's .45 caliber semiautomatic jumped into my hand the moment I lifted the lid. Del used the gun for target practice, insisting that I, too, become comfortable with its use. I checked to make sure the clip was out. His license to carry was under the gun.

A photograph of a young woman in a mid-1940s maternity blouse was beneath the gun license. She appeared to be twelve months pregnant. Beneath the picture, there was a death certificate for a Lassiter Harris, who I had to believe was the woman in the photograph particularly after Gail and I deciphered the cause of her demise—me. I had purportedly been born to a Lassiter and Chamberlin Harris on my correct birthday in Iberia Parish Louisiana. My mother died two days later.

"I wonder who Chamberlin Harris is." Gail fingered the picture. "Maybe Del did find you at the intersection of two gravel roads on a levee in the bayou. Maybe your real father abandoned you at that great big ol' plantation?" She didn't quite have Del down but as impressions went hers wasn't bad.

"What kind of a name is Stella Harris?" I held the birth certificate to the light so I could read the signatures only to discover my father's handwriting cruising across the line labeled father. As days went, this one had been a dilly, and the sun hadn't reached the yardarm of one of Price's pirate ships

"You'll always be my Olivia." Gail held out a hand for the certificate then held the document so close to her eyes I expected her to whip out a jeweler's loupe. "Stella Harris is spare, but it suits you."

Sometimes, Gail's bluntness exceeded her ability to apologize. I objected with a huff, "My passport says Olivia Lassiter as plain as day in regulation letters and everything."

Gail tilted her head, appraising my general state of being. "Olivia Lassiter—Lassiter Harris. That can't be coincidental. How did you get your passport?"

"Del always took care of getting both his and mine."

Gail stared at me with her carnelian lips pursed. "Del took care of it? How?"

"We went the Post Office. I had my picture taken. He filled out the form. I signed. He took it to the passport teller. That's how."

"You'd have to have a birth certificate with Olivia Lassiter on it or no go."

"Del took care of it." Tired of the conversation, I fingered the next item in the box, a soft, velvety ring box of the usual size.

"I wonder how he did it."

"Why could it possibly matter? I have a driver's license. I'm a licensed teacher. I have a passport. All of them read the same!" I snapped.

I bypassed the ring box, a flat square jewelry box, and a velvet bag in the dash to the bottom of the bin. There, in a nine-by-twelve-inch leather folder about an half-inch thick tied with a gross grain ribbon, we uncovered eighteen million dollars in recently drawn bearer bonds.

Gail fanned the lower right corners of the considerable stash. "Look at the dates on these." She fanned the bonds again. "They are all drawn recently from Barclays Bank in Bridgetown, Barbados. You're rich!"

"It must be for a new film. Bonds would be easy to transport."

Gail pursed her lips and narrowed her eyes, leaving me with the feeling that she was building Del's defense.

My nervous fingers worked the velvet drawstring bag. There was something long, bumpy, and hard inside. I couldn't resist. I unknotted the thin velvet drawstring, put a finger in and wiggled the neck of the bag open. Gail watched as an ancient key, bronze with an ornately scrolled finger-hold, a five-inch shaft, and long, split pins fell into my hand. I jammed the key back in the velvet bag then the velvet bag into my hobo purse. I planned to hang the artful key in my bedroom next to a feathered swagger stick Del had given me with a swish of my shoulder and a story of India during the Raj.

Gail opened the velvet ring box we skipped in our thirst for the buried treasure at the bottom of the box. It held what must have been my mother's wedding diamond. We both ogled the ring. Gail had the good sense to tilt the band so that we could read the engraving on the inside: *to my bonnie, Lassi.*

I slipped the ring on my ring finger. The diamond shot blue light into the room. I waggled my fingers. Gail batted one set of perfectly manicured carnelian-polished fake fingernails at the reflected light bobbing on the wall.

Tired of the game, I put the ring back in its box. Once the small ring case was in the safe deposit box, I opened the flat, square jewelry case perhaps eight-by-eight inches on a side. Our eyes must have been all whites, like old eggs freshly cracked in a frying pan. Coddled in blue satin was a necklace of pearls and rubies, two pearls then a ruby and so on. A large teardrop-shaped twenty karat ruby pendant surrounded by emeralds, the emeralds by pearls, pulsed heart-like from the center of the box.

Gail took a deep breath that reminded me to do the same. I snapped the lid shut and returned the box to its former position in the safe deposit box on top of the bonds.

"There is a story here, Liv," Gail said, "Such riches, riches like you imagine on Spanish galleons. I was reading about pirates last night, Blackbeard's crowd to be exact."

I replaced everything that remained, including the .45 with its pearl handle, in the safe deposit box, jammed the lid down, locked the box, and removed the key. I hung my hobo bag over my right shoulder ready to leave.

"So many pirates."

"So little time." Gail gave a Mae West laugh, followed by a sassy swivel of her hips then went to find the clerk. As we left the bank building, a gray sedan parked several cars down from Gail's Corvette. Price and Law—where had they been?

GAIL DROPPED ME OFF at the house. Once inside, I opened Del's wall safe hidden behind an oil painting that had been hanging on that exact spot on the wall since the day after we moved into the house. I placed the velvet bag with the key in the safe followed by a quick check for the papers Del kept in it. The house insurance and the deed were there, as expected.

Done checking, I went out into the now ninety-nine-degree day to finish mowing. I raked the cut grass. I edged the walks and driveway. I collected the grass in bags for the garbage man on Monday. I kept expecting Del to roar into the driveway, rush to the house and pour a gin tonic as he did every evening when he was in town. I tried rubbing the tire marks from his Jaguar out of the drive with my broom. But, no matter how I tried I couldn't make this day real.

I was still scrubbing when a white sedan parked at the curb. A magnetized sign stuck to the side read *Courier*. The driver, in a neat black suit, handed me a manila envelope with the hasp flattened under cellophane tape. I acknowledged that I was Olivia Lassiter. He requested my driver's license forcing me to make a quick trip to the entryway. He followed me, checked my ID, handed me a clipboard then pointed where I should sign.

As the courier drove off, I read the return address: *Perfidia, St. Philip, Barbados*. Wherever and whatever that was, the envelope had begun its travel to me three days earlier. I ripped off the tape then pinched the hasp open. A single sheet of folded paper was inside. I slid the sheet out. On the topside of the fold was a poorly drawn picture of something reminiscent of a circular staircase with bats. I turned the sheet over. A curvy letter P in a fancy typeface occupied the upper left corner of what appeared to be a note card.

I flipped the card open. In Del's imprecise, poor, pointy cursive, the note read: *Hey, darlin', by now you and Gail have been to the safe deposit box. Bring the key. By the way, I found you somethin' goin' to make you go all weak in the knees. It's what you need, Liv. Come on, girl!* He even wrote with a Southern accent.

I had a gyroscope once. I played with the thing constantly until I realized that when the gyroscope began to oscillate out of control, there was nothing I could do to intervene. I felt like that now, as though my only option was to let things go until they crashed to a nasty, bumpy halt. I sat on the driveway letting the hot cement warm the chill I felt.

I hugged my knees and rocked on my hips until the garage sale folks began to point and whisper. I put the note back in the big envelope then put the envelope on the front stoop. It must have cost hundreds of dollars to send. I suppose the expense underscored Del's desire for me to drop everything to bring him the key.

Whether I stayed or went, I needed to return the lawn tools to the garage. As I went about my chore, Del's voice nagged at me: *You're takin' this life thing way to serious, Liv. Sooner or later you gotta do one thing that don't make no dam' sense.* From the time I was twelve, my father found me predictable, dull, unattractive, over read, under-dated and, did I mention, dull. *It's what you need, Liv.*

The telephone was ringing. I trotted into the house quick enough to answer the extension in Del's office. A soft baritone with a touch of British said, "Miss Lassiter, this is Brendan Whitelaw. Our office represents your father in Bridgetown. I'm calling to ask if anyone has contacted you concerning your father's affairs."

"He was having affairs!"

"Sorry. His business affairs. Legal matters. I'm with Parradine and Whitelaw. He left us your number."

"My number?"

He began to speak very slowly as though to the hard of hearing or slightly daft, leaning heavily toward daft. "Telephone number. Your address. That sort of thing. You see, he's gone missing."

"Missing? The DEA didn't mention it while they were here?"

"There?"

Who sounded daft now?

"They told me that a cousin drowned. I don't have any cousins." My eyes drifted to the painting that disguised the wall safe. The painting was of the stone front of a house, its entrance graced by a shower of red flowers dangling from a tangle of branches on a massive old tree.

"Well, yes, Aaron is dead."

I fingered the thickly administered oil paint. "What's going on?"

"Aaron's death may have to do with a ship that grounded off Perfidia, the White Lady. Did your father ever mention the boat?"

"He never mentioned we had family, why would he mention some old boat." I sounded testy, but who wouldn't when faced with a dead cousin, a new name, a missing father, and profound, previously unknown riches.

"Not some old boat, the White Lady. She belonged to the deBancos of Pendu...in Columbia. Rumors hit the chop immediately."

"Rumors? DeBancos?"

"Drugs. That sort of thing. The White Lady was yar, could carry a bit of illegal below boards. She was hulled in the accident. Authorities found nothing." The staccato of a skilled typist clicked over the long distance line. "I don't suppose you would consider coming to Barbados? With Del gone missing, we may not be able to move forward without you."

The background clack of the keyboard produced a syncopated rhythm. Whoever was typing was fast and sure, surer than I was about almost anything at the moment.

"Mr. Whitelaw, I haven't got a clue what is going on or where Del is. He never spoke to me of relatives. In fact, he led me to believe he found me along the side of the road and stole me from some gators."

"Alligators?"

"A New Orleans thing," I said rather more N'awleans then not.

He cleared his throat but uttered nothing for a count of thirty. When he did speak, his voice was quiet, "If I were you, I would come."

I was picking at the thick strokes of oil on the painting, trying to decide if I'd been threatened or beckoned.

"Let me know when you arrive, better still give me the flight number I'll see that someone meets you."

When the line went dead, I went to Del's desk. I broke open the lock on the lower left file drawer sure that Price had pocketed the key. They had been back.

This bit of petty larceny was the reason we beat them to the bank. I knew what they found in the drawer, the combination to the wall safe—the one I had just been in, the one that carried nothing of greater portent than house papers and now the very key that Del had summoned. I took the velvet bag from the safe and stuffed it in my hobo bag.

Teacher in-services started next week during which the newest changes in the curriculum were introduced, a week later I would have eight-year-olds waiting for me whose older siblings had sung my praises. I was considered to be an excellent teacher by my peers. I was a sensible, single woman of an age when sensibility was about all I had to offer. I wasn't about to hightail it to this Perfidia, St. Philip, Barbados without thought and research.

I parked my trusty little gray and orange Gremlin in the shade of a big Amur Maple in the library lot then rolled the windows down an inch so the afternoon heat wouldn't crack the windshield. I bounced up the stairs to the library, went directly to the card file seeking books on Barbados and, for fun, pirates. I gathered books then settled at a lovely little carrel with a view of an ash tree. If I got bored, I could watch the tree grow. I ran a finger down the index in the first book until it came to the word Perfidia. I did the same with each book.

Perfidia appeared in Bajan history in the mid-1690s. The first reference was recorded slave sales to the Drax of Drax Hall, the first sugar plantation on Barbados established in the 1650s. After 1700, there were frequent references to Perfidia in regards to the sugar trade. She survived the great hurricane of 1831 which pretty well flattened most of the plantations in Barbados, leaving a count of only five. She nearly didn't last the regime of one Crispin St. John (pronounced Sinjin) Law, who made profligate into a verb. According to the books, Perfidia only survived through the emancipation in 1800 and general changes in the law of the land because of a Steadfast White. Records indicated that White may or may not have been Crispin's half-brother.

Later in the same century, the then master of Perfidia, Collier Law, gave his brothers each money, a ship, and a mission to buy land. They established outposts: a rubber plantation in Malaysia; a cattle ranch in Australia; a pineapple plantation in Hawaii; a cotton plantation in Louisiana; an orange grove in Florida; and coffee plantations in Colombia and Kenya. Not unlike the British Empire, by 1870, the sun never set on the Laws who reigned over their empire from the queen mother, Perfidia.

This diversification saved Perfidia as all but one of the other Barbadian plantations went bankrupt, were divided among family, were sold, or became pricey vacation spas. The six remaining Law plantations became a cooperative corporation named Bajan White, which to date operated well in the interest of its members. Perfidia still belonged to the descendants of the original owner, one Tad Law, not Thaddeus, not Todd, but Tad as in tadpole.

As for pirates in, of, or around the Caribbean, only Blackbeard, his crew, and one fitful reference to Jean Lafitte surfaced and, of course, Disneyland. Aargh!

By five o'clock, I had deduced that Del's disappearance had nothing to do with pirates and everything to do with a plantation and a wealthy man for his spinster daughter. The funny thing is, if I had searched using the right word, I would not have taken the key to Del or accepted Brendan Whitelaw's offer or threat or whatever it had been.

The correct reference would have provided plenty of research data on my cousins but by the time I first heard the word I was already part of the treasure hunt.

International Airport to Houston, to Miami, to San Juan, Puerto Rico then, finally, to Barbados. Staying? I'd barely had time to pack before driving to Los Angeles on Saturday night for my flight to Houston early Sunday morning.

"Mr. Whitelaw told me to let him know when I arrived. Is there another number where I can reach him?"

"It would be best to leave a message with me. I'm the Parradine in the firm's name."

"Tell him Olivia Lassiter will call at eight this evening."

"I'll leave the message. Whitelaw may be at his desk then, can't promise, I'm afraid," Parradine said in his burr-y voice. The telephone line went dead.

I slung my hobo bag over my shoulder, bought a newspaper from a young boy then took my place at the back of the rental car line. While waiting, I watched the semblance of perfect order in the taxi line disintegrate. A family, unable to stand in line a moment longer, tried to jam suitcases, children, plastic rafts, and stuffed animals into the third taxi in the queue. The maître-taxi in his starched white uniform all but bashed the mother over the head with his swagger stick. Soon, order was restored, the line was a line, and the world was once again safe for Victoria and God. On the surface, Barbados gave me that feeling; starchy, but not quite. And why not, the island had belonged lock, stock, and cane sugar to Great Britain until 1966, only eight short years ago.

When finally, the man at the car rental desk handed me a map and the keys to a nifty little Austin Morris, I asked only one question. Directions in hand, Austin wrapped around me, I turned right on H7 until it hooked into H5, where I took another right then followed the road toward the Ragged Point Lighthouse. The directions were quite clear. Don't take the turn-off to Sam Lord's Castle, when you pass Shrewsbury Chapel drive perhaps another mile, she'll be on your right. You can't miss her, our Perfidia.

I STRUGGLED WITH THE wrong side of the road thing until I realized that the steering wheel of the rental car was on the wrong side, too. So enlightened, I managed to stay on the correct side of the road. As the novelty wore off, my eyes began to wander to the scenery.

Small houses lined the roadside, each neatly balanced on a rock at each corner. Most had a square porch to the front. The homes, designed to be moved, were painted riotous colors intense enough to be used for directions in the United States; turn left at the blue house, the yellow house, turn now or be blinded by the color.

Away from the airport, the air smelled like a perfumery gone berserk, heavy on the musk, mango, and banana. Bajans walked along the roadway swaying to some unheard but godly tune. No wonder Del had kept this all a secret. Taking a deep breath, I overcame the urge to stop the car, take off my clothes and run to the nearest beach.

I drove my little white sedan around the bottom of the pear-shaped island. After a series of small towns, tasteful signs appeared indicating the turn to Sam Lord's Castle. I passed the turn to the Castle then passed Shrewsbury Chapel where the road began to drift slowly north. I drove another mile toward where my map showed Ragged Point Lighthouse to be. To my right, a hulking wrought iron gate, sagging on its hinges, marked the entrance to Perfidia. A new coat of black paint covered fresh welding in the scroll work of palm fronds. When both gates were closed, as they were now, the wrought-iron palm fronds created a curvy letter P.

I parked off the road then climbed out of the car, camera in hand. My camera was one of the new automatic 35mm with a zoom lens that easily attached to the in-camera lens. The camera with its case fit in my black leather hobo bag as did the zoom lens, and so into the boundaries of my life. The bag had two substantial shoulder straps, about an inch wide each, attached to two enormous rings at either end of the bag. An eighteen-inch zipper ran between the rings. All my teacher things fit comfortably into its magnificent gullet. I adored it.

I took a picture of the gate then screwed the zoom on for a photograph down the drive. No matter how far I zoomed, the house was still out of range, hidden behind trees that blazed in a red canopy of fragile blooms and palms that sent jagged fronds heavenward.

The shaded lane swayed like a Bajan's walk toward Perfidia. I clicked off shot after shot.

Tearing myself away from the glory, I got in my car then chugged back down the road, making a left turn at the signs to Sam Lord's Castle. Once parked, I wandered idly through the castle grounds to a bar that overlooked the southeastern cliffs.

I eased onto an empty bar stool from which I could observe the exclusive denizens of Sam Lord's Castle. The hotel provided lodging to the privileged few who could afford the tariff to stay in the small cabanas that ringed the old estate. A few, the blessed few, could afford luxurious rooms in the manor house itself according to the rate sheet conspicuously displayed in a clear glass rack on the bar. The twenty-four pound glossy paper of the rate sheet matched the prices, convincing me that I should have brought a least one bearer bond from the safe deposit box.

I ordered a rum punch from the bartender then returned to my viewing.

The bright, white castle appeared to be of the Georgian period. The large central section was set off by matching, set-back wings on either side. A veranda with a balcony overhead framed the entrance. The roofline was crenelated. Immaculate gardens punctuated by bougainvillea spread from the veranda down toward the swimming pool near the cliff's edge to the sea.

Wide stone stairs curved up to a piazza on either side of a parterre before rising to the formal entrance. Two fountains, one within the walkways, another at the base of the ornamental garden, mirrored each other.

The house was smaller than what one would consider a castle, but then, according to the cover of the matchbook from a snifter at the bar, the castle was self-proclaimed. And, as for Sam Lord, he was a Sam, but hardly a Lord. There was more the pirate about him. There was that word again. Aargh!

I toyed with the matchbook until the bartender delivered my drink. Palming the glass, I swiveled the bar stool to face the ocean. Perhaps twenty feet away, a businessman in a blue pinstripe, summer weight butter-wool suit caught my eye. He sat at a round table with three similarly dressed men.

I stared at his back, wondering who wore wool in this weather. He must have sensed me watching because he glanced over his shoulder. When that proved unsatisfactory, he hung an arm over the back of his chair twisting to see what or who was drilling eyes into the back of his head.

Dismissing me with a glance, he turned back to the others seated with him under an iridescent white umbrella. The soft island breeze lifted their hair so that now and then a manicured hand would have to finger-comb a lock back into place. The breeze continued to toy with their business as I ordered another rum punch.

"Careful, ma'am," the bartender said, "Deez are lustful drinks."

"And, if you have no one to lust with?" I quipped, blazing him with all of the pizzazz I saved for my third-grade students.

"I can't recommend more than one." He wiped a water ring from the bar while he watched me scrutinizing the businessmen. "Dem, dey know how to live, hey."

An untamed boy-man smile lit his face. The kind of smile you can only pull off if you're somewhere south of twenty-five, full-lipped, raven-eyed, and just plain cute. He caught the drift of my thoughts and reared his head like a colt. "You drink dat one and don't fall off your chair, ma'am, I'll buy you de third."

"Hey, mon, you got a name, den?" I teased.

"Not bad," he answered in flawless, lilting English. "Not bad for an American. Just a moment." He left to take care of another customer.

The businessmen seemed incongruous amid the tourists dressed in dayglo colors, basking in the sun, drinking cocktails garnished with citrus fruit. When the bartender returned, I asked, "Who are they?"

He threw his head in their general direction. "Hotel kings dividing up the riches of the island. Ever since they got their hands on Sam Lord's, there has been little stopping them." His eyes still on the party, he absently dried a glass with a starched white towel.

"You know any of them?"

"Just deBanco. He's the man in the pinstripe suit. He represents Bajan White, a consortium of growers." He set the clean glass next to others arrayed upside down on a bleached white towel with crisp blue stripes at each end.

His mention of Bajan White piqued my interest. "On my way here, I saw the letter P on a wrought iron gate."

"Perfidia, now there is de lady. She is one of only two plantation houses still occupied by the original family. Both still operate windmills and crushers. There are rumors dat de men dey want her."

"Perfidia," I said, "Tell me about...de lady?"

"I could tell you some local lore if you'd like?"

"I'd love," I said, drawing Mt. Gay rum through two tiny red straws. The chilled rum proceeded directly to my sinuses creating a sort of brain freeze. I wiped my nose with the back of my hand, laughing through the pain.

The bartender leaned on his elbows. Getting his intelligent brown eyes ten inches from mine, he said, "Sam Lord, as you read on your bar menu, mooncussed. On stormy nights, he would hang lanterns on the cliffs above the beach. He knew the great cutters laden with goods would begin the search for South Point almost immediately upon clearing Ragged Point. Next thing they knew they were aground, perhaps mistaking his light for South Point, no one is sure. He killed, he buried his loot, and he built his empire. Now, a hotel chain has his castle. But, there was another...."

He put his towel to another glass, wiping it until the crystal sang. The businessmen opened their appointment books. He watched their scribbles intently enough to read the date of their next meeting.

When they snapped their books shut, he took a breath. "Once upon a time, there was an island. A pleasant little island, not tall enough to be discovered by the Spanish, but low enough for the British, or so the main character of our story would have you believe. Barbados turned out, like many islands in the Caribbean, to be an excellent place to grow sugar. But, of course, this required laborers because the English gentry did not labor.

"Consequently, the English bought slaves or shipped over indentured servants making sure that they never obtained their freedom. A local legend claims that the mooncussing didn't begin with Sam at all, but with a boy shipped over from England for stealing a candle. The boy escaped from the prison ship by stowing away on a galley bound for Belize. Which, I'm sure you know starts with B that rhymes with T and stands for trouble."

"How very Dickensian." I sipped my drink. "Or, should I say, how very Professor Harold Hill-ian. Both." Aware I was babbling, I stopped.

My storyteller held up three fingers. "This boy had three assets. He hated the British. He knew how to steal, and he was intent on paying off his indenture. So, he learned a bit from the Pirates of Belize, some say even from Blackbeard. Once successful, he freelanced.

"While all the British pirates were doing the Spanish, he apparently did the British, even the odd British pirate. Then, his below decks filled with filthy lucre, he sailed cannons blazing into Carlisle Bay, strode up the steps of the Registry, paid off his indenture and bought most of St. Philip. All long before Sam Lord was a twinkle in his mother's eye. He hid the remainder of his treasure and retired to grow sugarcane. Except, on occasion, when the weather was most foul, he worked his trade."

"Cool," I said, "And this boy's name?"

"Tad Law."

"Law? Any relatives in the DEA?" I asked mischievously as a vision of Agent Law flickered through my mind.

He took my empty punch glass, smiled one of those smiles then went down the bar. First, the dark rum went in then the light then the lime juice then who knows what. Back, he set the drink in front of me where he dropped in two bright swizzle sticks each topped by a multi-colored macaw and squeezed a dash of lime over the top. With the middle finger of his right hand, he scooted the drink across the shiny mahogany bar. I sipped. My eyes rattled.

"For you, ma'am, a true rum punch."

"Waz the difference?" I slurred through what I hoped was an impish smile.

"Bajan White Dark Rum then Bajan White Light. Lots of rum."

"Indeed." I sipped the drink again. "Tell me more."

"Ah, dis is de part dese tourists dey like. Tad goes to his land. He starts amassing rocks. He builds a small stone house, a windmill of stone, a crushing house and slave quarters. Done, he has a fledgling plantation which he promptly names Perfidia."

"Why?"

"Dat de punchline to my story. Because he thinks the British are a perfidious bunch of thugs. Because he got the money to build through perfidy. Because de man, he hab a great sense of humor. Done naming the plantation, he calls his foul harbor Taddys Cove. No apostrophe."

"No way!"

He laughed, "Hey, ma'am, dat de story I raised on."

"Not the way you're used to telling it, though."

He shrugged. "My father is the foreman on Perfidia. I grew up in the north quarters. Before you go revisionist on me, in the late 1920s, the sixteen cabins, originally built around a courtyard with a cold kitchen in the middle, were joined to make four large houses. It was a great place to be reared. I got to watch the essence of who we were, who we are, every day. Dad went to school on the island. I went to Harvard. Not bad for the descendants of Tad Law's original black bull."

"Do you mind if I ask your name."

"Dave."

"Got a last one?"

"White," he smiled, "Where are you staying?"

"Nowhere," I wondered if, Dave White descended from Steadfast White from the history books.

Dave left to take care of a few more drinkers newly seated at the far end of the bar. Everyone wanted to have what I was having. Dave poured the rum punches, put in the tiny birds, squeezed the lime, all while keeping his eyes on the four men at the round table.

Back, Dave carefully smoothed out the folds of a napkin on the bar. Drawing a map upside down so I could see, he said, "Pass Shrewsbury Chapel, you know where it is from here? About a kilometer later there is a turn to the right onto a lane. The road looks rougher than it is. You'll see cliffs to your right. Don't stray. You've arrived when you see the south quarters, sixteen little cabins all set in a square. The diggers working on the current restoration project occupy most of the property, but there is one room available. Ask for John White. He'll make sure you get a place to stay."

"The slave quarters are a hotel?"

"Bed and breakfast. They only let the sixteen cabins, but staying is one of the best experiences on the island. Because the plantation is still operating, there will be places you can't go, including the manor house. Cane fields block it from view. Don't get any ideas about wandering through the cane, it is dangerous anytime, but particularly at night."

A hand brushed my shoulder. I swiveled on my stool. The businessman in the pinstriped suit said with starch in his voice, "I couldn't help but notice you."

"DeBanco," Dave acknowledged then moved down the bar. Soon, Dave was performing his native shtick for the happy planter's punch drinkers who oohed and ahhed in all the right places during the twice-told tale of Sam Lord.

Mr. deBanco's eyes were such a dark blue that they appeared black at first glance. A breeze blew his carefully cut, wavy hair onto his brow. He swiped the forelock back with a flick of his hand.

"Sorry, if I was rude. Four men in wool suits sitting out in the tropics caught my eye. I hadn't meant to stare."

His eyes, which were a smidge too close together, narrowed. "Mad dogs and Englishmen," he dismissed. "What brings you to our island?"

"Vacation."

"I would have guessed something more serious, in fact, you seem quite dour."

I waggled the wee macaws in my empty drink. He plucked one from my glass and tucked its bamboo stick behind my left ear. "The colors compliment your brunette curls."

He held out his hand. "Feron deBanco."

"Gail Kazarian." I hoped she wouldn't mind.

"Pleasure, perhaps we will bump into each other again. I'm usually here mid-day to do the spot of business."

"Perhaps," I said while hoping not and not particularly knowing why.

"Well then," he said, "Enjoy your vacation."

He left me with the odd sensation of having been checked out and found wanting. Well, that went both ways. Mr. deBanco left me with a goodly size case of goose bumps. Not easy to achieve on a perfect eighty-two-degree day wrapped in a wistfully warm breeze.

DeBanco followed the cobbled path towards the Castle. He brushed one hand over the bright red blooms of a tropical bush before stopping at the top of the gravel walk to look back my way. After only a moment of further speculation, he disappeared from sight.

I paid my bar tab, grabbed my napkin map, and waved the map at Dave, who was still performing. Dave was right. A good rum punch is indeed a lustful drink. A quick check of the tourists assured me that no one noticed my small trip over a flat stone. From now on, only one rum punch for de lady.

I drove out of Sam Lord's, my stomach doing rum dances. My head started with that tight piercing rum thing. Flying insects dominated the far reaches of my peripheral vision. I was flat out drunk. Del would have been proud.

AT H5, I TURNED right as instructed past the small Gothic, gray stone Shrewsbury Chapel. The lane Dave had drawn on the napkin arrived within the kilometer foretold but still caught me by surprise. I swerved off the road. The nose of the rental car hit the ground, giving a vicious bounce. The engine died with the rear of the car angled into traffic. With a honk, a light gray Mercedes missed my back bumper by inches.

After a few turns of the key, the car's engine whined back to life. The corduroy lane jarred like a good massage before smoothing out as Dave had predicted. The gravelly road angled to the east then gave a sharp turn northward skirting a cane field. Sugarcane formed a formidable fifteen-foot barrier on the left, so close to the road that leaves brushed the side of the car. On the right, the land swept down a bench to the sea. I pulled into the sparse grass ten feet from the end of the bench and walked, if a bit wobbly, to the edge.

I fought the rum back to toe the brink. Cliffs fell fifty feet to a turbulent, natural harbor. This foul harbor must be the one Tad Law, the mooncusser, had paid for with plunder from dead men. The turquoise sea pummeled a narrow strip of sand at the cliff's base. Screams for mercy rose with the waves breaking on the shores of Tad Law's haunting grounds. I listened to gulls screech over the cliffs and to the wind wail through rocks until sunset gathered over my right shoulder.

As the blue of the sky darkened, lights began to dance across the water. A small boat with an outboard motor rounded a landslip to the southwest. The skiff's pilot had a searchlight rigged to the bow. He flashed the light first on the cliffs then on the water. Finding some reference point, he threw his anchor overboard, shined the light on the water then settled down to fish. The sun gave a final flash that blazed the sea blood red. Night fell. The screams for mercy receded as I walked to the car with my back to the sea.

Driving on a strange road so near cliffs so late was nerve-wracking. The road never strayed far from the cliff until the last turn took off northeastward hugging the cane field. Lights beckoned in the distance. Through soft-needled trees, a light blinked on in a substantial shadow. Perfidia?

The car crunched on thick gravel at the edge of the quadrangle created by the sixteen former slave quarters. A tall, broad-shouldered black man with big workman's hands waited for me. He filled out his white Bermuda shorts and white shirt. The shirt bore an ornate lazy red letter P like a brand embroidered above the left pocket. As he strode to my car, his eyes sparked in the remaining light. He radiated impatience tempered by innate politeness.

I was late. Still, John White was as good as his son's word. The moment I exited the car, he slapped keys to cabin number 4 in my hand. John grabbed my suitcase and hobo bag from the trunk and took off down the quadrangle. I took a hop-step to overcome his long stride gaining enough edge to open the cabin door before he reached it. As I did, the hiss of the early evening breeze wove its way through the room to kiss my arms.

"You know about manchineel?" John's voice rumbled somewhere in the bass register. He pointed to a fifty-foot tree with a broad canopy.

"They're big trees?"

"Don't be sitting under dis tree in a rainstorm, dey drip acid. De milky sap will blister your skin." He shook a finger at me then pointed toward a squat building made of gray rock. "Breakfast is served in the kitchen. There is an open bar until eight o'clock each night. I hear the gin tonics are refreshing. We have lectures on plantation life for the restoration workers. None scheduled this week."

"What time is breakfast?"

"Six to ten o'clock every morning. Don't miss it. The eggs and sweetbreads are delicious."

"Where is the main house from here?"

"This is a working plantation. Obey the signs. You won't be in danger."

"Your son is terrific," I responded, trying to ignore the chiding rumble in his voice.

He gave a small smile. "He is that."

"He liked being a boy here."

"I'm late home. Have a good evening. Try a gin tonic before bed. They are known to smooth rum."

He strode away. When he reached the corner of the quadrangle, he glanced back. Seeing me, he waved. I smiled, but he was gone.

Inside the cabin, wooden Venetian blinds clutched the top of sashes painted dove gray. The furniture was rattan, painted in white enamel. Thick cushions covered in a print of yellow and green palm fronds made the chairs inviting, reminding me of Del's chosen home decor.

A white rattan armoire provided closet space. There was no television. A wind-up clock tocked the time from a glass-topped wicker nightstand. People had been born in this room, died here, loved here. I put my hands on the wall. Unlike the screaming ocean, these walls didn't weep.

The bed had a wicker headboard complemented by a firm, inviting mattress. The light bedspread had been turned back revealing scratchy bedclothes starched and ironed for my arrival.

I threw my suitcase on the luggage rack to unpack the few things that needed unpacking, including a small, framed picture of my family. Del was standing with a hand on my shoulder having just joined me as the timer tripped the camera. Light radiated from Del to the camera; he was born for Hollywood. Remembering that as of this moment no one but Parradine and Whitelaw knew I was Del's daughter, I tucked the photograph back in my case.

A black dial telephone, similar to mine at home, squatted on the nightstand. I read the dialing instructions before deciding that there was sufficient time to steam out some rum in a hot bath before calling Whitelaw. The bathroom had once been the closet, explaining the husky armoire. The architect who had converted the oblong cabin to a guest room had managed a serviceable bathroom without impinging on the living area.

A white pedestal sink graced the inside corner. The toilet was hidden behind the opened door. A huge cast iron tub perched on eagle's talons dominated the end of the small bathroom. Copper pipes soared from the tub to a tank overhead. When I turned the porcelain handles, lukewarm water splashed into the tub. I stripped off my clothes then clambered in over the tub wall.

The water heater kicked in with an astounding thump. Steam poured out of the faucet as the telephone in the room began to ring. I let it ring intent on a two-inch long reddish-brown bug squatting on the wall watching me bathe.

I shouldn't have. Whitelaw had called according to the handwritten message tacked by the night clerk to the small corkboard below the cabin number on the outside of the cabin door.

BATHED, I SAT ON the edge of the bed, wrapped in my plaid cotton bathrobe, my head doing the rumba. I sipped a gin tonic delivered from the kitchen at 7:59. The drink was as billed, light, refreshing, and able to round the sharp edges in my head. I dialed Whitelaw's number. The voice that answered wasn't the burr from my earlier call, but the baritone I'd heard over the telephone line in Bakersfield.

"This is Olivia Lassiter. Mr. Whitelaw?" I grabbed the pen and paper by the phone. During meetings and calls, I doodle. It must help me concentrate. It most certainly helps me forgive the drawings in the margins of my students' homework. I sipped my gin tonic. Another edge dissipated. I drew an eye. "When can we meet?"

"Tomorrow morning. Barclays. I have to stop by Morten's Mortuary, prior. Can we meet about 10:00? We need to speak to a Mr. Donovan at the bank. Do you have transport?"

"You know I do. You've had me watched?"

"No. I just arrived in, haven't had de time to arrange for thuggees."

I strained to understand his off British accent. His guard must have been down. I waited for him to break out in dem and dis. It made me wonder from which side of the culture he sprang.

"Then how did you know how to reach me."

The line grew quiet. Then a soft, "It doesn't matter."

"It does, rather. I don't like that you can find me whenever you want when I haven't met you."

A wry laugh wandered over the line. "Not particularly upset dat...sorry, I'm tired, that your father's gone missing, though."

"My emotions are none of your business."

"I see. Parradine told me you called and that you would call back at eight. I stopped for a drink with an old friend. He'd seen you. That's all. You think you're being followed?"

"Dave White?"

"Mm."

"Gray Mercedes."

"Ah! And to think you've only been here a few hours. Imagine what the future holds. Barbados is a small island, fourteen by twenty-one miles. There aren't many places to hide."

"Who would be following me?"

"Perhaps you're imagining."

The Mercedes had continued down the road. The driver had shown little interest in me other than the initial turnout of Sam Lord's Castle. "Perhaps."

"Barclays then. Park near Trafalgar, the bank is an easy find from there."

"If you're late should I wait for you?"

"No, go on. I'll find you."

"I'll be wearing..." The line went dead. Both partners of Parradine and Whitelaw seemed to have the unpleasant habit of hanging up on people.

I sat on the edge of the bed, trying not to let my third-grade teacher's imagination create drama where none existed. I lay back, my right hand behind my head, listening to the wind shush through the louvers.

I reread Del's couriered note half-expecting him to appear in the cabin doorway. He didn't.

I nodded off dreaming of Del. We were sharing a long, late, Caribbean dinner over the soft roll of steel drums. He slipped the bandleader bearer bonds asking that the band play the song *Perfidia*. Del asks me to dance and in dancing hands me off to another. I cannot see who he is because he is shadowed by the light. Del asks *Did you bring the key?* I nod. Del leaves me with the backlit man.

I woke with a start. I wasn't Olivia Lassiter. I was Stella Harris, somehow connected to Perfidia, home not of pirates but mooncussers, to the sale of drugs, to the dead, and to the gone missing.

I quickly changed into loose black cotton slacks and a black cotton tank top, grabbed my cabin key then went out walking to get as far from my dreams as possible. The night was lukewarm, perhaps in the low seventies. A warm breeze coddled me.

I walked the lane for about a half mile to the edge of the cane field. Dense foliage on either side of the path topped by the blackness of the sky created a tunnel alive with dappled shadows. I forced myself to take the first step into the dark. As I walked, lights began to twinkle deep in the cane like fireflies in a cornfield. I followed their dance.

When the fireflies turned into two flashlight beams, I stopped. The lights met. A hushed greeting followed. The lights went out. I was cane rows over, unable to see who whispered so urgently.

"Where are you holing up?" one man rasped.

"Sophie's."

"Figured her out yet?"

The other man must have given a shake of his head.

"I've got it from here."

"Try honey, not salt."

"What? Me? Too rough?"

The leaves of the sugar cane rattled. Another light flickered through the leaves. Whoever it was wasn't concerned about being seen. The meeting broke. Long strides took off to my left, as a man with a catlike gate angled behind me.

Whoever held the oncoming light had turned to follow the man to my left. The effect of the voices, the lights, even the tone was disquieting. Who was this Sophie? I should warn her, shouldn't I?

I spun ready to return to my cabin. The lights had lured me deep into the field, far from the lane. The ocean whispered to my left. I walked toward the water reassuring myself that once at cliff's edge, I could find my way to the bed and breakfast.

The cane closed in on me. I stretched my hands out in front to protect my eyes from the back-slash of the leaves. Their edges nicked my hands. A sharp noise at my back startled me. Someone called. I spun to my name. The cane snickered. I was impossibly lost.

"Del?" I waited. "Del if that's you, we need to talk."

No sound, no voice. Yet, something.

"I'm lost."

The wind clattered through the cane. My senses told me I wasn't alone, yet I'd never felt so alone in my life. A pinprick of light glinted through the cane. I narrowed my eyes but the light, if there had been one, was gone.

I took ten steps toward where the flickering light had been then ten more then forced myself to count off ten more steps. I emerged after much self-urging into a clearing. Overhead there were more stars than I'd ever seen. As I admired the stars, something erased them then put them slowly back one by twinkling one.

When my eyes became accustomed to the new lighting arrangement, I made out a massive sail clattering in the night breeze. The windmill was a conical mound of stones each fitted one on another without the benefit of mortar. I craned my neck to see the top of the cone. A tree-trunk sized wooden pole emerged from the mid-point.

Four wooden spars arrayed around a wooden gear attached to the pole. Each mast carried a canvas sail, unfurled and full to the wind. I guided myself around with one hand on the rock face.

On the far side, a wooden waterwheel rotated a large gear that turned a smaller one. Water sloshed into a centuries old hewn wooden trough that sluiced into the mill house. Slowly the smell of the place registered. A bitter sweetness mingled with a dense moldy, green smell—crushed cane. With my hand on the rocks, I continued around the base of the mill hoping for a door.

When I located a wooden door, it was locked. I put my ear to the wood. I could hear the grinding of stone on stone.

I leaned against the stone wall, enjoying the creaking sails coupled with the shushing of cascading water. Opposite me, a slight break interrupted the wall of cane, why not? I pushed off with a last lingering look at the magic at work in the clearing. The soft glow of ambient light radiated to my left marking where the plantation house must be. I meandered down the narrow path accompanied by the buzzing of night bugs and the chirruping of small tree frogs. The lane deposited me not ten feet from where I had plunged into the field. I had no idea how far I'd gone but knew I could find my way back to the enchanted mill.

Once in my room, I grabbed my turquoise and black geometric print shorty nightgown and adjourned to the bathroom to change for the night. A scrap of white college-lined paper taped to the outside of the lavatory window fluttered in the evening breeze.

I opened the window and flattened the flitting paper against the pane with the fingers of one hand. It read: *Be careful out in the fields, girl.*

Girl?

Someone had been spying on me, someone with access to cellophane tape, someone who knew which room I occupied. There seemed only one possibility, John White, but why? Why would he bother? I jammed the note in the envelope with Del's missive for safe-keeping, but really!

Girl?

Day Four

MY SLEEP WAS FILLED with memories of rainy nights, gauzy curtains, and a thousand bugs whining just outside the window screen. In my dream, no matter how I fought them, the curtains wound around me like a caterpillar's cocoon. I awoke to a wet, dense aired morning. My mood, the rain, my lack of sleep all befitted a day to meet someone I didn't know, at a bank where I didn't bank, to discuss a cousin I had never met.

Not at all sure what proper attire would be, I picked out a nice light green cotton skimmer, square-necked, and sleeveless. The dress glanced off my figure. I ran my wet hands, fingers wide, through my curls. My curls bounced to attention and would stay that way in the day's humidity. I reached into a pocket of my suitcase for a pair of hose. At the thought of nylon encased legs, I defiantly threw my multi-colored huaraches on the bare feet of my tanned legs, giving brief thanks to lawn mowing in short-shorts.

At the last minute, I dug deep into the same pocket of my suitcase to grab a bracelet of inlaid, painted tropical birds with interlocking wings. The birds flew around my wrist in raunchily bright colors.

Del had given me the bracelet on my twenty-fifth birthday accompanied by some cockamamie story about a long lost love. I put the bangle directly in the upper drawer of my chest of drawers where I forgot it until packing, sure at the time that he was making some point about how dull I was. Now I wondered if my mother had worn the bracelet; if she were the long lost love, if I were the love child of the story kidnaped to California.

Feeling more like the mysterious Stella than the famously dull Olivia, I ran to the kitchen dodging the warm rain that dripped from the branches of the manchineel.

John White was right. Breakfast was scrumptious though the coffee was weak. I ate a heaping plateful of scrambled eggs plucked fresh from under the chickens clucking in the yard, lightly fried tomatoes, peppers and onions, and thick slices of coconut bread. I wrapped two more slices of bread for the road. The cook, Nancy, according to the name embroidered on her uniform, assured me the rain wouldn't last. At least, I think that's what she meant when she said: *De rain, she neber stay her welcome.*

For now, squalls washed ashore in wind-driven waves. Out on the road, palms swayed heavily. A strong wind buffeted the sedan. I fought to stay in my lane. Not that there was much worry, few people were out, making the gray Mercedes coupe cruising an eighth of a mile behind all the more evident.

The wind increased parting the clouds to display the first hint of blue sky overhead. The squall she be blowing herself out. The patois was catching. The rain and wind had cleansed yesterday's dense smell. In its wake, delicate aromas were unleashed. With just the barest hint of sun, the island blossomed into colors straight off of a palate of primes. Breadfruit, banana palms, mangoes, coconut palms, heavy with fruit created a free fruit stand along the curving highway.

With the sun, people emerged. Tall, stately, people with dark, exotic eyes sauntered under the blossoming trees. Occasionally, I would drive past a woman carrying a basket of fruit on her brightly wrapped head. Mesmerized by the sights, I was slow to notice the landmarks of a large city crowding in on the road. Other cars, buses, and motor scooters joined me as traffic-clotted. I checked the rearview mirror for my traveling companion. The gray Mercedes was two cars back, nesting behind a small lorry.

One by one city houses lined the road. Unlike the small, brightly painted homes of the countryside, these were long-framed shiplap and gray stone houses with a capital B for British. They seemed built to last the Empire, which, of course, they had.

A rainbow lit Bridgetown. I wondered if one arch ended at Barclays Bank. In my musing, I barely missed ramming a bright red two-story red tour bus by steering hard to the left. The Mercedes pulled to the left as well. As quickly, it pulled back into line.

A policeman in a blazing white, starched shirt and shorts waved me forward with a warning shake of his finger. Tourists, afoot, joined the ordered queue of cars until forward progress was halting and erratic. Faced with the choice between a bridge choked with cars and pedestrians or the municipal parking lot, I parked. The gray Mercedes continued in the queue. I craned my neck to see who was driving, learning only that the driver was dark or tanned with dark hair and sunglasses.

As I walked across the gray stones of Chamberlin Bridge, I watched for Trafalgar Square. Then he was there, poor Admiral Nelson, a statue plop in the middle of an eroding triangle. His tri-corner hat bleached on top by pigeons, one arm resolutely stuffed in his uniform coat. He looked disapproving to downright disgruntled at the smallness of his monument, currently surrounded by taxis waiting for fares.

When I reached the relative haven of a sidewalk, I elbowed my way into a store. The time was 9:50 on a hot morning made sultrier by all the bodies. I was at the end of a formidable line of tall, thin, perfectly formed women buying British made bikinis at British West Indies prices, about half the U.S. dollar. When I finally reached the counter ten minutes later, the saleslady was very helpful. If I'd only turned left, I would have seen Barclays Bank.

Outside the store, people were everywhere, on the sidewalks, emerging from store fronts, crossing the streets. I elbowed my way out, inserting myself into the downstream flow. As I broke ranks to cross the street, a taxi driver yelled at me, the driver of another car honked, and a fellow heretic in a yellow checkered shirt pinched my rear. Despite all of these attempts to either kill or maim me, I opened the door to Barclays. A whoosh of chilled air greeted me, followed by silence, fractured by the occasional whisper.

No impatient men were tapping their feet waiting for the late Miss Lassiter. Everyone in the bank was either in line for a teller or with a clerk at one of the massive oak partner desks arranged along the back wall. I checked for a nameplate that read Mr. Donovan but saw none, so I queued with a polyglot of people behind a sign urging us to please wait for the next available teller.

When a female teller waved me over, I asked for Mr. Donovan. Shapely, overdressed and imperious, the teller pointed a finger that ended in an inch long down-curled fingernail. I followed the line of her finger, not the nail, to a desk. She curled the same finger once in a come here gesture.

A young man, tall, thin, with thinning blond hair stood. He adjusted his gray summer weight suit, buttoned the middle button, centered his tie, all while excusing himself from a man in a hot tropical print shirt and jeans. The man he had been speaking to spoke briefly to a sunny-faced clerk at the next desk over then left. Donovan approached me, his hand extended in greeting for half the passage of the room.

"Mr. Donovan," he said with a sweep of his hand toward his just vacated desk. I followed to the still warm chair he offered. Engraved lettering proclaimed him Mr. James Donovan. The business card in his crystal card holder described him as the Assistant Bank Manager. "Now, Miss, how may I help you?"

I reached into the depths of my hobo bag, pushing aside Sam Lord pamphlets, to pull out my passport. I handed him my passport then flipped the picture sleeves in my wallet to a small photo of Del.

All business, Mr. Donovan tapped the snapshot, "Name?"

"Delmar Lassiter."

He turned to search through hanging files in a credenza behind his desk. "We have no one by that name in our records. Did he go by another name?"

The answer was yes. Instead, I asked, "Do you have a file under my name?"

Donovan turned back to his archives. He cleared his throat each time I inhaled. Eventually, he placed an over-used manila file with bent corners, thick with papers on his desktop.

"Let me see your identification again, please? And, may I have your social security number."

"If I may know why?" I laid my passport on the desk, spinning it so that my photo and passport number were readable.

"This is difficult. I can't tell you why unless I have access to your account. I can't access your account without your social security number."

My account? Curiosity alone caused me to rattle off the nine numbers. He followed me pointing to each number on his record with the eraser end of a pencil. It was like ticking off lottery numbers. I hoped I won big.

"Now, Miss Lassiter, may I have your mother's maiden name?"

Once you've offered your social security number, there is no need to get coy about your mother's maiden name except I hadn't a clue what it was.

"Does Graydon sound familiar?" he offered, which given my experience with banks seemed an odd thing to do.

"Yes," I said, as familiar as any name, which meant not at all. At least, Graydon gave off waves of British stiff upper lip-ness.

Donovan made a note in the file before adding, "What information do you require concerning your account."

"What account?" I fondled an upholstery tack in the arm of the chair.

"Your trust." He tapped his pencil eraser on his blotter. "I'm sure there will be some tidying to do, but you will receive the remainder of the trust on your thirty-second birthday."

His eyes locked on my left hand as it toyed with the tack, leading me to believe he was checking me over for a ring of some sort.

"I'm unmarried, is that a problem?"

His eyes slid away from my hand. "No. Not really, but women typically have little experience with finances. It can be a benefit having someone to..."

"Handle the investments?" Which explained why the money was in trust until my thirty-second birthday, by then a father would assume his daughter married. "What tidying?"

"There was a run on Bajan White, a British corporation, about a month ago. A significant number of shares were sold, considerable bought. It was a good buy." He stopped with a semi-reptilian half-smile on his lips. "Sorry, indiscreet."

"And, my father withdrew funds from my trust to participate in the buying?" I guessed.

"Several hundreds of thousands of U.S." Donovan intertwined his hands then thumped them on his blotter.

"Who would a sell-off hurt?"

"All of the plantations that make up Bajan White, I suppose." Like deBanco, Donovan's eyes were too close together, but unlike deBanco's eyes, Donovan's were weak and revealing. Donovan pursed his lips, looked at his hands, checked his cuticles then folded his hands again. Finally, his eyes met mine. "Bit of a family tiff."

"Family tiff?"

"Bajan White is all Taddys. Over the centuries, some branches of the family have been more successful than others. The various holdings were incorporated into Bajan White to smooth out the bumps. The rivalries continue. I can't imagine what the jockeying must have been like when they cleared their scabbards."

"Duels? Who's most successful now?"

"At the moment, the wretched deBancos seem to be pulling the strings."

"DeBancos?" A few cherries on the slot machine of life clicked into place. "A Feron deBanco introduced himself to me yesterday, could he be doing business for Bajan White?"

"No, Bajan White is Lloyd Law-Maddock's sole purpose in life. Lloyd has been in London these last months. His brother died recently, so Lloyd's arrived back for the funeral. Feron usually shows when Lloyd's in London."

"How many plantations are represented by Bajan White?" I knew from my research at the library six remained.

"Apolima, Hawaii; Pendu, Colombia; Perfidia, Barbados; Maison Vol, Louisiana, Vent Amer, Malaysia; and Candle in Australia." He ticked them off with the eraser. "Headquarters for Bajan White are in London out of tradition more than anything."

"What service does Bajan White provide the world?" My fingers unwound the upholstery tack on the arm of the chair.

"Well, rum, sugar, molasses, wood, bananas, coffee, rice, spices, rubber, beef, that sort of thing." Donovan began to search for hangnails on his perfectly manicured hands, rubbing his thumb over the edge of each nail. "The deBancos operate Pendu. They grow and sell coffee, considered some of the finest in the world."

"Only coffee? That's all, nothing remotely illegal?"

"Family by-laws and all that." Donovan concentrated on rubbing his thumbnail with his index finger.

"It would be tempting, though?"

He continued to survey his hands. "Might be, but considering their antecedents, they seem to be a pretty lawful bunch."

"Tell me about Lloyd's brother's death." I shifted in the wingback chair, my fingers worrying the tack.

"Now we are far off the subject of your trust?" Donovan clasped his hands, raising and refolding each finger. "It is important for you to know that Aaron, Lloyd's brother, is—was Amanda Law-Maddock's son. Technically, he and, Lloyd, are direct descendants of Tad Law. Aaron drowned. Rumors flying about are that Aaron hijacked the White Lady from Pendu, drove her into Taddys Cove, grounded her then looted her of some priceless cargo."

"What about Brendan Whitelaw?" I managed the tack loose then began winding the spirochete in and out of the fabric.

Donovan unclasped his hands, laid them flat on his blotter then rechecked his manicure. When he was sure the half-moons were precise, he glanced at me. "What about him?"

"If Aaron did hijack the White Lady, and there was booty on board, is there any reason Whitelaw would be interested in the take?"

"Every reason in the world." He studied his hands. "If you believe the rumors."

"Which are?"

"So, Miss Lassiter," he said, changing the subject with little attempt at grace. "Your trust is restored though your father retains access to it. All of his other assets appear destined for Vent Amer."

"Excuse me? Isn't that the rubber plantation in Malaysia?"

"Of course, Vent Amer is the Harris family estate."

With that, another cherry dropped. I had family alright.

"I expected to meet Mr. Whitelaw," I said.

"Well, that is a problem. You might try the mortuary."

MORTEN'S MORTUARY WAS JUST off Trafalgar Square, in an alley that dodged behind St. Michael's Cathedral. Deposited in the parlor by the receptionist, I paced the black-veined, white marble floor. The walls were black from the marble floor to the chair rail and a creamy white above. The chair rail was lustrous brass.

The spicy aroma of dying flowers floated liberally around the room. Soothing music was playing so quietly that the hymn was nearly indistinguishable from a persistent white noise giving the impression that the overhead fan strummed the chords. The song was one of those printed in all Protestant hymnals. I recognized it but didn't know the words because my father, Del Lassiter, née Chamberlin Harris, referred to organized religion as that soulless enterprise that rapes your bank account. Still, I had gone to church with the odd friend, which is to say, my father thought them odd for attending church.

"Kell Morten, May I help you, ma'am," a cultured British voice asked, preceding a small, precise man in a neat black suit. His shoes, polished to a high luster, clicked on the marble as he came through a black door to my right. He had metal tips on the toes and heels like a tap dancer.

"I hoped to find Brendan Whitelaw here. We were to meet at Barclays. He never arrived." My introduction made; I took a step forward, standing out in my green dress against the black walls. To me, the room looked like an outside-in coffin.

Morten took a nervous step back and stuffed one hand in a suit coat pocket which appeared never to have held anything larger than a pen. "Busy man," he said, "Perhaps I can help you."

I hesitated, who did I want to be? I ran my hand over the chair rail; brass polish clung to my fingers. Decided, I said, "I'm Chamberlin Harris' daughter. Has Mr. Whitelaw been here?"

"He left a few moments ago. I'm surprised you didn't pass him."

No doubt Whitelaw was on his way to Barclays where he would learn about my trust from the indiscreet Mr. Donovan. We could continue this way for some time despite Whitelaw's claims that Barbados was a small island.

"May I ask what business he had here?"

"Aaron Law-Maddock's autopsy is just done. There will be a closed casket viewing this afternoon at two. You are most welcome then." Morten clasped his hands in front of his suit; the lapels fell in a parallel line. "The funeral will be tomorrow, also at two, I believe, at the chapel near her."

"By her, you mean Perfidia."

A shallow nod followed. "Of course, Mrs. Law-Maddock relies on Morten's for these sorts of arrangements."

"They are common then?" I smoothed the front of my green dress. He watched my hands leave streaks of brass polish down the green linen.

He ticked his head at my mess. "No, Miss Harris, they are not, common. But, she did lose her husband last year and now a son, poor dear."

"May I ask if you know my father?" I hung my hands at my sides at a complete loss as to what to do with them.

"Lin Harris," Morten said as though he had said the name many times before, "Of course."

"Mr. Whitelaw tells me that Mr. Harris has gone missing."

Morten nodded at his folded hands. "Bajan for he's chosen to hide-out."

"Are you sure?"

"Miss Lassiter, I've lived forty years on this island, buried all of the Taddys that have died during that time. Yes. I am sure that to go missing means to hide-out." He refolded his neat, clean, dainty little hands in front of his fly. "There are many Bajan sayings such as egg have no right at rockstone dance or fisherman never say dat 'e fish stink and dat man 'e go missing. I have heard that to go missing was the code for mooncussing."

"Are you implying..."

He waved a hand to deflect my question. "Certainly not. No ships have gone aground..."

"Since the White Lady," I interrupted. Was everything I'd ever believed about the father I adored a flat out cosmic lie? "Buried Taddys?"

"Yes, even they die." Morten shifted, the slight click of brass followed as the tip of his shoe met the highly polished marble floor.

"How many under suspicious circumstances?" I rummaged in my hobo bag for a tissue, even a used napkin, anything to wipe the brass polish off my fingers.

"If you consider drowning suspicious, then Aaron is not the only one." He folded his hands again. Every time Morten gave me a piece of meaningful information he appeared further emasculated.

I pulled out a napkin with golden arches embossed in white then wiped each finger while keeping my eyes on Mr. Morten. He cocked his head, seemingly bemused at my hand cleaning operation.

"Where is my father hiding out?" I finished off with my right pinkie.

"The usual places, I would think?"

"I'm new to the island. I'm new to the Taddys, as you call them, why would I have a clue what the usual places are?"

"Well, I only know of one, Lacy's. I've heard talk of others." He held a hand out for the used napkin. I handed it to him. He wadded the stained napkin into the palms of his hands then folded his hands back together.

"Lacy's? Is that a bar or something?"

"Heavens no...Parradine."

"As in Parradine and Whitelaw?"

Again he nodded, followed by another toe tap. I bet he was a blast at a dance.

"May I ask about Mr. Whitelaw?"

"I'm hardly the best source. We aren't generally in the same social circles." Morten gave me a sharp once over. "Follow please, I hear the family arriving."

Mr. Morten opened the door to the foyer. Hearing raised voices, he steered me to another exit. Morten's deft traffic control and quiet words couldn't cover a man hotly proclaiming: *you bastard, how dare you!* Morten raised one precise eyebrow as he helped me exit into an ancient alley lined by the walls of gray stone buildings.

An exposed brick-lined conduit mid-alley ran at my feet. It must once have served as the open-air city sewer system. From the smell, I was inclined to believe the channel still washed sewage to the sea. A thin tabby cat, its eyes dull from hunger, looked over my ankle. The cat followed me down the alley until I broke into a quick trot.

The alley dumped me out under a sign that read Roebuck Street. I wandered down the street toward the hurly-burly of town. A right at St. James Street brought me closer to the cacophony of people going about shopping, sight-seeing, and their business.

I strolled aimlessly up Coleridge Street wondering why Del had changed my name, why he raised me without family, why he had hidden me away, wondering about my trust fund, wondering who I was. Sadly, I had always been fond of Olivia Lassiter found at the four corners with her stuffed alligator.

MID-BLOCK A SMALL WOODEN sign hanging from a chain at either end proclaimed Parradine & Whitelaw. Red-flowered trees stippled the mortared gray stone building with white spots where the mid-day sun shined through their feathery leaves.

The wooden shutters, which edged each window of the building, were painted black. The shutters currently latched to the side of the building could be closed during high winds and hurricanes. Wide stone stairs with short risers swept up to a landing in front of the single door entrance. The door knocker was a brass monkey with clasped front paws below a screeching grin that displayed goodly sized eye-teeth. I turned the door handle rather than touch the howler.

The door opened into a foyer of dark wood, hand-oiled for centuries. A woman sat behind a mahogany desk, her back to me. A telephone exchange board with nine holes and two plugs was to her left, a manual typewriter to her right, and, on a credenza behind her, the latest telex and the finest electric typewriter that money could buy. Her back to me, she was typing at a prodigious rate.

I squinted to see the words she typed as a sheet of paper moved through the platen. She hit a key. The page rolled off the platen into her hand. She snapped the document once between her hands then swiveled in her desk chair to greet me.

She was not pretty, but she was handsome. A conservative, navy blue dress piped in white made her look crisp, efficient, and effortlessly trustworthy.

"Do you have an appointment with Mr. Parradine?" she asked in a clipped British accent.

"Actually, no," I said, "I'd hoped to see Mr. Whitelaw."

"He's not in." She shot a quick look at the closed door to her right.

"Then Chamberlin Harris. I heard he may have gone missing here."

She cocked her head. "Truly he hasn't. Last time I saw our Lin was three days ago."

"Did he arrange to courier a letter to Olivia Lassiter from here?"

"Perhaps, now how may I help you?" She clasped her hands on her blotter looking exactly like the watchdog secretary they warn you about in management books. A few years ago, Del had proclaimed that someday those third graders wouldn't be enough. When I insisted they would, he enrolled me in management courses at California State University Bakersfield, until I had a second degree in Business Administration. I still didn't have a clue why, though it had been a help with Mr. Donovan.

"Is that Whitelaw's office?" I crossed to the door on her right. The knob turned easily. The room was immaculate, not a paper on the desk, not a brief to be seen, not a dust mote in a corner.

No framed photographs leaned in the family pecking order on the ancient sideboy now serving as a credenza behind the desk. The blotter on the desk showed no drink rings, no telltale slips of a pen. This perfectly furnished law office included no engraved deskset with the standard gold pen, no nameplate, no business cards. No carbon-based life form used this space, except perhaps for the mouse that had deposited the droppings next to an empty silver candy dish. Even the two walls of law books, their bindings of the finest embossed leather, their edges smacked into place and held captive by a fine patina of dust on the shelf, showed no sign of use.

I opened the middle drawer of the desk as a slender older man, gray showing at his temples and shot through his mustache, walked into the room. No doubt, he had worn the gray suit for effect. The tidy legal secretary stood just to his left so that she too could see the action. I ignored them. There was nothing in the drawer, not even the leavings of lead dust and paper clips. As old as the desk was, it was hard to believe that anyone had ever sat at it to write a law brief, study precedence or prepare a defense.

"Miss?" the man said with the slight burr I'd heard over the telephone.

"Mr. Parradine?" I responded. "How long has it been since someone occupied this office? You can round to the nearest decade if it would be easier."

He recognized my voice as well. "Miss Lassiter, Mr. Whitelaw has been otherwise occupied. He rarely comes in of late. We assist when we can."

He watched me like any good lawyer. He may have been calculating my worth as well.

"Otherwise occupied?"

"He has considerable on his plate. Miss Smythe can confirm this." He turned to his assistant. She nodded her head displaying years of artful practice.

"Where does he spend his considerable time?" I slipped open the top drawer on the right. They weren't concerned, so I slid the drawer shut.

"The occasional tourist bar, he likes his scotch neat. He calls into the answering service on the odd occasion, but, in truth, we rarely know where he is."

"Does he exist?" I asked.

Parradine smiled, but the delighted giggle that escaped Miss Smythe was the giveaway. Parradine scolded her with his eyes.

"Very much so I'm afraid. I promised his father, Colin, my partner, that I would look after his son should Colin precede me in death. As he was much younger than me, I felt it was a reasonably safe wager. It wasn't. I've had Colin's boy, Brendan, since he was but eight. He was and continues to be a handful. Now, given that our Brendan isn't in and that Miss Smythe and I are covering for him, what can I do for you?"

"Tell me what's going on?"

"In general or the usual island gossip?" Parradine came through the door. I tensed. He stopped halfway. With his back to a section of the bookcase, he swept his hand from the waist towards the exit. I took the hint. When he continued to block my view of the books in the case, I wondered what he was hiding.

I reached behind his back and pulled out a dusty copy of a book titled *A History of Barbados* as told by Sam

Lord. I held the book out to him title out. He raised his eyebrows. I hugged the book to my chest.

In the outer foyer, I asked, "Tell me about Perfidia and the Taddys."

"Best thing to do, in that case, Miss Lassiter," he said, studying me before proceeding, "Is take a tour at Perfidia. Get Johnny to take you about if you can."

"John White."

"Indeed. Johnny gives a grand tour."

"Isn't he too busy for that?"

"He loves to show her off. They fawn over her, all of them, too much actually. Perfidia is just a house and fields, isn't she?"

"I haven't been to the house, Mr. Parradine, but I'm getting the impression that for some Perfidia is much more."

He glanced at Miss Smythe. "The problem is, Miss Lassiter, she is a bit of an albatross. The usual long-term erosion has gone on much as it has with the great houses in England. Of course, Taddys, as we call them, don't quit without a fight. Still, I think she is very much at risk."

"Why tell me this?"

"I don't like how little you think of our Brendan."

"What has any of this to do with your Brendan?"

While talking, Parradine had maneuvered me through the foyer to the main entrance. Having achieved his goal, he ushered me through the door to the front landing. The black door closed behind me. I opened the door and walked back in. Parradine was leaning over

Miss Smythe's desk. He turned at the sound of my huaraches.

"Your book," I said, offering him Sam Lord.

With a wave of his hand, he signaled the book was mine. I looked at the binding before opening the book to the flyleaf. The data on the page proclaimed it a first edition.

"Thank you," I said, stuffing the book in my increasingly bulky hobo bag. "One more thing, do you know where Lin Harris has gone missing?"

"He'll find you if he needs you, lass." Parradine crossed to me and put a hand on each of my shoulders, his eyes were quiet and kind. "Lin is excellent at this sort of thing."

"Hiding out!"

He squeezed my shoulders. "Relax, Olivia. He will find you. I feel confident he knows you are here."

"Feron deBanco?" I asked.

"Miss Smythe," he answered, with a remarkably straight face, "Would prefer if you did not swear in her presence."

"I see."

"Perhaps. Now if I were you, I'd go have Johnny show me about. Who knows what or who could be lurking out at the old mooncusser's lair?"

I left, almost. I planted myself on the dusty stair stoop plopping my bag on my lap, feeling closed in and closed out. Parradine was right about one thing; I needed that tour of Perfidia. As for Mr. Whitelaw, our Brendan, Danny, he had lied, as best I could tell, about needing me for Del's affairs.

I watched the hurry of people rushing to lunch dates, rushing to appointments, standing and gawking at the blend of tropic splendor and British colonialism while I considered what to do next. I could sit on these stairs staring at the odd passerby wondering about Brendan Whitelaw, his detractors, and his protectors. Or, I could go to the mooncusser's lair for that tour.

I DROVE SOUTH, IGNORING the glow of the island until I once again bumped over the lane towards the bed and breakfast. I stopped where the cliff's edge hung out over Taddys Cove, hoping, perhaps, to see the small boat in daylight. Once out of the car, I retrieved my camera from my bag, hung it around my neck by its black strap then locked the bag in the trunk.

At cliff's edge, I took off my huaraches and dangled my feet where they were misted by salty ocean spray. With each waggle of a leg, the order of events played across my mind. Del sold his shares of Bajan White. Aaron hijacked the White Lady. Del got a midnight call then left on family business. Somewhere in the churn below the White Lady went aground. Aaron drowned. Del had gone missing.

A small boat rounded the northern headlands into the cove, coming from Ragged Point, much as the White Lady may have done. The motor was barely audible above the roar of the waves that crashed against the rocky base of the cliff. A surge of water carried the boat into the cove. The small outboard motor managed the wave enough to keep the craft from being flung against the rocks.

At a point, perhaps 200 feet to my left and down, the motor stopped. I lifted my camera on its strap around my neck then screwed on the zoom lens to take a look. The boat came into sufficient focus for me to make out the essentials, if not the details.

The boat's pilot, a man, dropped anchor. The wooden skiff heaved in the gut-wrenching waves. Twice, the pilot was knocked off his feet, once landing sprawled, his kidneys splat against the seat of the boat. He wore a baseball cap and sunglasses that hid his features. Not that he would have been recognizable at this distance.

Other than the pilot, the boat carried a gasoline canister and a blue duffel bag. He rifled through the bag. It was like Thor's cup, out came a facemask then swim fins, a snorkel, a spear gun, and still there was more in it. He put the spear gun back in the bag then leaned over the right side of the boat to rinse out the face mask and strap it on. He pulled the band tight then, baseball cap still on, put his face below the churning surface.

A steadying hand on the gunwale, he shook the water off like a dog. He checked beneath the surface of the water several times. He must have spotted what he sought, because he strapped on the swim fins, grabbed the snorkel and dove straight into the onrushing waves. The baseball cap left his head riding the crest of the wave to a small inlet in the harbor.

I tried to follow the yellow tip of the snorkel through the sea foam as it moved closer to the rock wall. I clambered to my feet then ran along the cliff. Whoever this man was, he was hunting for something, something worth risking the sea.

Waves sprayed twenty-five feet up the cliff face. I was looking for a way down to the sea when the yellow tip began to make steady, sure progress back to the tossing boat, staying parallel with the cliff. He reached the wallowing boat, tossed the snorkel, mask, and fins over the gunwale then hauled himself aboard. The only sign of his workout was the few minutes he took to stare at the base of the rocks where a small sea-formed cave undermined the southern-most wall of the cliff. A quick rush of waves into the cave produced a thirty-foot high geyser.

With a shake of his dark-haired head, he started the motor, pulled up the anchor, putt-putting to a spot further around the cup of the natural harbor closer to where the cliff sagged into the ocean. The slump was grassed over in places. Tall, gangly palms clung to the upper edge indicating that the slide had happened long ago.

The boat idled where the landslide had slowed the water enough to cause a sandbar. At low tide, it would take a dexterous pilot to bring anything bigger than this skiff into the harbor, a pilot who knew the cove like the hairs on his chest. It was easy enough to see how a ship, like the White Lady, could run aground, but removing anything from below boards seemed impossible. It was not something one could do alone. Someone would have to stay with the grounded vessel, while the other rowed or motored ashore with the booty.

The man in the boat leaned over his blue bag. He pawed through the bag until he found what he wanted then turned, raising binoculars to his eyes. He scanned the cliff face until he found me. With my camera to my face, I was as indistinguishable as he. I waved in case the man eyeing me was Del then scrambled out of sight. Over the sound of the slamming ocean, the motor buzzed back out to sea.

I PARKED IN MY assigned space at the bed and breakfast. The quadrangle was quiet. All the restoration workers must have been at the site. The mottled shade of the trees cooled the square in the afternoon heat. I avoided the spreading branches of the manchineel tree. Though I admit a certain curiosity about the acid it secreted, I had no desire to use my skin as a test case.

The moment I entered my cabin, my internal alarm went off. My suitcase was opposite side out from where I'd left it on the luggage rack. The paperback I was reading was spine up, pages splayed, instead of closed with a bookmark in place. My room had been cleaned, the bed made, tiny shampoos set out on the bathroom counter, and clean towels with the washcloths folded into little birds hung on the towel rack. But what reason would a maid have to turn my luggage except to reach the far side pocket?

I telephoned the office.

As I waited for John White, I discovered that my couriered note from Del was gone. The pages on Perfidia photocopied at the library were missing, as well as the roll of undeveloped film taken at the gate. Strangest of all, my doodles from my phone call with Whitelaw had been lifted. For the life of me, I couldn't remember what I had doodled, a W, for sure, maybe the telephone number because I do that, then add the occasional watchful eye. It seemed an odd thing to take.

"I checked with the housekeeper. The keys were all on the rack. Was the door forced?" John rumbled, filling the door.

"I didn't notice anything as I entered."

He ran a big finger along the door frame. "Windows?"

"Possibly?"

"Anything of real value missing?"

"Just my sense of security."

He put a comforting hand on my shoulder. "Do you want me to call the police?"

I sat on the bed, taken by an overwhelming sense of the unreasonable. "Who? Why? John?"

"Someone like me who knows you're Lin's daughter." He walked to the far window. He stuck his hand through the open window and pulled the shutter closed.

"How do you?"

"You bear a strong family resemblance."

"I look like a Taddy?"

He nodded, seeming surprised I hadn't known.

"But, the family doesn't even know Del has a daughter."

He turned in response to that comment. "Oh, I think you're wrong on that count, Miss Olivia."

"They know about me?"

"Of course, they do. 'Twas right here your mother got pregnant. And, Lin, he brags about how he raised the perfect Taddy, pretty level-headed little girl will save y'all."

"D...Lin came here often?"

"All his life, even when we boys. His father wanted Lin close to Perfidia. Wanted he boy to know the way of de company. Lin caught a Graydon girl, and that was that. Off they go. She dies having herself a Taddy and that the last we know of you. But, Del, he keep comin'. He here for all the big news."

John sat in the wicker chair in the corner of the room his right leg crossed over his left at the knee. He rested his forearms on the arms of the chair, looked out the window for a moment then turned to me. "Maybe he tell you 'bout de White Lady what be on her. What dey do with all dem bags of white."

"Del was on the White Lady?"

"He find Aaron body. He carry dat boy in he arms all de way to de lady from de old landing." Then, like a quick rain, the patois ceased, "Who knows you're staying here?"

"The man in the gray Mercedes, your son, Dave, and Whitelaw."

"Who have you met?"

"Just you, Dave, Parradine, the banker, and the mortician. Feron deBanco approached me at Sam Lord's, he was meeting with a group of businessmen. Dave said they were hoteliers. But, thinking back, deBanco approached me and introduced himself as though he knew who I was."

"Everybody den!" John slapped his knee coupling it with a slight rock of his body.

"That's funny to you?"

With one hand, he pretended to tip a non-existent hat. "Hat's off, Miss Olivia, in barely a day, you've met all of our rogues. Now, dey be swarming around you like gnats."

I ran a hand through my curls. "Which one of them would do this, take such small things?"

"Anyone attempting to discover why you be here."

I stared at him from the edge of the bed. Del's request for the key in his couriered note would answer that question quickly enough. "Why?"

"Because of de lady, Miss Olivia. What go on is always over, about, and around her."

"Show her to me then?" I said, walking to the door in my polish-streaked green dress, happy bangle, and huaraches.

"With pleasure." John put a hand on the small of my back and ushered me into the quadrangle.

"Mr. Parradine recommends you as a guide."

"Lacy did, did he?"

"Well," I said as we left the quarters, "We're not exactly on a first name basis. Mr. Parradine did regale me sufficiently on the subject of Whitelaw's father to pique my curiosity. He was very fond of Colin. You knew him?"

"He was smart. Tough. Maybe a little too good. I don't know, girl. But, Colin, he never wrong about de business or de law." John gave a quick shake of his head.

"How old was Brendan when Colin died?"

"Seven, maybe eight." The same age Parradine had quoted.

"How did he die?"

"Damn Taddys are forever dueling. Over what? A piece of land, a harbor? There are some grand stories of great raids, a ship docking, men rampaging through the house, whisking the daughters to another plantation to keep Taddys' stock going. My favorite is the one where some Taddy had a daughter who was a ringer for Tad Law. She was most highly prized. Never mind that she was bred at Candle. You know dese places?"

"Candle is the one in Australia, right?" I asked aware he hadn't answered my first question.

"Ships arrived at Candle from both Maison Vol and Perfidia on the same night. Swashbuckling followed with the boys from Perfidia winning the fair Maddock maiden, Jane. Like a good broodmare, she bred true. Her sons, all six of them looked just like Tad Law. But, Jane saved her love for her daughter, even named her Best."

"Best?"

"Her full Christian name was Best Forlast." Laughing, I followed him down a dense path into the humid darkness of a cane field. "Watch the leaves, they cut."

We walked in a single file, John to the front. His basso profundo boomed back to me ricocheting off the walls of sugar cane. "Jane talked her oldest son, Collier, into buying his sister, Best, her own plantation then promised Best that once all of her brothers died, which given the family business they were most likely to do, Best would inherit Perfidia."

"Instead," I said, "Best deBanco was stuck at Pendu forever and was what? The chief architect of the wretched deBancos because her brother, Collier, didn't die, had sons and kept Perfidia?"

"Quick study. Best named the Colombian plantation Pendu. Follow the path. That's a girl. Granddad would tell us these grand tales, heard from his and so on. Wild and a wee dangerous the lot of them."

"And Collier's claim to fame?"

"He inherited a plantation in ruins then by sheer force of will rebuilt Perfidia and made her relevant again. He was the architect of the modern plantation, the modern manor house, and Bajan White."

I panted in the heat as I hop-stepped to keep up with John's long strides. He must have heard my death rattle because he slowed.

"Did Collier Law mooncuss?"

"Of course."

One step we were in a tunnel of cane, the next the great arms of a windmill appeared. Unlike the one I'd stumbled on the night before, this one was situated high on a windward cliff with nothing but sea to its back. With the sails unfurled, it would generate the crushing power needed to press the juice from the cane. Today, the sails were furled and neatly reefed with sisal.

"And, now, where are we in the Taddys' line?" I asked.

"Drayman Law had a son and two daughters. The son, Colin, is dead, and the daughters can't inherit."

"Isn't that a bit medieval?"

"Dat it be." John gestured toward the windmill. I followed his hand.

"So, who gets Perfidia? I mean, when did Drayman Law die?"

"1939."

"Thirty-five years ago? It's still not settled?"

"Not likely to be either, not without a fight. Here's the grinding house."

I HADN'T NOTICED THE lack of a waterwheel, at first, but without one, the structure looked more like a stone kiln than a mill. The furled sails of the windmill soared above the stone building, hiding massive wooden gears with hand hewn wooden pistons. The furled sails against the bright blue sky seemed pulled from the Dutch landscape painting minus the nodding heads of tulips. But unlike a watercolor landscape, the lines were harsh as if the wheel that the sails drove had been used to crush more than sugarcane to a pulp.

John opened the weathered, gray wooden door, each board held in place by hand-pounded iron stays nailed by a square iron nail at either end. As we entered, dank air rushed out.

The crushing stone dominated the interior. The floor was hard earth compacted by time and the feet of slaves then gangs. When the wind turned the crusher, the noise must have been excruciating to the men tethered in the harnesses still attached to each spoke of the great gear.

When John closed the door, the darkness ate at me. I turned my face toward a laser of sunlight piercing through the conical center of the mill. The light beam descended the piston but petered out before the meager ray reached the crushing stone.

We both looked up the shaft. I could feel the leather straps on my shoulders. I felt bowed under the imagined weight.

"Dave said your great, great, great was the first."

"Indeed, they called him, First. He never worked the crushing house. I think in the United States, they would have called him a house Negro." John leaned against the stone wall which pitched him slightly forward as it bent upward toward the piston. He put his hands behind his back, his feet out, and still his back curved.

I touched the pitted crushing stone. "First's sons worked the stone, though."

"A few of them did though Tad was fond of First's off-spring. I think there was a bit of a scoundrel about First. Legend has always included him in many of Tad's more colorful adventures. First never married, but had twelve sons. Some say that the high literacy rate the island prides itself on began when First, who learned from Beth Law, taught his children to read and write. Don't feel too sorry for First and his. They've always had the best of Perfidia...of Barbados."

"So much so," I asked, "that Perfidia seems more yours than, let's say, the Maddock's who are, at best, stewarding the plantation until an heir appears?"

He pushed himself off of the wall to open the door. I pressed my hands against the cool interior stone.

"The restoration crew has done a remarkable job. When I was a boy, her sails were tattered, stones had fallen from the walls, and the primary piston had rotted away. And, here, Miss Olivia is the boiling house." John made a sweeping gesture to his left as we exited the mill.

Workers crawled over the hand-mortared rock structure that surrounded the windmill. They were carefully placing stones. Each stone had a black number painted on the bottom side. One stone would be selected, the number checked, the mortar laid, all before the stone was rocked gently into position. The boiling house was being reconstructed, stone-by-stone.

"What happened?"

"The mortar was too unstable to allow tourists inside. So they have deconstructed the building, made a grid of each sector, numbered each stone, managed a wee archeological dig while the wall was rubble, and now are happily recreating the outbuilding."

The workers moved over the stonework like purposeful ants.

"The sugar was crushed in the mill then..."

"Yes. The resulting juice sluiced off the crusher to the boiling house. Do you want to go back to the wheel?"

I shook my head, watching another stone gently rolled into place then rocked until it fit. When pleased with the rock's seating, the worker selected another running his hands over it communing with its lumps and bumps like a phrenologist.

John stepped away from the workers. "In the boiling house, the cane juice was brought to a boil. They stoked the fire with bagasse—cane trash. The liquid was stirred as it boiled to steam out the water. Eventually, the liquid crystallized but not before molasses was extracted for rum. The end product was muscovado, brownish raw sugar. The muscovado was transported in hogsheads to the harbor, rolled out to dinghies and ferried to a waiting ship." He gestured in the general direction of the landslip.

"Sugar wasn't refined here?"

"Never. Perfidia grew cane. Muscovado was as close as she got. However, rum was and is made here."

"She helped grow a country, as well."

"Some would object loudly to that." John stepped away from me, leaving the impression he was one of them, perhaps believing that the Whites and others brought here against their will deserved more credit.

"I read that there was some problem in the cane industry in the thirties."

He looked me over, before locking on my face. "You look overheated."

I put a hand to my brow. My bangs had curled, but not kinked, a good sign. "Not so warm that I can't have the full tour. What would Mr. Parradine say if you took me back half-done?"

"More to the point, girl, what would he say if I took you back half-baked." He gestured to a table and chairs under a blue and gray striped market umbrella. John poured the contents of a half-full Styrofoam cup of what appeared lukewarm ice tea to the ground then tossed the cup.

He quickly wiped the table with a rasty, moth-eaten, windowpane checked, cotton towel. With a sweep of his arm, he invited me to sit. The shade of the umbrella did feel good. He pulled two canned iced teas from a red metal cooler shaded under the table and offered one to me.

"The cane?"

"Here we go then, girl. Dis be patented lecture number two: De Cane." He put his elbows on the table and folded his hands together. He gazed towards the sweep of the sea for a moment, maybe wondering which version of lecture number two to give. "Perfidia was always perfect for sugar. Not that you need much to grow cane other than sufficient water."

"Where does your water come from?"

"Below ground and above. The coral cleanses the below ground water. Wells bring the water to the surface, but we rarely need to irrigate. There is almost always sufficient rain."

"Would there have been a well near here?"

"For the quarters, for the livestock, to wash the cane at the mill."

"I haven't seen one at the bed and breakfast." I put my elbows on the table enjoying the breeze tickling my arms and drying my wet armpits.

"The wellhead is at the west corner of the kitchen, behind a door, under lock and key, to keep the odd worker's baby from taking the long fall. The kitchen staff oversees entry. If you'd like to see the well, you could ask Nancy to show it to you."

"How deep?"

"The ground water supply seems to be just above sea level." He studied me for a moment, his dark eyes making some reckoning of my thoughts, narrowed ever so slightly.

"So tell me about the cane?"

He sipped his ice tea, tilted his head then studied me a while before continuing. "The cane fields are prepared in the late summer. Plowed and fertilized. Sugarcane sprouts from short sections that contain nodes. The sections are planted end-to-end along a furrow with the furrows about six feet apart. The first shoots break the ground in about a week.

"Cane grows rapidly, requiring constant weeding until the field is impenetrable. The edges of immature cane are feathery but as it matures the leaves become sharp enough to cut easily through your skin. Barbadian cane is mature within a year. If you watch, you might see it grow. By harvest, the stalks reach fourteen or fifteen feet."

I bent my arms, elbows still on the table, and rested my head in my hands. John White's intense black eyes and rolling bass lulled me.

"When the crop is ripe, cane cutters use machetes to cut the sugarcane in swathes. The cutters are still called the great gang. Grueling work. Some plantations burn off the leaves before harvest; others set fire to the cut sugar cane so full of sweet juice, it is unharmed. In Tad's day the cut was loaded into two-wheeled, horse-drawn carts that carried it to the mill, now it's trucked. The harvest is washed then chopped into short sections and crushed.

"The roots are left in the ground to sprout. A single planting produces three crops. After the last harvest, the land is left fallow or planted in soybeans. Cane takes nitrogen out of the soil; soybeans return it. Before the 1930s, sugar was the dominant cash crop."

"Then in 1938 the sugar cane bubble burst?"

"The curse of the sugar beet. But, girl, you can tell the difference between the two. And, Bajan White sugar, she make de best rum."

"Having overdone a taste test only last night, I am your actual expert witness."

"Any questions?"

"How did the Taddys get the barrels to the harbor?"

"According to oral history, the ships stood off the bar at the southern headland near the slump and waited for high tide. Dinghies loaded with muscovado stood by in Taddys Cove to transfer the barrels. Big ships anchored off the sea side of the sandbar. Some of the ships sent their dinghies in, some required Perfidia to send her dinghies out. The captain of the sailing vessel had to be practiced because they had only the high point of the tide on which to load and get back out to sea."

"But, how did the barrels get down to the cove?" I pointed toward the cliff's edge for emphasis.

"Truth or myth?" John seemed wary of my question, which piqued my curiosity. He drank ice tea, his dark eyes distant, one finger plucked at the rim of the

Styrofoam cup. Like a prize student, I tried to re-engage the teacher.

"Heavy on the myth." I raised one shoulder as coyly as a girl called Sonny can, hoping to get back to the familiarity we had been sharing.

"Truth. Before the landslip, the crop was carted down a narrow road that Tad and his minions carved into the cliff head. Our current crop of archeologists has surmised that the heavy use of the shipping road and the slipshod way it was torn into the cliff eventually caused the slump."

"The road might simply have been a way for the family to reach the beach, might it not?"

"The family has many ways to the beach. Archeologist to preservationist to family, we all agree that the myth is impossible."

I cocked my head, hoping the myth jibed with a drawing of bats and a spiral staircase; the White Lady listing hulled in the bay, a jeweled necklace, and a key to Tad's treasure.

"Impossible?" I raised my eyebrows.

"Some say that Tad dug a vertical tunnel to a series of caves that led one to another and so to the harbor. Men stationed at the opening lowered sacks of muscovado by rope to men at the base of the shaft who hauled the muscovado through the interior of a hundred or so feet of earth. They placed the sacks in a staging cave on a tall bar of sand to keep the bags dry until the dinghies arrived for loading. This cave is only accessible to the men loading during low tide and to the dinghies during high tide. Nonsensical."

"Given that the headlands' road existed, when did the cliff slide to the sea?"

"A raiding party, possibly from one of the other plantations, in an attempt to break Perfidia's monopoly on the Lesser Antilles sugar production, caused the land to slide."

"When?"

"It occurred during Collier's years, which would make the raid about the time of your Civil War. Sugar was booming."

"So, the boys came in one night on the high tide and blew Collier's shipping road to hell? His own brothers!"

He gave me a brilliant, toothy smile showing off two gold molars as he swatted at a bug that flew too close to his right eye.

"What happened next?"

"Collier shrugged and sank one of their ships loaded with goods for the Confederacy, reaped that harvest, then called in an engineer and had a forty-foot, heavily reinforced crane built on the bluff. Until the thirties, they lowered the sugar from the cliffs near the north quarters."

"No caves."

"Disappointed? I was. I spent much of my youth looking for them with Colin as our dinghy pitched in the waves."

"But if Tad mooncussed there had to have been beach access invisible to the British authorities. He hardly would have sent his men scurrying up the cliff with looted goods for anyone to see. Road or no road."

"Most believe he just rowed into Taddys Cove."

"How believable is that?"

John stood. "Tad's booty has never been found. It may be only a small boy's myth. Or, perhaps he spent it or hid it so well it hasn't been found in generations."

I pushed my chair back from the table. "Some myth! Did Aaron mooncuss?"

"The White Lady went aground on the bar. It happens."

"Did he drowned before or after?" I rose from my chair ready to leave. "I had the DEA at my front door, was Aaron trafficking?"

"Come, girl, back into the cane." He turned for me to follow.

"I asked a question." His shoulders stiffened at my tone.

"To which there is no answer. Perfidia is an old plantation with old ghosts. You're coming late; you have only to be harmed." I took his comment for what it was—a threat delivered in a bass, not a baritone, voice.

John took off quick time, muttering: *Go home, girl*. I scrambled after him; carefully staying in the narrow path between the canes of sugar. He sped away leaving me alone, deep in the cane.

I swatted as small black bugs ringed my head in the unbearable heat. The acrid smell of smoke and the green of hot sugar cane scoured my nose. The increasingly pungent smell came from no discernible direction, descending in a thick band into the cane.

Fire!

I ran for the bed and breakfast with my hands out front to ward of the cane. I tried not to breathe, attempting to outrun flames I couldn't see even as smoke enveloped me in its phantom arms.

I needn't have bothered. Flames shot three feet out from the windows of cabin 4.

Restoration workers and the kitchen staff had formed a bucket brigade from the kitchen to my quarters. Buckets flew past me. Water, splashed through the windows by the bucketful, hissed. Though the flames came within inches of the next cabin, the stone walls contained it. A restoration worker hosed down the wooden shingled roof of the next cabin to keep the fire from spreading roof to roof.

I didn't try to save my few belongings. It was futile. The blazing fire had consumed them. Too hot, inexplicably hot, I overheard staff mumbling that the smell of gasoline was strong when they first arrived.

Two hours earlier, I had felt violated because someone stole a few belongings. Now I felt gang-raped by people who think they can do anything because they have money and power. And money. Go home were the last words I'd heard from John White. Well, if this was the Taddy way of making certain I did, they had misjudged me.

I sat on a bench just outside the kitchen and watched the struggle. When the interior of my cabin was embers and the ashes steamed, the firefighters quit their watch. By then, the sun had made its nightly dive into the sea.

I had no clothes. I had no identification. I had no money. I had no picture of Del, or notes, or photographs. My shelter was gone. The temperature dropped to the mid-seventies. My little green sleeveless dress, all the clothes I had, was too light for the night. Nancy, the cook, dragged me by the hand into the kitchen.

Nancy scrambled eggs. They went rather well with neat gin. As I sipped my gin, it became evident that John White had gone home for his evening meal. He hadn't responded to repeated calls, both vocal and by telephone. Not that he could have stopped the inevitable, but he should have been there as the foreman...as a friend.

I removed Mr. White from the ally list. I had no idea when I had begun the list or even what we were allied against, only that the list was decidedly short. The need for allies implied a war or quest. Quests required a goal, armament, knights—the usual. I was here for Del, but, of course, quests by their very nature are never about the obvious.

"Miss Olivia?" Nancy said wiping her hands on a towel tucked into the waist of her white uniform. The ever present P embroidered on the uniform's breast pocket moved as she continued to wipe the tables using a towel with interlocking red P's worked in the weave. "If I be you, I take me to de manor house. I march over and tell dem what happened at dey bed and breakfast, tell dem because of dem you hab no money, clothes or shelter. I would." She put her hands on her slender hips for emphasis.

"And they would, what?" I moaned into my gin.

"Take you in." She wiped the table next to me in a circular motion, quickly scooping up crumbs.

"This isn't *Jamaica Inn,*" I quipped.

She shook her head. "Alas, no. But, it would be nice, den we would have a Jem about."

"I've gathered Brendan Whitelaw serves that part."

"Danny got de sly about he all right." She began laughing, barely able to get words out she added, "Hard to trick, he be."

"Did you see anyone go near my room before the fire started?"

Nancy shook her head and wiped her hands on the towel at her waist.

"Would you tell me if you had?"

"Not my place. Nor theirs," she said, gesturing to include all who presently inhabited the bed and breakfast. "They know of the fire. They will report the loss or they won't." She wiped her face with her waist towel. "It has always been this way. What de lady want, she get."

"De lady." I gestured toward where I presumed Perfidia to be. Nancy patted my filthy, ash-covered arm. Seeming to notice my state of dishevelment for the first time, she turned to the kitchen. A moment later, tap water ran into a tin bowl. When she returned, she placed a bowl of water, a clean washcloth, and a bar of soap in front of me.

I took the hint.

AFTER MY SCRUBBING, I walked the two miles to Sam Lord's Castle, if my kilometer to miles conversion was correct. My rental car, useless to me without keys, stayed parked in front of the burned out cabin, minus the history as told by Sam Lord, retrieved from the floor of the passenger seat. I arrived after the thirty-minute walk in my green skimmer streaked with ash and brass polish, hot, sweaty, and smelling romantically of acrid smoke.

I sat on a barstool, my back to the bar, scanning the assembly of people enjoying themselves. Couples shared glances as they entwined their fingers on starched white tablecloths. Swaying palms tatted shadows on the grass beneath a sliver of moon.

A steel drum band played the *1812 Overture* then quickly segued into *I'll Be Seeing You*. Hand-in-hand couples wove through tables to the dance floor nestled in the lower gardens of the estate. Couples who started in ballroom stances soon laid their heads on their partners' shoulders. The men's hands journeyed down the women's backs. Every one of them knew who they were and where and with whom he or she was staying that night. I had never dreamed that having a bed or one name to call your own could be such a luxury.

"De lady, she is here," Dave White said over my shoulder.

I swiveled on the seat. "As you no doubt know by now, de lady, she be homeless and penniless."

He cupped my hands around a rum punch in a tall dewy glass. "As comfort goes, the offering is not much, but the drink is on the house."

I sipped as the steel drums began the first notes of *Perfidia*. A chill, like the tingle when your fingers wake from sleep, pricked my back. I took my hand from the glass as though the cold was making me shiver then swirled to scan the crowd for a small-minded, cruel man. Instead, hands were squeezed, cheeks pecked, and offers to dance accepted. Few couples could resist the Latin beat ringing out from the steel drums; even my tired toes attempted the rhythm.

"Miss Olivia," Dave said, "Telephone."

I grabbed the receiver from his hand. "Yes?"

"Sorry about missing you at the bank," Whitelaw responded in his melodious baritone.

"Sorry about the bank!" I shrieked into the telephone. Every reveler at the bar shot a blurry-eyed gawp my way. Dave tried to motion me behind a tall potted plant with spiky red flowers. I stayed seated. "Do you know what has happened to me? Have you any idea?"

"We need to talk," Whitelaw said, his soothing voice a little too gentle for my mood.

"Who do you think you are? How can you treat someone this way? I'm Del's daughter. I belong here. What's the matter with you?" I gripped the receiver with such might that my fingers cramped.

"Are you slowing down at all or just flinging angst into the moonlit air."

"Where are you?" I narrowed my eyes and made a visual sweep of the tables, checking for a man with the telephone receiver to his ear. "Are you watching me?"

"Of course, I am."

"Right now?" I carried the phone as far as I could given the length of the cord, to get a view down the bar, across the restaurant to the dance floor.

"Well, not at this precise moment."

I plunked the phone down so hard on the mahogany bar that the telephone jangled. "What am I going to do?"

"Tell Dave to get you a place to stay and some clothes to wear. He knows I always pay my riders."

"And if he won't?"

"Put him on the phone if you're lax to ask a man's help. Perhaps you are the kind of woman who has never had to rely on the kindness of men. True?"

"Oh, my, we've read Tennessee Williams. I'm not impressed." I stopped long enough to regain my breath. The other end of the line was similarly silent. "Say, Dave finds me shelter then what?"

"Attend Aaron's funeral."

In the silence, the rumble of the ocean came clearly over the line.

"Will you be there?" I switched hands, doing mini push-ups on the bar top with my right hand to loosen the cramp.

"Had a spot of a run-in with a member of the family today, so only as long as necessary. I'll find a way to keep in contact if you've got the nerve to stay on the island. I am truly sorry about the fire. Were you able to recover anything?" He knew, of course. He probably lit it to get his hands on the key.

"Tell me something that will make me stay when I have nothing left and no reason to care."

"I'm watching you now." Hearing the cadence of waves on the beach over the handset, I peered down the gardens toward the edge of the water. A dusting of tables nestled in clusters of multi-flowered bushes along the walkway to the beach. The door of a striped canvas cabana well down the path was open. A tall, slender man leaned on the doorframe.

"Make sure Dave finds you a place with a tub. I happen to know that you like baths," Whitelaw quipped. He had been in the cane field, he had taped the note to my cabin window! Maybe not, I had been in the bath when he first called.

The line went dead. The door of the cabana closed. The light went out in the window. I watched a shadowy figure glide to the garden walkway where it turned into a man with his hands stuffed in the pockets of a pair of light dress slacks.

His unbuttoned shirt was a dark print, flapping over a white undershirt; the kind I'd heard called a wife-beater. He dodged through the lower bushes quickly disappearing into the shrubbery. He was gone, leaving me with his sensuous, frightening voice echoing in my ear. I thumped the telephone to the bar.

Dave emerged from a door on the other side of the counter carrying a case of beer.

"Mr. Whitelaw says you will stand me to a bed and a fresh set of clothes, he'll pay you back." I slid the telephone towards Dave then folded my hands around my drink. I sucked in a huge straw full of rum punch. The planter's punch met the gin and eggs, my stomach made a sound reminiscent of the waves crashing in the harbor. I took another slurp.

"Danny said that, did he?" Dave said, looking over my shoulder.

I swiveled so fast in my chair I slid out of it to standing. No one was there, maybe the back of a tropical print shirt, maybe that.

"I've got an extra room. You're welcome to it. I'm off in an hour."

"You don't still live on Perfidia, do you?"

He laughed at the pathetic whine in my voice. "No, I live above Danny's law offices. Rent from Lacy. He's got two apartments in the back wing. I have the front apartment, Danny the back."

"Did your Dad light the fire in my room?"

"No." At the look of disbelief on my face, he added, "He wouldn't."

"I took his tour and lost everything."

Dave stowed the beer on a shelf near the floor then poured a whiskey for a man down the bar. "Then why trust me?"

"Because Whitelaw told me I should?" I answered with more of a question in my voice than meant.

That great boyish smile smeared across his face; the laugh came right from the belly. "He'll appreciate the hell out of that. I'll try to get someone to cover for me so I can close out a bit early tonight."

Dave's eyes shot over my shoulder and widened. I turned. Feron deBanco approached, his hips swaying to the beat of the steel drums, one hand held out toward me.

"I see you're back. It's a lovely night. Would you care to dance?" deBanco asked.

The steel drums twanged in a spicy beat. I wasn't a dancer. In fact, no one had ever invited me to dance without coercion from my father. Yet, here was a man exuding maleness, I could smell it, asking me to dance despite my smelly, smoky dress.

I shook my head.

Feron grabbed my hand. I was pretty sure I hadn't accepted, but here I was walking behind him as though his arm was a leash. The minute we gained the dance floor, he rolled me into his arms, one hand on the small of my back, the other holding my right hand. At the first step, I knew I was in trouble.

He was smooth. He must have spent his youth in cotillion. He not only smelled male; he smelled like money, lots of it, as though he had been rubbed in it since childhood. His too close together eyes were a deep, dark blue with black corona. His umber hair would have been in ringlets if not for the expensive, stylish cut that left it long in the back and waving over his ears.

His lawn shirt was so soft it felt like silk, the batik print was various rich browns, perfect with his tan slacks and the loafers on his sockless feet. Money smelled good.

"So, you've been here a day, what do you think of our little island?"

"Not much."

He rolled me out to arm's length then back returning his hand to the small of my back, perhaps lower. He cocked his head as a question.

"My cabin burned. My clothes are gone. Nothing left. I need to go to the U. S. Embassy to get a passport and the money for a ticket home."

"Sucks." His lopsided grin was catching, a dimple on the right, lower on the left.

Next thing I knew, I was twirling. As the music spun down, he dipped me until my chin length hair brushed the stone dance floor.

"Anything I can help you find?" he asked, lifting me easily from the crazy angle.

"No. Mr. Whitelaw has offered to buy me some clothes. He asked Dave White to give me a place to sleep for the night. I'm okay for now."

"Whitelaw? He was here?" DeBanco surveyed the gardens seeming more than a bit caught off-guard.

"I guess. He telephoned just before you asked me to dance."

As the band broke for a rest, deBanco dragged me back to the bar. I felt I should apologize for my dancing, for not smelling like money, for being dreary. He deposited me on my bar stool.

"Hardly anyone can dance a real salsa." He patted my shoulder. "You did fine if that's what worries you."

"I'm worried about my father—my clothes—getting home, not about my dancing." But, I was. For some reason, I wanted this man to think well of me. I was pretty sure I'd already blown that. Besides, I'd talked too much. He couldn't have known my predicament. If he had, how had he?

DeBanco pulled a gold money clip from the front pocket of his perfectly pleated tan pants then peeled off four hundred BWI. "Consider it an investment. Not enough to get you home, but enough to keep you within reach."

I handed it back to him. He folded my hands over the bills.

"Can I buy you a drink then?"

He gave a swift, engaging grin then took off in long strides toward the car park. The sound of Dave White clearing his throat brought me back to the bar. He was standing with his hands on his hips staring at my empty glass and fist full of money.

Day Five

I SPENT THE NIGHT at Parradine's feeling incredibly safe tucked under the mosquito netting in Dave White's spare bedroom. Dave lent me an extra-large tee-shirt that proclaimed itself to be from HARVARD. The soft cotton knit shirt covered me to mid-thigh. I lay listening to the sounds of a crowded tropical city, which included a wild night of revelry spurred on by Australian sailors fresh off their ship. Somewhere after three a.m. when the city quieted, I fell into a sound sleep.

At breakfast, Mr. Parradine kindly asked me to call him Lacy. Lacy excused Dave's absence saying that Dave had a few errands to run before Aaron's funeral. Parradine sat across from me, deeply engaged in the London Times. He had a wonderfully tweedy feel to him, a kind of solid goodness that draped him nicely like the very best suit coat.

"Who set the fire in my room?" I asked, still ensconced in Dave's tee-shirt, my mostly naked legs and bare feet tucked under the oaken table in a salute to the modesty of Lacy's dining room.

The dining room was wallpapered in a soft floral print. A built-in, glass-fronted hutch had three drawers below, three shelves above. The table was a light oak, as was the wainscoting. The table chairs were oak as well, with rattan seats woven in an intricate flower pattern. Paintings on the wall were of the flowers that bloomed in the trees everywhere on the island.

There were two exits from the dining room; one led to a sitting room reachable through the back door as well as from the offices. The other doorway opened into the kitchen. What I could see of the kitchen was old fashioned, with flour and salt drawers, window-paned cabinets, and an ancient stove that looked converted from wood-burning—or perhaps not. I had noticed a stack of wood outside the back door when I arrived in the night.

The coffee was excellent, brewed by pouring hot water over grounds into a glass flask. The method was new to me. I poured myself a second cup.

Lacy lowered the newspaper to peer at me. He pursed his lips, bushing his gray mustache, before sighing and raising the paper with a crinkle, which, I suppose meant, he had no idea. A moment later, he lowered the newspaper again. "Better not to ask, lass."

"You took Whitelaw in?" I took a slurp of coffee with a bite of the ever-present coconut bread.

The newspaper rustled as he put it down. "After his father's death, yes. Being a confirmed bachelor, an eight-year-old boy was a mystery to me. Made a hash of raising him, I'm afraid."

"What happened to his mother?"

"She rose one morning, took off her cotton nightgown and folded it neatly. Naked, she said goodbye to her four-year-old son then hanged herself in the middle of her cabin. Brendan's father, Colin, found her when he came home that night."

"How did his father learn about the folding and everything?"

"The lad told him, plus the boy left her things undisturbed." Lacy's sad eyes said everything; he needn't have bothered with the shake of his head.

"Whitelaw doesn't think..."

"No, lass. Maybe when Danny was a wee lad, maybe then for a time. He stayed in the cabin all day with her hanging there." He shook his head again. "Imagine."

"Why?" I fingered a bite off of the coconut bread, played with the crumb a moment before stuffing the sweet bread in my mouth.

"The best we could tell was that she didn't want to be trouble to Colin. She left a lovely note about how sorry she was that she was pregnant."

I snipped another chunk of coconut bread off with my fingers, wondering why a second pregnancy would matter.

Reading my mind, Lacy answered, "Funny thing, Danny was the problem. Another baby couldn't have mattered. The damage was done. Colin loved her very,

very much. She was a lovely girl. He'd known her all his life."

"What am I missing?" I fingered more coconut bread.

Lacy patted my hand. "Nothing, lass. Not one thing."

"Then tell me about Collier Law and Perfidia."

"Forever why?" Lacy folded his newspaper very precisely, even dog-earing the page he had been on when we began to talk.

"John White got me started. The fire got us off course."

"To get back on we need to go a tad further back than Collier. Did our Johnny tell you that the Whites, in the main, were house servants and overseers?"

I nodded, reaching for more coconut bread. Lacy watched me snatch the slice with his sly blue eyes. For the briefest of moments, I expected him to whack my fingers with the butter knife. Instead, he pushed the butter my way. I waggled my finger no.

"Eventually, the Whites took to the Church of England, took to literacy, placed themselves well as foreman, overseers, lady's maids, especially after a few generations of..." He hesitated.

"Miscegenation?" I offered.

He pursed his lips, squinted and poured himself a cup of coffee. "There's that then."

"Making them family?"

"Not family, not exactly. Half are trying to prove they belong in the big house, the other half are still slaves to it."

"I read that Steadfast White saved the place?"

"Well? Taking advantage of one of the few slave uprisings in Barbados, he killed the idiot Crispin Law then took over the main house claiming he was a direct descendant from Tad Law and by rights should inherit."

"He was family, wasn't he?" I rested my chin in my hands, my elbows on the table, completely enthralled by Lacy's easy ramblings and his pleasant burr.

"He was a descendant but not in line to inherit. Crispin had sons."

"And Steadfast?"

"Unfortunately for Steadfast, Crispin's grandson, Collier, the man you asked about, walked up the stairs into the drawing-room where Steadfast was holding court and shot him steadfastly between the eyes. Forget Steadfast and Crispin, the boy, Collier, rebuilt Perfidia."

"Boy?"

"He was seventeen. Never went to school. Never went to England. Bolstered the family coffers, which had slimmed noticeably after the hurricane, by a spot of mooncussing."

"No one ever challenged him?"

"He fought three duels, won them all. As a result, he sent his youngest brother to Hawaii to grow sugar, one of his middle brothers to Malaysia for rubber, the other to Australia for cattle. His sister, Best, was famously in Colombia. Made them change their surnames so that nothing could be traced back to Perfidia if the investment went bad. The investments didn't go bad; they bloomed. Now we have the Winslow, Harris, Maddock and deBanco families among others."

"What happened to Collier?" I snatched more coconut bread.

"He died at eighty-three having sex in the Great Hall on a tapestry rug beneath Estella."

I raised an eyebrow. "Estella?"

"Oh, you'll meet her soon enough, lass. She's been the official site of many a family adventure."

I munched happily, my mind filled with duels, miscegenation, and the rug on the Great Hall floor. Somehow this was my legacy. I hadn't placed myself in the panoply as of yet, but I recognized something in me that had lain dormant all my life, something I had dragged with me to adulthood.

When I was small, I would lock my bedroom door and imagine I was a pirate. I sailed my twin bed ship, sheets full to the wind, battens cracking, into harbor after harbor, my trusty sword my only companion. Ahoy!

"One of Collier's grandsons challenged him for power. The old boy told him to choose his weapon. The grandson picked any woman on the drawing room floor. Eight people witnessed the duel. The grandson took over Perfidia, ran her well too, which would have put a smile on old Collier's face."

The image of Collier dead on the carpet, exhausted by his endeavor, too proud to yell uncle, fanned my whimsy. "Which brings us to...?"

"Eventually to Drayman Law, who died in 1939 and left two daughters and one lively son who lived hard, loved hard and died hard at twenty-eight. Tell you, lass, Colin was not only my partner but my joy, if it weren't for his son, I don't know what I would have done with my sorrow."

"How did Colin die?"

"They found him at the base of the cliffs with his brains bashed in."

"Was his killer found?" I watched Lacy over the rim of my coffee cup.

He fingered the newspaper, deciding what to say or just how to say it. "No one was ever arrested if that's what you mean. No proof, you see. Had there been, I would have taken some action. Wish I had. Now especially. Well, you've made me speak out of turn. That is the short version of a history that took over two centuries to write."

I looked at his gentle, pale blue eyes, wishing I could string everything I'd learned together to intuit the meaning. But I was missing an essential element, like hydrogen, that was so basic to the Taddys that it was everything and everywhere.

Lacy's tale of Whitelaw's mother hanging in her cabin and his father's murder disturbed me. It made me want to show Whitelaw that I had what it took to stay and to earn deBanco's bribe.

"Are you going to the funeral, then?" Lacy asked, snapping his paper open to the dog-eared page. "You'll want something more than Davey's Harvard tee-shirt to wear."

He folded the newspaper, stood, and crossed over to what should have been the flatware drawer. With a hand on each scrolled drawer pull, he slid the drawer open. "House funds," he said turning back with a handful of bills. "Leave the green dress on your bed. It'll get a good wash."

"It's all I have to wear." I pulled the tee-shirt down to cover my thighs as I stood.

Lacy gave me a solid once over then walked out onto the sun porch. He returned with a pair of worn, frayed blue jeans thrown over his left arm like a sommelier's serviette at a fancy restaurant.

"Danny left these jeans the last time he stopped round." Lacy handed the button-fly blue jeans to me, checked me over again, adding, "The shirt will cover whatever is left out."

Whitelaw, from the size of his pants, was a good two inches narrower in the hip and four longer in the leg which would make him minimally six feet tall. The shirt did cover what was left out, everything from the second button to the top. The jeans smelled of saltwater. The fabric scratched, too, as though recently wet and stiffened as the ocean salt dried in the fabric.

Within the hour, I returned to the house on Coleridge Street with an appropriately somber dress purchased at Cave-Shepherd.

SMALL, TATTED WHITE FLOWERS rimmed the scoop neck of my new black dress and highlighted the empire waist cinched by a bow in the back. A pair of black Mary Janes and a black boater hat with a white gross grain ribbon completed my ensemble. I bought the hat at the last minute because my church-going friends had told me that a lady always wore a hat to church.

When I came down the stairs, Lacy, in a dark gray double-breasted suit, said, "Boaters always put me in the mood for Benny Goodman."

We listened to big band tunes on the Rediffusion as I drove Lacy's black Mercedes sedan towards St. Philip. At Lacy's direction, I turned into the drive of a well-maintained chapel surrounded by mahogany trees perhaps two kilometers past the gates to Perfidia.

The chapel looked stolen block by block from an English estate in Surrey, except that its gently sloping lawn overlooked the north quarters of Perfidia built on a benchland that stretched to the Atlantic Ocean.

Dave White directed us into a parking spot. Lacy rushed around to open the driver-side door for me, only to find me on tiptoe peering over the top of his car checking the parked cars for a gray Mercedes. One was parked just off the road, one tire in a slight ditch.

Lacy navigated me toward the chapel with a hand on my upper arm. The church was a simple stone structure, with three lovely Gothic stained-glass windows arrayed down each side. Instead of a bell tower, the bell hung in an arch of gray stone at the roofline above the door.

A graveyard next to the chapel enclosed by a gray stone wall protected worn headstones jumbled in with crypts so long weathered that the stone surface was made knobby by centuries of tropical rains. People were milling on the Bermuda grass clawing its way through the sand between headstones.

Some mourners stopped to set one or two flowers in small metal vases atop the headstones or paused in passing to pat a vase-less headstone. Predominant in the green and quiet was one new hole, dug at the side of a limestone crypt. The tombstone read: *Aaron Michael Law-Maddock, February 14, 1950-August 21, 1974, Born to the storm.*

"Lacy!" a woman, who looked to be in her early fifties, called taking decisive steps in our direction. Her black, silk shirt dress emphasized her quick gate and firm, slim body. Lacy openly admired her wicked trot as her three-inch spikes aerated the turf. She reached for his extended hand. He gave her an elegant old world smile as he kissed it.

"Lacy, love, I am so glad you are here. I was afraid...ah, I should have known better." She looked speculatively at me through narrowed gray eyes. "Lacy?"

"Amanda Law-Maddock," he said, "May I present Olivia Lassiter. Amanda is one of Drayman Law's two fine daughters."

Amanda clasped my hand in two small hands that looked far too well-bred to have a grip like a vice.

"My dear! Lin's daughter!" she said, squeezing harder. At my flinch, she dropped my hand then looked at hers as though surprised they were at the end of her wrists. "I'm so sorry!"

"Shouldn't I be offering my condolences to you?"

"Awful. What must you think of us? Your father comes to us and goes missing."

"I think," I said with care, "you lost a son. How hard Aaron's death must be for you."

"Not pleasant, not at all. Then Lloyd has a row at the funeral parlor. Poor Aaron, I was quite embarrassed. Oh, there, they're playing that song."

She grabbed my left hand with remarkable familiarity and dragged me towards the country church now thronged with people, so many that every pew was filled, leaving latecomers to stand at the back of the small nave. The western sun blazed on the stained glass of the Gothic windows splashing ribbons of color across those assembled. The rosette window set in the wall above the pulpit blazed a multi-colored quatrefoil on the aisle.

Amanda stopped at the front left pew. A brass marker proclaimed that this carved piece of wood belonged to the family Law. Only one person sat in the row. A youngish man immediately rose to his feet, his hand extended. He couldn't have seemed more British if he had smelled like wet wool.

"Lloyd Law-Maddock," he said, as we shook. He had pleasant lines under his dark, summer-weight suit, broad at the shoulder, narrow at the hip. The term well-knit came immediately to mind quickly followed by tightly knit.

Tension lines marred the corners of his light eyes. His brown hair was poking out in several directions. The reason became evident when he rammed splayed fingers through his unruly waves. Something had recently distressed him, something more than this funeral. He motioned for me to sit next to him.

There was continued commotion at the back of the church as men opened and positioned folding chairs in the entry, those unable to find seats, waited in the wings. The church doors were opened wide for those forced to stand outside. The majority of those in attendance were Bajan. Until now, I had been traveling surrounded by visitors and workers from Canada, Great Britain, and the United States. It struck me then that white Anglo-Saxon Barbadians were few, an imbalance that was as old as the initial arrival of the slave ships.

That song turned out to be *Nearer My God to Thee.* Del's absolute least favorite. He always said the hymn made him think of a boat adrift without engines while a huge something lurked in the dark.

Across the aisle to my right, Feron deBanco leaned around the person seated next to him and gave me a crooked smile. I nodded to him then sat with my back starchily straight against the pew and tried not to hope for dancing at the wake. Amanda patted my knee.

Lloyd stood so quickly that the bench jarred back a few inches almost ejecting me via the slippery, highly polished mahogany seat. He nudged his way past our legs. Crossing the aisle, he reached over the man in the aisle seat and grabbed deBanco by the elbow. DeBanco stood. They spat words at each other until Feron pulled free. As deBanco sat, he made a point of pulling up his pant leg to avoid destroying the sharp crease in the expensive fabric of his suit.

Lloyd returned to the family pew accompanied by whispers weaving through the congregants gathered in the nave. Looking even more disheveled, he sat, not at all concerned about his crease.

Amanda reached across me to pat her son's knee. "There dear. You can't have expected him to change feathers just because your brother is dead."

To no one in particular, in a voice that echoed off the back of the church, Lloyd responded, "And, a bloody thug as well!"

A few voices could be heard demanding to know what had been said. The minister cleared his throat to shush them. Silence fell as the pastor began the final farewells. When he sensed discomfort with his impersonal eulogy via the shifting bottoms of the mourners, he nodded toward our pew.

Lloyd rose, carefully buttoning his suit coat. He brushed a shaky hand through his mussed hair. Curls immediately fell back across his brow. As he stepped to the lectern, he raised red-rimmed eyes to the gathered mourners. He cleared his throat—hesitated then cleared his throat again.

A brief, embarrassed smile flickered across his lips. The pink tip of his tongue flicked out to wet them. With trembling hands, he pulled a three-by-five note card from his breast pocket. He read the card to himself, his lips moving unselfconsciously. His eyes rose to those gathered.

"Aaron loved Perfidia, the good and the bad of her." Lloyd's British accent rounded the edges of his words, lending them the tone of an Auden poem. "He relished her legends, he played pirate on her beaches and like every little boy before him he sought out her treasures."

A soft chuckle worked its way through the church.

Lloyd glanced at the card quaking in his anxious grip. "Aargh, me matey and now that I have your booty; I will burn your ship and ravish your fair daughter."

People shifted in their pews. DeBanco, his back hard against the bench back, studied me until I google-eyed him. He snorted and slid a finger up one nostril. After that, I kept my eyes on Lloyd.

"So imagine how startled I was to realize I would never see Aaron again, only this stiff wooden box. He'd always been in movement, my fair brother, filled to the brim with life, most especially with a storm rising. Tonight, I will drink one last toast to the mooncusser."

Surprised titters filtered through the tiny church. Lloyd walked down the steps to the casket. He ran his knuckles down the coffin to the massive carpet of roses draping it. He plucked a single white rose from the arrangement which he tucked in the buttonhole of his suit coat. "Goodbye, dear brother."

Lloyd swiped his hair from his eyes as he trotted down the center aisle and straight out the church doors. Within a heartbeat, Feron deBanco followed. The rest of us sat undecided as to etiquette forced to imagine what ensued in the churchyard.

Nearer My God to Thee signaled the arrival of the pallbearers. The family pew, Lloyd's words, the country church facing out across the dark cliffs, was Del's huge something Perfidia risen for Aaron like the glacier's calf?

The pallbearers, six men of varying ages, arrayed themselves around the coffin. Lacy Parradine assumed the middle left. John White took the front right corner. A lithe man, perhaps Bajan, perhaps not, put a shoulder to the front left corner. With a nod of his head, the casket began to glide toward the door. Amanda reached out and touched the man's elbow as they passed. He acknowledged her with a fleeting smile. Even with the weight of the casket on one shoulder, he moved with the fluid grace of the man from the cabana, but so did Feron deBanco and Lloyd Law-Maddock.

AARON'S PALLBEARERS CONTINUED IN step down the aisle. As the coffin cleared the Law pew, an usher appeared. He gave a nod to Amanda. She grasped my hand. We followed the coffin through the doors, Amanda huffing with impatience. Once outside, the bearers bore to the right down a manicured path. Amanda hauled me to the left through the humped grass to the gravesite.

Feron and Lloyd had preceded us.

DeBanco had Lloyd pinned against the rough stone of a crypt bearing the name Collier Law. Lloyd, his hands splayed behind him on the gravestone, was attempting to push off. As we neared, Feron's words drifted to us in a harsh whisper, "I did it at her behest! Ask!" Feron looked around the graveyard before adding, "You're no better, you weak-kneed sod."

Lloyd showed signs of melting under the assault. He laid his head against the stone then his knees gave a bit until he began to ooze down the crypt wall.

Amanda snapped off a sharp, "Lloyd!"

Her strident voice got Lloyd upright in time for a quick shove from deBanco that bounced him off the stone. DeBanco glared at Lloyd while adjusting the sleeves of his suit coat until they covered all but the last half-inch of his shirt cuffs. Neatened, Feron turned to Amanda, gave her a half-smile under hooded, cold eyes then strode off, his open suit coat blowing in the soft breeze.

Lloyd wiped his sweaty palms on his slacks. Embarrassed for him, I studied the headstone. Lloyd cocked his head before turning away, misunderstanding me completely.

As the pallbearers neared the crypt with the coffin, I noted the name on each headstone. Centuries of Laws, Whites, and Chapels dominated the graveyard. On one headstone, someone had chiseled a hyphen after White and engraved Law beneath it.

A tarnished silver vase, beneath the name, Sophie White-Law, held a bouquet of mixed fronds. Was this the Sophie of Sophie's where one of the men I'd overheard in the cane field was staying? If it was, she couldn't have been the topic of the meeting?

At the lane, deBanco climbed into a Jaguar sedan. He didn't start the car; rather he watched the bearers set the coffin on a pedestal over the grave. As soon as the bearers stepped back from the coffin, the Jaguar's engine growled to life. Instead of driving off, deBanco glanced to the right of the churchyard.

Tracking Feron's line of sight, I saw Del's back disappear around the far side of the chapel. I started after him. DeBanco opened the car door. He was halfway up the walk, when Dave White stopped me at the side gate, don't follow written all over his face. As Dave walked me back toward Lloyd and Amanda, deBanco, back in his car, pounded on the Jaguar's steering wheel.

Amanda stood next to Lloyd, raised slightly on her toes, her lips not three inches from his left ear. I couldn't hear the conversation, but from the hiss of her words, I understood there was venom. Seeing me, she narrowed her eyes at Lloyd, who, on command, patted his right side indicating I was to stand next to him. As the Jaguar's back wheels shot gravel onto the church lawn, I scanned the churchyard, the parked cars, the horizon, and the edges of the cane field for my father. He had gone missing. Again.

Amanda leaned behind her son, murmuring, "I'm sorry for Lloyd's behavior. He's a bit distressed by the day."

Lloyd kept his red-rimmed eyes on his brother's casket. As the clack of the hand-winch signaled the coffin's journey into the grave, I put my left hand on Lloyd's right sleeve, kneading a piece of the suit fabric between my fingers. He turned his head slightly, smiling a small smile at my tweaking fingers as his brother's wooden coffin creaked out of sight.

We stood side-by-side, my hand clutching Lloyd's sleeve until the creaking stopped. Lloyd stepped forward. Bending, he grabbed a handful of the loose dirt from the pile next to the coffin. Stepping to the mid-point of the coffin, he cast the dirt into the grave where clots rattled off the coffin. I followed suit. Behind us, Amanda said, "They'll expect us at the gate."

At her command, we turned in unison. Amanda ran quick hands down the front of her narrow skirt to straighten imaginary wrinkles. She adjusted the wide belt at her small waist, checked the French twist in her blond hair for stray strands, moistened her lips then strode away at an astounding clip. Ten feet on she motioned to us. We hastened to catch her.

The funeral attendees queued at the open picket gate to the graveyard. We formed a line, Amanda, Lloyd then me wondering if I was at Lloyd's side as part of Del's plans. If Lloyd was to make me all weak in the knees, Del knew less about his daughter than she did about him, which at this point was to say everything.

Where had Del been during the ceremony? For that matter, why hadn't he contacted me in the two plus days I'd been on the island? Why appear now only to evaporate behind the long, wispy needles of a stand of Casuarina leaving me stranded among strangers. Avoiding me made no sense. He'd lured me here, and here I was. My eyes slid to the Casuarina trees. Del was well and truly gone.

Amanda nudged me to pay attention to the people in line. Each person who stopped had a small signal for his or her sympathy, sometimes a light touch, sometimes a light word, each far more affecting than the funeral. I accepted their condolences while berating myself for researching pirate at the library when every breadcrumb in the card file and in the texts had led to mooncusser.

"Hello, I'm Topper Law," a tall, elegant black man said extending his hand.

"Olivia Lassiter," I responded, taking the hand of DEA Agent Law.

"I'm a musician. I perform here and there on the island. We should talk sometime. Here's my card." He smiled a big cat grin like a panther on the scent, as my life took yet another complicated turn.

"Where's Agent Price?"

Topper nodded to Lloyd. Lloyd shot his free hand through his increasingly out-of-control waves, keeping his narrowed blue eyes on Law. Law blew Lloyd a kiss. With a small shake of his head, Lloyd turned his attention to the next person in line.

Topper kept my hand longer than necessary. I didn't like the familiarity.

"You haven't answered my question, where's Price?"

He leaned in to whisper in my ear, "Local copper."

Amanda yanked me out of line hissing, "Ignore him."

I stepped back into the line. Topper held his hand to his ear, thumb and little finger out, "Call."

Topper strode out the gate and across the lawn to the gray Mercedes parked in front of a green Healey. Lloyd's eyes followed Law's gliding steps as my wondering grew. Topper drove off in the Mercedes, answering any questions I had as to who had been following me.

Topper Law had come or been sent to Bakersfield for a purpose. Though the house, safe, and safe deposit box must have provided some temptations, he hadn't taken anything. Price and Law had arrived at the bank as Gail and I left. I had the key by then. It was all I had taken from the box. Was that why he was following me? Had he searched my cabin? Had he lit the fire?

"Sods the lot of them," Lloyd said to no one in particular.

"Lloyd, son, you are far too stressed," Lacy said, bypassing Lloyd for me.

I grabbed Lacy's hand like a lifeline. "I didn't see you in the chapel, until you..."

"Oh, my dear, lass, I was in the back pew watching. I always just lurk at these outings. It's most amusing. I guess I'm last. Ride on?"

"She's with us, now," Lloyd stated, taking possession of me with his right hand on my upper arm.

"Indeed," Lacy answered, "Have her then."

Lacy unbuttoned his suit coat, took out a small, flat, brown leather key case from which he removed one key. He handed me the key. His eyes on Lloyd's, he said to me, "To the back door, Danny would be most disappointed if I didn't offer refuge."

I took the key, momentarily torn between the safety of Parradine's and the unknown of Perfidia. "I'll just go with Lacy."

"No, you won't," Amanda said joining us, "You must come to Perfidia. We have been waiting for you."

Lacy raised an eyebrow. "Well then, lass, that's settled. Amanda will see to you."

He curled my fingers around the key. After a moment of consideration, he took Amanda's face between his hands and gave her a quick kiss. "You, my dear, you be careful, now."

He kissed her on the top of the head then walked to his car. Only two vehicles remained at the graveyard a big, black, Bentley and the green Healey. I guessed correctly. Amanda took off at a near run for the Bentley.

"There will be a wake." Amanda opened the left front door and climbed into the car.

Lloyd ran a hand through his curls before opening the door behind the driver's seat for me. "I hope you aren't disappointed, so many are."

"With?"

"Perfidia. People often are. They expect Gothic."

"Get in," Amanda ordered, "She'll see soon enough what you are all sparring over."

WE PULLED OUT ONTO H7, less than a quarter mile later Lloyd turned down a rutted, narrow lane. There were no gates to greet us, no sign that the road went anywhere but to the sea. Even the Bentley rattled like a stagecoach clambering west. Soon the ever present cane fields walled us into deeper ruts and a narrower passage.

"Shortcut," Amanda said, keeping a death grip on the armrest.

The lane smoothed as two carved wooden pillars, washed by rain, eroded by time appeared. The delicacy of the carving on the pillars was still identifiable. Clean strokes of a blade had carved ever narrowing spirals up each column ending in a deft, intricate explosion of palm fronds. The pillars were no more than ten feet high; the tooled fronds somehow arched heavenward above that height.

Palm trees lined the lane ahead. The first palms of the rank and file had been planted one behind each pillar, the others followed in perfect symmetry as far as the eye could see. Soaring seventy-five feet overhead, they danced shadows down the forgotten road.

Worn hinges showed where a gate had hung. Pieces of rounded wood and chunks of cast iron lay scattered to the left as though on one particular day the gate had opened never to shut.

"Will you do the honors and close the gate?" Lloyd quipped.

A tiny ripple of delight coursed through me. The situation was, in fact, most perfectly Gothic, a woman shanghaied down a rutted road through a mysterious long disused gate that linked mooncussers to their treasure.

Lloyd's amused eyes were reflected in the rearview mirror.

As we passed between the pillars, the road smoothed to a carefully maintained path with worn tire marks on either side of a ridge of green grass. I turned in my seat. From this direction, the pillars looked to welcome travelers. When I turned back, a bulky silhouette darkened the end of the lane. Lloyd stopped the car. "Would you like to walk the rest of the way?"

"For God's sake!" Amanda snapped, "Just drive to the porte-cochère and let us out!"

I opened the car door in response.

They pulled away, leaving me under the seventy-five-foot palms that arched the drive, swishing their fronds in the breeze. I glanced back to the pillars waiting until the purr of the Bentley faded. I wanted to meet Perfidia for the first time without an automobile in my view, without the rearview mirror obstructing my line of sight, and, particularly, without Amanda's foot-stomping edginess.

When quiet came, I ambled down the lane toward Perfidia. The building flickered in and out of view as the palms sambaed overhead. The line of palms ended where the road swerved past a single story, solid block building that seemed part of the earth rather than from the built world, hunkered as though daring the wind to mess with her.

Mahogany and Casuarina trees shaded the front lawn, punctuated by the flaming red flowers of two immense Flamboyant trees that shaded the side entry to the fortress-like structure at the southeastern end of the building. What appeared to my uneducated eyes to be hand-hewn blocks of gray stone were mortared together creating a thirty-five foot long, perhaps thirty-five-foot deep single story structure with an L to the back. A larger two or three story structure of white stone had been added into the L at some later time. Gray quoins highlighted each corner of the white building, nominally marrying the two buildings. Each structure had a hipped slate roof.

I walked down the southern line of the gray stone fortress. A second story started fifteen feet to the south. At thirty-five feet, the gray stones jutted inward fifteen feet to join the white stone addition that continued easily thirty feet further toward the ocean, though I didn't pace if off. Five windows below and five windows above marched in perfect symmetry from where the original building joined the new structure to the gray quoined corner thirty feet later. The windows with twelve-over-twelve paned windows were in ranks. The bubbled flaws of old glass shimmered in each wood framed pane.

A few small narrow slits sliced through the second story of the old structure. There were no windows anywhere else in the stonework, not to the side, nor to the front. I walked the front of the gray stone section until it ended at an angled set of stairs that stepped from the lawn onto a porch shadowed under a corrugated metal roof. Flamboyant trees laid their flame-colored flowers like poinsettia across the porch roof so that it seemed to drip with fire. These were the trees, the roof, and the blossoms in the painting that hid Del's wall safe in Bakersfield.

Carved palm columns with arching fronds held each corner of the angled porch roof aloft. The white-stone structure brightened one wall of the porch. A door constructed of massive mahogany planks with iron cross pieces opened into the original structure. Narrow windows, wide enough for a musket barrel, sliced through the blocks on both sides of the door.

I returned to the edge of the road to study where the two buildings met. A massive chimney jutted up between the old second story and the new, seeming to belong to neither building. Crenellation edged the second story section of the old structure ending at the chimney, where the new structure's hip roof took over.

A smaller hip roof joined the first story of the old structure to the new at a massive gully-washer gutter. The drain that ran between the two roofs funneled into a gray stone pipe tucked behind one of the columns on the porch. The pipe would deliver run-off directly to the ground. Perhaps there was a cistern below that captured the water for reuse or to refresh the aquifer.

No wonder Lloyd had worried. The plantation house was far from Gothic, it was a mess of ugly misfit stone buildings, styles, and architectural periods.

I continued down the line of the white structure north a good seventy feet. Tall twelve-over-twelve paned windows ran the remaining length, on both floors, five feet apart. Black shutters were latched open between the windows on the first floor. On the third floor, the windows were smaller and paned six-over-six.

When the white stone wing ended to the north, I turned right. Fifteen paces, later a single story porte-cochère jutted out a good twenty feet to protect weary travelers from the vagaries of tropical rain. Mahogany pillars of carved palm supported the roof of the carport spreading their fronds against the whitewash of the ship-lapped ceiling. A balcony with white railings and balusters occupied the second story. Two bright umbrellas were unfurled on the deck above.

A single pair of glass doors bore iron grillwork that created a central letter P. The doors served as the entrance to the white stone wing from the porte-cochère. On either side of the French doors, two tall, narrow windows were shuttered. The louvered shutters, like those at the front, were painted black. A pair of stone kangaroos sat to each side of the door. One clutched a bright cerise umbrella between its small front paws. Perhaps, they had been a gift from Candle, the plantation in Australia.

Through the porte-cochère, there was a large gravel parking area. The mourner's automobiles were parked there willy-nilly, some blocking others. At the back of the lot, doors to a stone four-car garage were open displaying the Bentley, a Jaguar, a green Healey, and a bright red Jeep. The native gray stone garage sat at a distance to the back and north of the house. The garage was likely the original carriage house given the small paddock of bright green grass that adjoined it.

I skirted the garage, walking to the east. A stone pillar delineated the north edge of an expansive, manicured lawn, across which the north pillar's south twin was barely visible. I wouldn't have noticed the columns, except for the privet hedge that ran between them, separating the lawn from cliff's edge. At a small gate centered in the hedge, rickety stairs zigzagged down the cliff wall to a narrow strip of beach in Taddys Cove.

At the gate, I turned to the house, the ocean at my back. The lawn swept from the cliff to the iridescent white of the plantation house. From my limited knowledge of architecture, I believed the new structure was Georgian like Sam Lord's Castle. A double veranda ran the full one hundred twenty-five foot length of her. The second story's covered balcony was protected by the massive hip roof of the structure and was easily twelve feet wide.

At ten foot intervals, columns carved to mimic bundled sugar cane held the balcony aloft over the veranda and the roof over the balcony. Leaves at the top of each sheaf of cane seemed to bend under the weight of first the balcony and then the roof.

A set of French doors centered between each pillar punctuated each room on the balcony. Nearly every paned door was thrown open with fluttering curtains sucked out by the freshening sea breeze. Narrow windows with louvered shutters were to each side of each set of doors. Furniture, visible through the slats of the balusters on the railing, populated the balcony.

At the south end of the second floor, a wooden staircase turned at a landing then descended to connect with the veranda. At the north end, the balcony bloomed into the sitting area over the porte-cochère from which another set of stairs mirrored the southern stairs to connect with the veranda. It was as though the porte-cochère had been added to balance the small second story of the original gray stone house.

Eight sets of French doors on the veranda matched the doors on the balcony above. The doors were flung open exposing the interior of the house to the veranda, to the lawn, to the cane field on the northeast, to the garden-like wilderness to the southwest. On either side of the ranked doors, tall paned windows marched to the corners of the building. The black shutters for each window were opened and latched together, ready to close in case of high winds or hurricane.

Three stairs, the full length of her, stepped up to the veranda from the lawn that stretched a hundred feet or so to where I stood. A small parterre decorated the corner created by the garage and porte-cochère. Other than an elaborate fountain that carried forward the bundled cane motif, grass filled the area between the walks that wove around the fountain in a quatrefoil pattern.

I spun to the sea, the house at my back.

The sun dazzled over the water so that the waves danced, sparkling in the foreground, only to become breakers as they tore into Taddys Cove. No ship could have ridden undetected into Taddys Cove or rounded the headlands from Ragged Point heading southwest without being observed by Tad Law or the generations that followed.

Perfidia, the high white lady, rode the crest of the cliff. From the sea, she must have looked like a comber herself. I sighed, letting free the breath I had taken upon turning to the ocean. Of course, they wanted her for a hotel. The rich would clamber to stay here imagining the colonial days. They would sip their gin tonics at tables scattered across the lawn, waiting for a waiter who dashed in and out of the French doors at their whim.

I sauntered across the long stretch of green grass, the sea to my back, not anxious to join the wake for a mooncusser I had never met. With each step, voices from within the plantation house grew more distinct. Snatches of laughter floated my way, followed by the clink of crystal.

Two men stepped out onto the veranda. Each held a tumbler of gin tonic, a twist, ice, and swizzle stick gave their drink preference away. They stood side by side. The eyes of the older of the two raked over the lawn. He posed with his left fist on his waist, his suit coat tucked behind his fisted hand. They were two of the hoteliers deBanco had been entertaining at Sam Lord's Castle.

I extended my right hand in greeting. The younger of the two shuffled his drink to free his hand, the older man, left his fist on his hip. He appraised me top to toe then took a sip from his glass. I shook hands with the younger man. "I'm Olivia Lassiter. You are?"

"Friends of the family," the older man answered quickly.

"Weren't you at Sam Lord's with Mr. deBanco? I believe he said you were interested in purchasing Perfidia."

DeBanco hadn't, of course, but they couldn't know. The younger man colored slightly.

The older man said, "You'll have to talk to deBanco." Something in the way he said deBanco showed disrespect, leaving the impression that the man thought highly of himself and few others.

I brushed past them into what could only be the Great Hall. The room was perhaps twenty-five feet wide by seventy-five feet long. As I entered, I conjured that the furnishings would reveal a genteel shabbiness, as though the owners had lived with them forever never quite able to afford new. Chairs would be upholstered in hand-woven tapestries fraying at the edges, the planked floors covered in Oriental carpets worn and rewoven.

If any of this were true, work had been done by master restorers. Chairs and settees, from every period of the last two hundred years, were scattered about the hall with little semblance of order, yet the balance seemed perfect. Mourners sat next to tables from all periods and of all materials, wood to wicker, many laden with wine stems or liquor glasses and plates of hors d'oeuvre. There were few rugs to fray. The floor was a deep burnished wood, polished to a wet look. A visible path was worn from an interior archway to the middle set of French doors on the veranda. How many centuries of footfalls were necessary to wear a path in hardwood?

Portraits hung the length of the back wall. A stone fireplace perhaps eight feet wide, four feet deep, and six feet high dominated the south end of the room. The mahogany mantel was at least two feet in width. The figurehead of a woman carved in wood with her feet planted mid-mantel reduced the enormous fireplace to a footnote.

The figurehead soared into the room. Her right hand extended beckoning, her dress, a soft, aged-red clung to her ample body in an imagined wind that blew freely around her ankles. A carved wooden rope wound waist to shoulder, like a bandoleer, bound her to the wooden spar that ran up her back. The beam was buried deep in the wall, emerging above the mantel and angling through the ceiling into the floor above. Whoever she was, she was part of the architecture of the house.

"Meet Estella," Lloyd said over my shoulder, "May I offer you a drink?"

I pointed to Estella.

"Stay," Lloyd waved one finger then left me. I studied Estella, the beckoner, siren, figurehead, witness to duels, possibly my namesake, and by legend, from the prow of a ship sunk by Tad Law.

As I waited for Lloyd's return, I studied two portraits one on either side of Estella. The painting to the right was a slip of a girl, her dark hair blowing in the wind, her blue eyes tranquil. Done in the style of Gainsborough, she was surrounded by palms and puppies. In the far distance, a clipper ship rounded a verdant bluff. Her dress was soft pink. Her apron had small, embroidered rosebuds at each corner. One hand held a Bible; the other rested on a mother-of-pearl rose centered on an ornately carved wooden box on a table.

To the left, a portrait of a young man stared down the length of the Great Hall. His hair was the darkest brown, curling close around his ears. His eyes were startling for their clarity, almost without color—gray, then. The boy wore the raised collar of the time, waistcoat, trousers, and leggings but looked as though he wanted to strip them off and run for the beach carefully painted behind him.

An ornate, bejeweled key hung from a chain or fob at his waist. I stared at the key instinctively reaching for my hobo bag. My fingers crabbed. I fought down the urge to dash to the south quarters and paw through the charred remains of cabin 4 for my bag containing the key, my passport, my money, my whole life really.

I stepped closer to read the small brass tags under each portrait even though I had guessed the boy's identity. He was a boy named Tad, she a girl named Beth. They were impossibly young.

Lloyd touched an icy glass to the back of my left hand. I turned to him.

"There is a more respectable portrait of Tad in the dining room, but this is my favorite."

"He's a boy."

"They sent him packing when he was eleven."

"Tad Law?" I asked, running my hand across the brass plaque.

After a moment, Lloyd said, "Records indicate that he was indentured as Tad Law. Maybe they misunderstood him. He was quite young, or maybe they just wanted to get him out of Great Britain." Lloyd sipped his drink. "No one knew who he was for generations."

"He *was* just a street urchin?"

"Oh, quite, you've read too much Dickens if you think otherwise. While studying at Oxford, some great, great or so grandfather found reference to a birth in Whitechapel lockup that proved to be him. His mother seems to have been a prostitute who had herself nabbed to give her a place for the birthing. There was, of course, no surname, so a silly note at the side of the notation read: *we have named the boy Law for the law who stood mid-wife.*"

"White and Law?"

"No coincidence, there. Tad surnamed the slaves in the south quarters White and north quarters Chapel. Chapels emancipated themselves in 1800." He fingered his glass.

"More please?"

"Tad was indentured at eleven. He never forgave the British or his mother from what we can tell. You should read the family law about illegitimacy. Not pretty."

"Family laws?" Lloyd locked his arm comfortably in mine.

"Not to be confused with the family Law. Once Beth taught Tad to write, there was hell to pay. The originals of the Code are under lock and key, specially treated and all that."

"Beth?"

Lloyd bumped me with his hip, my drink sloshed a bit. "Beth was the nubile young daughter of the captain of the ship that bore Estella. Tad killed Beth's father to get what he wanted. Not just Beth, but chests of bullion Beth's father had taken from a Spanish galleon. Tad enjoyed the irony of entertaining other ships' captains at Estella's feet."

"In a peculiar way, you have to admire the hell out of him."

Lloyd jostled me again. "Tad Law never admitted he murdered or mooncussed, you know."

I studied Lloyd then the portrait. "There is a family resemblance even after all these generations."

He blushed then cleared his throat. "Only on the surface, I assure you. Another?" Lloyd took my glass on his way to the bar set up at the far end of the Great Hall.

The moment he was gone, Feron deBanco appeared on my right. After the scene at the cemetery, I was surprised to see him at Perfidia. In his British accent colored by something softer, something Latin, he said, "So, Cousin Olivia, you have finally come home to roost."

When I didn't respond, his manufactured smile slid into wariness. His suit, of the darkest charcoal, had been tailored for him. It did nothing to inhibit the indecent smell of too much money. Still, he was an elegant man, a man who would never tolerate a spot or wrinkle or hair out of place. As if to prove it, he reached up to flick an errant wave back over one ear.

"I haven't properly thanked you for the dance and your generosity. I appreciated both. Truly."

As Feron sipped his drink, I could see Tad in his features as well. The old pirate must have had some potent genes.

Feron flipped his head toward the portrait. "Grandda."

"Since we first met on Monday, I've been wondering by what authority you deal with hoteliers?"

A quick flick of deBanco's eyelashes signaled his surprise at my question, he stumbled to answer, "Lloyd was in London. Amanda asked me to do the dirties. Though Lloyd is clearly put off by it."

"The cemetery? Still, Amanda doesn't appear to favor you any more than Lloyd does."

"When she needs me, she's willing."

DeBanco clutched a cut crystal low ball glass of whiskey in his manicured right hand, sipping his drink sparingly. He tucked his left hand in the hip pocket of his knife-creased trousers like a man in a Brooks Brothers advertisement.

"So, Feron deBanco, how much money did Pendu lose during the run on Bajan White stock?"

"Nothing, my dear, not a damn pound." His fingers fidgeted with his glass until a bit of liquid splashed on the floor.

"The market slumped. You lost a ship, White Lady. Come on, Feron, how much did you lose?"

"Did you know that Lin, excuse me, Del was aboard the White Lady with Aaron?" Feron leaned against the mantel, his hand in his pocket, his suit coat scrunched behind, giving off waves of green. As if realizing he was destroying the line of his suit, he removed his hand from his pocket. The coat fell neatly into place, not so his hand; he didn't seem to have an idea what to do with it. I had struck some nerve.

"John White told me Del brought Aaron's body to the house. So, my dear Feron, what was on the White Lady?" I challenged.

A sly smile pressed the corners of his mouth. "Aaron—and Lin."

"How did the accident happen?"

"Poor judgment or so we are to believe. The night was a rotter. Heavy winds and rain, still Aaron knew the coast. A call came in that the White Lady was aground on the bar and breaking up. The salvagers floated her off early the next morning."

"Nothing missing?"

"Aaron," deBanco sipped his gin. "Don't put on airs, Miss Lassiter, you're no better than the rest of us."

"Damn you, deBanco!" Lloyd snarled, inserting himself between us.

"Get off your bloody high horse, Maddock. We're all after the same thing." His eyes roved over my body, leaving me wondering if I was the thing.

Done with his survey, Feron sipped his drink, his eyes on Lloyd the while. Finished, deBanco set the glass on the mantel. Giving a glance toward the French doors, he left us to join the hoteliers on the veranda.

"Did deBanco bother you?" Lloyd stood so close that our shoulders rubbed.

"Not at all. Can I ask you something very personal?"

"Of course, you are family," he said, but his whole being said no.

"How much trouble is Perfidia in?" I gestured to where Feron talked to the hotel magnates. Lloyd's eyes followed my gesture, narrowing as he watched Feron intently enough to read his lips.

Lloyd shook his head to break the spell. "Why do you ask?"

"I talked to a Mr. Donovan at Barclays. He briefed me on the Harris accounts." I sipped my drink as an excuse to watch Lloyd's reaction. I was sorely disappointed. He wasn't shocked, worried, or even frightened by what I may have heard.

Lloyd turned back to the portraits. "See the key on Tad's fob. According to our oral history, that's supposed to be the key to Tad's cache. It is the key to the inheritance box, the one under Beth's hand."

"Lloyd, I overheard Feron at the funeral. What did he do and at whose behest? Perhaps, if someone would confide in me..."

"I didn't mean...I'm sorry if you...oh, Olivia, what must you think of us?"

"What must *I* think? My father has, euphemistically, gone missing. One of you murdered Aaron, possibly for drugs. From comments by both Lacy and John, Perfidia is up for grabs. It seems like rich, idle men are playing some version of king of the hill with Perfidia the prize. That's what I think." I put my hand on the sleeve of his suit coat to soften my words. He looked down at my hand then to my eyes. "You asked me. What was Aaron doing with the White Lady?"

He covered my hand with his. "I wish I knew."

Topper Law approached us, his tall body and lithe walk broadcasting his sensuality. He didn't seem to care which of us received his message.

Lloyd's forearm tensed under my hand. "Topper, how be you?"

"Fine given the circumstances. I see you're showing Olivia our Estella."

We turned under Estella's breasts only to stare at her bare feet planted firmly against the southern wall. Lloyd removed Feron's glass from the mantel. He looked into the drink for a moment. "I miss Aaron. The house seems so barren without his comings and goings."

"Barren, intriguing word choice," Topper said, "There are no heirs and no hope of one for the moment. Just Amanda, the bastard, and the bachelor." He put a hand on Lloyd's shoulder. "Heard anything about the transfer yet?"

"Excuse me?" I asked.

"Perfidia changes hands on the heir's thirty-second birthday plus six months. Amanda's kept Perfidia running since her husband, John Stoddard Maddock, died last year. Lloyd's just had his thirty-third," Topper answered, squeezing Lloyd's shoulder.

Lloyd sipped his gin tonic.

"But, wouldn't the oldest male child automatically inherit?" I asked.

"Who said Perfidia went to the oldest?" Topper casually slung an arm over Lloyd's shoulders.

"I assumed, sorry."

Lloyd appeared comfortable with Topper draped on him. No one else in the room seemed to notice or care either.

"I'm afraid Tad was a bit more careful than that. The heir must look like Tad, dark curly hair, light eyes, and have his build. Then, he has to prove himself by some set of rules known only to the previous heir. With the plantation came a good bit of power as delineated by documents in the inheritance box, some amended by Collier in the 1850s, but not since. Only the chosen heir can open the box. But, the box has been missing since my grandfather, Drayman, fumbled the pass to his son, my uncle, Colin," Lloyd explained. "With the box gone, no one is at all certain who the heir is or even what he gets. Messy, rather."

"Must the heir be raised at Perfidia?" I asked. They both nodded. "Then it must be you, Lloyd."

"Except I'm the Chief Operating Officer of Bajan White. The heir runs Perfidia. Nothing else and has typically been the ne'er do well of the family. The black sheep if you'd rather."

"Aaron?"

"Aaron was as blond as my mother," Lloyd responded.

So, Amanda was blonde. I'd have guessed otherwise.

"There is Colin's son," Topper said, removing his arm from Lloyd's shoulders. He placed a hand over a gold star painted on the top of Estella's right foot. Did the star represent Stella's name or had it named her?

"There is that," Lloyd said, "And, forgive me, there is the other."

Lacy had said the same to me over our morning coffee though morning felt forever ago. Colin's son was many things, but strictly Anglo-Saxon was not one of them. I wondered about the prescribed formula.

Topper took Feron's empty glass. "Have you had the opportunity to consider the government's offer any further?"

"The offer isn't an option at the moment."

"It will become other than an option soon enough if you're not careful." They checked the veranda for Feron's progress with the hotel men.

Lloyd covered Topper's hand with his. "I'd like to see her preserved."

"You are your father's son, Lloyd. I'd be careful of that. One might even remind that he was a stupid man." Law turned Feron's glass so that the last of the liquid in the tumbler dripped on the sanded, polished, mahogany floor planks. Lloyd's eyes followed the alcohol down.

Meantime, Topper crossed the room like a jaguar claiming the veldt.

Lloyd squeezed my hand guiding me toward the far wall between the mourners. "Topper has a bit of a chip. It got him where he is. He is a gifted musician when he bothers which he hasn't of late."

"Topper Law, dare I ask?"

"There's more than one bastard in the family. Amanda found our Topper swaddled in a basket in the dining hall screaming his head off, figured he was a Law, not a Maddock, I gather. I was maybe five."

I raised my eyebrows, surprised by the dismissive tone of his answer given what I'd witnessed between the two men.

"What government offer?" I asked, instead of pursuing my curiosity about Topper.

"The historical society wants to buy Perfidia and open her to the public. The family could stay to work her for a share of the profits until the last of us is gone." We stopped mid-way down the west wall. "Here they are."

Behind us, Amanda was holding court seated in a red leather chair, leaning with interest toward Lacy Parradine, who sat to her right. He held her pale hand in his.

Amanda was in her element, her French twist still perfect, the black silk of her skirt still unwrinkled, her voice distilled with gin. She gave me a small wave of her polished fingertips. The other mourners were gathered around a grand piano, sipping their drinks, whispering as Topper Law applied his elegant long-fingered hands to Grieg's *Largo* from the *Pier Gynt*.

Lloyd gave my hand a tug directing my attention to the portrait hanging behind us. A beautiful woman with dark hair sat on Del's lap in a wicker chair on Perfidia's veranda. French doors framed them, a hint of the lawn reflected in the glass. She glowed. One hand rested on the soft swell of her belly. Del had a hand around her waist; the other rested on the arm of the chair. A half-smile grazed his face. His crystal blue eyes looked lit with fresh laughter. They were beautiful. They were happy. They had everything. She was dead. He had gone missing.

"Your mother," Lloyd motioned with a sweep of his hand.

The plaque read: *Lassiter and Chamberlin Harris, Perfidia, 1946.*

"This is their wedding portrait. They were married at Perfidia. Lassi was one of the Graydon girls, island merchants. Lin was just out of the British Army."

"She died in childbirth," I said, flatly. My radiant mother and my British Army veteran father were unknown to me. Del had spoken of the Second World War but always off-handedly as though it were a rite of passage for all young men of the era, never as though he had participated in any meaningful way.

"Yes, I believe she did, Amanda would have the details." Lloyd put a comforting arm around my shoulder, accompanied by a quick, brotherly hug. "You have your mother's eyes. Flat on the bottom, round at the top, they smile. Mischievous eyes. And, her nose, I think."

"I didn't know she was beautiful. My father never spoke of her nor were there any pictures." I lowered my right hand from my heart feeling exposed by the gesture. "How can you stand by while this happens to Perfidia?"

"Stand by? Olivia, I've been in London trying my damnedest to straighten this out. The straightening is beyond my abilities." He ran his free hand through his hair. "So, please, dear, please, if Del has told you anything, no matter how small, that might help, please tell me."

Lloyd wore begging like a man who had never tried it on before.

"Del wrote he had found me something nice that would make me go all weak in the knees. That's it."

"Oh, my dear girl, you can't think me?"

"Topper would be a bit disappointed, wouldn't he?"

Lloyd tilted his head to check my eyes trying to surmise my level of understanding or perhaps surprised by my sophistication. It wasn't sophistication; it was inexperience. I had never loved, man or woman, except Del. So, it all seemed equally foreign to me.

"Truly, Olivia, Aaron had a plan to save her. He didn't share it with me. Someone stopped him before he could succeed. I'm bereft of ideas as to what it was. Is that the answer you wanted?"

"No. But, I'll accept your words for now."

He gripped my shoulder. "What has Del told you?"

"Nothing, Lloyd. Absolutely nothing."

"I can hardly imagine that. The way he talks about you, his bonnie daughter who made him proud every day of the week."

"He's lived two lives—two complete lives. You know him more than I ever could." I ran my hand through my curls then shuddered at the gesture. "Don't you see? What he told you is what he wanted for me."

"He also said you were stunning—no a stunner."

"As I said." I waved my hand up and down my long, unglamorous, unisex frame.

"No, you are, you move beautifully, your laugh makes me want to roll on the lawn like I did as a child. Your eyes make me smile. Just being near you, I feel freer than I have in years."

"If I didn't know the facts, Lloyd, I'd think you were flirting with me. So, let's get to business, Perfidia is besieged on all fronts, isn't she? DeBancos, hotels, the government, just like the banker, Mr. Donovan, hinted at, and what the hell was Topper Law doing on my doorstep two days after Del found Aaron's body?"

Lloyd squeezed my hand. "The recent furious sell-off of family shares weakened the deBancos. They may no longer have a controlling interest in Bajan White, which would be a blessing on several fronts. So, yes and no."

"And Topper? By the way, he makes a believable hard ass."

"I asked him. Feron was busy. I was still in London. We thought...oh, what we thought doesn't matter anymore. It was Topper's idea to take Officer Price on a free trip to California."

"Did you meet Whitelaw at the mortuary yesterday?"

"Why?" he asked.

"You called someone a bastard."

"Cousin Brendan," he mocked, "is, of course, quite literally the family bastard, and a bit of a spanner in line to the throne as he is. But, I'm afraid I was speaking to deBanco." He put a hand on my arm and pulled me in for a quick hug to whisper, "Though you'd do good to keep an eye on Whitelaw."

"I would if I ever saw him."

Lloyd kissed the top of my head just as Amanda made her grand entrance into the hallway announcing with a flip of her lacquered fingernails, "They're gone!"

AMANDA YANKED ME OUT of Lloyd's arms and marched me out the French doors to the veranda. Her stiletto heels beat a tattoo on the wood, leaving a divot when the pressure of her stride was more than the aging wood could handle. At the northern staircase, she dragged me up the stairs. Never breaking stride, or breathing hard, she towed me down the balcony to a set of doors near the middle of the second floor.

With a sweep of her arm, Amanda said, "My morning room is yours. I've locked the adjoining door. If the daybed is too uncomfortable, we can move a real bed in for you. I like to curl up on the daybed in the afternoon sun to nap. Will you be comfortable here?"

The room was gorgeous, a woman's room, with a small mahogany escritoire, though it had an odd, musty odor. A view across the lawn, encompassing a sweep of the cliffs, the slip to the west, ragged coast to the east, and the boiling ocean was framed by the double set of French doors. "I should think so, thank you."

"Of course, you won't have to unpack. We'll see what we can do for clothes. You're taller and thinner than me. So mine won't do. We'll have to go shopping. Have you anything at all to wear?" Amanda flicked her polished fingertips at the dress I had hand-picked for the funeral as though I had hand-picked it at a swap shop.

I smoothed the skirt of my black dress. "This dress plus what is in the jute basket that Mr. Parradine brought in from his car."

"Those blue jeans, that green thing!" Amanda pointed at the colorful basket with handles that Lacy had set on the coverlet of the daybed. She sized me up. "Tomorrow then, the green thing will have to do for tonight."

"Tonight?"

"Dinner is at seven. We dress for it. One should never be late for a meal, too rude. Tonight's dinner will be attended by the usual people, except for you, of course. You should know that Lloyd's room is to your left, Feron's two doors down on the right, and, of course, I'm right next door." Amanda's hands rested on her hips as she looked me over. By now, I knew what was coming. "Has Del said anything to you?"

"No."

Amanda threw her head. A tiny hair escaped from her French twist. She spat on her right thumb and index finger then reached back with her spit-wetted fingers to slick down the stray hair. "My son is dead, likely murdered. Did you think I didn't care?"

She paced around the spacious morning room before whirling back to me. "You must think I am an absolute bitch."

"Quite honestly, Mrs. Law-Maddock, I don't know what to think about any of you." I pulled my horribly wrinkled green dress from the bag. I would have to wear the sheath with my huaraches, which I suspected, as I eyeballed Amanda's black Ferragamo spikes, wouldn't pass muster.

Amanda continued pacing. At a small chest of drawers, she pointed and asked, "What are these?"

I walked to her side. Del's courier envelope, one roll of film, and doodles around Whitelaw's number lay fanned on the chest. My heart thumped. "Mine."

"Then that," she said gesturing behind the escritoire, "must be yours as well."

I peered over her shoulder. The stench of smoke leaked out of my suitcase. The only thing still missing seemed to be my hobo bag.

"Air the suitcase out, won't you?"

"Of course," I said, "In case anything is salvageable, is there somewhere I could do some laundry?"

She eyed the suitcase. "I'll send Peggy."

Amanda left, sucking most of the air out of the room. I sank to the daybed overcome. Someone had pulled my belongings from the fire, the same someone, from the reappearance of the doodles who had searched my room in the first place. With one read of Del's note, the thief knew I had brought the key. The thief then returned for my suitcase, makeup case, and hobo bag to search at his or her leisure, lighting the fire to cover the theft. The key hadn't been in my suitcase or makeup case, and here they were.

I was sitting in the same spot in the same position when Peggy, a striking Bajan woman in the ever present white uniform with embroidered P, arrived. We decided to take the suitcase to the fresh air of the balcony. She was lax to carry the sooty, smelly bag, so I did.

I set the bag on a round, white wicker table on the balcony. Soot powdered the suitcase so that my fingers were black by the time I had the hasp open. I didn't hold much hope for my clothes or the white table but, though the smell was quite acrid, my clothes seemed to have escaped the worst of it. Peggy bundled my few things into a laundry basket taking great care to keep the edges of my suitcase away from the white of her uniform.

"Dis be bad business," Peggy muttered, carrying the laundry basket at arm's length as she trundled down the long balcony to the nearest staircase.

I locked the French doors. Amanda's day room was perhaps sixteen-by-sixteen. A tall rectangular louvered window graced either side of the French doors at the entrance. Light poured through the louvers splashing over an oriental rug of sea green with yellow roses embroidered at each corner.

The rose theme was repeated in the cushions and pillows of the wicker chairs. A stark white coverlet with hand-quilted roses at each corner graced the daybed, whose pillows also bore roses.

A portrait of a more mature Beth than the one over the fireplace in the Great Hall hung above the escritoire. Beth's burnt umber hair, now streaked with gray, was in a severe bun knotted low at the back of her neck. She wore a storm gray dress, under a white apron with yellow roses embroidered in each corner. With one hand Beth hugged a Bible to her chest. With the other, she clutched a linen whose embroidered yellow roses mirrored those on her apron. A key hung from a length of chain around her waist.

A handkerchief with roses, a blowsy woman, gauzy drapes, all those dreams from my childhood, had I been here before? The mossy oaks, the Louisiana four-corners alone screamed no. Had Del taken me to Maison Vol? Why? Why had he kept me from this?

I fingered Del's sooty note, trying to rub the letters until they made some sense, but in their stubbornness, they wouldn't smear much less provide me telepathic guidance. The first tear of frustration fell to my cheek followed by the second then a great squall hit me. I gave in to the tears plopping myself, legs crossed, on the floor, crying until my back hurt, my nose ran, and hiccups passed for breaths.

Behind me, the wind rattled the French doors. Through sobs and hiccups, I realized the rattle was too modulated for the wind. Someone was whispering my name. I crawled to the door, reaching up with one arm to turn the knob. Lloyd pushed his way in to join me.

"Oh, Olivia," Lloyd murmured, sitting next to me on the floor his back against the windows. He wiped my eyes with a clean handkerchief pulled from his trouser pocket. When I hiccupped and started all over again, he handed me the handkerchief. When I didn't stop, he pulled my head to his shoulder.

I sniffed then snuffled then hiccupped then sobbed. Sometimes, I alternated, sobbing first. Eventually, Lloyd helped me to stand then steered me to the daybed where he sat next to me, keeping one arm around my shoulders.

"Somebody brought all my stuff back," I whined, handing Lloyd his wet, snotty handkerchief. He gestured it back to me. I balled it into my hand then lay my head on his shoulder until I was quite done crying.

LLOYD AND I WERE late for Amanda's precious dinner. I was in that green thing, which, with my red-rimmed eyes made me look more like a Christmas tree than a youngish, confused woman. DeBanco joined us. I wasn't sure how I felt about him being in a bedroom two doors down from me, other than it felt too close.

The dining hall was a moderately sized room with a gray stone floor. The walls were stone, as well, and kept the room cool. The only furnishings were a table and chairs with ornately crafted legs, a breakfront, and a buffet.

The head of the table was empty though a place had been set. A portrait of Tad, more formal than the one in the Great Hall, hung directly behind the place setting as though he would be joining us for dinner, if not in body then in spirit.

The man in the painting was older than the boy in the Great Hall, wiser from the lines marring the corners of his eyes. His brunette hair was in a ponytail; ringlets drifted around his face. His gray eyes were hardened, but a half-smile still kissed his lips. He was not beautiful, not etched, not heroic, just an ordinary, slightly more than pleasant looking pirate who had stolen a candle then built an empire.

Tad must not have forgotten the shame of his crime. The only explanation for the breakfront that contained nothing but beeswax candles, hundreds of them, behind its glass doors. The breakfront dominated the wall next to the portrait. A carefully cross-stitched sampler rested on an easel on the sideboard below the cabinet. Beth, perhaps, had stitched: *"If you are without light, if your wick be down, if you are lost in the dark, take one. They are for all who find rest here."*

I batted back more tears. When I lifted my head, Amanda, Feron, and Lloyd were watching me.

"The candles were their joke," Amanda said.

I thought not.

"Poor dear, you have had a grueling couple of days. What say, shall we forgive Olivia her tears?"

Lloyd applied his eyes to his plate. Feron stared at Amanda, as though her hair had sprouted leaves. Amanda planted a little rigor mortis of a smile on Feron. After which, we ate in silence. Lloyd sneaked the occasional look at me. Amanda watched Lloyd. Feron speculated, his too close together eyes on Amanda, then me, then Lloyd, then me.

I considered whether the iron door at the far end of the room led to the wine cellar. The old door looked to have an industrial strength lock. When the door lost my interest, I ate like I hadn't eaten in recent memory, trying to quell the uneasiness in my stomach with food. Glasses ticked against stoneware, forks rattled, leaded crystal stems sang upon meeting the neck of the wine bottle at each refill. The forced silence was most exquisitely uncomfortable.

"I have business in Bridgetown," Feron announced, thankfully breaking the silence. He placed his crumpled linen napkin on his emptied plate then scooted back his chair. Rising, he took one last sip of wine, gave a slight bow my way then left through the arched entry into the Great Hall.

"I hope," Amanda said, "he hits a tree and flies lay eggs in his eyes before they find him!"

"Mother!" Lloyd scolded for the both of us.

Amanda pushed herself away from the table. "Lloyd, we need to attend to Law family business. Olivia, please excuse us."

"Should I wait?" I asked.

"Our business will go late." Amanda smoothed the elegant natural silk skirt she had changed into for dinner. "Come," she said, as Lloyd fell in line like a gosling on the way to a pond.

I sat at the table for a few minutes observing Tad's portrait. In the end, we had an understanding. So, I took one of his candles as a talisman against the darkness that had fallen as we ate.

The sliver of a moon had not risen. The lawn was unlit, giving one the sense that it stretched out for eternity. Eternity defined by a privet hedge at cliff's edge. Scant light glowed from the bedrooms on the second floor. My room was dark, as was Amanda's. But for all the darkness, the night slipped around me like a soft cloth enticing me to wander in its warm folds. I accepted, deciding that a stroll of the perimeter of the yard would be safe enough.

The same cars, minus the green Healey, were tucked in their same spaces in the stone garage. A washing machine thumped in a room to the right of the parked cars. I kept one hand on the garage's rough stone wall until the wall turned the corner to the western cane field.

As they had two nights ago, lights bobbed amid the cane like fireflies rising for their evening caper. I was determined to break-up tonight's whispered meeting, determined to learn about Sophie, her cabin, and why it was important to understand her—or me, in case I was the *her* in question. The flitting lights stayed just ahead, a little to my left or my right. Soon enough, the lights merged into one.

I checked my bearings. A brief triangle of light marked Perfidia at about my four o'clock. I had been enticed through the tall, stifling cane northeast toward the cliffs. I touched the edge of a cane leaf. Though immature, the small blade was sharp enough to make me withdraw my hand. A flashlight beam flickered between the stalks. I fought deeper and deeper into the cane guided by the twinkling beam. With each step, I stroked down the leaves of cane, like the spines of a catfish, hoping to avoid a stinging cut.

I never saw him, never heard him until my body was hard against his, his hand clasped over my mouth. I went limp like Del had taught me to do if mugged. My attacker was powerful. He dragged me. I kicked. I bit his hand. When that didn't stop him, I went stiff. He continued to half-carry, half-push me until the sound of the ocean fussed at the rocks just below.

"Want to dance?" deBanco sneered, ratcheting me around until my back was to the sea. I bobbled from the spin. He let me go with a little flair. I teetered on the edge of the cliff, one heel at the brink, the other with a few inches to spare. I stepped toward him. He stood with his hands at his sides, his head cocked, studying me.

I didn't give ground. I had little choice. Chastising myself for an idiot, Feron's Jaguar had been in its garage stall.

"Why did you come? What are you after?" Feron snarled.

"My father asked me to come. I'm after nothing," I answered.

A sharp slap rang off my cheek. "Now?"

Tears stung at my left eye. I managed to stay upright clinging by a toehold to the cliff's edge. I tried to merge this man with the man on the dance floor, the man who had given me sympathy and money. He had tried honey to induce me to stay, now this.

His body, under his elegant charcoal suit, was fit, capable of harming me far more than a mere slap. He sucked on the edge of his hand where I'd bitten it.

"Where is it?" he demanded.

I took a breath. "You'd risk another body?"

"You're distraught," he said, "I have witnesses. Little Lloyd, Amanda."

DeBanco grabbed my upper right arm. My skin oozed between his fingers. He gave me a sharp jolt. My right foot lost ground. I slipped to my right knee. Feron never loosened his grip, burning my skin as he wrenched me to my feet. I bowed my head, closed my eyes, afraid to speak, to move, to do anything to spur him on in his game of Let's Terrify Olivia.

DeBanco put a finger under my chin and raised my face to his. His wintry eyes met mine. The second backhand caught me off balance. I covered my face with my left hand. He grabbed that wrist, demanding, "What did your father tell you?"

"If you kill me, you'll never know."

"Bull, dear girl." He pushed me off with ease, like a gnat, or a fly. Tad's candle popped loose of my hand. I fell back, hands grabbing. For a moment, I had his sleeve. He staggered toward me. A second push sent me over the edge.

My arms windmilled. My back slammed against something rigid. My legs jammed against the cliff. Pain shot through my head as it rattled against something solid. But, I fell no further.

"Olivia?" Feron called, "Olivia?"

I froze, afraid any movement would give me away. When I didn't answer, deBanco pivoted sending a shower of dirt cascading over the cliff. Small rocks, bits of dirt pinged off me. Eventually, his footsteps faded away. Words and voices rolled around my head. It had been deBanco in the cane field that first night who had quipped: *What? Rough? Me?* to his accomplice. Who was the other man? Del? Whitelaw? For that matter where did Topper Law spend his nights?

The raging of the ocean, unchecked by the bulk of the cliffs, pounded in my ears. Air greeted tentative groping by my right hand, the same for my left.

I put both hands behind my back to discover what held me in place. The trunk of a small palm tree curved out from the cliff to cradle me. The tree vibrated as I moved, dislodging chunks of dirt from the cliff wall. I shut my eyes determined to stay supported by the fragile tree until morning when Amanda would certainly notice I was late for breakfast.

The waves roared. My hair was soon wet from sea spray. Morning no longer seemed like a viable option. I felt the cliff in front of me for a handhold. Dirt broke free. Wet chunks skittered around me. I waited until the trunk quit shaking.

I expected to fall. When I didn't, I took my time studying the roots of the palm. I stuck my hand between them. The tree would tumble down the cliff soon.

A soft-needled Casuarina clung to the edge of the cliff sending feelers in and out of the crumbling dirt. I yanked on a root that disappeared into the cliff just over my head. When the root didn't give, I dug behind it until my fingers could grip.

Using the wooden handle I'd dug out, I managed to perch one foot on the palm stalk. Clumps of dirt showered into the night. I got a death grip on the Casuarina root, lifted my other foot to the palm then shimmied onto the cliff on my stomach.

I rolled to my back, my green dress scrunched around my bottom, accepting the safety of the warm earth beneath me. I imagined the fall to the beach, the quick end when the vertebrae broke, the nerve split and the mind just quit sending messages.

I tried moving. Everything seemed to work. I made it to my knees. With the able assistance of the Casuarina, I got to my feet. I leaned on the tree, wondering where Perfidia had gone. No triangle of soft lights lit her now. In fact, there was no light at all. Just squeaks, chirrups, cracks, and thumps, every little night sound amplified by the dark.

The manor had been at my four o'clock when I charged into the cane. I had gone northeast after that. I pointed myself in the direction I thought was southwest. I stumbled through the cane, no longer worried about the sharp edges of the leaves, wanting only to keep the ocean to my back, praying to see the lights of Perfidia ahead.

The wind had freshened. It roared through the cane, smacking stalks together in Calypso rhythms. The thunder of the ocean disappeared in the cacophony. I tried to hear the waves above the wind. Another sound cut under the clacking cane, stealthy footsteps. I ran down the narrow cane row. At first, I could feel each cut to my hands then I didn't care.

I snagged my foot on a root. It threw me face down in the dirt, bleeding and exhausted. I hadn't a clue where I was. I lifted my head, hoping to see something I recognized from John White's tour.

An old board and batten cabin surrounded by sugar cane on three sides occupied a small clearing. I scrambled to my feet and ran to the door which swung in the wind from years loose on its hinges. Cane rattled on the tin roof, slapped at the windows, tore at the meager shutters, yet the cabin would shelter me, without regard for who might be lurking I stumbled in, the door whacked closed behind me.

A bed with a sleeping bag crumpled on top occupied one corner. I needed no more invitation. I climbed into the sleeping bag, swaddling within its folds. A flash of light crossed the cabin window. I covered my head, closed my eyes, and waited.

THE DOOR CREAKED OPEN on its rusty hinges. The old batten walls breathed. Footsteps crossed directly to the cot. To me! I held my breath.

"Liv, darlin', climb out from unner that bag, will you? Look, I followed you in I reckon you're unner there."

In a tiny, tinny voice, muffled by all the batting, I asked, "Del?"

"Fraid so."

I stuck my head out from under the sleeping bag, my body quaking. I rubbed my arms with my hands. The act of self-comforting calmed me.

The cot creaked as Del sat on the edge. He shined the light on me. He stroked my bruised cheek with his fingertips.

"Don't." I brushed his hand away.

"That's okay, you're fine now," he said, asking, "DeBanco?"

I swam my way out of the sleeping bag, my green dress hiked high around my hips. Del tossed the folds of the sleeping bag over my exposed legs.

"Feron knew the ledge was there. He didn't mean to kill you. Jus' scare you."

"It worked. What if the tree hadn't held? Like it didn't! What then? Ledge?"

"Ledge. I 'spect Feron just gave you enough twist to get you to it. You've fallen further out hikin', Liv, whaz the matter with you?"

"Ledge?" From the moment Feron broke up the dinner party, he was lying in wait for me, his flashlight at the ready. He hadn't tried to kill me, just scare me. Well, he'd accomplished that, I was still shaking.

"What'd deBanco ask you?"

"He wanted to know what I had, what you'd told me."

Del gave a quick whistle accompanied by a nod. "We have a bit to talk about." He stroked my cheek with the back of his left hand.

"A bit?" I grabbed the flashlight and shined the light on his face. "Where the hell have you been?"

"Around. Found Aaron, hon, had to see the tale to the end. I've done what I can. Now, I need to hear from you."

"Were you in the cane field two nights ago?"

"No. Did see you at the funeral. Why?"

"I was lost and scared. Someone called my name."

Del kissed the top of my head. "There, girl, nothin' to be scared of. Reckon the good guys are keepin' an eye on you, tha's all. Prolly that no good Whitelaw out messin' in the suga' heard you, maybe saw you an' tried to make contact, maybe that ol' boy."

"You can drop the Southern-fried, Chamberlin," I said.

Del sniggered, "Oh, hell, Liv, been talkin' like this fo' so long I'm not sure I can, but for you, I'll try."

"Not a bad start, but shouldn't you have a British accent? Shouldn't you tell me about my mother? About the British Army? About Vent Amer? About everything? Oh, Del?"

"We get outta this mess, girl, and I'll tell you stories that'll make your hair not only stand on end but ignite, tha's a promise," he said, hugging me.

"Let me start, to go missing means to go mooncussing."

"My dear, who have you been hangin' out with?"

"The good guys," I responded with sugar in my voice.

Del grabbed my upper arm to pull my ear close to his lips. "Liv," Del whispered lending gravitas to what followed, "Perfidia is in real danger. Her situation was grim before the White Lady went aground, now Aaron's gamble has tightened the vice. We're all struggling to put the thing right and time is running out. Once she's gone, they all are. She's the queen, she is she, not just a house, she's..."

"Everything," I interrupted, "But, Del, I don't know what the key opens. I don't understand why you wanted me to bring it.

"You brought the key?" he asked, surprised. Maybe I wasn't so dull and predictable after all. Or was it that he hadn't found it when he searched my room and suitcase? Why would he, though, when all he had to do was ask me for it?

"I did, it was in my hobo bag. I haven't seen my bag since the fire, why?"

Del sighed, sadly. "Got the key from Colin Law, years ago. He handed it to me, said keep it safe. I did. Now the key is gone. I was goin' to give it to Amanda."

"But Del, it looks so much like the key in the portrait of Tad Law that hangs next to Estella, is it?"

"All I know is Colin gave it to me. Who has it?"

"I don't know. I don't like these people. I don't like this game. I want to go home or to Lacy's, he gave me a key to his house."

"You can't, you're my eyes and ears. You've made it to Perfidia, now make hay."

"I'm no good to you. I haven't figured out what the bats and the staircase mean on your note. I don't know what was on the White Lady if there was anything. I know Feron is brokering Perfidia to a hotel company, but I don't know which one. I don't know what or who you found for me. I only know I'm not who I thought.

Instead, I'm Stella Harris, cousin to modern day pirates who think somehow I have the answer to it all!"

"First of all, I grabbed that sheet of paper off the White Lady then scribbled the note to you. Whatever else was on the paper was Aaron's. Bats, staircases? Ridiculous. He was a ridiculous boy in many ways. Trust me. I knew his father. Second, Aaron hijacked the White Lady to tweak deBanco."

"Then why is he dead?"

"Don't know, Liv. Once we called for a tow, Aaron headed for shore in the dinghy. I stayed aboard. Amanda was frantic when I got back to the house next morning. I went down to the beach to search for him. Unfortunately, Aaron was two days dead before I found him."

Del squinted at me then raised his right hand, two fingers up. "I assure you, there was nothing aboard her. Aaron just drove the White Lady onto the sandbar in the harbor, slick as owl snot. We downed a bottle of champagne. Didn't call for a tow 'til we were damn sure the White Lady was all but ruined. She was a pathetic sight once they floated her off the bar, but a wonderful one."

"And to think they call them the wretched deBancos, do they have a name for the Harris."

My father hugged me again. "Brave, bold, loyal, charismatic, dashing—there's barely a superlative that hasn't been used."

"Oh, Del, don't leave me ever." I kissed Del's cheek, eager as a puppy. I might as well have licked it. "But, who...what do I get?"

"You'll know, sweet Liv, you'll know."

I watched him, wondering if I would ever know, how I would know, but asked again instead, "If there was nothing on the White Lady, why is Aaron dead?"

"The seas were rough, waves pounding into the cove. The dinghy was kindling. Aaron was in the wreckage. Made me wonder if he expected to load her, not empty her. I wondered if he had found Colin's stash."

"Colin's stash?" I gasped, "Colin Law mooncussed!"

Del shook his head in dismay. He tucked a strand of my hair behind my ear, looking as though he couldn't believe that I couldn't believe. "There wasn't a stormy night that man didn't love. God, he could sail!"

"This is the twentieth century, you know," I admonished my father's glee.

"Damn!" Del looked so dashing with his dusky, Loosiana smile, his hair all hanging in his blue eyes that I didn't need my imagination to see the mooncusser in his broad shoulders and trim body. He only lacked a knife clutched in his teeth.

"Where's Colin's stash, then?" I bumped him with my shoulder.

"Well then, Liv, tha's the problem isn't it?" He bumped back.

"And, everyone is crawling all over this plantation looking for Colin's booty?"

With a slight bump back, Del ignored my question. "Sonny, for us findin' the stash is salvation if it isn't long gone like the treasure in Tut's tomb?"

"And for the others?"

Del shrugged. "We'll find the stash, Liv. The alternative isn't acceptable. Trust me?"

"Whose cabin?" I asked, finally checking my surroundings.

Yellowed clothing, brittle from the years, hung from hooks screwed into a board to my left. A rocking chair with a sewing drawer sat under an isinglass window. Tools rested just inside the door, a shovel, a machete, a bucket, and some gloves. An empty coffee cup, next to some crumbs on the table, a man's shirt hanging by the collar on a nail by the door, and a whiff of a chamber pot were new additions.

The interior walls were unfinished, the studs exposed, in every cranny, a small shelf had been made from scraps of two-by-four toe-nailed into the studs. The shelves held canning jars filled with small rounded green or blue sea glass. A drawing of an earthen cliff slammed by the waves, done by a child struggling to grasp the crayon, hung proudly from a rusty tack thumbed in one of the sixteen-inch centers.

"Sophie White lived here until the day she hung herself. Right there." Del pointed to a crossbeam in the ceiling.

"Whitelaw's mother? Have you been staying here?" I held up an edge of the sleeping bag, thinking there had been three men in the field. It would explain why he hadn't contacted me, deBanco kept him informed of my whereabouts.

"No, not here."

"When do I get Vent Amer," I teased, tucking my head into his shoulder. I loved leaning against my father on the rickety old cot, in the rickety old cabin, surrounded by the croaking of frogs, the rustling of sugar cane, and the whisper of wind through the cracks in the wood framing.

Del kissed the top of my head. "Play your cards right, you get Perfidia," then, with a fingertip brush of my bare thigh, added, "Nasty scrape. You'll want some washing. Feeling strong enough to make the trip back to the house? Peggy will have your nightie clean by now. A long bath, a good rough, dry down, you'll be ready for tuck in."

"I did the right thing, coming, I mean, despite everything?"

Del stood offering me his right hand; I clutched it, distracted that he knew Peggy was washing my clothes, more distracted that he knew I'd packed my nightie. But, then again, he was my father and Barbados is hot.

"I counted on you. Hang out with the boys, fin' that ol' stash so we can rescue de lady."

"Del?" A sudden wave of apprehension washed over me, accelerated by the vivid memory of deBanco's eyes as he pushed me off the cliff. "Don't let anything happen to you."

"If it does, hell will follow." Del used my elbow as a tiller and guided me out the door of the cabin. My leg hurt, my back hurt, my pride hurt. I was a frightened girlie mess. Del would have been horrified if he knew. He had made me pinky swear never to become *that* kind of girl, pointing to my best friend, Gail Kazarian, as he did.

"Is there an heir to Perfidia?" I asked, squeezing his hand.

He pointed to the picture on the wall. "Not a legitimate one."

Thinking of Sophie's gravestone, I couldn't help wondering when White-Law had lost its hyphen and why?

Day Six

After a bath, I opened the windows to the night breeze then crawled into the daybed and fell asleep with Del sleeping strung between two of the wicker chairs in the room. He was gone when I awoke before sunrise. I nodded back off.

The surf suffused the air with a studied pounding that suffused my dreams. I fell into the rolling combers, my body pounded against the rocks, my spine snapped. A flashlight swept over my body. I woke covered in a sweat wondering where Del had gone in the half-light of dawn. I must have dozed off again because when I woke, the sun was sufficiently high in the sky that a gin tonic could have been considered appropriate beverage for breakfast. I was sure Amanda would be furious. Not as furious as I was at deBanco, who I considered hunting down in his bedroom and slapping until the urge passed.

I slipped into a pair of white cotton slacks that smelled only mildly of smoke and a blue plaid camp shirt. I wasn't a fashion plate, but I felt like me. I was just deciding how to approach Amanda when she backed in the French doors balancing a tray full of food, dishes, linens, and a silver coffeepot. Steam rose out of the delicate curlicue of the coffeepot's spout.

"Give a hand, make us a place by the big window, one of those wicker tables will do."

I pulled the nearest white wicker table into position by the window with the best view as well as two of the smaller chairs. Amanda set the tray on the desk then spread the linen over the table's glass top. She plunked a lush, pink tropical flower in a crystal vase in the middle of the cloth. Satisfied, Amanda set two places with porcelain so delicate I could see through it. Done, she motioned me to sit.

"I have always enjoyed breakfast here." She poured us each a cup of coffee. A rich, dark brew with a heady aroma likely roasted at Pendu. I was afraid the heat would shatter the fragile coffee cup. It didn't.

With a flourish, Amanda lifted the lid from a covered, mirror-shined, silver serving platter. Wielding a large silver spoon, her pinky raised, she served us each a poached egg on a slice of ham. The eggs were followed by thickly sliced coconut bread. "The sweetmeat is freshly made. I thought a delicious breakfast might help heal bruises."

I took a bite. "Tell me about my mother."

"Emily Lassiter Graydon. Always went by her mother's maiden name, even at boarding school. She didn't realize until she was in her teens that Lassi sounded best on a dog. Lin Harris summered with us every year. His father would do anything to get him out of the Malay quagmire during typhoon season, so Lin was and remained a constant in our lives until the war broke out.

"Returning after, Lin took one look at Lassi and that, well, was that. I think they made love in the old spring house. She was clearly with child when they married. You, my dear." Amanda sipped her coffee. Carefully placing the cup in its saucer, she reached for my hand. "She was lovely, a beautiful girl. You remind me of her. She was full of light.

"Bajan White sent Lin to Louisiana to oversee Maison Vol for the LeChances, which he did under the assumption that when the British repatriated the properties in Malaysia, he would take his new experience to Vent Amer. Lassi hated Maison Vol. She had a terrible pregnancy, cried all the time, chafed when she wasn't crying. She complained about the heat, Del, and even my sister, Celia.

"Lassi was convinced that Celia's husband, Jerome, peeped through her windows at night. More likely it was the Yankee ghost checking her out. I saw him once myself in his muddy uniform, all moldy with a bullet hole where an eye should have been. Your mother died two days after you were born, shouldn't have, did." Amanda sipped her coffee, nibbled her coconut bread, and watched my awestruck face.

"And Del moved me to California and changed our names?"

She put her hand on my arm. "Not immediately. When Vent Amer was returned, he left you with my sister."

"I remember a soft southern lady hugging me. Mostly, I remember feeling abandonned, orphaned, I suppose."

"Dondé LeChance, the matron, was all billowy like one of those powdery Southern ladies in *To Kill a Mockingbird*. It must have been she. My sister, Celia, is much like me, only dark, like our father." Amanda poured me another cup of coffee from the silver pot and put another slab of coconut bread on my plate all without answering my question.

Thinking of the drawing on Sophie's wall, I asked, "Tell me about Brendan Whitelaw."

She looked out over the lawn to the clouds forming for the afternoon's showers. "To do that, I'll have to tell you about my brother, Colin. About us all, I suspect."

Amanda fiddled with the curve of her scoop-neck silk blouse then checked the tightness of the belt at her waist. She put both elbows on the table, realized how many codes of etiquette she had just broken and removed them, checking to see if I had noticed.

There wasn't a hint of gray in Amanda's hair or dullness in her light eyes. Even her hands were unspotted and smooth skinned.

"How old were you when Lloyd was born?"

"Not nearly old enough."

I ate some eggs. They were delicious. I finished most of what was on my plate before Amanda spoke again.

"My father, Drayman, sent to Candle for John Stoddard Maddock. He was the oldest of the Maddock boys, second born, but one of those big, tough Australians. He had dark hair. I think Dad hoped to cure the blond streak he had introduced with Mum. Father claimed John Stoddard was the smartest of the litter." Amanda raised an eyebrow. "Wasn't much of a judge of brains, Dad. I was madly in love with Crispin deBanco. In many ways, our relationship might have worked out, given how things turned out."

"With Colin and Perfidia?"

"With John Stoddard. Drayman, Dad, hung onto Perfidia through the thirties when the market went. Dad diversified by calling in markers from Candle and Maison Vol owed to Perfidia for years, investing them wisely in Bajan White and other stocks while adding land in New Zealand and Canada to the portfolio. When I was fifteen, Drayman sat me down and ordered me to forget Crispin because the deBancos were no longer a threat to Perfidia, instead, he advised me that it was necessary for me to marry a Maddock to strengthen our ties to Candle. By the time I was eighteen, I had Lloyd, and my father was two years' dead."

Amanda slathered a thick piece of coconut bread with lemon curd. She licked lemon curd from one sloppy corner before she took a bite of the wicked thing. "All along friends had been telling my father to keep an eye on my brother. They intimated that Colin stole, that he lied and that he didn't discriminate with his conquests. Dad never listened."

Amanda's description didn't jibe well with the picture both Lacy and John had painted of Colin Law like mismatched sides of a broken coin.

"When Dad died, John Stoddard took over Perfidia knowing he was at best a conservator. John Stoddard was in his thirties, been in the army, all that. Never mind that he didn't have a God-given brain in his head. John Stoddard couldn't add a column of figures with a ten-key. Colin could do advanced equations in his head. Instead, Colin did Sophie White. Sophie was my lady's maid. She lived here. I should have wondered when she moved out to the cabin. Colin followed her. They shacked up like common Bajans.

"Sophie walked to the manor for work each day. Then there was the second baby. The scandal by then was terrible. One day Sophie just hung herself. Peggy took over Sophie's duties. Worked out fine, I always preferred Peggy.

"Shortly after, I discovered that John Stoddard was heavily in debt to Pendu. I still haven't a clue what he did with all of Dad's money. Crispin practically moved here, like Feron now. He watched over every decision John Stoddard made, each one designed to increase Pendu's hold over us. John Stoddard never understood Crispin's gambit. I went to Colin."

"Colin was to inherit wasn't he?"

"Of course, but he was disgraced and five years shy of the appointed birthday. John Stoddard was spending so prodigiously there wouldn't have been anything left to inherit. Colin still had the rights to much of the cane production, not only here but at Apolima in Hawaii. He took control of that, infuriating John Stoddard. Their rivalry became impossible to bear. In eight months, Colin had Perfidia on her feet. We were still in debt to Pendu, but the current taxes were paid, and Laws held controlling interest in Bajan White."

"And, so Crispin murdered Colin?"

Amanda's fork rattled against her plate. She wiped her mouth with a linen napkin embroidered with a P. "No."

"You're sure."

"Crispin and I were lovers."

"Please don't tell me Feron is your son."

A guffaw roared through the room. Amanda shook her head. "Crispin was with me the night Colin died."

"Who then?"

She shrugged. "I should tell you that Colin had been smuggling drugs for years. He bought back our shares with drug money. He said it was the perfect gambit."

"How did he manage his exchanges?"

"I have always had the habit of sitting out on the balcony until the Southern Cross is visible. Then, my nightly vigil was how I avoided my husband. It was also how Crispin knew I could come to him. Occasionally, I would see a ship ride into Taddys Cove. The next morning, it was gone. Another would follow within a day or two. Once, to tease Colin, I keep a record on my calendar."

"Caves?" The drawing on Sophie's wall showed the tide coming in, rushing into an opening that looked everything like a cave.

Amanda raised her neatly darkened blonde eyebrows.

"Aaron's doodles...spiral staircases? Bats?" I explained.

"Bats in the attic maybe."

What cave doesn't have bats? Aaron's doodles must mean something, though both Del and now Amanda denied it.

"Who killed Colin?"

She sighed, "From the morning that they found my brother's body to John Stoddard's death, I never slept with the bastard. I couldn't do much, but I could make damn sure Lloyd and Aaron were all the sons he ever got."

"What happened to John Stoddard?"

"Crispin did kill him." Amanda wiped her lips. "I asked nicely."

"Am I allowed to know why?"

Amanda spooned lemon curd onto another piece of coconut bread spreading the curd with the back of her spoon. She took a sip of freshly poured coffee then a bite. She chewed for a while. "Rain will come before three today. Unusual."

"Amanda?"

"John Stoddard told Lloyd he would inherit. Meaning Perfidia would be Lloyd's and pass through his line. Of course, Lloyd hasn't got a line, and not bloody likely to either, though I think he is trying one on you." She watched me over her sloppy coconut bread. "Don't trust Lloyd, he's cut so many deals hoping to keep Bajan White afloat he has no soul."

"You had Crispin kill John Stoddard because he said Lloyd would inherit?"

"John Stoddard had no right to tell anyone anything as regards Perfidia. With my father and brother and the inheritance box gone, the heirs, the rules for succession, and the tools to keep Perfidia safe were gone, too. No key. No ceremony. My brother and I promised our father as he died that we would protect Perfidia, whatever the cost. It cost my brother his life. In turn, I promised my brother his son would inherit."

"But..."

Amanda clapped her hands. "If Brendan were illegitimate, it would be a problem, but Colin gave me the marriage certificate for safe keeping. Whitelaw meets all of the requirements according to the Code. We think. It's a little difficult to know for sure without someone to pass the torch."

"Any idea who has the box?" I asked.

"There would have been nothing left if John Stoddard had lived. As it is, Perfidia is heavily in debt to both Bajan White and the Bajan government. We haven't paid taxes in anyone's memory. You must have found or figured that out by now. What you don't know is that Bajan White put a call in on some loans, one huge one in particular. The deBancos began demanding repayment because they could, and because, it has become apparent that the deBancos may no longer control Bajan White. We have only a few days left on a 60-day call.

"Crispin has kindly offered to buy the second mortgage, and forget the rest of our debts if we'll just let the wretched deBancos have Perfidia. The bright spot is that if Crispin knew Feron was with the hotel magnates, he would kill the weasel." She stopped, brightened, then continued, "Anyway, D-day for Perfidia is September 1, this Sunday."

"The box?" I asked again.

"It would be most lovely if you discovered what Aaron planned. The money would come in handy right now."

"Del thinks that Aaron found Colin's stash. I assume it is drugs. If Aaron did, and it was found, would Whitelaw be of help?"

"Brendan could move drugs, but your father has more established connections." Amanda began to pile dishes back on the tray. "I think we understand each other."

I nodded, as one thing became crystalline; Del was to Perfidia as fence was to coke. No wonder the DEA kept showing up at our door in Bakersfield.

Amanda rang the bell for Peggy to retrieve the tray. Instead, Peggy entered with three planter's punches balanced on a silver tray. Peggy pulled up a large rattan rocker then plunked her ample hips into the seat.

"So, Peg, where is Colin's stash?" Amanda asked.

Peggy drank for a minute, wiped her lips, took the cherry by the stem, wrapped her tongue around the fruit then sucked the cherry into her full-lipped mouth. "I remember dat Colin and dat no good John out looking for Tad stash, all over dem cliffs, just looking an' looking. One time dey got all excited 'cause they found dem a cave, but it no cave at all. Da hole be fill wid water, can't hide no booty in a cave like dat. Dem two.

Took to digging 'round de rubble at de bottom of de cliff, found nothin'." Peggy shook her head while taking a deep slurp of planter's punch. "But Colin stash? Maybe he find Tad stash, use it."

"I do miss my brother," Amanda said.

Peggy pointed to Amanda with her thumb. "Colin always was de only one who could keep that nasty John Stoddard in check. Boy, did dey go about it. Yellin' and screamin' and threatenin'. Dat John Stoddard, he one dum', vicious man. Best day we had be the day dat old man die."

Amanda raised a finger. "A year ago, God bless. One day he's out yelling at the great gang, the next he's gone." She sipped her rum punch.

I raised an eyebrow. If Crispin deBanco had killed Maddock, it had been accomplished such that no one's eyebrows but mine were raised.

"Had a hell of a party didn't we, Peg?"

"Best old wake dis place seen since I was a girl. Amanda, she so happy!"

"I just smiled all night long," Amanda agreed.

"Dat John Stoddard worry Amanda something fierce with he roving eye and mean ways. Amanda only have one job, keepin' Perfidia for de family. One job." Peggy rocked in her chair.

"Have you worked here all your life?" I asked.

Amanda looked away seemingly embarrassed by my question. The patois gone, Peggy said in the lilting British accent of the island, "I don't work here. I live here, just like Sophie, like her mother and hers and hers and so on. There is always a White lady for the mistress."

"Do you have a family?"

Peggy returned to the patois. I sensed that the patois was a defense mechanism, something to hide behind, a relic of slave culture that joined Bajans into a tribe.

"When I was a girl, my father he de foreman. Dey live in the south quarters. Still. Daddy gone, though. Long time. But, my brother, he family, he girl, dey down there. John, he de foreman now. Taddy always take care of dey people."

"It's symbiotic and don't ask." Amanda sighed as some palpable tension washed away as if she were worried about something Peggy might say.

What had Lacy said about the Whites? Some worked in the big house, and some were still slaves to it.

Peggy pushed her way out of the rocking chair. She patted Amanda on the shoulder then lifted the empty tray. "If symbiotic means we all work out our problem like she's ours, then that be true."

"She?"

"Perfidia, you poop!" Amanda said, throwing back the remainder of her planter's punch. As Amanda stood to leave, she pointed one coral polished fingernail at me. "Rest. You need it. You've got the most awful bags under your eyes."

I napped until Peggy brought dinner to my room. By then, I was beyond well-rested and into restless.

𝒫

AMANDA SCUFFED ONE OF the wicker chairs to the railing then sat and adjusted a light cardigan slung over her shoulders in preparation for her nightly wait on the Southern Cross. I stepped out of my French doors to enjoy the evening as well. Lloyd was leaning against the railing outside his room. There was something communal in the wait. When the Southern Cross skimmed the horizon its stipes tipped toward the sea, Lloyd waved and returned to his room shutting and latching the doors behind him. When the crescent moon dimmed the constellation, Amanda returned the wicker chair to just outside her doors and entered her room. She clicked on a light by her writing desk. The night was so lovely it seemed a shame to retire early, but, then, I'd slept most of the day.

The stars were thick overhead. The thrum of a small engine rose over the crash of the waves in Taddys Cove.

Curiosity got the better of me. I changed into Whitelaw's discarded jeans and a freshly laundered black sleeveless top from my suitcase. Armed with a flashlight found in the hold of Amanda's escritoire, I descended the south stairs to the veranda then down the two steps to the lawn.

I trotted across the gray-green of the moonlit grass toward the small gate tucked in the hedgerow of privet. The Southern Cross was still lazy low in the sky though fainter as the still ascending crescent moon laid a glade of pale light across the clipped grass. I slipped my wrist through a cord attached to my flashlight then flashed the beam side to side like a blind man's cane. I prayed I didn't beam up the ghost of Tad Law standing by the privet staring hopefully out to sea for an unsuspecting clipper ship. I felt jumpy and restless enough for two without his specter for companionship.

The gate through the privet angled open four inches. Grass grew thick between the gateposts. The rusty hinges screeched but didn't resist. At the verge of the cliff, only the roots of the shrubbery kept the undermined ledge from plunging straight into the harbor.

The cliff wall below the ledge appeared stable enough though exceedingly steep. The wooden staircase, riser ends to the cliff wall, zigged first to the right, going down ten feet before zagging to the left down another number of feet and so eventually reaching the waters below. I oozed through the gate, keeping a solid hold on one gatepost.

At the base of the stairs, a small crescent of beach glittered in the growing moonlight. I suspected that the denizens of de lady made the odd night assault for skinny dipping and frippery down these very stairs. The thought that the stairs were used even now helped to calm my worry about descending the grayed wood. The thin putt-putt of the boat's motor reminded me that it was the under-glub that had drawn me across the night-shadowed lawn.

A shallow, flat-bottomed skiff raced from the south toward the base of the stairs, its pointed bow cutting from wave crest to crest. The night, the boat, the brilliant stars continued to call me out to play. The pilot flashed a light over the cliff face, dancing it away from the stairs long before it reached me. His next sweep of the light was higher. The light continued to arc, as the person in the boat searched for someone or something on the beach. Certain it wasn't me, I turned off my flashlight. He turned off his.

Flashlight still extinguished, I bounced one foot on the first stair to check that it would hold my weight, which was silly considering the possible consequences. When it held, I did the same on the second stair. Reassured, I continued gingerly down, keeping a death grip on the wobbly wooden handrail. A thin sliver of the weathered wood scored my palm. With a shake of my hand, I descended the rickety stairs drawn by the tiny motor, the dancing light, and the beach below.

On the last zag, the skiff disappeared among the waves. I squinted to separate the white hull of the boat from the combers and saw a shadow bouncing to my left. The pilot was searching the bottom boards, perhaps for a blue bag with snorkel gear like the one on the first boat I had seen.

The sea was rough. At night, Taddys Cove would be treacherous for anyone who didn't know its bars and beaches. There were few reasons to be out now, not to be seen, not to be followed, not to be found out. But, here I was, as well. The pilot sat with his head cocked, trying to pull a sound from the air. A moment later, I heard a deep rumble.

A second larger motor growled out past the bar. A launch, easily three times the size of the skiff, appeared at the headland. Rounding into the cove, it thundered through the surf to the middle of the small bay. The driver made a slight correction then sped, full throttle, straight for the cliffs.

The skiff bounced over the swell to be pitched bow down in the trough. The outboard, out of the water, died. Wallowing as waves washed over the gunwales, the pilot yanked the motor's rope repeatedly, trying to start it with each pull...one, two...five. The skiff pilot never took his eyes off the launch as it tore towards where he floundered in the smaller craft.

The man in the skiff turned a knob on a hose that ran from a gas tank to the boat's motor, adjusting the mix, or gas line or both then pulled the rope again...one...two. The engine whined to life. The pilot reached back for the tiller, cutting an angle for open water. The small boat's bow lurched over the waves. The motor died, the propeller spun to a stop. The skiff rode the swell, each wave bringing it closer to shore. The pilot pulled the cord on the outboard. Again. Then again.

The launch, blue on top, white below, adjusted the angle of attack, gathering speed until the powerful inboard motor slashed through the waves.

The skiff pilot glanced toward shore. He pulled off his shoes. With one look at the onrushing launch, he reconsidered abandoning his boat for the pounding surf. Taking to the oars, he alternately stroked and surfed the current toward shore.

With a deep growl, the launch gorged on the skiff.

The impact reverberated through the wooden railing into my hands.

The skiff's hull disintegrated. Wood splinters shot into the air, falling like hail to the beach. The launch cut to the right, skirting a hidden rock, to idle mid-cove. Whoever piloted the launch knew the rocks and shoals of the cove as though tattooed on his forearm. A man dressed in black came onto the deck from the launch's cabin. He scanned the wreckage with binoculars; his legs set shoulder-width apart to overcome the pitch.

I raced down the remainder of the stairs, ignoring the screeching wood threatening to rip loose from the cliff wall with each footfall. Of course, the man on the launch saw my mad race. Of course, the bright beam of the launch's searchlight lit my descent. Of course, I flipped him off as I ran pell-mell down the stairs screaming: *I'm coming!*

Next moment, I clung to the railing, one foot in mid-air, balanced on the tiptoe of the other, suspended twelve feet from the beach.

The last flight of stairs was gone—as in not there.

The wood lay shattered amongst boulders pitched on the beach as though a tsunami had rolled them for drinks. Rocky gravel ground by the waves and ancient wood dribbled to the waterline.

"Stay where you are!" A voice hissed from a dark crevice of rocks to my left.

I swung my head. Another warning sounded. The man the skiff had come to meet scrambled toward me over the night shaded rocks.

I wasn't to be stopped, not while there was hope that the man in the boat lived. I hung from the last stair; one foot pointed and dangling to reach the first boulder, a jagged beast embedded in the sand during some previous thrashing. Splintered wood littered the crevices of the jumble of rocks, not trees tossed ashore, but milled wood ground to matchsticks. I gingerly let go of the last vestiges of the stairs for the water sprayed boulder and slid.

My rope-soled shoes were like skates on the wet surface. I sat on the tipped rock to take off my shoes then threw them to the beach, hoping to find them once I gained the sand. I checked over my shoulder; the waiting man was a shadow deep in the rocks. Whatever had been planned hadn't been legal. The launch had intervened. I signaled for him to come to help.

When I took off at a run, no one followed.

My bare feet, toughened by Bakersfield summers, did just fine until they met the mix of rocks and coral beaten to a granular pulp that passed for sand. The coral bit into the soles of my feet. The beach, the lovely little crescent of inviting skinny-dipping beach, was covered in razor-like sand and was half the size it had been when I started my headlong rush down the stairs.

One of my shoes floated by as the water receded to the sea. I grabbed it from the surf and put it on. A moan, more a groan, like the sounds of an animal in pain, distressed, hurt, calling for help spurred me across the beach.

I have no experience with real pain, real wounds. I've seen my share of scraped knees, bloody noses, and black eyes. But, eight-year-olds either cried or sniffled, they didn't moan like their next breath would be their last.

Not like this.

With one shoe off and one shoe on, I made my diddle-diddle-dumpling way toward the softening groans through the deepening water. With each step, my feet sank into the oozing tidal sand. I fought through the sucking surf on aching legs until I reached the shattered remains of the small boat.

The lights of the launch lit the cliff wall like daylight. Why? What did the man or men on the launch hope to see? Me? The yacht continued to idle fifty feet off shore. With my way lit, I scrambled through the splintered boards of the skiff, struggling to reach the diminishing cries for help.

I began to fling boards aside, calling now, not caring who heard or saw me. I gestured for the launch to shine their damn searchlight down the wreckage. With a roar of the motor, the yacht tore around the slump, leaving rough seas in its wake. I shook my fist at it as its waves set the beach awash. No one saw. The boat was already well out past the bar.

Another faint groan was followed by one still fainter. I dug through the rubble. A face mask, a blue bag filled with snorkel gear, an underwater torch, a gibberish of stuff, even a pickax, luckily buried pick first in the sand and not in the man who groaned. Pulling the bag from the rising water, I uncovered a tennis shoe shod foot. I lifted what appeared to be the seat of the boat, exposing a leg—a gashed, broken leg—the mangle showing brilliantly through torn slacks. I raced to uncover the rest of the body.

Del was unconscious. His head was battered. His breath was shallow. I could barely feel it on my cheek. His pulse was rapid. Water lapped his knees. The beach would be awash in half an hour with all but the tallest rocks under the hurtling waves. I couldn't help him. I couldn't. I squeezed his hand in mine. I called his name softly. I babbled, "Del, don't leave me. Don't. I'm going to get help. Now. Hang on, please, Daddy, please."

I placed my hands under Del's armpits, dragging him up the beach until his back rested against the cliff wall. The pain must have been horrific. Thankfully, he couldn't feel it, or so I chose to believe. I scrabbled around until I uncovered two gunny sacks under a piece of the broken hull. I used the hopsacking to cover his shoulders hoping to ward off the chill of the ocean driven breeze.

Satisfied that he was safe from exposure, I went back to the wreckage for wood to use as a splint. Finding two leg-length boards, I carried them to where Del lay. I placed a board on either side of his tortured leg then gently straightened it.

No rope! Back in the rubble, I located a length of sisal attached to what had been the bow. After struggling to untie the wet knot, I brought my prize back to Del and wound the rope around the two boards. Whenever Del groaned, I stopped. My heart stopped. I held my breath until my chest demanded I breathe. When he would take a breath, I would begin again.

I took off my tee-shirt, folded it six times then jammed it under the rope and over the wound, hoping to stanch at least some of the bleeding. My work wouldn't win a badge, but the splint and the wadding might keep him alive.

There was nothing left to do but go for help. To do that I had to sneak past the man hidden deep in the rocks to reach the sea swept stairs. There was no time for a delay. I grabbed a piece of driftwood for use as a weapon.

P

I SLOSHED THROUGH DEEPENING water, not caring where my feet landed or on what they landed. I scrambled over the rocks to the base of the stairs. Spray blown off the breakers dried my lips and encrusted my body. My bra, now nearly invisible, offered no insulation against the sea breeze. I quivered from the cold.

I checked for a shadow in the rocks. Seeing no one, I put down my chunk of driftwood to climb the large, tilted rock directly beneath the stairs then, on tiptoe, jumped to grab the bottom stair. The weather-beaten board split. I jolted to my rump on the crest of the rock then slid. I sat at the base seeking the strength within to tackle the gap to the steps before my father's life was washed away in the tide.

A hand touched my forearm.

I filled my lungs to give a healthy, adult female scream, the type that just reverberates, the kind they record for horror movies—that scream. A decidedly male hand covered my mouth. I squirmed. Another hand grabbed my waist, lifting me to my feet, pressing me to my captor's body. A mouth came to my ear. The voice from earlier hissed into my hair, "They're on the beach."

I wrenched myself free. The powerful man jerked me face-first to his well-muscled chest, holding me there with a hand clutched in my hair. My breath escaped me. It wouldn't come back. I gasped like a goldfish on the sidewalk. Out of options, I went limp. He held me upright.

"Get your legs under you girl, hide, quick. They're coming. Get, now, please?"

Please? I knew this voice.

Whitelaw shoved me behind a pile of scree loose from the cliff. I rode the scrambling pebbles deep into the shadows then scurried for a view of the beach, my feet creating a small avalanche of rocky sand. Thankfully, the rushing sand went unnoticed by the three men jogging around an outcropping of rocks to my left.

I raised myself enough to peer over the rubble. One of the men was taller than the other two who were matched in size. All were dressed in black from ankles to the tops of their watch-capped heads and armed. One held a gun in his hand; another had a holster across his chest.

They ran through the surf, legs high, plunging through the waves. My missing shoe chose that moment to float high on a wave past the tallest of the three men. He grabbed the sandal from the surf. Scanning the cliff face, he loped to catch the others. Topper Law.

As they neared the crushed hull, I readied to make a disturbance. The crisp snap of a bullet hitting rock echoed around the cove, a chunk of stone broke free. Rocks tumbled down the bluff toward the wreckage. Topper's next shot loosened a small landslide of scree that carried debris with it. The third shot caused hull boards to jump in the wreckage.

These men were dangerous, this wasn't a pirate movie. There was no romance to it. My father's life would end on the beach, under flotsam, covered in seaweed. Would they find his corpse and say he drowned?

I thought of Aaron.

Angry voices echoed off the rocks.

The three men jogged back towards me. I made myself as small as I could hunkering behind a pile of stones. When the light they strafed along the beach was a pinprick on the southern headland, I scrambled up the tilted rock. On my toes, arms stretched overhead, I somehow grabbed a stair.

The stair held. I clutched the board with my right hand while summoning the strength to reach over my head to the back of the next stair with my left hand. Gripping so hard my fingernails dug into the old wood, I walked my feet up the face of the wall.

Dirt and rocks bounced to the beach as my left foot gained purchase on an exposed root. My right foot, toe pointed, found the lowest stair. I hooked my foot and muscled my leg onto the stair. After a moment's rest, hanging upside down like a sloth, I crabbed my left leg to join my right then hauled myself to standing. I clambered up the shaky stairs, praying with each step that the rotting wood would hold to the top.

Gaining the lawn, I squeezed back through the gate, dashed to the south stairs then scrambled up them. In my borrowed room, I threw on a shirt and covered the splinter in my hand with Lloyd's handkerchief before going for help. The men on the beach hadn't found Del. Where was he? Where was Whitelaw?

At a small noise, I looked up. Whitelaw stood in my doorway, his wet shirt clinging to his chest, as graceful as he was powerful, a roguish smile on his full mouth. His eyes, as gray as those in Tad's portrait, checked me from head to toe. My heart hit eighty. I flushed at the memory of his hands crushing me to his chest. He put one finger to his lips then rolled out of the door frame onto the balcony. I rushed to follow him, but he was gone, leaving only the light echo of his steps on the south stairs.

If Whitelaw was here, Del was here.

The next moment every light on the balcony blazed. A short man with a robin's chest trotted up the stairs to a room mid-balcony. Amanda flew out of her bedroom, her bathrobe flouncing behind her, her hips swaying in pink furry, spiked-heeled mules, her long hair, out of its French twist, bouncing over her shoulders. Her mouth, in an O, was covered by her pink-polished fingertips. Peggy thundered by a few moments later.

I followed them to an open set of French doors three doors down the balcony. The short man leaned over the bed where Del had been taken, his stethoscope over Del's heart. Del's broken leg lay on top of the bedclothes at an odd angle held straight by my ridiculous splint. Amanda gently washed his face with a face cloth. Peggy was standing by the doctor's bag, prepared to hand him what he needed. As I rounded the doorframe, Feron deBanco pushed me aside and strode through the door, five shades whiter than he should have been.

He snapped, "What's happened?"

"It's Lin," Amanda said, wringing out the cloth, "Someone's tried to kill him."

I surged to Del's side. Feron backed away then tore out of the room. As he left, I noticed his dry business suit, every pleat was pressed, his shoes were shiny—he hadn't been near the beach. Del's eyes fluttered open, he whimpered, "Whitelaw."

I pivoted to the door. The frame was empty until Lloyd came from the balcony straight over to me. Taking my hand, Lloyd said, "Olivia, my dear, you look a fright."

The doctor studied me for a moment then fingered the purple bruise rising on my upper arm. I put my hand out to stop him. He saw the rough bandage on it and gently uncovered the wound. Peggy clucked when she saw the channel left by the splinter. She whispered in the doctor's ear. He gestured yes.

Lloyd lifted me in his arms, as though I weren't almost as tall as he, as though I didn't weigh a thing, as though he hefted women every single day. He carried me down the balcony to my room. Peggy followed batting him out of the room like dust from a rug. Lloyd touched my knee with his fingertips then exited opposite where the doctor tended Del, leaving me wondering about his effortless strength.

Peggy disappeared down the hall returning with a black medical bag covered in leather so cracked it appeared to have survived the wrecking of many a ship. She snapped the bag open, dug around for a moment then pulled out an amber bottle and a gauze bandage. So armed, she pointed at the bathtub. I took the hint. Once I bathed, Peggy removed the splinter and wrapped my hand.

She folded back the bedding on the daybed then helped me into Dave's freshly laundered tee-shirt. I snuggled into the softness of the shirt. Nestled under the covers of the daybed, I stared at the portrait of Beth, the freedom and joy of her youth spent. What must she have seen?

As the adrenaline of my night's adventures began to wane, Peggy returned with a gin tonic and a slab of coconut bread. I refused the sweet bread, not the gin tonic.

"He be fine girl," Peggy said, "Dat Del be fine. Dr. Smythe has bound he wounds before. He be fine." She patted my sheet-covered leg. "Don't you worry, doctor make he good as new."

"Peggy?" She heard the question in my voice and held one finger to her lips. She waggled her finger for emphasis. I refused her waggle. "Peggy, what did...does Tad's key open? The key in his portrait."

"De big ol' box, de one in Beth painting. Only dat box." Peggy narrowed her glorious dark eyes. The frown that followed seemed incongruous on her generous, open face.

"And the key in Beth's portrait," I pointed at the painting, "The one on the chain around her waist? Is it the same key?"

Peggy's head bobbed. With a quick upturn of the corners of her mouth, she said, "Dat key open the well-house door. A chil' fell into the open well, one of Beth baby. Dat what dey say. So, Tad have a wall and a door built. De Lady's key kept by the lady maid always. Nobody know where dat key is not since 'bout thirty years. Dat key just gone."

When my head hit the pillow, Peggy swayed out the door closing it behind her. I watched the light from the balcony play across the ceiling. A bat, a circular staircase, a trail to the water, a walled in wellhead, two keys, Tad's and the Lady's key, a child's drawing of a cave being pounded by water, and Colin's cache all pinwheeled through my mind. The soft burble of voices caring for Del provided my lullaby.

I don't know how long I slept, only that I was wakened from a deep sleep by stealthy movement at my French door. The knob turned. The gauzy drapes blew in on the tidal breeze. I lay still, my eyes shut, willing the intruder away yet comforted by the knowledge that tonight my scream would bring others running.

The door closed. The breeze ceased. The latch caught. The lock was set. The room was stifling. The intruder had drawn the shutters. Soft footsteps neared me.

I waited for a hand across my mouth. Instead, gentle fingers ran down my exposed upper arm. When the fingers reached the bruise, there was a soft intake of breath.

"I did this?" Whitelaw asked. He lifted my bandaged hand. "And this?"

He kissed my fingers.

"I'm sorry, then." He leaned over me. I thought he would kiss me, perhaps, hoped he would. Instead, he brushed the hair from my eyes, said nothing, just stared a moment before standing. He ran his hand down the back of my arm then strode for the door, leaving behind goosebumps.

I whispered to stop him, longing for his touch, "Del's going to be okay. You saw to that. How did you get him off the beach?"

"I didn't. We hid in a crack in the cliff, behind the sand. I had a boat. When they rounded the headland, I carried Lin out then motored to the north landing. I radioed ahead, Lloyd was waiting for us," he answered, one hand on the door knob, ready to exit.

Whitelaw had been skulking about on the beach for a reason. Had Del been expecting Whitelaw? Had Whitelaw expected Del? Whichever, they were both involved in activities that could only be done during high tide and undercover of night.

Whitelaw had depended on me to make my way back to the manor. Now, he had come to see that I was safe or to ask something of me. I played trump. "Where's the Lady's key? Peggy said it had been missing for thirty years. I got the impression that your mother was Amanda's lady-maid then."

"Key?" Whitelaw raised his raven eyebrows. "I remember my mother hanging a key on a chain on a nail by the door each night. She claimed it was the key to my father's heart. That's the only key she had. It opened a closet." He closed his eyes, some thought, not a pleasant one, stole across his face.

"The key to Colin's heart? It is sweet, but it doesn't make any sense, does it?" I asked.

Whitelaw cocked his head and ran his eyes over the light sheet covering my form. With a lopsided grin, he said, "You looked smashing in your bra and my jeans."

I climbed out of bed, but he was out the door. I checked the balcony, he was gone—again. Before crawling back under the sheet, I opened the shutters and louvers to let the breeze usher me to sleep.

In the dark, propped up against my pillows, the sheet covering my legs, I struggled to make sense of what Sophie had told her son. Del claimed that there wasn't a moonless night that Colin hadn't loved. According to Sophie, the key unlocked Colin Law's heart. Colin's cache? Was that the meaning of the circular staircase drawn on Aaron's notecard? Were the drawings Aaron made the map to the cache?

Questions without answers, but there were. My brain just refused them.

Day Seven

SUN STREAMED THROUGH MY windows long before I woke. I climbed out of the daybed feeling every bruise, every bump from the night before. With every move I made, the salt dried in Whitelaw's jeans burned the scrapes on my legs. The bruise on my arm was brilliant, just below the embroidered puff sleeve on my peasant blouse with its drawstring neckline that, magically, had survived both the fire and Peggy's wash job. I snapped on my happy bangle for something bright.

Three doors to my right, Del, his eyes bruised from pain, his leg stiffly splinted, his head bandaged, lay on the bed. Amanda was asleep on a huge rattan chaise lounge in the far corner of the room with one arm hanging over the side, a soft blanket draped over her legs.

Del was as white as the eyelet coverlet tucked under his chin. I touched him just to feel that he was warm. His eyes flickered open. When he saw me, a drugged, lazy smile lifted the corners of his mouth. I knelt beside him to whisper in his ear, "Is there anything I can do for you?"

He took a deep breath as his eyes slid to where Amanda slept. He made a writing motion. A small pad bearing instructions for his care occupied one corner of the nightstand next to his bed, a pencil tucked neatly at the pad's side. I handed pad and pencil to him. Del wrote, tore off his note with the next two pages then gave them to me.

He mimicked reading what he had written then crumpling the paper and swallowing. It niggled that Del knew a pencil would leave an imprint. I had to read it in a mystery novel. He tore the three pages off like he did it every day.

When I lit a fake match, Del nodded his approval. I read his pointy message, crumpled all three sheets then scurried out of the room before Amanda awakened. I burned the note to ashes in a silver tray in my room then stirred them. I carried the tray onto the balcony letting the ashes drift in the wash of the breeze off the cliffs.

At my request, Amanda lent me a car and one of the cars I got—the red Jeep with a torn seat and a left-handed steering wheel. Having just learned to drive steering wheel on the wrong side in, I now had to adapt to steering wheel out. Somehow, I managed my way around the southern point of the Island to Bridgetown without hitting a child, a donkey or a motorcyclist.

I parked near Admiral Nelson. If possible, the Admiral looked more disgruntled than he had the first time we met. Upon leaving the car, I ducked into a throng of freshly landed cruise participants to evade Topper Law, five cars back, in the gray Mercedes. I mingled my way through Cave-Shepherd to Coleridge Street. I would like to say I jogged up the steps to Parradine and Whitelaw, but I did not. My legs hurt, my hand hurt and, in fact, my head hurt, likely due to my late night snack of gin.

I ignored the disfigured monkey knocker and bulled into the reception room. Ms. Smythe smiled her most business-like smile over hands she had clasped on her blotter. The platinum band on her ring finger convinced me that she was the wife of Dr. Smythe, who fixed the bones and ills of de lady. That seemed to be the way things worked. The family of de lady kept everyone close.

"Is Lacy in?" I asked.

She cleared her throat as she tapped her fisted hands on her blotter, three taps; loud enough to be heard behind Parradine's closed doors.

I stared at her. She stared at me. "Mr. Parradine is with his partner."

"May I see them, then?"

Ms. Smythe cleared her throat, stood, and pulled down her skin-tight navy blue straight skirt then her flowered peplum blouse. With steps narrowed by her skirt, she did the rhumba to Parradine's door. Lacy's burr answered her knock. In a stage whisper, she said, dramatically, "She's here."

The door flew open. Lacy emerged with his arms out. "My dear!"

Over Lacy's shoulder, his partner, Brendan Whitelaw, climbed out the window. So, we were back to that. I accepted Lacy's hug managing to dance him into his office. I closed the door behind us nearly taking Miss Smythe's nose off in the process. When I was sure I was out of her hearing, I held the palm of my left hand out to him. "Del says you have Tad's key."

Lacy pulled me away from the door, depositing me by the window. He scowled for a moment, started to speak, stopped, positioned a piece of paper on his desk then shut his eyes.

"Well?"

"You want the key? The one Del asked you to bring? That one? Tad's key? The key that went missing when Colin died? The one to the inheritance box, missing since the day Drayman died? The key to the succession, that's what it is called in the Code and wills. Sounds like the open sesame to the kingdom, doesn't it? That key? Really? Olivia!" His voice rose as he spoke.

Parradine stared anywhere but at me. He made fists of his hands. His whole demeanor had changed from warm and fuzzy to fight.

"You gave Tad's key to Whitelaw!" I pointed out the window. "He just climbed out like some two-bit cat burglar. You gave the key to him!"

"No. I did not," Parradine said, his jaw firm, his burr crisp as though that alone would make me believe him. "I'm sorry, my dear. I simply don't have anything of Lin's."

Lacy made it sound as though he would never, ever have anything of Del's.

That quick, the fists were gone. He wasn't angry at me, what then? He patted my arm.

"I do have something of yours, though. Something, I think you'd like back. Johnny had your rental car towed to the airport. You must have left Parradine and Whitelaw as your local number, the rental company called here. It seems that you left your purse thing in the trunk. I was going to drive the bag out to you, but now you're here."

He pointed to a black lump next to his desk. My hobo bag! I reached down and lifted the huge double-strapped bag onto his desk. I unzipped the central pocket then jammed my hand into the opening. When my fingers met the velvet key bag, my world began to slip back into orbit. I kissed Lacy on the cheek.

"Feeling better?"

"Feeling more together." I slipped my passport from the bag to show him.

"Good…good," he said, absently. "Then you'll be on your way. Hate to rush you, lass, but I've got an appointment due."

I stared at the debonair bachelor surprised. My belief that Parradine did nothing but pander to Perfidia wasn't the case. He had real clients.

With a gentle, almost mocking smile, Lacy led me by the upper arm out his office door. He shuffled me through the entry and face to face with the ugly monkey. I slung my bag over my shoulder. One strap immediately cruised down my arm.

Feron deBanco, dressed as ever in a suit, lazed against a tree just outside. As I passed him, he two-fingered the strap back onto my shoulder. Humming something unrecognizable, he took all three stairs in one leap.

Lacy's business was Perfidia. Feron was here. Del knew I had brought the key, but lost it. He knew that my hobo bag was at Lacy's and presumed the key was in it. Whitelaw had just crawled out the window. One of these men had rummaged through my suitcase, taken my small things only to return them after reading Del's note in which he asked me to bring the key. Likely, the same man had taken my suitcase and whatever else was left in cabin 4 before lighting the fire and searched it, only to be disappointed. Given they all knew my bag was found, why was the key still in it?

Despite all of the unanswered questions, it was Lacy's hurt and anger that occupied my mind.

BY THE TIME I reached Perfidia, Del was sitting snuggled in a host of pillows with some color back in his cheeks, talking in hushed tones to Topper Law. I watched from the doorway for a moment, speculating. When their voices rose, I left them to their jousting. After last night, goading Topper seemed dangerous to me, but Del seemed to be enjoying himself.

In my room, I dropped my hobo bag to the floor then reconsidered. I unzipped the cover of one of the rose embroidered throw pillows then removed the key from my bag and tucked it deep in the batting. Pillow re-zipped, I jammed it behind all of the other pillows strewn on the daybed. If someone rearranged the pillows, the key might be lost forever. Feeling comfortable with my deceit, I went in search of Amanda.

Seated at a delicate white desk in her bedroom next door, Amanda was busily writing thank you notes to people who had attended Aaron's funeral. It seemed a bit odd but very polite. I sat on one of her wicker chairs, my hands on my lap waiting for her to acknowledge my presence.

Amanda finished writing a note on a card with a P in the corner, signed with a flourish then dunked the nib of her pen in an inkwell before looking in my direction. She was wearing pedal-pushers in an adamant pink with a sleeveless seersucker blouse of the same shade. The shirt was tight in the front, billowy in the back. Her feet were shoved into pink sandals with three-inch spiked heels.

My own legs were ensconced in Whitelaw's jeans. My peasant blouse was colorfully set off by the bruise on my arm. My multi-colored bracelet gaudily circled my wrist, matching nothing. My hair had descended into a brown curly mob at ocean-side last night. It refused to uncurl.

Amanda studied my state of dishevelment. By the slight cock of her head, I knew what was coming.

Instead, she said, "That bracelet is from Apolima. I remember now, Del stopped there on his way back after the war. He gave it to your mother. Garish damn thing! The man has no taste, never did."

I stared at the birds thinly outlined in the same brass that backed the bracelet, stunned she hadn't asked for the key. She had to know I had it; even that it was in my hobo bag. News traveled faster than a wave here, besides what Parradine knew, Amanda knew.

"All that gold!"

"Gold?"

"Gold. Excellent workmanship, though, it always reminded me of something a drunken Tiffany might have made."

My hand locked over the bracelet. Del must have been disappointed when I never wore it. Had it not been for this trip, it would have languished forever in my lingerie drawer. It was gaudy. It was garish. He had given it to my mother. Now, it felt priceless.

My fingers traced the lines of gold as if by touching them I could somehow know my mother. In truth, it wouldn't, couldn't. Del had driven us away from his memories of Lassiter Harris in that rickety old Dodge and fabricated my creation myth, telling all and sundry that he had found me with my alligator, Bontemps, at the four corners. Amanda drummed her lacquered fingernails on her desk, bored by my roiling emotions.

"Why wouldn't Del have kept my mother's memory alive for me?"

Amanda shook her head. Her fingernails tapped on the desktop. Her eyes shifted to her closet then back to me. "Lacy called, he said you'd found your bag thing. That was where Tad's key was, right? Show it to me."

She fluttered her pink fingernails towards my room. When I didn't respond quickly enough, Amanda crossed to unlock the adjoining door. I pushed her aside, entered my own room, shutting and locking her on her side of the connecting door. I retrieved the key from the pillow. Del had asked me to bring the key to him. Shouldn't I march down the balcony to his room? Shouldn't I?

Amanda swayed in through my French doors, her hand held out.

"Give me the key, Olivia."

"It's Del's."

"It's Perfidia's. It belongs to her. Just give it to me."

Amanda wiggled her fingers. I placed the key in her palm. She ogled it, stroking the hold as though expecting a genie to appear. Finally, she handed it back. I hadn't expected that. I'm not sure what I had expected, maybe that she would streak from the morning room yelling that she had the key—maybe that.

Amanda took my hand. Her stiletto heels chipped the fresh white paint on the balcony floor as she dragged me back to her room. She closed the French doors, drew the gossamer drapes, slapped closed the shutters on the other windows then shushed me with a finger to her lips though I hadn't made a noise. She shushed me again as she walked to a painting of water frothing in Taddys Cove that hung above her table and chairs.

She lifted the watercolor from its nail. A small key was taped to the back of the canvas with silver duct tape, the kind of tape available at any hardware store. The type of tape not recommended for use on original artwork. She ripped the tape off of the canvas then showed the key to me with a modicum of swash.

Next thing I knew, Amanda was deep into her closet, designed for furs, ball gowns, cocktail dresses, and a thousand shoes, rooting amongst the shoes like a truffle pig. I tiptoed over to peer in the closet door. She was on her hands and knees opening a small square door hidden behind shoeboxes for well over a quarter century, given the styles of the shoes strewn on the floor.

Sensing that I was behind her, Amanda said, "I liberated the key to this door one day while playing in our mother's room. She'd left it in the lock. The crawlspace under the eave was empty. I always kept my favorite things here: Mom's diamond fingernail file, Celia's hula skirt and coconut bra, Colin's toy sword—that sort of thing. It came in handy."

Dust poured out of the door as Amanda crawled in under the eave. By the hollow sound that followed, she was flinging cardboard boxes aside. Her head reappeared. She shoved a box with an intricate mother of pearl rose carved on the top ahead of her out the small door. That box. The one in Beth's portrait.

Once out the door, Amanda sat cross-legged, her bejeweled sandals forgotten, her pedal-pushers hiked to her knees, her blouse covered in dust, her nose dirty, her hair hanging free from its latest do, surrounded by hopelessly out-of-fashion shoes. She fondled the box.

"I'd gone to see Drayman. John Stoddard was there. I watched through the louvers. John Stoddard opened the box with Drayman gasping his last on the bed! He read some of the papers. It wasn't right. Colin came roaring past me. He hit John Stoddard so hard that John Stoddard bounced off one of the bed posts. I think Colin wanted to kill him. John Stoddard tore past me out of the room. Dad died. Next minute, Colin flipped the box open. There was a painting on the inside of the lid. He glanced at it, I swear that was all. He handed me the box. He told me to hide it. He pocketed the key to the box. Oh, Olivia! Want to see?"

I shook my head. I wasn't the heir. It wasn't my box.

"Lacy told me Del had the key. All this time?" Lacy's incredulity was echoed in Amanda's words.

"In a safe deposit box." Colin had taken the key. My father, Del, had it. Colin had given it to him for safekeeping, as he had given Amanda the box.

Like Lacy, Amanda's lovely eyes grew cold, the tip of her dirty nose reddened. Tears gathered in the corners of her eyes until they pooled over. The dirt from her face ran in rivulets to her chin. Her tears dripped from there to her bright pink blouse leaving little muddy stains.

"Put the box back, Amanda. It's been safe enough all these years. I won't say a word, but please keep it hidden and don't tell another soul you have it."

She was well back into the hole, only her butt showing as I turned to leave. A shadow bled down the balcony; leaving me with the impression of broad shoulders. Someone had been peeping. Panicking, I tucked Tad's key in Whitelaw's jeans at the small of my back then adjusted my peasant blouse over the circular bow as though I was packing a revolver.

I exited Amanda's room intent on returning the key to its hiding place. Lloyd grabbed my hand. I jumped. He gave me a puzzled look. I realized he thought I'd recoiled at his touch. I kept on course for my room.

"I need to speak to you," he said, a short step behind me. He was a handsome man, no doubt, well-kept and well dressed. Today, he was casual in khaki slacks and a crisp white polo shirt, his initials embroidered on the upper left chest where a pocket should have been.

I opened the doors to my room.

"Not here. Meet me in the study."

Lloyd strode for the stairs, cantering down them. I followed a few moments later hoping to track his shadow to the requisite room. I need not have worried. He was standing by the door when I reached him. He ushered me in with a sweep of his hand.

"They've upped the call. You've got to help. I'm desperate. They can't have her…" He wrung his hands.

"Is that it? Is that what was so important? You know what I have." He had sent Topper. Topper had seen the riches of the Harris family in Del's safe deposit box. He had rifled through the bearer bonds, seen the necklace, the ring. It could be enough to save Perfidia this one time. It certainly was enough for a dowry of old, enough for me to quit teaching third graders.

"Olivia, you must realize the lengths the deBancos will go. After the other night…" He waved a hand as his words dribbled away.

"Feron?" I said with sudden clarity.

"Conflicted. Someone's broken into Lacy's files and mine. It appears to be Feron. He would do it for his father...for Pendu...for Perfidia. The problem is he's Chief of Security for Bajan White."

"What's missing?" I asked, trying to digest this new bit of information.

"Nothing. Lacy had duplicates of some inheritance box papers at Drayman's bidding. They are still in Lacy's files, but out of order. Feron subsequently told

Lacy something he could only have learned from the documents. We think. It is possible Crispin somehow had the information. Whichever, Lacy is convinced that Crispin deBanco is armed to win Perfidia. She is the key to all of the other plantations. The information taken is helpful only to whoever seizes power."

The unseen Crispin deBanco seemed the stuff of legends. Did he wear black, carry a gun, and stalk beaches? Likely not, he probably wore the same cologne as his son—money.

"What happened here?"

"I left the safe open and went for a gin tonic. When I came back, the door was wide. When I returned the documents were fanned out, plot plans, house plans, that sort of thing like someone had photographed them. I told no one I was so embarrassed. What am I going to do?"

"You know, I don't know, what's more, I don't care!" I slammed out of the study, bad move, impossibly the key slipped deeper into my jeans, his jeans, our jeans. What was the matter with me?

Lloyd came barreling out of the study brandishing an epée. He put the tip to my sternum and backed me against the wall of the Great Hall just below a painting of Collier, who had died fornicating on the rug beneath Estella. I raised my hands over my head. The key slipped thankfully into my bikini pants and stayed.

"With the key and the box, we could stop Crispin."

I brushed the sword away with my bandaged hand. Lloyd glared at the tip as though the sword had grown from his fist. He dropped the epée to the floor. The twang vibrated down the Great Hall.

He whirled into the study. His shoulders slumped. His feet barely cleared the door sill. I sucked in my stomach and recovered the key from my crack. The key recovered and safe in the back pocket of my jeans, I leaned over for the epée. Epée in hand, I strode into the library.

Lloyd was sitting behind a desk so massive that the room must have been built around it. His elbows were on a marble writing surface embedded in the desktop. His head was in his hands, his hands in his curls.

Bookshelves covered two walls of the room, each shelf overflowed with volumes, some ancient. Light seeped through cracks in the russet colored velvet drapes drawn over the windows on the outside wall. The fourth wall was covered with swords and daggers floor to ceiling. I returned the epée to its appointed slot. The room smelled of old paper, old leather, and heartache.

"You know, of course, that your mother has the inheritance box?"

His only response was to tighten his grip on his hair. Curls ranged between his fingers wrapping themselves so tightly into knots I worried that he would be forced to cut his hair to remove his hands.

"She's hidden it all these years. I have the key." I pulled it out of my back pocket, holding it out to him. "We could look. If it is true that the map to the cache is inside, you could save de lady. Preempt all the piracy."

He gulped but didn't respond.

"Topper must have told you about the necklace, the ring, and the bearer bonds. Where did Del get the necklace? Lloyd? Where?"

His eyes were so bereft that my heart broke.

"It was a wedding gift. There are still a few pieces in the safe behind me. It means nothing."

"It's worth a fortune. I could have my lawyer sell it."

He stared at the black lines of the marble worming their way across the desk. "Technically, no, it should have reverted on your mother's death. It was on loan. It belongs to Perfidia." He shook his head with his fingers still knotted in his hair. "The box, the key, the necklace, none of it is mine. My whole life...." His voice dwindled away. He unwound his fingers. He folded his arms on the desk and lowered his head to their pillow.

I walked over and wove my fingers through his hair. It was all I could think to do.

I HELD A BOWL of Peggy's chicken and rice soup within range of the soup spoon Del manhandled. He slurped as I related my somewhat amended adventures, no Amanda weeping as she held the box, but the epée and key in the pants incident to Del's great amusement.

"Wha's next?" Del slurred.

"Don't know. For the key to be of any use, I would need the lock it fit. Maybe everyone is right, maybe there aren't any stashes or caves." He shot his blue eyes to mine telegraphing *liar* wordlessly. "Oh, Del."

"Oh, Liv," Del mocked.

"Are you going to be okay?" I fussed over my father. He gave me his bootlegger's smile. I fussed a bit more, arranging the water cup with a straw on the nightstand so that he could reach the tall cup handily.

Del touched my hand. I glanced at him. He raised his eyebrows. "Gonna be fine. You gonna be fine, you figured out yet 'bout what's gonna make you go all weak at the knees?"

"He's lovely," popped out of my mouth.

Del leaned back into his pillows. "Lovely is a word I've never heard applied."

"I think life has been hard for him. No parents, just Lacy doing his bachelor best." I fiddled with the delicately embroidered ecru flowers that ran down the edges of the top pillow.

"What we talkin' 'bout?" Del seemed annoyed. But, Del was the one who said if I played my cards right I would get Perfidia. It had to be Whitelaw; he was the heir.

"Why I don't know, you all gonna tell me one of these here days?" I asked with as much honey in my voice as I could muster.

"Tol' you gal, you gotta figure the riddle out all on your own. Thought you had, thought you had las' night."

Thought I had, too. I smiled knowingly though my stomach agitated for an antacid.

Sitting in one of the wicker chairs, I read to Del from a leather-bound copy of the poems of Rudyard Kipling that had been sitting spine up on the nightstand beside his bed. The displeasure, if that is what it was, ebbed from his eyes. When he nodded off, I sauntered down the balcony, swaying to my room in the soft, humid air.

Feron's job was to protect Perfidia, Crispin deBanco to have her. Topper wanted to protect Lloyd. Lloyd wanted to continue to manage Bajan White, which he did well, given that his father, John Stoddard, had drained the company down to parchment. Amanda wanted to hand Perfidia off to the heir—Whitelaw. And Del?

De lady was in debt, on call, and losing old money, not new. The value of Bajan White stock had dropped like a rock. Who bought? According to Amanda, someone had purchased enough stock to change the power equation? Who owned the majority of Bajan White stock, right now, this minute?

I HAD REACHED MY room before I had time to fully assess all of the damage a change in power at Bajan White would rain on the attempt to save Perfidia, guessing only that it would depend on who held the majority of the shares. DeBancos had and still might. Law-Maddocks hadn't and still didn't.

With a shake of my head, I dug through the available pillows making a nest behind me like a gopher makes a hill, determined to spend the day down the hall from my father at his beck and call. With my nest assembled, I settled onto the feather pillows on the floor. I adjusted the louvers on the windows so that sunlight flooded over me. Once comfortable, I opened the autobiography of Sam Lord liberated from Whitelaw's office.

Sam Lord had been a rapscallion, no doubt. But, he hadn't been Tad Law. In fact, Sam Lord wasn't a match for Mr. Law, who he post-dated by near 100 years. The book, written supposedly by Samuel Hall Lord in 1843, waxed poetic about pirating and mooncussing. He described how the tall ships would round Ragged Point Lighthouse laden with goods on their way to South Point then into Carlisle Bay to unload, waiting for high tide to avoid sandbars and rocks. Heavy with goods they were lured easily into the foul harbors of St. Philip.

Taddys Cove was renowned for its sand bar. The bar neither came nor went. It just stayed, invisible in high tide, an obstacle when the water ebbed. The fan of reef, rock, and sand was so persistent that it blocked the sea from Taddys Cove during the lowest tides making the whole cove a beach. What was the legend, a cave where the waters never reached the booty, yet the booty could reach the sea?

I admit to being as befuddled as when I started to read. My eyes rested on the zebra stripe reflection of the louvers against the far wall. The shadow of a broad-shouldered man appeared on the wall broken by the dark bands from the blinds. The padded shoulders of his business suit gave deBanco away.

Amanda's door opened. DeBanco turned to her voice. From the cadence of the words, she chided Feron. His response was muffled, but not his footfalls which vibrated down the wooden balcony. When Amanda began to rustle around in her room, I went back to my book.

When it came to mooncussing, Sam Lord, or his ghostwriter, played coy, writing legend says this and legend says that, but clearly and carefully he implicated others nearby. Sam had a theory, too. He believed that ships lured into Taddys Cove saw a beacon, not at cliff's edge, but higher. He suggested that the light would have been perhaps 100 feet from the cliff and another twenty feet above ground so that it would appear to be a lighthouse to approaching ships. He included a crude illustration.

The arching fronds of the palms outside my room whipped against the balcony rail. The deep distant rumble of the ocean seemed to grow closer. I visualized cruising into Taddys Cove on a tall ship; my sails full, making a run for safety.

My reverie was disrupted by a vivid picture of Perfidia as I'd first seen her. Rushing out the door, I left Sam Lord's book, parchment pages askew, in a heap on the floor. I trotted down the balcony stairs, past the porte-cochère to the front of the house.

It began to squall, the rain blasting through in sheets. Lightning slammed the water. The wind thrashed. The ocean roared. The original structure of cut limestone blocks, the ubiquitous gray blocks quarried, according to Sam Lord, on the north of the island, hunkered against the storm like a drenched, dumpy maiden. I ran down the old lane, my pants wicking water from contact with the grass.

Water ran down my back. My blouse clung to my spine. My feet squished in my huaraches. Reaching the point where Perfidia was first visible from the lane, I sighted down the original squat structure. The massive flame trees that laid their blazing flowers across the roofline drew one's attention away from the second story, even the small Casuarina clumped at the corner seemed to diminish the height of the building. I had been in the stone dining room for every meal. There were no stairs at all, no room for stairs, but there right before my eyes was the second story, a crenelated second story! A tower!

I eyed the slits in the tower and, from my recent reading, recognized them for what they were: gun emplacements.

One embrasure overlooked the lawn to the front; the second faced the timber on the southern side and the third the sea. A lookout positioned at the loophole could defend and advise the people atop the tower the moment a boat cleared the northern headland, or the British came into sight on the road.

The second story that sprouted from the old bunker met all of Sam Lord's posits. It was 100 feet from the cliff and 20 feet high. If you were at sea in a storm using a spyglass, you would see a blazing light signaling a place of haven.

I ran through the rain to the hip roof of the angled front porch. The front door was made of scrolled, pounded iron work and mahogany wood. The heavy door opened with a wild pig squeal. I scrambled inside putting my back to the door to close it. An ancient crossbar once braced through iron loops attached to iron bars nailed by iron nails to the mahogany was the only lock. The crossbar leaned against the wall in a pounded copper umbrella stand.

The room was small with an archway into the house. A rectangular room was to my right through the arch, with the dining room to my left. The vaulted ceiling continued to the Great Hall. The end walls in the dining room, kitchen, and pantry were straight with no obvious access points to the tower.

Back in the entry, I walked toward the southern wall. I passed through an arch into the first room, whose archway connected the old structure with the new. I could see the veranda from where I stood. Fifteen feet to my right was a limestone wall. I worked my palms slowly over the limestone. My fingers found nothing, not a rock out of place.

There were no electric lights in this section of the house. Sconces with beveled glass and beeswax candles clung to the rock wall at five-foot intervals. An ancient tool used to light the candles leaned in the corner behind the first arch. More practically, a box of utility matches sat in a recess built into the rock face just inside the archway.

I struggled to light one of the utility matches on the damp box strip then I lit the sconce closest to the arch for light. The light was dim. It heightened the shadows before being absorbed by the gray of the rock. I took a candle from the next sconce then lit it and so on. When I reached the sconce nearest the far wall, there was no candle. I thought of Beth's crewelwork. *If you have no light, if your wick be down*...I ran through the archway into the dining room. I re-read the crewel work. Perhaps. I took a candle.

Beeswax candle in hand, I removed the glass chimney from the last sconce and placed it in the alcove where the matchbox had been. Back at the sconce, the candle slid deeply into the holder, much deeper than the candles in the other sconces. After a moment staring at the construction of the candleholder, I grasped the candle as though it were a handle then rotated it toward the floor, reasoning that if there were any resistance, I would stop.

Instead, a bolt shot back. Creaky hinges grated. A two-inch thick wooden door with a limestone block fascia opened to reveal a staircase. I charged up the stairs without a flashlight, without a buddy, without having told a single soul where I was going.

A trapdoor blocked my access to the roof. A metal bar an inch in diameter slid easily from the metal hasp that held the trapdoor closed. I freed the bar then pushed on the trapdoor with all my might. The door budged, but barely.

On the top step, I planted my palms on the wall opposite then with my back against the trapdoor, walked my hands up the wall. The flat of my back provided enough pressure to produce a groan from the door. As it slowly rose, I grabbed the edge of the opening, praying the door wouldn't thunder shut and catch me like a rat in a trap. With this small purchase, I used my back to heave the trapdoor. At apogee, the hatch slammed to the roof with a punch that shook the staircase.

I climbed to the roof, tripping on a band of copper or brass edging designed to kept rain from slopping down the stairs. Something oozed into my huaraches. A two-inch bed of wet charcoal flowed across the stone surface of the tower and out a drain hole into the gutter that joined the two buildings. The trough carried the sludge to below grounds after each heavy rain. The oozing coals I stood in couldn't be more than a few months old. There was nothing ancient about them.

I struggled to raise the trapdoor from where it had fallen flat on the roof, putting my knees and back to the task. When the door closed with a rattling crash, the source of the extra weight became apparent. A single sheet of iron that still bore the anvil marks of its forging topped the trapdoor. When the trapdoor was shut, the tower floor was entirely paved in limestone and iron.

A wide, shallow fire bowl was off center in the floor to be closer to the sea. The mooncussers hadn't used a torch to emulate a lighthouse; they lit a signal fire, a huge one, which required a supply of wood.

With the stairs cut off, there was no way to the tower. I surveyed the surroundings from my perch. The singular purpose of the small wilderness to the south of the house must be to provide mahogany and Casuarina logs for the fire. Though someone could bring the wood up the stairs before lighting the fire, a mooncusser would need an ongoing source of fuel, wouldn't he, if the fire were to last the storm?

A two-foot high crenelated parapet circled the tower. It provided some protection from the updraft of the wind off the water. On my knees, I checked the edges and outside of the parapet. A quick circuit produced no groove worn in the rock face where the wood had been hauled up by rope to the firepot. I rocked back on my calves, my hands on the wet knees of Whitelaw's jeans, both hands and knees blackened by charcoal and ashes, channeling Tad Law's deviousness.

The enormous chimney, nearly the length of the tower, was constructed of the ubiquitous gray rock. The wall blocked any ashes or embers caught on the breeze from reaching the roof of the new addition. It would also prevent the northeastern wind from scuttling the fire.

There was an arched opening in one side of the chimney. From below, the arch appeared to be a decorative element but up close it masked a recessed metal door. Using the palm of my hand, I fought the door's heavy metal latch out of the eye. Inside, a rope dangled on either side of a pulley. I pulled the rope hand over hand. After much straining, a dumbwaiter brimming with chunks of wood and bagasse appeared from below.

The reverse action lowered the platform to the base of the chimney for reloading. Once enough wood was atop the tower, the dumbwaiter would be returned to resting either at Estella's feet or in the kitchen among piles of cut wood.

And that was how they restocked their wood!

The storm had passed. The sky had become dusky. I was wet, filthy, and pleased with myself though no closer to finding any stashes. The existence of the tower convinced me that the doubters were wrong. There had to be a way to the sea from the house. What mooncusser would build a tower without access to the beach and the boats he wrecked?

The lit fire would be manned. Accomplices would scamper down the tower stairs then through another hidden door, no doubt hiding circular stairs occupied by bats, to a beach exposed during low tide. As the ship was crippled, those waiting would row out to the sandbar. They would kill survivors and loot the galleon then row back to hide the loot in the cache. Their work completed, the mooncussers would douse the fire, close the stone door, and be reading innocently by firelight when the British arrived. It had to be. I felt it in my genetically mutated pirate bones.

Perched on the edge of the tower dangling my feet, I dreamed of mooncussing. The ocean poured into the cove, clouds dusted the dimming horizon, and the tree frogs chortled in the coming dark. Snapping out of it, I lit one of my stolen matches to illuminate the dial of my watch. If I hurried, I could bathe before dinner. I circumnavigated the fire ring without regard for the wet ashes then yanked on the ring recessed in the trapdoor

The door didn't give a groan. Remembering I had used my back to raise it, I put my knees into the lifting. It didn't budge. Didn't budge as in someone had quite deliberately locked me in.

I sat on the parapet considering my options. The best way down was for me to lower myself to the hip roof of the porch, crawl across the slope to one of the flame trees then climb down the tree to the front entry. As I summoned the courage to fling my leg over the parapet, two sharp backfires popped to my left. A scream ripped through the early evening. Lights blazed on at the back of the house. Voices babbled off the balcony.

"Where is she? Where is Olivia? Someone find her!" Lloyd yelled.

Footsteps rang down the balcony then galloped down the stairs. Topper Law ran to the gate in the privet at the edge of the cliff. He started down the beach stairs, stopped then ran back across the lawn to the house. I would have signaled if I'd had a flashlight or if it hadn't been Topper. Instead, I hid in the shadow of the chimney.

In front, a figure roared in from the cane field to the north, Whitelaw by the flow of his movement. I fought the strip on the box to light a match, gave up and struck it on the stone. When it blazed, I held the match high over my head, hoping only one person saw my signal.

The front door screamed open. Topper strolled far enough out onto the front lawn to have a view of the tower. Without slowing, Whitelaw shoved Law hard on the chest then barreled for the house. Rapid footsteps skipped lightly up the balcony stairs. I moved to the balcony side of the tower to eavesdrop.

Whitelaw ordered, "Get the doctor."

"No, no, no," Amanda yelled in ever increasing decibels. "Lloyd, get the Bentley, take him to town. I'll call ahead. Topper you go with… Do it right, can you manage? This once!"

More footsteps, then Topper and Whitelaw met Lloyd at the Bentley, supporting Del's body between them. They loaded Del awkwardly into the backseat. Satisfied that he was in, they covered him with a touring blanket. At Whitelaw's rap on the side window, the Bentley roared off into the night, Lloyd at the wheel.

The moment the taillights disappeared Whitelaw laid a blow on Topper's jaw that staggered him. Amanda threw herself between the two men, her hands in the universal gesture to stop.

"Where is she?" Whitelaw hissed, "If any harm has come to her, I'll kill you, you conniving bastard."

Topper bolted past Whitelaw, showing no damage until he reached his gray Mercedes. As he opened the driver-side door, Topper put the back of his right hand to his cheek. So, Whitelaw was left handed? What a stupid thing to think when your father could be dying.

Law wheeled the Mercedes down the lane in the Bentley's wake, just missing the Jaguar.

I put one leg over the parapet, readying to lower myself just as the stanchion below the trapdoor slid with a screech. The heavy door rose slowly. I expected Whitelaw; I got deBanco.

DeBanco took one look at me, at the roof, at my clothes, at the charcoal, at me and said, "Whitelaw sent me. Said he saw signals in the tower. You're filthy."

"I know, I want a good scrubbing."

Feron reached back to help me down the stairs.

"Del?" I asked.

"He's gone," deBanco answered perhaps unthinkingly, or perhaps not. How could he look so unruffled in his damn suit? He stood there, offering his hand, not a hair out of place, his shoes spit-shined, and his shirt so white it glowed light blue in the dark.

"Why rush then? Why take him to the hospital, why..."

He drew me to his side and kissed the top of my head. "Sorry."

"No, you're not. You're all scared of what Del knows, what Del knows about you!"

He held me a little tighter. "You're hysterical, girl."

Girl? Really? Me? The one who found the signal fire? Or maybe not, either Whitelaw or deBanco or both had known how to free me from the tower.

"With Lin gone, I'm not sure we can save her," deBanco said, sounding deadly serious as though the endgame had ended, as though what hope there was had evaporated which didn't sit well with me. Still, I rested my head on his shoulder thinking that with Del gone I wasn't sure I wanted Perfidia saved.

Now, more than ever, I needed to know who held controlling interest in Bajan White.

Feron walked me into the Great Hall still tucked in his shoulder, oblivious to the stains he was acquiring down the right side of his thousand dollar suit. Whitelaw was waiting in Estella's shadow with one arm draped over the mantel. He glared at deBanco as we entered.

"I found the signal fire," I crowed.

Feron gave me a squeeze accompanied by a knowing grin. I tried to keep the disappointment out of my voice, without success. "You've both used the fire ring."

Whitelaw narrowed his eyes then snorted. He held his right hand out for me as he walked toward the door. "I'll drive you to Lacy's. I assume that's where they'll take Lin. It is the safest place in town."

"But...," I managed, a quaver in my voice that I hadn't meant to be there. Whitelaw grabbed my hand and dragged me out the front door. We were halfway to Bridgetown in the green Healey before he glanced at me.

I raised a hand, palm out. "I need a bath."

Whitelaw yanked the convertible's steering wheel hard to the left. We jolted to a stop on the verge. He climbed out, bolted around the car, opened my door, pulled me out, put his hands behind my head, and kissed me hard enough to keep me kissed for a couple of years. I folded willy-nilly in a wet, drippy, mud puddle, staring gape-mouthed at him.

"Yes," he said, hefting me to my feet, left hand to my right. "You need a bath, but you need to deal with Lin first. Then you're mine."

Hadn't he meant: then you're mine, girl?

Deal with Del? Really!

WHITELAW DELIVERED ME TO Lacy's filthy, shaken, and confused. Hearing voices at the back of the house, I took the stairs two at a time to Dave White's apartment.

Del wore a happy grin and a crocheted bed shawl. His broken leg was stretched on top of a multi-covered quilt. He looked positively in his element.

Filthy as I was, I was afraid to touch him, so without a word I went into an open bathroom to bathe. I left a brown ring of grime two inches up the tub wall. Someone had kindly laid out clean clothes for me. They looked suspiciously like another pair of Whitelaw's slacks, though these were white linen. A tropical print cotton shirt was included that I was sure I had last seen at both Barclays Bank and Sam Lord's Castle.

I rejoined the lively group, asking only, "What happened?"

Del chortled, "While you were playing mooncusser, someone fired two rounds into my pillows. I'm surprised you didn't hear them being up there and all."

"Who?"

Lacy stepped forward just a smidge, a grim look on his kind face. "We all suspect Feron."

Where was Feron? For that matter, where was Whitelaw? Whitelaw had all but ravaged me on the road, laying his claim to me like the hero out of some dime novel and now had disappeared like one.

I shook my head. I'd seen Topper Law rush from the house, Whitelaw rush to the house, heard Lloyd call for Amanda and me. But, I hadn't seen or heard Feron or Peggy. Peggy had no reason to shoot at my father. Feron, either, really. But, why was I so sure it hadn't been deBanco. Because, Topper Law, in the Mercedes, had passed the Jaguar on the drive. "He wasn't at the house. Why do you suspect him?"

"So you are the filthy beast everyone has been gossiping about. Did you see all that from your aerie?" A man scoffed as he stepped out of the shadow behind the door. "They suspect my son because of the break-ins and documents either photographed or removed from Perfidia and Parradine. Because they think he was complicit in the hijacking of the White Lady."

Crispin deBanco...at last.

"That doesn't make any sense at all. I've heard rumors that Aaron stole the White Lady to mess with Feron, well the deBancos. I wouldn't be surprised if Aaron hoped to have the White Lady packed with drugs when the salvagers came to force action against Feron." I rested my back against one of the nine-over-nine paned windows at the front of the room. The bustle of Bridgetown sneaked through the old glass. Del's eyes were on me, his head cocked, his lips pursed.

"Really? Sounds as though my son had plenty of reason to shoot." With a sharp glance at Del, Crispin asked, "Where did these rumors originate?"

"Except, he wasn't there. Besides, who doesn't matter, why matters." I said, dodging tattling on Del. I dove into the why of it not caring how foolish I sounded, making up my response as I rolled along. "I think the shooter thinks Del knows what Aaron was really doing in the cove that night, believes Aaron located Colin's cache, believes that if he can only get his hands on the loot, he can save Perfidia. Aaron's actions to disgrace Feron may have led in part to his own death, but Feron didn't shoot at Del. The person who fired those shots thinks Del knows what Aaron found. Do you Del?"

Both Del and Lacy chuckled, not the kind of derisive laugh you give when someone is clever stupid, but when they are clever smart.

"No, Liv, I don't. But I agree it wasn't Feron who took the potshot at me, poor boy. He wouldn't have missed."

"He is a professional, you know, ex-SAS and all that," Crispin deBanco defended his son. DeBanco senior was around five foot ten, dark-haired, graying at the temples and darker in aspect than the other Taddys I'd met. His eyes were a deep dark brown. His toothy smile coupled with his ease let anyone know that he had just what he wanted.

And, he kept looking at her.

Amanda smiled at Crispin as though he had just inherited the world; as though he was smarter than us all; as though he could make this all make sense.

Amanda sat on the other side of Del's bed, her hands folded in the lap of her silk skirt of a rose color so rich the fabric should have given off fragrance. A thin, sleeveless flowered silk shirt with a scoop neck flared over the skirt. A double loop of diamonds glittered around her neck. Diamonds dripped from her ears. She dazzled in Dave White's modest room.

Crispin stared at me until my skin tingled. Like everyone else, he had to know that I had the key to the inheritance box. "If Aaron was trying to discredit Feron, he did so because he believed Feron had a head start in the endless game of who gets Perfidia. But, girl, whatever Aaron was going to load he obtained."

Amanda checked her fingernail polish then smoothed her skirt.

"You're wrong, Mr. deBanco. Aaron hadn't obtained it, he'd found it."

"Whose then?" Crispin snarked, "Waste of a damn fine ship!" Crispin realized how he sounded and sent a tender smile across the room to Amanda before lowering his head to pick at imaginary calluses on his well-tended hands.

Lacy glanced out the window as though he longed to join the partying in the streets.

"You've been observing, just like me, Lacy. This isn't complicated. Help me."

Parradine in gray flannels and a crisp white shirt turned back to the group. "I can't, Olivia. I wish I could, I wish I knew, but I don't."

Del cleared his throat, waiting until he had everyone's attention before he spoke. "When I finally located Aaron, Whitelaw was knee deep in the water searching his body. He's been on my back ever since. Whitelaw was on the beach when the launch drove me ashore. Why? So he could finish me off? He's narrowing the competition—the little bastard heir is. You all know how dangerous he is. You all know what he is capable of doing. We've all paid for his transgressions. The only reason I made it off that beach at all was that Olivia saw Whitelaw lying in wait for me. The heir presumptive couldn't kill me, not with Olivia there, so the little bastard had a go at me tonight."

Del held his right hand out for me, when I realized how nicely I had set Whitelaw up, I huffed out of the room. And, though Whitelaw had come from the cane field after the shots were fired, he *had* been on the beach waiting for Del.

Day Eight

Lacy assigned me Whitelaw's spare bedroom for the night. A twin bed took up most of the room. The bed was tight under a window that overlooked a cobbled patio and the entrance to the kitchen. Unlike Whitelaw's office, this room was chock full of memories, a cricket bat, a hat, a small bookshelf of boy's adventure books. A child-size three drawer dresser served as both a chest of drawers and a nightstand. Model ships manned by wee pirates, painted by the shaky hand of a boy, littered the top of the chest. The pirates stood on rocks and boxes and atop masts.

A photograph of a man and a woman hung on the wall next to the bed. The woman had golden brown Nefertiti eyes, her lips full and smiling, her skin a sensual café au lait, light on the cream. The man's hair was a sun-streaked mob of brown curls. His eyes were gray, his smile easy and engaging. Colin had one hand around Sophie's waist. Brendan sat on the other, one tiny hand in Colin's curls.

Someone had snatched these hearts from Whitelaw's grasp, he had never been held the same, he had never been so precious, he had lost not only his mother and his father but what might have been.

Angry and muddled, I thought of Colin's battered body then of Aaron's. Aaron had rowed to shore leaving Del aboard the White Lady. Del claimed Whitelaw had been on the beach. Had Whitelaw forced Aaron to tell him his plan before he killed him?

Around and around my brain went, until like a hypnotist's watch, it put me to sleep. I snored into the morning. My dreams defined my next steps so clearly that even the voices trickling through the walls of Del's room didn't tempt me. I donned Whitelaw's clothes then slipped down the front stairs past the monkey into the wall of mid-day heat on the street.

On the short walk to Broad Street where Barclays squatted, I was buffeted by a crowd of tourist loosed from a cruise ship docked at the deep-water harbor. I glimpsed a woman leaving Cave-Shepard that reminded me I hadn't called Gail. She looked that much like her.

My restless night, the crowd, the small dark-haired woman made me anxious and tense, as though there was no one left to trust and nowhere to run. Aaron must have felt the same on the beach when he saw who waited. I swung through the doors to Barclays, glad to be alive.

Mr. Donovan rose the minute he saw me. I strode across the floor to him in Whitelaw's lovely linen trousers, with my grimy huaraches rudely slapping the floor. Donovan stared at my feet then at the mucky black tracks my huaraches left on the white marble. He pursed his lips. I signaled one question with my index finger.

He turned to his desk. As Donovan sat, he pushed his chair as far from me as he could. I sat in the chair opposite his, the very one I had occupied on my first visit when none of this made any sense—like now.

He cleared his throat, checked his manicure, took a sip of tea, cleared his throat again, splayed his hands on his knees, all before asking, "Yes?"

"Who has the controlling interest in Bajan White?" I queried, skipping right over all the formalities.

"Whoever owns the majority of the stock." It was an altogether pristine meaningless answer.

I gripped the edge of his desk. Leaning over my hands, I hissed, "You know exactly what I mean. Right now, after the recent stock activity, who owns the majority of the stock in Bajan White? Or, should I say, did Del, excuse me, Chamberlin Harris drive down the price of Bajan White then buy up as many shares as he humanly could with what was to have been my dowry?"

Donovan smoothed the front of his navy blue blazer complete with bright gold embroidered crest on the pocket.

"It isn't a trick question."

His watery blue eyes met mine. He placed his hands back on his blotter, his eyes on mine. "You."

"Who else knows?"

"Your father, Brendan Whitelaw, and Lloyd Law-Maddock."

"Thank you." I walked out of the bank.

I fought the crowd until I turned up St. Michael to Morten's. Whitelaw had been asked to view Aaron's body while doing so he'd had a run-in with a family member. I needed to know why he had been sent to view Aaron's body, what he saw, and what the cause of the argument had been.

It didn't take long. The police had requested that someone review the official postmortem, Amanda couldn't bear to be the one. She asked Whitelaw, the man who seemed to do for Perfidia whatever the others couldn't bear, to do the honors. Having stood over Aaron's body on the beach, Whitelaw knew before he was told that Aaron had been beaten, not by the surf, but by man. The closed casket was at Whitelaw's request to save Amanda the horror of seeing the maimed remains of her fair-haired son. Outside of the mortician, only three men knew the extent of Aaron's injuries: Brendan Whitelaw, Chamberlin Harris, and his killer.

As for the incident at Morten's, Morten resisted me at first then, his hands held tightly in front of his fly, shared that deBanco had threatened to jail Whitelaw. Morten was clear, he remembered it precisely. "The White Lady! The goddamn body! One more thing, you're in lockup!"

Whitelaw was one of two who knew Aaron was assaulted. He was one of three who knew I held Bajan White. If Whitelaw had killed Aaron, it was a waste, because all he had to do to save Perfidia was woo me like he had last night. Del was right: *I didn't know nothin' 'bout boys.*

INSTEAD OF GOING BACK to Lacy's to hang out with Del and Crispin, the old pirates; I took the island bus to St. Philip. The bus driver dropped me off at the gate to Perfidia. I strolled down the overgrown lane enjoying the palms swaying and the puffy pre-afternoon rain clouds scudding by overhead.

When de lady appeared, I studied her gray stone walls enjoying the second story on the old front wing knowing the secret it hid. I absorbed the hipped porch roof covered in the scarlet flowers, no longer wondering why Del had chosen that image to cover his safe. He wanted her. Now, I was Bajan White. Using what Del had set in play, Perfidia was mine. Not for me, for him. When he wrote *somethin' goin' to make me all weak in the knees,* he meant her—Perfidia.

Fiercely angry, I ran up the stairs and slammed through the French doors into my borrowed room to change into my own clothes, intent on ending the grasping and murdering. I could stop the call, I could stand down Crispin deBanco, I could clear Feron. I could win. I was Bajan White now all I had to do was find what Aaron had found to save Perfidia.

It turned out my own clothes had become Whitelaw's jeans, my camp shirt, and my rope-soled shoes. I jammed Lloyd's freshly laundered handkerchief, a flashlight, the box of matches from the hall, and some candles in my bag. I double-checked for Tad's key. After a moment, I threw in a towel. I was hoping to get wet, praying I would need a whopping good bath. I wished for a knapsack but settled for putting my arms through the two straps of my hobo bag. The heft of the bag rested on my lower back.

I scampered onto the balcony as Peggy reached the top stair. I waved to her and went the opposite direction, trotting down the stairs to the left. I plunged deep into the cane field my eyes sighting on the sails of the windmill I'd first found while lost in the cane convinced it held Aaron's staircase, the entrance to Tad's mythical tunnel. It was the one structure visible from the tower. A torch held overhead would be the signal that a ship had been grounded as the match had been for me. It only made sense.

The magical windmill's sails were still full to the wind as they had been the first night I saw it. The clearing was quiet. A check of the sky, my hand shielding my eyes from the sun, revealed rolling bands of clouds on the eastern horizon.

The sea was a pale, almost turquoise, blue, the swell small as though the real fury had been sucked out to sea ready to return in one tumultuous ripping wave. In all the excitement with Del, not one of us had checked the weather, but why would we? Day in and day out the temperature was between 72-85 degrees Fahrenheit with rain at 3:00 p.m., about as unexciting as weather can be.

The door to the windmill was locked. The padlock appeared flimsy. I scuffed around the grass looking for something to pry it open, unearthing a small metal rod two feet long, half-inch or so thick. I jammed the iron shaft through the shackle of the padlock until it popped open.

Inside the dark mill, ghosts soon plagued me. Their grunts as the great wheel turned accompanied by the shuffling of bare feet in the grainy dirt still vibrated within the stone walls. The sails creaked. I jumped, brandishing my new metal rod like a weapon.

Chagrinned, I stuck the length of rebar into my bag for just in case and rummaged for the slide box of utility matches I'd taken from the front entry and lit one of the oil lanterns that hung at intervals on the stone walls. Light filtered across the dirt floor; shadows danced as the wick drew oil from the font. When the lantern was burning steadily, I surveyed the walls.

I pulled a knob on a small door recessed in the wall and was rewarded with ages of dust, filth, dead bugs and a can of mustache wax on a thin wooden shelf. I turned the crusty can of wax with one finger. The advertising on the back of the can provided no clue other than the last time anyone had opened the cupboard had been roughly a hundred years ago.

I made a foot-stomping circuit of the windmill searching the floor for the door to circular stairs that would lead me deep into the cliff. Dust covered my shoes and the ankles of my jeans. Every step sounded just like the last. I leaned on one of the wooden arms of the crusher. If there was access to a staircase, if there was a staircase, it wasn't here.

The wind had picked up. The overhead gear driven by the turning sails groaned. The crusher arms began to move, the noise of the crushing stones, the water filtering through, sounded like voices laughing and screaming. What were they trying to tell me?

This windmill, unlike the one being restored, was in use, the reason the water still ran through the trace, and the sails were full to the wind. During harvest, someone would be at the crusher twenty-four hours a day, making it inappropriate for use by mooncussers then and now. Wherever it was, access to a staircase would be unguarded and unmanned at night.

If there were stairs, they would be behind a locked door in a building. The Taddys, all of them, knew of the tower. The stone door to the tower was meant to keep interlopers out, not family. The opening to the staircase would be the same.

If Aaron's doodles meant anything at all, the stairs were circular. There were bats. The presence of bats indicated access to the cove. Was the circular staircase in the house as well? The original stone structure was visible from the tower, particularly the entry. Perfidia was a hundred feet from the crumbling cliff. If the stairs were within, it meant that either the ocean or Tad had carved a cave one hundred feet into the cliff to meet the vertical shaft of a circular staircase.

The launch had driven Del ashore near where I'd seen other boaters either fishing or snorkeling. All had focused on the same point in the cove near a small crevice that drove deep into the cliff, perhaps the rock behind which Whitelaw had hidden Del.

If the crevice undermined the cliff, there might be a like fissure topside that would provide the location of the descending well. I was grasping. I had to grasp; I had to find the staircase if I was to find what Aaron had.

I JOGGED DOWN THE thin lane through the cane toward the main house. Rain began to splat on my head, not wimpy summer shower droplets but big old fat, wet, windblown drops that went straight from the outside to the inside of my clothes.

Though miserably wet, I searched the cliff's edge. Waves crashed then cascaded on the rocks far below. I walked with my head bent looking for a fissure, or any flaw in the cliff face near where I had found Del. I kicked at the grass. I scuffed my feet. Next thing I knew, my right foot broke the surface up to my calf.

After much yanking, my stove-piped foot grudgingly popped loose minus my shoe. By sticking my arm in the crack up to my elbow, I managed to recover the shoe and glimpse the rocks on the beach below. I sat in the wet grass slipping on my shoe staring at the south end of Perfidia that housed Estella and the archway to the entry of the old stone wing.

I trotted to the manor in as direct a line as I could manage through the pounding rain with the rolling roar of the surf muddling my equilibrium. My tracks through the wet grass marked my trajectory, maybe not a direct line but good enough. I passed the new addition, skimming next to it. I came to a stop at the long, wide chimney. Right there, somewhere right there, there was a staircase.

I entered the Great Hall through a set of open French doors then made a quick left. The fireplace under Estella's feet blocked me from reaching the identified spot. I placed my palms on the bricks, pushing on any one that seemed lighter or darker or farther out than its neighbor. Stumped, I sat dripping wet on one of the silk upholstered wing-backed chairs, leaving water stains wherever my body met fabric.

"I can light a fire if you're cold," Lloyd offered, as he crossed from the study on his way to close the French doors. As soon as he had the doors locked, the wind gusted, rattling them against the hook and eye latch.

"I'd like that." I folded my hands in my lap at a total loss as to what to do or say. "I need a bath."

Lloyd glanced at me. "No. You're quite fetching, even in men's clothes."

He watched me for a moment, gave me a half-smile then began to stack kindling in the fireplace. When he was pleased with his work, he lit one match and held it to the bagasse stuffed beneath the twigs. The fuel caught. As the fire flared, the fierceness of the storm outside seemed diminished.

At some moment, he alone intuited, he placed a log on the growing flames. Shortly, the wood caught.

Pleased with the fire, Lloyd took my hands in his and pulled me to my feet. Seeing a fierce passion in his eyes, I blushed. His kiss culminated some war he had been waging, something he hadn't wanted to admit to himself, something that changed the whole equation. He wanted Perfidia to hold and preserve. If loving me would get it for him, he would.

"What will Topper think?"

"Not much," he answered with a catch in his voice. He put his arms to the small of my back then nibbled on my neck.

"But…"

"I've wanted to do that since I laid eyes on you at the funeral. Since you tried to protect me before you knew who I was or what was at stake."

He drew one hand through his curls. I put my hand to the nape of his neck. His ringlets wrapped over my fingers. His head came to my shoulder seeming to belong there.

"Really?" Amanda snarled through the archway from the dining room into the Great Hall.

Lloyd pivoted to her voice. He gave me one last look of sheer longing then roared out of the French doors to the lawn.

"He's homosexual. You do know that." Amanda stalked in her spikes. As she crossed to me, I couldn't help thinking she hadn't seen his eyes. He wasn't homosexual, maybe bisexual, though I knew nothing about either. I did know that I'm not the sort of woman a man changes his stripes for if that were even possible.

If Whitelaw left me both shaken and stirred, Lloyd left me bewildered. Perhaps it was the gin he had been drinking, given his breath, or perhaps I represented freedom which might make any woman alluring.

"He was married once. Topper won," Amanda commented. She stared out the closed French doors across the lawn to the vast, roiling, storm-tossed ocean. "Have you seen the height of the rollers today? I keep waiting for the cliff face to rumble down to the cove turning this relic into rubble. That would teach them all. Damn, it would!"

"What's on the other side of the fireplace," I asked to her back.

Eyes still on the storm, one hand holding her waist, the other propped on a perfect hip, Amanda answered, "The old wellhead. When Collier rebuilt, he incorporated it into the dining room rather than the kitchen thereby enlarging the kitchen. When I was small, I dreamed that someone was imprisoned in there. I was sure I heard voices calling to me. Too much Poe, I suspect."

"The wine cellar?"

"You thought that? Beth kept the key to the wellhead around her waist. When she passed, the key was placed in the custody of the Lady's maid." She laughed as she turned to face me. "You wouldn't have *that* key, would you?"

"Just controlling interest in Bajan White, other than that I have nothing more than I did yesterday. Let Lloyd know that I've postponed the call for now, will you."

"Postponing the call is just the beginning. We could stem the tide if we opened the box." Amanda searched my eyes, her hands on her hips, her stance hopeful.

"We who? The two of us or you and Crispin? No."

"Whose side are you on!" Amanda snapped. She left me with an elegant flip of her middle finger as she stalked down the Great Hall, her tight ass sashaying with every strident step.

Since last night, I was on my side.

When the sound of Amanda ruining the hardwood floors dissipated, I walked through the archway into the dining room. The portrait of the older Tad hung opposite the metal door. Beth's portrait hung in Amanda's morning room. Every morning, I woke to see her standing resolute and aging in front of the iron door to the well, the key hanging from her waist, though I hadn't recognized the door. Like the sampler had led to the tower, her portrait was the clue to the well.

A keyhole was dead center in a brass plate nailed to the wellhead door. Ornate ironwork ringed the edges.

I dug in my hobo bag until my fingers wrapped around Tad's key. I jammed the key in the keyhole expecting resistance before the bolt shot back. After a fleeting moment of willfulness, during which my hopes ramped up disproportionately, the key turned easily. Tad's key didn't open this door. I needed the Lady's key.

I plopped in one of the captain's chairs, never wondering from whose looted ship they were taken. I rested my elbows on the table, the key between my elbows, and my head in my hands. Why would the key to the treasure be entrusted to the Lady's maid? Why wouldn't the old pirate keep it on his person?

Peggy came into the dining room, her arms loaded with dishes and silverware for the table. She hummed as she set the see-through porcelain edged in small, hand-painted flowers at six places around the table. Peggy straightened a knife then left the room. I stuffed the key back in my purse, listening to Peggy hum *Yellow Bird* while she clattered in the butler's pantry.

Peggy returned carrying six freshly laundered damask serviettes with the traditional letter P embroidered in one corner. She set them on the table. As she shoved the napkins toward me, something scraped along the worn wood of the tabletop. Satisfied that I had heard, Peggy walked to the opposite end of the table where she sat in the captain's chair under Tad's portrait.

I slid my hand under the napkins. My fingers wrapped around the bow of what could only be the Lady's key.

I slipped the key from under the damask. Standing, with my back to Peggy, I worked the Lady's key into the iron lock. There wasn't even a brief moment of hope, not a click, nothing. I pivoted to Peggy. She looked as disappointed as I felt. I sat back down, my elbows on the table, my fingers pulling on my curls.

"It suppos' to work. Suppos' to."

I retrieved Tad's key from my bag. We stared at the two keys from opposite ends of the table. They were so alike but so dissimilar. It was stupid of us. Anyone of the men could have swooped into the room. But, they didn't. My hands wound in the curls at each of my temples. Eventually, I loosened my right hand from my ringlets, using it to turn the keys so that the bits faced the same direction.

After more study, I ran my fingers down the shank of the Lady's key. A small channel ran the length of it. A complementary ridge ran down Tad's key from the bow to the collar. The collar was flat on the back, as was the throating and pin.

I turned the Lady's key over; the same was true. After several fits and starts, the ridge on Tad's key fit tightly into the channel on the Lady's key, melding the intricate fretwork of their bows into one long piece. The seams and notches of each key were flush, the key wards and bits a single unit.

Peggy used the table to hoist herself out of her seat then walked, straight-backed to the sideboard where she selected finely etched crystal wine glasses to complement the evening's china. Peggy placed a wine glass at each place setting. She rolled the damask serviettes, tucking each into a silver ring before putting one across the top of each plate, ending where I sat.

She reached down to finger the keys. Hearing footsteps in the hall, she hustled through the arch. Amanda asked her about the next day's menu. Peggy diverted Amanda into the kitchen and so managed to keep the angry riff-raff out of my way.

Their voices grew faint. I peered out the archway into the Great Hall. I was alone. At the vault door, the conjoined key slid in like butter on warm coconut bread. I turned the key ready for disappointment. The bolt shot back. With my pull, the door moved a scant inch outward. I pulled harder.

The metal door swung on hinges into a channel in the brick disappearing all but three inches into the crevice. Mid-way on the edge of the door, there was a pop-up grip for use in extracting the door from the slot. I grabbed the flashlight from my bag and shined it into a small chamber.

Three solid brick walls bounced light back at me. There were no sconces for torches, nor any other lighting system. There was no staircase, just the three brick walls, the door and an open, eight-foot, circular hole in the floor. The wind echoed around the brick shaft, howling like the damned.

I directed the flashlight down the wide hole. Bricks, embedded in the side of the wall, spiraled down as far as my light lit. Each set of three blocks stuck out six inches from the wall. Each brick stair was a stride length from the next winding perpetually down into the darkness below.

The bricks were moss covered, some green, some white with lichen. The words slippery and treacherous crossed my mind. I sat on the brink of what could only be Aaron's spiral staircase, wondering how he had gotten in since it had taken both keys to gain access.

Hearing the door pulled from the recess, I scrambled to my feet. As the door slammed, I glimpsed the shadow of a broad-shouldered man, which narrowed my jailer down to everyone. I pushed. The door moved. I called out. Someone shoved against my push. The bolt was shot. I pounded on the sound-deadening stone door.

I ran my hands over the door then the wall looking for a way to open the door from my side. But, there was none. I was trapped. All traces of my presence in the dining room were with me. Would they miss me, would Peggy lead them here? Would my jailer lead them away? How stupid was I to leave the door wide? How stupid?

I hoped the man who shut me in would hear my cries forever. I hoped he rotted in hell, I hoped his body washed ashore, his arms and legs akimbo. I hoped flies laid eggs in his eyes!

I had the only key. Though Aaron had gained access somehow, he was dead, his secret buried with him. No one was getting in, even if Peggy led them to the door, not without a locksmith.

I either made my way down the circular stairs or succumbed to the damp chill and eventual starvation. With me dead, what would Del's plans for Bajan White be? I'm sure he had conjured something—old pirate.

I sat on the edge of the hole, kicking my feet, developing a strategy for my descent. If a small ledge made by each set of three raggedy bricks worried me, the lack of a handrail intimidated me. My left foot hit a pipe in the middle of the hole hard enough to make it twang down then reverberate up the shaft. I lifted my leg until it made contact with the pipe. The pipe must have served as the railing. Standing, I gingerly reached for the pole trying to judge if I had the wingspan to grasp it while winding my way down the scant brick stairs. My fingers wrapped around the pole sufficiently to make going down possible.

I dug in my bag for something to tie the flashlight to my waist to light my descent. A key, a metal rod, a wallet, a passport, the keys to the house in Bakersfield—nothing with string or strength enough to use as a makeshift carabineer. The moment before panic grabbed me, my fingers brushed the web belt that served no purpose in the pair of Whitelaw's pants I wore. It had a metal clip on one end and a slide through metal buckle on the other.

After pulling the belt from my waist, I angled the metal clip through the ring at the top of the flashlight. I threaded the belt through a belt loop then ran the clip through the buckle, doubling it over so that it wouldn't slip out. The flashlight hung down my right thigh lighting points directly beneath me. It lit nothingness.

After a deep breath to quell my rising timidity, I stuck my arms through the two straps of my bag, knapsack style. I looked longingly at the locked door then grabbed the pole with my right hand. I stayed canted over the hole motionless for eons before placing my left foot on the first set of bricks.

The worn, moss covered bricks depressed with my weight. Clumps of mortar skittered off the brick wall. I expelled all my breath as though it would lighten me sufficiently to stop a plummet down the hole. After a reasonable amount of time had passed without the bricks breaking free, I took the next step with my right foot.

I felt the imbalance immediately. Each brick stair was a foot down and a two-foot stride. When my right foot was on the bricks, my left leg was pinned against the wall ratcheting me at a preposterous angle over the hole.

The pole swayed. Cold, wet, fresh air washed over me, reassuring me that the well somehow accessed the sea. I had to choose, slow, treacherous progress down the bricks or a helpless tumble down the hole. I freed my left foot.

Going down didn't get easier with technique. Every five steps or so, I stopped to rest. The combination of wailing wind, darkness, and anxiety was disorienting. The dangling flashlight cast random patterns of light on the brick so that the steps shimmied in the light. When the light stopped arcing, my dizziness passed, and I stepped.

When I could see neither the top nor the bottom of the well, I stalled overcome by the foul smell and the constant dripping. Down was thunderous, pounding water. Up was an impossibility away. The thought of dying in the dripping, reeking dark alone, locked in, unfound, made me regret missing my proms, regret the times I mowed the lawn instead of dating and all the decisions that had led me to dangle from this pole in a well to nowhere.

A bell clanged below me. The persistent tolling further frayed my nerves. I took a step. The pole moved more freely. A sharp clank followed.

I took another deep breath, followed by another step. The bricks gave. I stumbled to the next step. The pole listed heavily to the right, angling me over the hole. I crammed my left foot against the wall of the well, my right foot tread air. My right hand clutched the swaying pole. I tried for the next step. Each attempt angled me further over the hole.

I pivoted on my left foot to face the pole then reached for it with my left hand. The pole moved farther away, pitching me, two hands on the pole, feet on the bricks, at a forty-five-degree angle to the hole. With a death grip on the slippery brass, I jumped. The pole hit the opposite wall then swung back. I wrapped my legs fireman style around it. The step loosened in my lunge ricocheted down the brick hole. The pole shuddered. Righting itself, it produced a sharp clanking noise.

There was no bell! The pole was free at the base!

Vibrations from whatever was oscillating the pole stole into my hands. Only the old, weakened mortar above the wellhead was keeping the pole centered. Clinging, I closed my eyes, because closed eyes make every deathly situation better. Embarrassed, I opened them.

My crabbed fingers loosened. I slid, gaining speed as I descended. Bricks flipped by in the wobbling flashlight. Bleached marks on the wall tore past. The next moment, the raging sounds I'd heard from above were awash me.

I plunged into the swirling, frothing water fomenting over rocks, coral, and crabs. I hadn't had time to catch my breath. Flailing up my rising bubbles, I broke the surface and scrambled onto a pile of sand washed into the well by the unrelenting sea.

I clawed the wet, giving sands until I gained the top of the eight-foot-high pile of sand and scree inside the ocean washed cave. I lay on the ridge breathing, too glad of that to consider the next step.

After twenty minutes of wallowing in exhaustion examining my scrapes and bruises, I walked on a ledge cut into the rock wall of the cave with the water tearing in and out below me. Perhaps thirty feet later, a crack of daylight appeared. When the ledge ran out, I dove into the undermining water and swam until a wave carried me out in a wild burst of frothing, undulating water into the ocean.

Deposited unceremoniously on a massive rock face, I clung by my fingertips to a crack in the limestone. The water sucked with such force that each receding wave pulled my dangling legs seaward. In a brief break between waves, I hauled myself up the face of the rock then perched atop it one leg on each side of the crest.

Del's trashed boat was ten feet to my right. The cliff stairs dangled to my left. My perch was mid-way between the two, where it hid the mouth of the cave from casual boats in the harbor. I leaned over the seaward side of the rock. A deep channel had been cut in the face leaving a lopsided letter P.

The cleverness of the mark struck me immediately. Everyone knew that Perfidia rode this cliff, no one would think twice about a rock with a P on it in Taddys Cove. Picnickers probably slid behind the rock when it was accessible just to see what was behind the P. The whole island probably knew of the cave.

Whitelaw brought Del here and hid him behind the sandbar deep within the cave. The search for Colin's stash centered on the P. Like the tower, it was no secret, but how could they have accessed the staircase without both keys.

Rain battered me; waves tore at my shoes. The waves broke higher with each subsequent burst. Clinging mightily to the surf-strewn rocks, I edged my way to the base of stairs. Only two days ago the distance between the tilted top stone and the bottom stair had seemed far out of reach; today I launched myself high enough to grab the bottom stair. I ratcheted a leg up, caught the second stair then used the handrail to gain the stairs.

At a thunderous roar, I risked a quick peek over my shoulder. A slab of the southern headland slumped into the sea. The seismic wave it produced rushed into the cove. I climbed the stairs as fast as I could on my overused legs.

The wave hit. Wood snapped. The bottom stairs, the very stairs I had been on moments before, were swept away on the tide. On the return, chunks of wood were flung on the remains of Del's boat. That small inlet was a magnet for flotsam and jetsam, no wonder the search centered there.

I climbed the remaining stairs expecting with each handhold on the weak rail to flail back to the sea. At the top of the cliff, I flung myself headlong onto the grass, grabbed a goodly chunk of mother earth in each fist and let the rain pummel my back.

I might have been there through the dinner hour if my delicious enjoyment of life had gone uninterrupted.

"Olivia, you'd best come in. The dinner hour is near. You know how Amanda is about not being clean and well-dressed for meals."

What was Feron deBanco doing at the gate in the privet in a raging storm?

When I managed to look up into his handsome, narrow-eyed face, he started to laugh. With considerable glee, he reached down to help me to my feet.

I muttered, "Are you going to throw me back in?"

He put an arm around me to guide me to the house. "I'm sorry about that. I didn't mean for you to be hurt, just scared. The ledge is sturdy enough."

"Don't try to scare me again. I'll cut you out of Bajan White. Do we understand each other?"

He flashed a wicked smile. "Only too well."

The niggling thought that maybe things with deBanco weren't as they seemed cruised through my bedraggled brain.

I DRESSED FOR DINNER in my green sheath, adding a length of white beads with spacers of smaller gold beads found mysteriously on the daybed. Peggy or Amanda must have left them to add a little glitter to my dullness. I assumed the gold wasn't gold, but who knew after the whole Apolima bracelet episode. The white stones were iridescent. Pray, I wasn't going to dinner in gold and opals over a fifteen dollar dress and filthy five dollar sandals.

I slapped across the floor of the Great Hall in my sandals. The wind whistled a minor symphony through each set of French doors ranked along the veranda, the doors susurrated under the pressure of the wind providing percussion to the howling music. Estella, feet braced on the hearth, seemed unperturbed having ridden out gales much worse.

The moment I entered the archway to the dining room, the gentlemen scurried to push their chairs back from the table. They stood, all of them, ready for inspection, both deBancos, and Lloyd, who rushed to pull the seat out for me. All waited like the Queen's guard for me to sit. When I sat, Lloyd lifted my chair and scooted me under the table, managing a quick pat on my right shoulder as he did. A sly smile lifted one corner of Feron's expressive mouth.

Once we were seated with soup served, Crispin cleared his throat. "You do know that the wooden stairs have long since rotted out. The last of them fell to the base of the well a half-century ago. The bricks weren't the stairs but held the stairs that ran circularly around the pole to the base. You do know that?"

I hadn't, but wooden stairs made more sense to me than all of the men around the table knowing of the stairs' existence. I had the keys. I had figured out how they worked. Me.

I checked each face at the table. Crispin's eyes were speculative, Feron's withdrawn, Lloyd's were sweetly on me, and Amanda's were questioningly on Lloyd.

"How did you get in?" I asked.

"We're smart enough to get a key made, girl," Crispin said, the derision in his voice hard to misinterpret.

Girl? Again? The tone was corroding.

"But, did you descend?"

"Hell, no. Once we knew, we looked for the entrance along the shore. We've been in that cave repeatedly since Colin's body was found nearby with his head bashed in but no booty. Do you take us all for idiots?" Crispin's raptor eyes tried to sculpt out my darkest thought, which was that yes, they were idiots, unscrupulous, grasping idiots.

"You're right, of course. But, I survived my descent. Perhaps, for me, my bliss is the journey. So far, I've discovered the tower that you've been using for years, the staircase that you haven't used, and the cave that isn't a secret. I think I've done rather well, don't you?"

I glared at Crispin as I selected the right spoon for the clear soup served in a wide-brimmed shallow bowl. I scooped the spoon away from me, my eyes still on Crispin. If I had learned nothing else, I had learned the etiquette of formal place settings.

"Not an hour ago, my son found you clinging like a half-mad ground squirrel to the grass."

"My point exactly," I challenged, "What was your son doing on the cliff head in a raging storm?" I glanced at the men. Maybe Feron hadn't been checking for me, but for ships to lure with the fire. "Is the signal fire lit even now while we're chatting?"

Feron gave a great gut laugh that changed his whole character. When his father's eyes censured him, Feron lifted his napkin to cover his mouth, but he couldn't hide the delight in his eyes. Crispin threw his napkin on the table. He shoved his chair back, stood wordlessly, likely leaving to tend the fire. The raging storm made for a perfect night to mooncuss.

"We need to talk," Lloyd said when Crispin's steps no longer counter-pointed the opus of the wind.

"About?" I asked, wiping my mouth. "How disappointed Amanda was when the key Crispin made didn't fit the inheritance box?"

"How dare you!" Amanda yelped. "All holier than thou just because you refused to open it, don't think that bought my trust. Not after last night!"

"Mother." Lloyd placed a hand on Amanda's arm. She narrowed her heavily mascaraed eyes at me. Across the table, Lloyd begged, "Liv, behave yourself, please. We're grateful you've delayed Bajan White's call on the loans, but there are others. Perhaps, you were unaware of the extent of our misery."

Perhaps? Absolutely. "Who?"

"Well, for one, the man you just pissed away." Lloyd made a fleeting gesture toward the Great Hall.

"Then there is another rather huge amount from Lloyd's of London, not Lloyd of Perfidia." He grinned at his small joke.

"A ship they had ensured was lost in our harbor. Not recently, mind you, we lost the settlement; they took shares in Bajan White in lieu of cash. With the sharp devaluation of the shares, they are demanding payment for the difference. I came back from London with that happy news. We've borrowed from Barclays against this year's crop. Then, of course, there are the current taxes and the liens on the mortgages, both first and second. Add the back taxes. Her troubles do seem endless, don't they?"

"John Stoddard didn't manage all of this."

"No." Lloyd wiped his mouth with the edge of his napkin. "We've been in trouble since about 1831."

Lloyd shut Feron's laugh down with a rapier look. Amanda folded her napkin next to her soup bowl. A lemon sherbet in silver stemmed bowls soon arrived. No matter how dire the circumstances may be, one should always clear one's palette.

"Surely not since 1831?"

Feron answered, "No but since the last war. Now that the country has gone independent the British markets aren't guaranteed. Bajan White is playing on a much larger stage. I'm not sure anyone, not even our Lacy, can disentangle the bloody mess. Some of the debts and liens overlap."

Feron tipped his empty wine glass toward Lloyd, "I salute Lloyd's ability to balance all of the factions sufficiently to keep them off his back until now. Since the debacle with the shares, they're like hyenas on a blood trail.

"Amanda asked me to meet the hoteliers to find out what they were offering, to hold them off, if possible. The hotels approached about purchase only after the stock run; as if someone tipped them that our inability to pay her debts would make us hungry to sell. Or, perhaps, whoever tipped them off hoped that the unseemly interest of the hoteliers would highlight our predicament to the government. Further, they were prepared to discuss an arrangement to pay her debts instead of payment to the family. I say over Tad's dead body!"

"Bajan White is solid-ish," Lloyd wavered one hand, "but endangered specifically by Lloyd's. The lawsuit was against the company, not de lady. Though the conundrum is this, Bajan White wouldn't owe Lloyd's if the stock hadn't dropped and because of the drop, can't pay them. By agreement with the other members of

Bajan White, the payment has to come from Perfidia. Sucks, rather."

Lloyd held his wine glass over his shoulder as if a fountain of wine would appear. It did. A server emerged from the Butler's pantry to fill Lloyd's raised glass then filled those of the rest of the diners. Dinner would be fish, the wine was white.

"How much?" I gulped.

"Twenty million," he answered. "Just to Lloyd's."

I washed his answer down with wine. Everyone around the table knew of Del's eighteen million in bearer bonds from Topper's romp through Del's safe deposit box. "Could Bajan White front two million?"

"We considered that you would offer. It requires a vote. I don't see the other members agreeing. They blame us, they truly do." Lloyd put his glass down. "Whitelaw arranged the con. The ship was a big old barge loaded with containers on its way to Venezuela. She broke up off the headlands. The recovery folks swooped in, managing to save most of the containers. They floated the ship sufficiently to take her into the deep water harbor then sued Bajan White."

"But why?"

"Because they couldn't sue Perfidia, she was as broke then as now. Bajan White voted to take on the liability as long as Perfidia paid it back in monthly installments that haven't been paid in three years."

"Whitelaw couldn't have lured the barge into the cove. A ship of that size would have had the finest navigational gear aboard."

"He offered to take a container of tennis shoes off the captain's hands once the ship made the bar."

I sipped the wine in my cut crystal glass. "But, the captain had to have been in on the operation."

"He was. He's in prison." Lloyd cleared his throat.

"The tennis shoes?" The server dashed my sherbet away so quickly that the essence of the cumin in the soup lingered in my mouth.

"Nike wasn't happy. Been a few years now, we're inclined to think they've absorbed the loss."

"The money from the resale of the shoes?"

"Went toward payments, I assure you. Feron shook Whitelaw down until the money popped loose of his pockets."

Feron the enforcer, things were beginning to coalesce though not as I had expected. The information did help clarify Feron's behavior towards me, the interloper with millions.

"Lacy's done a masterful job of keeping us out of the news and a step ahead of the coppers. Now, with Aaron's hijacking of the White Lady, Lloyd's is in another uproar," Lloyd explained.

Feron continued, "Lloyd's insured White Lady. They are not inclined to believe she accidentally went aground within twenty feet of where the freighter did. They won't pay. The White Lady is registered to Crispin. He's furious, convinced he sees Whitelaw's hands in this. They're playing cat and mouse at the moment."

"Making the question of what Aaron intended to load of interest." I clasped my hands in my lap working my serviette between my fingers waiting for both food and explanation. "What do you expect from me?"

"Del told us that you would save us," Lloyd answered.

"I own fifty-two per cent of Bajan White. When I postponed that call, I did what I could with that resource. You know how much liquidity I have. I can't pay off your debts. And, since you seem to know everything else, I assume that you know that Del engineered the run on the shares then bought?"

Feron and Lloyd exchanged a quick look. Amanda clapped her hands for the main course. The server delivered fried flying fish rolled in coconut, rice pilaf, and fried bananas. My stomach let out a growl heard over the roar of the wind.

"The half-mad ground squirrel demands food." Feron raised his glass to me. I couldn't help it I blazed a happy smile back at him with my mouthful of rice. Lloyd looked away. Feron showed me his.

I twiddled with the napkin. "Where did Del join Aaron?"

"Here, but not by invitation," Lloyd said, reaching across the table for my hand, knowing why I had asked, no doubt wondering what had taken me so long. He had considered it by his next words. "Aaron seems to have rowed ashore. Del was waiting. Del rowed back out and grounded the White Lady, or maybe she grounded herself while they were ashore."

"Was Whitelaw involved?"

Both Feron and Lloyd shrugged like puppets attached to the same string.

"Do either of you know where Aaron searched?" I dived into my flying fish.

"The usual places. The rubble mid-cliff, the cave near where Colin was found, and the base of the gravel to its left. Makes you wonder if Aaron was just goofing, he did that you know," Feron noted. "Aaron was his father's blond-headed son, he had a streak of stupid mean in him a mile wide. He may have read Lacy's papers and strolled through Lloyd's safe. He had access to both."

"There are so many hands in this. So many. It makes me wonder about the old pirates?" I asked with my mouthful of fish this time.

Lloyd sipped his wine, his eyes remaining on me. But it was Feron who answered, "De lady, always de lady. Crispin promised her to Amanda as a wedding gift. Lin needs her for power. I would suspect they've worked out a deal."

"As in you get me de lady, I give you the lady?" I quipped.

Amanda shifted in her seat. Her eyes gave nothing away though her fingers played the stem of her wine glass like a concert pianist. Lloyd and Feron toasted, their leaded crystal wine glasses leaving behind a bright ringing.

"So," I said shoveling in another mouthful of flying fish, "Feron, how did you end up with the Olivia watch?"

"Whitelaw and I flipped. Not sure who won, though. I think Whitelaw got the easier chore."

"Meaning?" I asked, staring into his dark blue eyes.

"You're a handful, Miss Olivia."

"What now?"

"Find the stash," Feron answered.

"Then we need de rain to neber stay her welcome."

At that moment, one pair of French doors blew inward spilling rain and wind across the planked flooring of the Great Hall. Lloyd jumped to his feet. His chair screeched on the rock of the floor. He dashed into the Hall where he struggled to close the twin doors. Once closed, he jammed a chair under the knob. Lloyd stared into the howling night, his hands on his hips, his eyes on the horizon wondering like me, I suspected, if finding the cache was worth all the death.

"Olivia," Lloyd asked of the French doors, "Marry me?"

My eyes jumped to Feron's. His hand reached for mine. Amanda's laugh broke across the night. And, so help me, all I could see was a pair of gray eyes furious at me for even considering Feron deBanco's touch.

"I can't, Lloyd, I simply can't. Not now."

Lloyd nodded. Feron withdrew his empty hand.

Day Nine

THE STORM RAGED ALL night. I cowered in the daybed waiting for glass shards blown in from ruptured windows to rip my body open and for the sea, having risen above the headlands, to swallow me whole. I dreamed of falling into the raging sea to be bashed helplessly against the rocks of Taddys Cove, of Aaron' lifeless body bumping across the ocean floor, of Colin's like death. I dreamed of Colin's best friend, Lin Harris and his 18 million in bearer bonds. I dreamed of my unknown mother, of the rupture her death left in my life. I dreamed my father murdered Colin Law.

I woke exhausted knowing that at last, I'd had an offer of marriage.

Whitelaw's linen slacks had been cleaned. I struggled to pull them on then decided to wear my peasant blouse to complete the ensemble. My clothes were light and airy if I was not. I knocked on the French doors next to mine. Amanda answered, looking bleary-eyed, unkempt, and for the first time nearer sixty than twenty. She waved me in grabbing a satin robe to cover her diaphanous negligee. She called down to the kitchen for coffee. We sat each in a white rattan chair at a small table to the left of the French doors.

Moments later the coffee arrived on a tray with two porcelain coffee cups and a plate of the ubiquitous coconut bread. Peggy poured the coffee, hesitated as if waiting for an invitation. When none came, she huffed out. Amanda and I took stock of each other.

"Tell me about my father."

"Why should I? I brought the box out for you. For you! You wouldn't betray him."

"Not so! You trusted me with your greatest secret. We each maintained our integrity by keeping the genie in the box." I watched her struggle with my answer as I sipped my coffee.

She tapped her coffee cup while staring at the stacked shoeboxes that hid the small door in her closet. "I don't see why we can't open the box."

"Whatever is in that box has kept Perfidia safe since Tad put it in there. It would be wrong in so many ways for anyone but the heir to open it, which is why you kept it hidden all of these years. Why would you want to open it now?"

"Because of Del, because of Aaron, so we can get the jump on whoever knows its secrets. Don't you see?"

"No one knows its secrets. If they did, Aaron would be alive. They wouldn't be falling all over each other. There wouldn't be drownings and shootings. They wouldn't be following me around assuming I had the keys and knew where the kingdom was. No one knows what is in that box, with the possible exception of Lacy. He won't give it up, especially when the wrong man might hear it. Tell me about my father, I need to understand."

She shook her head.

"Amanda, I know he killed Colin."

She stared out the French doors. "I still miss my brother. We were such good friends, even after Sophie, even after that horrible mistake."

"Please?"

Amanda pulled her robe tight as if a chill had invaded the room though the room was stifling. She wrapped her hands tightly around her coffee cup, raising her shoulders then letting them sag, working through some inner struggle. I broke off a piece of coconut bread and waited.

"I'm sorry," she said, "Sorry for Aaron, sorry for Colin, sorry for all of us, sorry Lin ever came into our lives. Not before, but after the war. The Harris land and property were confiscated when the Japanese invaded Malaysia. Lin's father and brother enslaved on the railroads were never heard from again. The boat carrying his mother and sister to safety sank. No one survived. Lin was in the British Army serving in Africa, the second son. He vowed even then to get the property back.

"After the war, Vent Amer was returned, but the rubber plantation was in ruins. Lin was bereft. The idea blossomed to grow something else. He did. He was hauled away by Bajan White, not disinherited, but given a good kick in the pants. The custody of the property was entrusted to a distant cousin—our Colin. Lin and Colin were great friends from childhood, but the loss of the land split them like a cleaver. Colin tried to make amends, offering Lin the foremanship if he would agree to grow only rubber. It was a way back for Lin. Lin never got over what he considered a betrayal, never got quite right."

"What about Topper?" I asked the question I had wanted to ask since the day at the cemetery when I truly looked into Topper's eyes. Mine. His chin. Mine. His walk. Del's. Even before, I was told the story of his abandonment or about Amanda's gift of a surname, I had wondered.

Amanda patted my leg. "Peggy left us for a while in 1947 to try her hand at living in New York City with the other expatriates. I missed her, called her back down. She left me her baby to stage his abandonment. I provided a surname. Peggy asked John White to raise the boy with his. She officially returned to Perfidia from New York two weeks later, having been in St. Lucy with a friend the whole time."

She patted me again. There was enough fuel to start a fire and enough abandonment to keep it stoked. Had it been John on the beach with Topper, if so, who was the other man? Not Dave, I didn't want to believe it was Dave.

"Peggy's not fond of Lin." Amanda tweaked at the robe over her negligee.

"Did Peggy shoot at Del?" I asked amazed how little I was shocked that Topper was my half-brother and that Peggy was his mother.

"No," Amanda chuckled, a good deep rumbly chuckle, "Though she has reason enough. He raped her. She had gone to see her cousin Sophie to help with her boy. Del waited for her in the cane. When Peggy let herself in that night, I was sitting in the dark on the settee in front of Estella. Peggy's dress was torn. She was holding the front closed. She was a beautiful girl, not as beautiful as Sophie, but stunning in a way. I always believed that John Stoddard was seeing Peggy. She still swears no."

"What made you think that?"

"When I was with Crispin, John Stoddard was with someone. I would see him walking towards the quarters."

"Topper?"

"Lin never admitted the boy was his, never gave Peggy a cent. He swore he had no money. Peggy was engaged to one of the Chapel boys from the north quarters. Even though many Bajan women have their children then marry the father years later, her fiancé was too established in Island society to stand by Peggy. The Chapels are as close as Barbados has to a Bajan landed gentry with property that stretches from Perfidia to near Bathsheba. He married a lovely British girl. Peggy married Perfidia."

"Del and I were at Maison Vol?"

"Yes and no. I had asked my sister, Celia, to offer Lin a job at Maison Vol while he waited for the repatriation of Vent Amer. When Vent Amer was returned, he left you with Celia and Dondé. You were a month or two old. At first, Vent Amer seemed to be thriving. It wasn't until late 1949, we knew why. The scandal broke Christmas. Colin took over the property, he ordered Lin back to his job at Maison Vol. Not a year later, Colin was dead."

"What happened in 1953 that..."

"The police broke up a drug running operation deep in Maison Vol's bayou. Lin claimed innocence, but he turned around and kidnaped you. Celia hired a detective and an adoption lawyer. The investigator reported that you were thriving. We had no grounds to take you away from Lin." She patted my hand. "Poor dear."

I stared out the window at the sea wishing they had kidnaped me back, wishing I had been truly loved, remembering Donde's arms around me, feeling hate reach for my heart.

"Vent Amer is entailed through Del to you. Crispin is appointed to ensure your interests are protected. Still, Del keeps his fingers in the management of the estate. He's been there and here often. Even with Crispin's oversight, Lloyd believes Del is skimming. We were reviewing the second quarter reports the night of Aaron's funeral."

"Like Lacy, you knew that Del killed Colin. Why didn't you stop him?"

"We had no proof, not until you showed us Tad's key. The last time either of us saw the key, Colin had it. He wouldn't have given the key to anyone for safe keeping. Lin's done nothing but bring disgrace on the family. Now this, he's engineered it all, even you. He raised you to take revenge on us."

"He bungled it. I'm a third-grade teacher. I'm out of my league…"

"You're here with me. You've charmed us all with your gallivanting. You found the signal fire, the stairs, the same old cave, and you found them all in three days. Being Taddy is about proving yourself, showing courage."

"Or stupidity."

"Or that." Amanda gave me a brilliant smile, but her fingers worked the fabric of her robe. "You're anything but stupid. Brendan is fearless. Lloyd is careful. Feron is rash. So what? This isn't a production of the Wizard of Oz. All that matters is that we can't let Lin have Perfidia."

I left, wondering if there was truly anything that could be done to stop Del, short of what he had done to Colin and Aaron. I wondered at my inability to feel anything.

At a feather-light touch on my shoulder, I turned. Peggy pointed me not into Amanda's morning room but into a much smaller room one door down fitted with children's furniture. Her medical bag was stashed behind the door where it had once been most needed.

"This room was for our babies when there be babies, hasn't been for the longest time. We need to have some again. It would make this ol' house joyous."

I lowered my eyes to the ABC rug under my feet. My eyes came to rest on the tattered letter P.

"Amanda, she told you about Topper? I'll just get on from there. Your papa, he just want to destroy things like a five-year-old who had he train set taken. He hurt me because he could. I got my boy, except Topper's never been much good. He got a wild heart. Topper believe any old thing John tell him, 'cause John raise him. But, he always had airs like he belong in de big house. I think he messed Lloyd's marriage to get what he want. In."

"Did Topper shoot at Del?"

Peggy leveled steady brown eyes on me which I took for an answer. Fathers and abandoned sons, whole novels had been written about the permutation of possible outcomes, hardly ever anything good.

"Is that why you gave me the key?"

"I had it since Sophie die. She gave it to me. She said that somebody been using it. Been in her house. Told me to hide it until Tad's key come round. It was the very night Lin came for me."

"He must have..."

"He searched me alright. But, he didn't find it 'cause we saw he shadow. There dis spot by the window in Sophie house you can't see from the outside. I handed it back just there. Sophie brought it to me the next day."

I gulped before asking the hard question, "Did Sophie hang herself?"

"Have to ask de boy. De boy de only one there." By the look in her eyes, she didn't know.

"You told me once there weren't any caves."

"The island is coral limestone, some clay in the middle. We have blowholes, we have fallen in caves, but we don't have caves that go so deep, not naturally. The truth is in the box with everything else. No one be in that box since the day Amanda hide it. Good thing no one kill her. Whatever the truth is, it isn't caves, not like the caves they say."

"Del knew, Crispin knew, Colin knew that Amanda had the box, why *didn't* they take it from her?"

Peggy gave a great heave of her shoulders. "We just girl."

"What does that mean?"

"Means I see things. Amanda see things. Nobody see us. What I figure is that Colin had Tad's key, Sophie had the Lady's key. I think Colin was who Sophie worried about taking her Lady's key. But it was too late, he already found de cache. Dat what I think."

"You've not told a soul in all these years?"

"They all be gone, Sophie, Colin, Drayman, the box, Tad's key, the Lady's key. I guess I the only one didn't know Amanda have the box. All these years, I only had the Lady's key. No matter what you told, there be no for sure heir. No one left to identify the heir except Celia and Amanda. Dey girls. Bajan White has to vote."

"Amanda told me she has the marriage certificate."

"She can fight, but she might not win. Sometime Danny he worst enemy. Only two believe in him. We don't count. We girls. But de girls, dey keep all de secrets at dis old place. Ever since Tad, dat what my mama told me."

Peggy shook her head. Her beautiful dark eyes with their flying eyebrows gave me a look of such knowing that I hugged her. She wrapped her ample arms around me, pulled my head to her shoulder, and began to rock me. I stayed cocooned for a remarkably long time feeling precious for the first time since the soft powdery Dondé had tried to hold me tight enough to keep.

"If I was goin' to look for gold and treasures beyond imagination," Peggy said, stroking my hair, "I'd follow my name. I would. Maybe you the key Del mean to bring. Tad key was safer where it was. I don't know for sure, but I always wondered, since I was sitting pretty with my Amanda on de balcony watching for de stars."

"Peggy!" I squealed, raising my head to look into her mirthful eyes.

"Once, I see my Colin. He body was happy. You ever see a man when he body happy? He bounce. He bounce all de way to Sophie house. Next day, she asked me to keep de Lady's key. She worried about her man. I can add, I can."

With her hands on my shoulders, Peggy turned me out the door walking me to the edge of the balcony. She positioned me until I faced the ocean. Clouds swirled at the fringes of the horizon. More rain. The open gate bisected the privet. But, what else was there to see?

Peggy slid her hand down the balcony railing. Her fingers pointed down the privet to where the hedge ended in the southern pillar, a scant two feet from cliff's edge, so near that some future storm would soon topple it into the sea. The pillar's twin guarding the north end of the privet remained ten feet back from the ledge.

"Were there columns at the gate, too?"

"Not in my time, dey only be de two stelas marking Perfidia from the sea."

She saw my sharp glance. She had expected me to make the leap. Estella, Stella, stela, marker, star. When visible, the stipes of the Southern Cross would point directly to the southern stela.

"Do you think I need a key?"

"There is a reason the key have two parts. Sophie say the Lady's key open the well door, but it didn't, not alone. Everyone know Tad key open the box, maybe once the cache. Always two key, not one, not one like de men think, except Lin. He know. He know since he rape me since he kill Colin."

Peggy gave my forearm a loving squeeze.

"Peg, who do I trust?"

She hugged me so tight I worried my head would pop loose. After a second quick hug, Peggy walked off humming *Perfidia*, not to a Latin, but to a calypso beat. My fingers picked the beat out on the balcony rail.

Me...I was who I could trust.

I GRABBED THE KEYS from their latest hiding place in my room under the writing paper at the back of Amanda's escritoire then transferred them into my still wet hobo bag. Dressed in white as I was, I could hardly slip unseen across the lawn, so I used the south stairs then slunk up the side in the shadow of the Casuarina at the edge of the grounds.

The stela was limestone pitted by rain. The side toward the sea had sunk two inches into the ground so that the peak pitched a good six inches toward the cliff's edge. A crack tore its jagged way through the mortar. A cast iron P swung limply from the bottom nail, like a distress signal. I ran my hands over the knobby gray blocks. There was no magic door, no keyhole, no block that popped loose to reveal stairs, just an old, pitted six-foot stela.

I leaned against each side of the stela starting seaward where the vast horizon rode unobscured all the way to Africa. I shifted to the left. Hundreds of feet of privet separated the two columns with the gate in the dead center. Should the British or other authorities arrive unannounced after a shipwreck, the woods would not be easy to defend. Opposite the sea, the gray stone wing of de lady segued into the new.

Facing back seaward, I used my hand to mimic the position of the Southern Cross. The stipes of the Cross pointed to the horizon, as did one side of the patibulum. No hints there. The constellation was so low in the sky that the five stars were only visible if the night was void of clouds or heavy seas. I glanced back to the balcony.

Amanda, Peggy, even the men waited on the balcony each night for the Cross to rise. I got it! When the Cross was visible, the women knew no ships, no men, no family were endangered. They relaxed and went to sleep. The men sought the opposite. No Cross predicted a night ripe for mooncussing. I thought of Amanda and Lloyd out on the balcony, I wondered if it was a tradition now or necessity. I thought of the two inches of sooty muck trapped in the fire basin on the tower.

The tower was part of the house. The circular staircase was hidden within a well never used for water. What was the likelihood that Tad had dug another shaft under the old foundation? After all, there are just so many shafts you can dig in the earth before the foundation crumbles. Tad had kept everything very close to de lady, not only to keep a keen watch on what was his but to maintain absolute control over those who accessed it.

I waited for an epiphany at least as good as the one regarding the Southern Cross. My eyes kept wandering back to the narrow path through the cane to the bed and breakfast. The restoration workers would be at lunch. They might know where the earth could sustain a long, deep tunnel to the sea without crumbling.

Warm lights glimmered through the slatted windows of the bed and breakfast kitchen. When I entered, Nancy was setting platters of fried flying fish, plain rice, and coconut bread on a trestle table. A flurry of arms ensued as the workers dished their lunches. I sat down with them. Nancy brought me a plate accompanied by her brilliant smile.

"So, what's the latest buzz?" I asked the workers.

A long, long, long explanation about the thrill of finding the foundation for an old wall, no one seemed to know existed, bounced around the room from worker to worker.

"Why is the find so important?" I asked when I could take no more.

"We thought we were restoring the oldest working windmill on the island, but what we found is older and looks like the foundations for a crusher. Our latest thought is that the original structure didn't survive the hurricane of 1831, that the Laws built the standing mill on the crusher site."

Nancy put her hands on her hips. After a moment of consideration, she said, "Rumor always be the only thing here that survived the great blow is this kitchen and the storage cellar." She pointed to the wide planks beneath her feet.

The foreman stomped his foot on the floor. "Can I take a look?"

I tagged along. Nancy opened the back door of the kitchen then leaned over a pair of shed doors angled close to the ground. The hinges groaned. She let the doors drop to the grass before descending a short flight of stone stairs, flipping on overhead lights as she did. The cellar was majestic in size, dirt-floored, and dry. The subterranean room stored the needs of the bed and breakfast including enough toilet paper to TP Perfidia.

The foreman ran his hands down an unobstructed stretch of the dirt wall. "There's no foundation?"

Nancy pointed to one stone wall hidden behind shelves filled to brimming with rum, Coca-Cola, gin, tonic, burlap bags of sugarcane, rice, and flour. The foreman found an area of exposed limestone. He flicked out a blade from a Swiss Army knife pulled from his pocket and scratched on the wall with the tip. The stone was solid. There was no seepage. He seemed satisfied that the stones had withstood the gales of time. He thanked Nancy for showing the cellar to him while I wondered what the bags hid.

"Anything behind the bags, he should be interested in?"

Nancy put her hands on her hips. "Like a door to a secret tunnel? No, not even a tiny wee mouse door. Dis wall is just solid limestone. Dat stone be used on the ocean side to keep what be stored from spoiling."

The foreman agreed with her. "We've seen one wall, sometimes two, at various other locations where the cellars are near the ocean. So, I'm not surprised. But, I'm a bit surprised that Miss Lassiter is still looking for tunnels. The hurricane so changed the shape of the island that any cave or ocean access older than 1831 is part of the sea now. Tad Law was nearly a century gone by then."

"But he was pretty crafty. Besides, Perfidia survived, unlike the others."

"So, why couldn't his purported undermining? The damage to the island was extensive, especially on the Atlantic side from St. Philip to the north. As we just heard, the crusher was destroyed. Every part of the main house was either blown in or burned out."

"All of it?"

"The tower withstood the blow." Even the foreman of the dig knew about the tower. Had he been up there? Had everyone?

"And the wellhead?"

"The bunker made it. But, the addition didn't, much of it was timber. It was more modest and frankly, from drawings that survived, blended the two sections together better than the new. Before the storm, the back lawn stretched forty feet past the two stelas. The old well is now open to the sea behind a rock marked with a P. That's the kind of damage we are talking about."

I shut my eyes envisioning the egress from the brick cave filled with thrashing sea water. The walls were shaped, the ledge above the water purposeful. "The well always opened to the sea. I'm sure of it."

"Maybe, still, if it weren't for the rubble, which acts like rip-rap, Perfidia would be as gone as Tad's pillage."

"Gone?" I said stupidly, following Nancy and the foreman back to the kitchen. The pillage couldn't be gone. Too many had died for it to be gone. Stela, Stella, Estella, and star.

I made my goodbyes at the kitchen door quickly retracing my steps to the pillar. I leaned on the side facing the house. The sun lit the French doors in the Great Hall. A sunbeam ran across the wood floors shadowing where Estella carved through the room as though still on the prow of Beth's father's ship. Stela, Stella, Estella, star! De lady, so far each of Tad's clues had been associated with Beth, Beth's sampler, and Beth's portrait.

I ran back down the path to the bed and breakfast kitchen. The poor foreman had the fork half-way to his lips when I burst in panting. "Was Estella part of the original house—the fortress?"

The foreman twisted to face me. "No. Estella was out in the elements. When Tad put her up, there was no veranda or balcony, certainly no Great Hall."

"But the fireplace, the massive open hearth—the mantel?"

"They were added. Collier built Estella into the house after the hurricane." His eyes checked Nancy, who went about her work.

I sat so heavily on one end of a bench that three restoration workers rode the wave up then down. "The dining room?"

"Was the original parlor, I guess you'd say."

"But part of the original structure?"

"That, the old kitchen, the tower with the embrasures, and the odd rectangular room directly after the archway, which was where Tad and Beth slept until the first child was born. Imagine a soddy on steroids."

The hmm I thought must have slipped my lips because the foreman said, "Indeed."

If Tad's cache still existed, it was accessible from somewhere in the original structure. Peggy believed Colin had found it. He had taken his news to Sophie's isolated cabin. Both keys had been there for a time.

Some link existed between Sophie and Tad's cache, some bit of evidence that bound the two together. Perhaps it was the Lady's key, the key to Colin's heart. On a whim, I detoured for Sophie's.

THE NIGHT I FIRST stumbled across Sophie's cabin, someone had been using it. It wasn't just the sleeping bag that gave its use away, but a dirty coffee cup, crumbs on the table, and the male smell of an empty chamber pot sitting in one corner. Del denied it was him.

I was now certain that I had overheard deBanco and Whitelaw in the cane field that first night. One had gone toward the ocean. The other had circled behind me to the cabin. It would have been Whitelaw. Was he here now?

I opened the door.

Whitelaw was sitting at the small table under the window writing. He stood as I entered. He was as ever in jeans and a tropical print shirt. His shirt was unbuttoned revealing a sterling set of abdominal muscles.

He held out his hand.

I put the Lady's key in it, hoping it would help uncover the link between Sophie and Tad.

"Your mother gave the key to Peggy. She would have gotten it with the job, but Sophie thought someone was after it. She told Peggy to hide it until Tad's key surfaced. Peggy hid it all these years."

Whitelaw took the key, turning towards a small door. I grabbed his shirt. He touched my hand, his eyes puzzled.

"The day your...?"

He took a deep breath. His startling gray eyes, lighter for the black corona, sought neutral ground over my shoulder. I steeled myself for the truth.

"Dad had gone to work. I was asleep behind the curtain. Another man stopped by. I didn't recognize the man's voice then. I did later. There was an argument about the baby. She wouldn't kill it. That's what the man wanted. The door slammed. She began to cry. The soft sound of her tears put me to sleep. Can you imagine?"

Whitelaw pulled me into his arms. He leaned his chin on the top of my head, his hands interlaced behind my back. His chest rose and fell beneath my cheek. I took a step back, not away, but back to better see his face with its arching brows, and straight nose. His lower lip was longer than the upper, so he seemed always to wear a slight smile.

"Her kiss woke me, just a shadowy thing. I crawled out of my bed. I think I called to her. She was standing, where you are now, like you are now, her hands busy folding the clothes she had just taken off. She was naked. I never knew why. Still, don't. Do you know why?"

I shook my head. I needn't have bothered; he couldn't have seen it not where his heart was.

"She turned me away, around. Told me to sing my favorite song, a silly thing, but long. When I turned back, she was hanging. I touched her foot. I called for help. I ran into the cane. No one came. I played with my toys. All day. Afraid to look. It was dark when Dad came home. The man who came didn't hang her, but he killed her. Is that what...?"

I pulled his head to my shoulder; sure it had been Del. I couldn't ask. I clucked as I rocked him. "Anything else I should know about your mother or father?"

"She was beautiful, truly. Tall, slender, long legs, perfect really. I look like her, but I don't, too much of Dad in me I think. My mother's eyes were so...almond shaped, slanting gently up at the corners, big walk-in eyes. She would hold me in the chair in the corner. We would sing my silly songs. She rocked me until I fell asleep."

He pulled away, wiped his eyes then gave me a mercurial smile.

After a deep breath, he added, "Later, Dad told me I was the heir and that I should do as the inheritance box said, it would save de lady, always. He confessed that he had borrowed the Lady's key from my mother. Dad said he put it back each time. But he seemed worried that her death and the key were linked. It disappeared just before."

"Peggy. Did he say what was in the box that could save Perfidia?"

"Lacy has hinted that the other plantations are leaseholds, but without the box, it can't be proved."

"Crispin must know? Feron must know."

"Crispin must hope. They all must hope that the box is gone for good. Thirty-nine years of unpaid ground rent alone would be enough to save Perfidia. No one will need Tad's stash if there is one?"

"Amanda has the..."

"Box? She brought it out for you?" His voice held as much wonder as it did question.

"When I told her Del had Tad's key. Then."

"You have to hand it to them, the ladies. Peggy with the Lady's key. Amanda with the box. I hope they get their wish."

"You, you're their wish." I squeezed his hand.

He pecked me on the cheek. "I might be their nightmare. I win, Crispin loses. Lin loses. If I'm lucky, I can keep Perfidia, keep her going, get her back on her feet. Twenty-four years is a long time to wait, too much time to brood. I'm afraid I have a lot of anger in me."

"I don't believe that."

Whitelaw turned to the closet, inserting the key in a narrow carved opening. As he turned it, the paneling opened revealing a space deep enough to hang a shirt. It was empty, even the shelf that ran across the top. He stepped back to let me see. His head hovered above mine as we stared into the small space. He knelt to feel for brass rings, handles, hollow boards, anything but the dirt below.

"Damn," we said in tandem.

Whitelaw got off his knees, brushing the ages off his pant legs. He clasped his hands behind his back as though commanding a great sailing ship and stared into the small closet. A moment later, he reached above his head as far back on the shelf as his hand would go. His fingers brushed something they recognized. He went for one of the chairs in the main room, dragging the ladder back chair from the small table under the isinglass window to the closet.

He stepped up on the seat to reach deeper into the shelf. The distinctive scrape of wood on wood followed. He stood on his toes, the muscles in his back bunched under his shirt. He scooted whatever he had found to the edge of the shelf. I held up my hands; he lowered a dusty shoebox tied firmly in the middle with a bright blue satin ribbon.

I carried the shoebox into the main room, untying the ribbon as I walked. Whitelaw was so close on my heels that he nabbed one of my huaraches with the toe of his shoe.

I placed the shoebox on the table. He lifted the lid. The corner of a swatch of royal purple velvet slithered out. I took a corner of the cloth in each hand and lifted. A heart-shaped, blue diamond as big as a silver dollar nested within the purple velvet.

I had seen a drawing of this exact jewel in my library research. The necklace had been on a ship bound for Belize. Treasure hunters still sought the ship along the Lesser Antilles route. The jewel here meant the galleon had gone aground in Taddys Cove.

"My father found Tad's stash," Whitelaw said, joy lilting his baritone. "He found Tad's stash! Dad brought this to my mother, Colin's Heart, his promise to her. He loved her very much, you know."

He echoed Lacy word-for-word. Sophie or Perfidia, what had Colin loved most; the beautiful White girl or the worthless tangled historical mess that was Perfidia replete with messy family?

Whichever, there was only relief in his son's face. Not want, not desire, not anger, not loss, just release in this relic of his father's undying love.

Whitelaw put the diamond back in the box, taking the time to refold the purple velvet and re-tie the ribbon. He stepped onto the chair to return the box to the small recess. Done, he jumped to the floor, shut and locked the closet then handed me the Lady's key.

I took his hand. "I have to ask? Aaron needed help loading whatever he had found. Del said he found you searching Aaron's body, is that true? Were you in on this with Aaron?

Whitelaw turned my hand over in his and kissed the mound of my palm. "Aaron radioed he was coming in. I was at the north dock waiting. That's the last I remember. Feron found me head down on the beach, unconscious, the tide coming in. The White Lady was aground. Salvagers were towing her with Del aboard. Feron brought me here. By the time I got my legs under me, Amanda was in a state about Aaron. Aaron confided to me that he'd found Dad's stash. Aaron wanted to load it, take it out, sell it and save her. But, he didn't tell me where, or Del, or whoever killed him. I searched Aaron hoping to find some clue."

"Del killed him," I mumbled, ashamed of my part in this, even if it was by proxy.

"Del murdered my father. He may not have killed Aaron." Whitelaw ran a finger down my palm. "Del's not the only one in this game."

I searched Whitelaw's face for some indication he was telling the truth. He may have seen hope in mine. He kissed my palm again.

"Crispin?"

"John White, Dave—I've been shadowing them. It wasn't Feron who went through Lacy's files. It was Dave. I watched. I walked in on him when it looked like he might get somewhere. I expect John went through Lloyd's files. He was talking business with Amanda. He left about the time Lloyd went for his drink." He ran a finger down my wrist.

"Why try to kill Del, why did they do that?"

"You showed up with Tad's key, we thought Del had gotten the location out of Aaron. Feron has been trying to keep you safe while I've been skulking about watching Del. Del kept going back to the P. I wasn't the only one watching. The Whites made their move hoping to make Del talk, kill him then loot it. But you showed up, so they waited."

"It's not at the P, I'm sure of that."

Whitelaw shook his head, kissed my palm then folded my hand one finger at a time.

"Before the crane, sugar was lowered down the center of the stairs and loaded to skiffs using the ledge to get it to the water. It was safe there except for the highest tides. That was its only use. Until Aaron swore it to me, I never believed Dad had a stash. Though I was only eight, I knew Dad was up to something, but not mooncussing, whatever it was it appealed to the wild and the just in him. There was something in the taking that Dad loved. He didn't run drugs. I'm sure of it.

Whitelaw unfolded my fingers.

"Was it you that led me out of the cane field that first night? Did you leave the note on my window?"

He kissed my palm. I took it as a yes.

"Now what?"

"Now we have bigger fish to fry, girl."

"Tad's cache?"

"Aaron found Dad's cache, Tad's must be near, but still more cunningly hidden, or Aaron would have found it. His body was at the base of the slip just to the left of the gyre. I've been over every bloody nook and cranny of it. Nothing!"

"Gyre?"

"During high tide, the waves break creating a sort of whirlpool, all the flotsam and jetsam is gyrated into the rocks. It's near the P. You likely were in it when you emerged from the well."

I felt the tug of the swirling water at my ankles as I fought to climb the rock face to safety.

"Peggy says I'm the key. It's up to me."

He kissed my ear, turned me for the door and patted me on the butt. "Then what's keeping you?"

Indeed.

I only knew one way back to Perfidia. I followed the cliff edge past where Feron had forced me off. The thump and thunder of the bay kept me company until John White joined me. We walked side-by-side in silence. When we reached a fork in the path, he left me for the quadrangle. His closeness was threat enough.

Back at the stela, I leaned against the stone with my eyes closed. The ambient heat of the sun warmed my back. My hobo bag with the keys rested on my right ankle.

"Sunning?" Feron, my watchdog, asked standing on the verdant grass of the lawn.

"I am." I shaded my eyes to see him against the sun's glare.

"I'm driving into town. Want a hop into Bridgetown to see your father?"

I studied his face. Maybe his blue eyes weren't that close together. He brushed my hand against his. I took it.

We walked across the lawn to the garage, our locked hands swinging between us. The closeness was comfortable, even the silence.

When we reached the Bentley, he opened the door for me. I settled in as he came around the car dragging his knuckles over the shine. He climbed in beside me but didn't turn the ignition.

I turned to study his profile. His lips were pursed under his slightly Roman nose, making me wonder if there wasn't a Latin or two in his lineage. He had the kind of chin that keeps a turtleneck sweater in its place.

He reached forward to turn the key in the ignition, stopped, turned to me, ran his hand down my arm, all before saying, "Topper."

"I've known since this morning."

"That he shot at your father?"

I must have looked puzzled. "That Topper's my half-brother."

Feron took a deep breath. "I've wondered. There's enough of Lin in both of you to create an odd symmetry. Topper can be pretty rough, you should be aware of that."

"Rougher than you?"

"I was beside myself. With you bungling around Bridgetown, what were any of us to think?"

"Bungling?"

"Bungling," Feron said, pulling the car out of the drive. "And bungling with the Whites."

Feron piloted us through the small towns, past belching buses, past women strolling down the verge one hand balancing rattan platters of fresh fruit on their heads. He changed lanes to avoid naked children playing at the central water fountain in one town. He detoured down St. Lawrence Gap to point out a few night spots. We laughed at a small man who called out *morning* to the passing cars. DeBanco deftly negotiated Bridgetown's streets to park in front of Parradine and Whitelaw. I got out. He didn't.

I leaned in the window. "You're leaving me alone to face the old pirate?"

He shot me the crooked smile that I was beginning to adore. "Have my own old pirate to face. And, I hope to run into a younger one."

"When I was here last, he went missing through the office window."

Feron snorted. My arms dropped to my sides as the car lurched forward. I skipped up the stairs then past the monkey, nodding at Mrs. Smythe on my way to the second floor. She clattered up the stairs behind me, detouring to Whitelaw's apartment.

Del was tucked deep in bed with his leg in a more traditional cast. He was playing backgammon with Lacy. He wore his usual happy grin, making it difficult to cast the ol' boy in the part of a cold-blooded murderer and rapist, who deserved to be shot by his bastard son.

Del acknowledged me as I plowed into the room, his eyes a joyful blue. Lacy glanced past me. I heard Ms. Smythe talking to someone in hushed tones, a woman from the tenor of the answering voice.

"So, Del, have you committed two murders and countless crimes to get your hands on Perfidia?" I leaned against the inside of the door frame awaiting the denial.

"I'm supposed to answer that while playing backgammon with the family lawyer?" Del gestured at Lacy with a black checker.

"Lacy is well aware that you murdered Colin Law. Did you think this bunch of pirates wouldn't find out about the key, did you! It took them one day!" I pointed, as the truth hit. "You lit the fire. You did. You wanted me to deliver the key to Barbados! I was just your courier."

"Lots of conclusions bein' jumped to Sonny." He moved his checker, as the anger I'd seen earlier returned to his eyes.

"Don't call me Sonny. Ever! I'm not your son. I'm not your handmaiden of doom. I'll not let you succeed. You're a murderer. And, you're in cahoots with Crispin. You've made some deal with that black-hearted deBanco."

"Cahoots? Oh, my, dear Liv, nobody, but nobody uses that word anymor'. Well, maybe Lloyd, he might. I hear he proposed to you all las' night."

"Drop the accent," I said, putting as much chill in my voice as I could muster. "I'm the prize with my shares in Bajan White. I get it. I decide who gets Perfidia! DeBancos get Perfidia if Feron marries me. Whitelaw gets Perfidia if *he* marries me. Even Lloyd. You've introduced me for breeding like a Taddy mare. You thought if I got Perfidia for you, you'd win. That you would wrangle control from me. Think again."

"Wrangle?" Del patted Lacy's knee to let him know the next move was his. "They took everything from me.

Drayman, Colin—my friend Colin, you'll never know what he did, ever!"

"I will and when I find out, I'm...I'm out of your life. If I've learned anything, I've learned that Taddys know how to take care of business. They'll get you, Del. They will. And, know what, you'll deserve it."

Sun filtered into the room through the opened louvers as did a soft breeze making the temperature quite comfortable despite the wet heat outside.

"They won't, not this time." By the chill in his eyes, he meant what he claimed. He pounded a checker over his heart. "I know where the inheritance box is. Looks like I should have wooed Amanda like old Crispin."

Del rolled the dice then placed his checker. A small vein pulsed just over his left eye. In twenty-seven years, I'd never seen him either tense or angry. The smile, always the smile, the disingenuous lazy Southern-ness of it underneath which he operated at an unfathomable level of deceit. I gulped air to calm myself. It was as though a 10,000-watt charge drained from the room.

I sat at the corner of the bed, near where Del's cast ended, but as far from him as possible. I brightened my mother's eyes, produced my mother's smile and patted his bare toes. "Why now?"

"With the presumed incumbent nearing thirty-two years, the only way to stop the inevitable is by assuming control via a hostile takeover, a vote, or death. No one at Bajan White is going to vote me in, not even you. That Bajan boy's head is harder than a coconut shell, hard to kill; he is. Leaves me with a raid. There have been other raids."

"A century ago by brigands."

"Oh, my, Liv, oh, my, brigands?"

"I'm just a tool. I mean nothing to you. You stole me from my family. For all I know, you killed my mother."

"You think I denied you your family. This family, these people, they destroyed me."

How could Lacy move his backgammon piece, how could he sit there without hate in his eyes? He loved Colin Law; he raised his son. But, here he was playing backgammon as cool as one can be in an Egyptian cotton shirt on a Barbadian day. I didn't understand any of them, or it, or anything.

"I'm going to make this right, somehow. I take my trust, my shares with your 18 million in bearer bonds, and I make this right."

"You can't save her. You're a girl. You need a man to overcome Tad's misogynistic Code just to have access to the box. You're not the only game in town, Sonny. You're just the one I spent my life shaping. Don't get too righteous. You don't work out..." He shrugged and threw the dice.

"When were you going to tell me about my half-brother?"

"Wasn't, wasn't gonna tell you. Why ever would I do that, girl?"

"Because I have one!" I yelled, standing. "What about the other one? What about the one unborn?"

"Does it matter I don't know what you're talking about? Does it?" With an angry nod, he moved his checker. The vein over his eye was pulsing in a rhythm

Bob Marley could have made into a hit. "Man can't have secrets? A few secrets, Liv, tha's all, I deserve this?""

"Sophie!" I screamed.

"Sophie? Never touched that girl—just Peggy. Peggy must have had that key stuck where the sun don't shine. Never found it. Searched Sophie's, too. You telling me that second baby wasn't Colin's?"

Lacy's eyes met mine. He touched a red checker to his lips. I'd gone too far. I'd passed some threshold. I didn't like what I saw in Del's eyes. All the happy was gone, replaced by pure cunning. I regretted forcing Whitelaw to haul Del's broken body off the beach. Had it not been for me, this would have been over.

"You took everything from Brendan Whitelaw. You need to make it right."

As I stomped out the door and down the hall, someone closed the door to Whitelaw's spare bedroom. I knocked. No one answered. I rattled the knob. The door was locked. Someone was in there with Whitelaw's little toy soldiers, that bothered me. The same someone had heard my tirade. Lacy had tried to warn me when he put the checker to his lips. He had. Poor Lacy forced to care for the man who had left him bereft with an eight-year-old boy to raise. I put my hand to my mouth in horror. I had destroyed everything.

Feron peered around the corner of the newel post at the base of the stairs. "Ready?"

"Any luck with the young pirate?" I asked curbing the self-loathing that grasped my ankles preparing to crawl up my legs and consume me. Feron brushed a hand down my arm. He knew. Had he heard, too? I followed him, past the hideous monkey, down the stairs to the street where the Bentley sat illegally parked at the curb.

"Did what I came to do if that is what you're asking?"

The shadow of a woman watched us from the window where Del convalesced. Repugnance worked its way to my stomach and hate reached for my heart.

I was not the only game in town. Another woman was waiting in the wings. I hoped it wasn't Gail Kazarian. I hoped it wasn't my best friend.

"Which was?"

"Made sure your father can't get his hands on Perfidia. With Tad's key, we have Lin certain sure for Colin's death. Got it formally recorded at Bajan White."

"Formally recorded?" I snorted, opening the passenger-side door. The shadow left the window.

Feron narrowed his eyes at me. "We've long censured murder. We're not all immoral prigs. Can't do much, though, still not sure Del doesn't know where Colin stashed his take."

As I clambered into the seat, I sighed, one of those deep sighs that just sits at the bottom of the diaphragm. Apparently, killing during mooncussing was business, but premeditated murder was—well—murder?

"Oh, sigh!" Feron laughed, "You've gone all damsel in distress."

"Have not!"

A crazy wildness invaded his eyes. "Have too!"

I bumped my head on his shoulder. He put his arm around me. "He's evil, Feron. My father is evil."

Feron started the car after a quick, cutting glance. "We've lived it for so long it is hard to fathom that you didn't know."

I stared at my hands. Feron put an arm on the back of my seat as he pulled out into the street. From that vantage point, he played with the curls at the nape of my neck. What was the matter with me? Only days ago, he had tried to kill me, okay, scare me, off a cliff. I could have fallen to my death even with the ledge beneath me. There was a hair's breadth of difference between scaring and succeeding, or between my father and Feron's actions.

I waited for him to propose as he piloted us companionably back. The proposal didn't come on the ride to Perfidia, or during dinner. I was sure it was on his mind. I was the prize. Peggy had been right about that, not the key, but the prize. I held the majority of shares in Bajan White. Where I went, so went Perfidia.

When dinner ended with me un-affianced, I settled myself in the Great Hall on a divan, likely from Vent Amer, given the tigers woven in gold in the upholstery. I tucked my legs under me and stared at Estella.

Feron nudged his way next to me on the divan. He stretched his long legs out, feet flat on the floor. He put his hands behind his head then followed my eyes to Estella.

"Who needs a figurehead in their Hall anyway?" he asked.

"The foreman of the dig says she was here before the addition was built."

He cocked his head until vertebrae cracked. Next thing, his head was on my lap. I idly ran my fingers through the dark waves of hair lapping his ears.

"Certainly, they didn't move her when they remodeled. She's huge!"

"Maybe she was lashed to the tower, initially?"

Feron grabbed my hand. "From the sea, it must have looked like some cheap pirate ship sent down from the heavens, signal fire ablaze, Estella at the prow. I wonder if the mooncussers of yore ran up a jolly roger."

"Yo, ho, ho..." I ran a finger around the edge of his ear. "Tell me this, have you all been searching the cliffs and caves since Drayman died."

He stopped my fingers with his hand, "No. No reason to go hunting. Perfidia limped along. With the cliffs fallen in, no one believes Tad's stash still exists. As kids, we all prospected at the base of the rubble for fun, sort of a rite of passage, like hunting lion. If we'd ever found anything, we'd have passed out cold."

"Did Whitelaw's impending thirty-second plus six, set Del off? He says it did but what if it was what Aaron found that spurred him to action? Let's say Aaron just stumbles on the prize that can undo all of Del's work, because, be clear, he steered Perfidia's predicament to the point where she was his for the taking, heir be damned."

"Indeed, we had balance; now you've got control! Bloody hell, girl, what are you going to do with it!"

When he bolted upright, I scrambled to my feet and ran for the French doors to gain the veranda. He trotted after me. I ran down the gallery to the balcony stairs.

Feron caught me mid-stairs. Placing a hand on each shoulder, he backed me against the stair rail. I struggled. He pinned my shoulders against the railing like I was a walnut he intended to crack open in the vise of his hands.

"Don't you know?" He kissed me so hard my head bounced off the wall. The second kiss was gentler. The third time, I gave in slinging my arms around his shoulders. I waited for him to lift me in his arms expecting him to take the stairs two at a time and deposit me in the daybed. Instead, he raised my arms from around his neck, pecked my cheek then bounded up the remaining stairs.

When Feron's doors closed, I climbed to my room. There, I waited for that moment when the lights went out, when the Southern Cross bloomed, when Stella, me, could descend undetected to Estella, the star.

Day Ten

WHEN THE SOUTHERN CROSS lay low on the horizon and clouds scudded across the night sky, I changed into my camp shirt and Whitelaw's salty, worn jeans. I put the keys in the velvet bag from the safe deposit box then ran my belt through the loop and tucked the bag and keys in the front pocket of my pants. At the last minute, I grabbed the iron rod from the windmill from my hobo bag, hidden behind the door in a lump on the floor. Unsure what to do with the rod, I jammed it into the back pocket of my jeans where most of it stuck out. So, I stuck it through the front belt loops, ungainly, but safe and easy to grab.

I briefly considered rousing Feron but changed my mind, this was mine to do. Armed with my flashlight, I trod down the balcony stairs on tiptoe. A glance at my moonlit shadow revealed a half-mad ground squirrel up to no good with scant time to make this right.

I slid through the middle set of French doors into the Great Hall, crossing quickly to where Estella's feet stood on the mantel. She wore sandals carved in relief, a leather thong between her big toe and the rest. A star was painted in gold on her right foot, but not her left. On my tiptoes, I reached above my head to press on the star. Nothing moved.

Estella had to be the open sesame! I took two steps back. A rattle at the French doors made me turn. I thought I saw a shadow as windblown clouds tore towards the moon. A moon glade rippled across the shiny old mahogany leaving dark images laced across the floor. My shadow had been this and nothing more. The moon laid its soft light over the folds of Estella's dress.

The faint gold star on Estella's right foot wasn't alone, only brighter than the four others painted on her robe amid the binding rope. She bore the mark of the Southern Cross, the angle of the stipes pointing to the far corner of the fortress.

The original entry was through the archway leading to the old bastion. The walls of the front entrance hid the door to the tower. The wellhead was in the dining room. Other than the kitchen, Tad's bedroom was the only room whose secrets had not been revealed. Two walls of the kitchen bore windows, the third the hearth. After some searching, I found the rigging for the dumbwaiter to the tower in the fourth wall. The wood, when lowered, came to rest next to the original fireplace now open to the Hall via a decorative archway, most likely a Collier renovation. It had always been the two of them,

Tad building, Collier perfecting. As for Tad, he had never used a room twice.

With the kitchen out of the running, I went to Tad's bedroom. Three walls were limestone. The interior wall was river stone, rounded and mortared in no particular pattern. I studied the river rocks. The stones came in a variety of colors, from mottled brown to shimmering mica-engrained granite that reflected my light.

Stela, Stella, Estella. With the beam of my flashlight, I gathered five glittering stones into the stars of the Cross. The stipes was nose down to the floor, the patibulum at an angle on the wall, just like the Cross sat in the southern sky. I followed the lowest star in the patibulum to the highest. At a slight flaw in the wall, I pushed on the rock star. I twisted the stone. I pushed up on it. I pulled down.

The rock star slid neatly into a mortared space below to reveal a keyhole surrounded by greened brass. It hadn't been opened for a very long time. I jumped at another rattle of the doors, even imagining I heard stealthy footsteps. I checked through the archway. No one was there.

Back at the lock, I took both keys from the velvet bag. Tad's key didn't fit. Peggy's admonition of two keys, always two keys rang in my ears.

The Lady's key did.

A bolt slid back. A spring sprung. The section of wall bearing the Southern Cross opened on relic hinges. I flashed a beam of light into the opening. A flight of stairs descended a narrow bricked in shaft. The walls were no more than thirty inches apart, the height perhaps seven feet. No rail, just walls of rough limestone blocks.

In the dim light from the Hall, I made out a small handle on the inside of the door. I yanked the heavy old door shut using the interior grip. The minute the door closed, a bolt shot. I pulled down on the handle. The door remained locked. I pulled up. The lock remained shot. I pushed out. I pushed in. The bolt slowly receded. I could get out.

The stairs were limestone. Worn in spots, cracked in others, some edges sharp, some splintered, a fall would be deadly. I took the first step, dragging my left hand down the brick wall for balance while shining the flashlight down the stairs with my right. With each step the brick shaft grew colder, a weird clammy cold, rot mixed with dirt mixed with water.

Thirty-two stairs later, the down shaft ended at a brick wall. A wooden door held together by rusty iron braces was embedded in the bricks to my left. The middle bracket bore a keyhole. Tad's key worked this time. The corroded metal hinges on the door were stiff. I got a finger hold in the crack, breaking a nail for my efforts. Undaunted, I withdrew the iron rod from my belt loops and forced it into the crack, leveraging the thick door open enough to squeeze through into an antechamber, perhaps six feet square and seven feet tall.

Three tunnels branched, one in each wall like a chicken's foot. The left-hand tunnel ended fifteen paces down at a door. I tried the Lady's key. It didn't work. I tried Tad's key. It didn't work. Nor did the two keys assembled into one. Frustrated, I inserted the rod between the door and the jamb. The door opened easily.

The brick-lined cave was stuffed wall-to-wall, and floor to ceiling with white bricks encased in plastic. A half-inch layer of dust or mold covered the sheeting. Whitelaw's conviction that his father had never run drugs be damned. Millions of dollars' worth of white powder were evidence enough, minus two bricks, that this was Colin's stash.

Or was it? Amanda was sure Colin had paid off Perfidia's debts with the drugs he ran. Whitelaw believed his father was grifting someone who deserved it. Lacy's belief in Colin was absolute.

Del's words came rushing back: *Colin...my friend Colin, you'll never know what he did, ever!* But I did. Colin had mooncussed Del's shipments. Colin paid off Perfidia's debts with Del's drugs! Del hadn't killed Colin to get Tad's fortune, but to retrieve his own. Poor Aaron! I staggered out of the room under the weight of my certainty, only to see chipped wood around the bolt.

Aaron had forced the door open, the reason neither of the keys worked. I put the keys back in the velvet bag and tucked it into the front of my pants. Aaron had expected Whitelaw to fence the drugs, Del found out. Who had told him? Who would have known? I didn't like the answer, but I knew it had been Dave White. Aaron's friend, Whitelaw's neighbor. I would bet Colin's stash on it.

I pulled the door closed. Aaron's jimmy job had left the bolt perpetually open. I wedged the door with a chunk of loose brick from inside the chamber. It did the trick. Satisfied with what I'd found, I retraced my steps to the antechamber. The snicker of rock on wood came from the stair door. I rattled the door. I had the key needed to open it. Still. I waited. Silence. I flashed my beam down the tunnel to the right. I could just make out another door about twelve feet down. I ignored it and concentrated on the middle branch because I could see a downward slope to the shaft.

The central tunnel descended at a slow angle. My flashlight bounced off walls covered in slimy green mold. A drip hit the brick floor now and then. Otherwise, it was quiet. Not even the ever-present ocean roared.

Sixty paces on, disturbed cave dwellers swished their wings like leaves in the wind, readying to take flight. Soft squeaking followed. Eighteen paces later, the sloshing sound of waves in the cove echoed off the brick walls. Here, bats hung cheek to cheek from the ceiling. They rustled as I passed then refolded their wings until they looked like dark tear drops ready to fall. The bats reassured me that Aaron had found his way into this tunnel. Twenty-one steps more, the tunnel came to an end a narrow cleft hidden in thick brush.

The exit, through a tangle of small, prickly bushes, was angled thirty feet above the beach. A pyramid of limestone bricks was strewn down the cliff wall ending in a mound of rubble where the great hurricane had tumbled it. Rusting iron was tangled with weathered wood in the ruins. Dirt, gravel and more rocks rested atop the shredded metal. Five large stones, worn on one side, dirt covered on the other, lay newly over the jumble deposited by the slides.

A shelf of limestone jutted out over the tunnel opening, shadowing it night and day. Two palms had found enough traction to grow in the slumped earth at the reaches of the opening, one on each side. Once the palms had grabbed hold, bushes had followed stabilizing the soil. The narrow horizontal opening was invisible from above and below and when rocked in would have been impossible to find.

But, Aaron had found it then dug his way in, the only explanation for the newer rocks below and those carefully lining the tunnel walls. What little thing had led Aaron to discover it after centuries? He had left the answer with his doodled bats. He must have been on the beach either at dusk or dawn. The bats taking flight had caught his attention and his imagination. He watched for their return, maybe scrambled up the rocks toward where he had first seen them then dug his way into the tunnel.

I sprawled on my stomach close enough to the edge to see through the bushes. Crossing my arms, I rested my chin in their fold. The tunnel was well constructed and reinforced. It was the way in, just as the well had been the way down. Pick marks on the brick walls indicated the tools used to reopen the tunnel after the hurricane. Collier's work.

Tad, and for all I knew, Collier, deposited his take somewhere within these tunnels. The cache Colin adopted was either empty when he found it, or he emptied it, using its contents to pay Perfidia's way out of debt. Still, it seemed too easy to find to have been Tad's cache. Whatever had been or was in the first two caches hadn't mattered much to Tad. Because when it mattered, Tad built blinds and double blinds, keys that worked alone and in tandem, walls that moved, left clues for the generations and used a constellation as his code. Though the cliff wall had extended another forty feet before the hurricane, Colin's Heart and Collier's excavation were enduring proof that Tad's keyed-cache remained hidden in this tunnel behind yet another clue. Or, so I wanted to believe.

The shudder of rocks down a slope drew my attention to the beach. I parted the bushes using the back of my hands. Something wispy tickled my left hand. I reached for it.

A small bit of thread pulled from a knit shirt hung from a broken twig on one of the bushes. I knotted the thread between my fingers. How happy Aaron must have been with his delightful, well-conceived plan designed to do the most damage to weaken the deBancos while saving Perfidia. It might have worked except that Del had greeted him, not Whitelaw.

Whoever was on the beach tonight wasn't worried about being heard. Three men jogged down the beach, the quarter moon lighting their way. They stopped at the entrance to the cave behind the P. The tallest man raked his flashlight beam across the base of the cliff then into the cave.

Topper—it was Topper—left his companions at a trot his gun swinging in his hand with each stride. He fired into a crevice. The shot sent a fourth man scurrying under an outcropping, ducking rocks loosed by the bullet. Whitelaw by the way he moved.

Startled by the reverberation off the cliff wall, bats exited the tunnel in mass, flapping so near that my hair fluttered with the beat of their wings. The men looked up. It gave Whitelaw the opportunity to shimmy over an outcropping into a deep fissure.

Topper pointed to where the bats had exited. Dave and John started up the rubble. They were here because of me; because I asked Del about Aaron's bats. Del had been bat hunting the evening the Whites drove him aground. He hadn't been expecting someone, he had expected something. Because of me.

Topper's next shot ricocheted off the tumble of rocks to my left. Whitelaw pushed deeper into the fold of the cliff. Topper responded to the slightest sound of dirt snickering, firing first then repositioning to get a better angle on where Whitelaw hid before firing. Atop one of the large boulders, Topper fired two more shots that ricocheted from rock to rock.

When I heard a soft grunt, I waited, knowing I should do something, unsure what it could be. One thing I could do—I pulled the key bag from my jeans and dug a small hole under the rocks to the left of the opening. I stuffed the bag into the hole, dusted it with dirt and covered it with palm fronds. I kept the rod.

At another gunshot, I scooted forward for a better view. A rock pinged from the mouth of the tunnel to the rubble. John flashed his beam up the riprap toward where I hid. By whatever radar bats worked, they wheeled back at me full speed. I ducked. When they settled, I looked out.

Dave White was there, John in his shadow.

I scrambled back into the cave, stood and ran. Dave grabbed my hair. I jabbed back with the rod. He wrenched it from my hands. I grabbed his wrist and scissor kicked with all my might. Breath exploded from his lungs. I sprinted up the tunnel. My flashlight bobbed. Someone was between me and the stairs.

Feron!

"Liv," he said seductively, "Come."

I stopped, out of options. Feron blocked the stairs, Dave, the tunnel.

Dave trotted towards me. Feron covered the ten feet between us throwing me roughly behind him. I bounced off the bricks but stayed standing, pummeling his back with my fists. DeBanco backed, trying to trap me against the wall. I fought him. He shoved me hard enough to slam me into the stairway door, snarling, "The stairs."

Dave rammed his head into Feron's chest. Feron flew into me. I crashed into the door and oozed to the floor in a heap. Feron and I tangoed for a moment, Feron doddering in my feet. Dave took the advantage and swung the iron rod.

Feron's head bounced off the bricks. DeBanco lost his footing and fell askew in the tunnel. Dave kicked Feron in the left side once, twice...too many times. Feron clawed at the bricks trying to gain his feet. I screamed. It was too late. With one more blow, Feron was down.

Dave grabbed my hair, dragging me over Feron sprawled in the tunnel, his head at an odd angle on the wall. He wasn't moving. Blood darkened one eye. I think my light went out.

𝒫

I REGAINED CONSCIOUSNESS WITH an oily rag in my mouth, my hands tied to the roots of washed up palms deep in the crevice where I had last seen Whitelaw. The back of my head throbbed, my peripheral vision dazzled.

I tried to remember what had happened...none of it made sense. I must have dreamed Feron in the tunnel. I must have wanted him to save me. I must have. I had the only keys.

I spit out the gag and let loose a scream that echoed off the cliff wall. It brought Topper. He gave me a lazy grin, all the worse because it looked so much like Del's slippery Loosiana smile. Topper wrung the excess sea water out of the gag before stuffing it back in my mouth. He pulled a shoelace from one of his wet tennis shoes, placing it over the gag and cinching it at the back of my head. I struggled. The bindings on my hands tightened, cutting into my wrists. Topper checked them, patted me on the head then followed John and Dave up the scree to the tunnel's mouth.

The rising tide pulled me seaward. The moon set. A thousand pinpricks blazed light through the black fabric of the universe.

A log bumped against me.

I pushed it away with my right foot. It bumped back. Whatever it was, it was warm.

I rattled the palm to move the object away from my body. It rolled toward me on the next wave. Whitelaw. Blood flowed from a wound to his shoulder, leaving a thin red trail in the water. A raft of fronds and boards flung together by the sea kept him afloat. He must have struggled his way into the flotsam. Now, he was being pummeled by the clothes washer water into the gyre. We would die this way, Brendan Whitelaw and me.

I struggled to break my bonds. Rewarded by the snap of a palm frond, I pulled harder. Something sharp tore at my wrist. I tried to grasp it. Whatever it had been it disappeared with the next eddy. I stretched out my right foot to steady the raft debris trying to keep Whitelaw's head above water.

Hearing raised voices, I stole a look up at the tunnel. Topper stood on the edge stacking the white bricks as John handed them to him.

My foot cramped; the flotsam rolled heavily to the left. I tried to right it. It drifted out of my reach slowly rotating Whitelaw beneath its fronds.

For several agonizing minutes, I struggled to snag the raft with my right foot. A comber tore into the gyre, roiling the debris against a slab of limestone, surfacing Whitelaw's body. He sputtered to consciousness. Shivering from the damp and gasping for air in quick, racking breaths, he fought his way from the flotsam and got his knees under him. He shook his head, droplets flew off his hair, he ran his eyes over the cliff to orient himself. A wave tore around him slamming him to his knees. As he went down, he saw me. He struggled back to his feet fighting his way through the gyrating water to reach me. He pulled the shoelace from my mouth.

I spat out the gag and croaked, "Topper!"

Whitelaw picked at the knots in the wet rope that bound my hands, leaning heavily on me as he did. Done, he turned to me cushioning his left arm with his right hand at the elbow. "Topper shot, next thing I knew I was in the water. I floated out. When I came to, I saw the raft of flotsam. Not thinking, just trying to survive. It got caught in the tide, washed me into the whirlpool. Lucky!"

"Can we make it out?"

For an answer, he sat next to me. His teeth were chattering. I pulled him into the cusp of my left shoulder and rubbed his arm to warm him. He gasped. I stopped. My hand was warm from his blood.

"They've got Colin's Heart. John took it. They'll sell the stone—my stone. The stone was for us."

"I need to know who asked your mother to kill her baby?"

"In case, we don't make it?" he asked, quaking in my arms.

"No, in case it was Del."

Instead of answering, Whitelaw passed out. I needed to stop the bleeding then I needed to get him warm and somewhere safe. My gag had disappeared in the breaker tousled cove. I cushioned Whitelaw in the fronds then pulled my camp shirt over my head and folded it several times. With the bandage made, I yanked Whitelaw's web belt out of the belt loops. On my knees, I placed my blouse over the wound and used the belt to hold it in place.

Whitelaw put a hand over my hand as I exerted pressure on the makeshift bandage. "John Stoddard. I think she be ashamed to tell Dad."

At a clink on the rocks, I lay next to him in the fronds and pulled him back into my arms, trying to give him whatever warmth my body retained. It wasn't until a large chunk of Del's boat came at us that I realized the circulation in the gyre was increasing with the rising water. I held Whitelaw's head to my shoulder, and scooted us deeper into the palm fronds and roots, anchoring us, as he had done in the flotsam, high enough to keep our heads above water.

The bats soared out of the cave as the White's took new positions. Dave restacked the bricks at the crest of the pyramid. John took them down the riprap to the beach. Topper hauled them to a boat and loaded them aboard.

When the freeboard of the skiff was a scant three inches above the water, Topper revved the motor and sputtered around the southern headland. He was back within the hour, by then Whitelaw and I were afloat circulating and bumping off rocks with each blast from the ocean. Whitelaw lay chilled against me. There was nothing I could do to warm him. The breeze from the breakers was stealing both of our lives away.

Topper made three jaw-dropping trips around the headlands, the boat overloaded with Colin's stash, enough money to ensure the Whites were nobody's slaves or slaves to cane. The last load in the skiff, John and Dave joined Topper. The boat chugged toward the southern headlands, water lapping the gunwale.

A wave tore between the two rocks that formed the gyre and buffeted Whitelaw and me against the cliff wall. A piece of our raft pulsed out to sea. Whitelaw slipped from my arms and under the water. I grabbed for him. The fronds took me down. I grabbed the back of his shirt and rolled him over, just as the next blast hit us. I caught the fronds with one arm, cushioning Whitelaw with the other. We had to get out of the whirlpool before we were either pulled into the open ocean or pummeled in debris. I was chilled through and losing my fight. The backs of my naked shoulders were raw from rubbing in the palms. I could feel my strength ebbing, soon I would be unconscious.

They would win. Topper would return to release my body from the palm roots, expecting to find Whitelaw floating in the cove, crashing on the rocks like Aaron or Colin battered and fish eaten. I would join him.

Palm fronds, wood, seaweed, fish all swirled around us in an ever deepening whirlpool. A dark blue baseball hat with L.A. Dodgers embroidered across the front floated into my lap. Del hated baseball, but our next door neighbor did not. He bought the cap from her for ten cents at last year's garage sale. It had been he that day in the cove.

Del had done this, created this, arranged his own daughter's death. I hated him.

"Whitelaw." Despite the sound of the motorboat still pounding toward the headland, I knew that I had to get him to safety.

"Danny, please, girl," he murmured. I was glad of any response.

"Danny, then, we've got to go. It's our only chance." I put his good arm around my shoulder and stood. With the help of the roots, he got to his feet. We battled our way out of the gyre, fighting to keep above the circulating water, flung apart in the surf more than once.

The boat idled at the bar. Light bobbed across the water. The sound of our struggles must have carried over the water. Their searchlight scanned the whirlpool coming to rest on the fronds then glancing over the rocks where we hid. Another breaker crashed in and sucked us down. When the boat growled and turned out to sea, we emerged spluttering.

Wind, waves, weakness tormented us as we fought to gain footing in the riprap. Whitelaw slipped. We fell in a heap. I shoved him to his knees. He clambered up the rocks until of a single mind we reached the rubble beneath the tunnel. He lay on his back in the riprap struggling to breathe.

"Can you go on?"

He rocked to his knees and labored up the first boulder. The second one was too much for him. I knelt and signaled for him to step on my back. He shook his head. I wanted to scream, rely on me, but waited through two more weakening attempts. We made the remaining six feet to the tunnel. There was nothing to do except hope that the deepening tide washed our tracks and his blood away before the Whites returned to recover our bodies.

Whitelaw shimmied into the tunnel on his stomach. His head hit the limestone with a thud. I urged him deeper. He responded by crawling to mid-tunnel before collapsing. I tightened the belt putting more pressure on his wound. His gray eyes tweaked. His hands cramped from the pain then he passed out.

𝒫

I RAN BACK TO the cave entrance for the keys. I hated leaving Whitelaw, but I had no other choice. Del had made me recite the signs of exposure to him while on our hiking trips. Whitelaw had them all, plus the bandage was wet and likely doing little to stanch any bleeding. I coursed up the tunnel. I found the iron rod from the windmill in the antechamber. The end was tacky with blood. Dried blood was smeared on the wall. I rested hands on my knees to catch my breath before tackling the door and the thirty-two stairs. Panting furiously, I stared at the door to the stairs.

Feron had flung me behind him. I had pummeled him; he had tried to protect me. Because of me, Dave had beaten Feron with my iron rod with long latent fury, until deBanco was unconscious and helpless, or dead. I touched the dried blood, horrified at my culpability. What had they done with his body? Wrestling the key from the bag, I bumped the door. It opened. Feron had jammed the lock with a toothpick. All I had to do was push on the door, and we would have been safe. I fell to my knees, pounding on the stone wall. I gasped for control, stood, ran up the stairs to the small landing and pushed in on the knob. Once in Tad's bedroom, I shut the door behind me and shoved the rock star over the keyhole.

I took the balcony stairs two at a time, roared into the nursery and grabbed Peggy's medical bag from behind the door where she kept it. I checked Feron's room just in case; it was empty.

As I thundered across the Great Hall, footsteps echoed behind me. I didn't look. I recognized Lloyd's step.

I galloped down the stairs.

Lloyd grabbed the medical bag from my hand. "Where are we going?"

Reaching Tad's bedroom, I slid the small star rock down and shoved the Lady's key in the lock, the bolt shot back. At Lloyd's touch, we switched on our flashlights and descended the stairs.

I had left the door at the base of the stairs open. I pointed down the tunnel. Lloyd followed my finger. I stopped him when the thunder of the waves was loud on the riprap, and the bats began to stir. We stared at a pool of blood on the brick floor. Whitelaw was gone. I ran my hands over the walls. I trotted to the tunnel opening. I peered out.

A bloody hand print like a petroglyph marked the entrance. Why hadn't I seen it? Why hadn't I noticed? The White's had found Danny. Feron? Were they both awash in the raging sea?

Lloyd remained focused on the dark pool at his feet. I stayed out of his way. He flashed the beam over the tunnel walls. Stopping, he rubbed a spot on the wall then rubbed his fingers together.

He motioned me over with his flashlight. When I reached him, he played the beam over a rusty print on the wall. A scramble of bricks jutted out from the wall a scant half-inch appearing mislaid or shifted by time.

Lloyd handed me his flashlight. He put both of his hands on the middle brick then pushed.

He pushed again.

Tad had done this brickwork or possibly Collier. Beth provided all the clues: her portrait, her father's figurehead, her crewelwork, I kicked the brick closest to the floor. What clue did she offer this time?

Nothing. Lloyd shrugged. I shrugged back. Beth...what was left?

The original portrait of Beth was the only Beth icon I could fathom that hadn't, as of yet, provided a clue. Her hand rested on the rose carved around the keyhole of the inheritance box, yellow roses at the corners of her apron, roses on the pillows and comforters. Colin and his son had instinctively known how to gain access.

"A rose."

Lloyd backed against the wall and shined his light on the brickwork. A rose emerged in the shadows of the jutting bricks.

We stood, our heads cocked. We divided the work, each pushing on bricks. Lloyd flashed the light back on the rose, a P appeared, as well. I shoved the one block both designs shared. A rock-faced door swung open into a small tunnel. A bloody handprint gleamed on the jamb, another on the floor.

Lloyd signaled for me to crawl into the three foot by four foot high tunnel. I did. Immediately, the door shut. I kept crawling accustomed by now to being locked in.

The door opened. I heard Lloyd jamming something under it.

The tunnel took a sharp turn back into the cliff ten feet later. I made the corner. Five feet later, my way was blocked by Whitelaw's feet. I shined the flashlight up his body. He had passed out with one bloody hand pressed against an iron door. I shook him. He moaned.

I crawled back to the main shaft calling out, "He's unconscious."

Lloyd motioned me out, saying as he crawled in, "Watch the door, it swings shut."

As he scuttled in on the bricks, the sound of his shuffling knees filled the small space. Lloyd disappeared around the corner. He said something indistinct. He spoke again. A sharp noise that I hoped wasn't a slap was followed by scuffling.

"Danny, it's your brother. Dan."

A grunt rode the brick walls to me.

"Come on. Remember the time you jumped off the cliff. It's not that bad, not as much blood for sure. Can you crawl?"

A thud like a log hitting loam came round the corner.

"Look, you either bleed to death in here, or you crawl out."

The sounds of their pant legs chafing on the bricks stopped three times. Each time, Lloyd cajoled. Once,

Whitelaw must have hit the wall with his wounded shoulder. The whimper tore at me.

"Can you give us a hand, Olivia?"

I leaned in on my knees. Whitelaw crumbled five feet from the door. I got my hands under his arms and pulled him into the main tunnel far enough that Lloyd scrambled out.

At Lloyd's signal, I took Whitelaw's feet. We lifted him between us. Lloyd, at his shoulders, backed up the tunnel. Getting him through the narrow opening to the stairs proved a challenge until Lloyd got an arm under Danny and managed him through on his feet.

I stumbled on the bottom stair on shaking legs, trying to catch my breath. Lloyd motioned me aside. He lifted Whitelaw onto his shoulder and carried him fireman style up the thirty-two stairs. Whitelaw's back scraped along the ceiling.

I crawled up behind them. By the time I made the door, Whitelaw was on the floor in Tad's bedroom bleeding freely through my sorry bandage onto one of the precious hand-knotted wool rugs. Lloyd was bent over with his hands on his knees, huffing like a pile driver.

Amanda tottered into the entry in her spike-heeled mules. She dropped to the floor next to Whitelaw and immediately put pressure on the wound, cooing to him as she did. She gave Lloyd a sharp look. Lloyd took his hands off his knees long enough to point at me.

Peggy made the corner from the kitchen carrying a wool blanket that she laid out on the floor. We lifted Whitelaw onto it then each took a corner of the makeshift litter and carried him through the Hall and up the stairs to the room where he had taken Del.

Peggy took over from there, clucking to Whitelaw as she undressed him. She gave him a spit bath before tucking him into the lovely soft white bedding. Dr. Smythe soon arrived, scatting us out with both hands. Peggy stayed.

Amanda arranged herself in one of the wicker chairs on the balcony to wait. Lloyd took my hand and led me down the stairs, flashlights in hand. We fairly skipped through the Great Hall to the bloody rug in Tad's bedroom. The tunnel door was still open. We turned on our flashlights. Two steps later, I slid the door closed behind us.

We descended to the rose. Lloyd opened the door. It immediately swung shut. I played my light over the bricks. When I nodded, he pushed the block that opened the door. I shoved a brick near the hinge; it moved far enough to jam the door open. I waited for him where we had found Whitelaw. Just there the tunnel widened and heightened to accommodate the wood and iron door to the keep. The door was solidly locked. I fitted the two keys together. The key slipped in. After a moment of revolt, the bolt slowly retracted.

I shoved the armored door in.

We both took a deep breath then as of a single mind turned our flashlights into the man-made cave of limestone blocks. The room was seventy feet from cliff's edge, even now.

Tad had been a careful, organized man.

The gold and silver chains were on the left, all the set jewels on the right, gold coins cascaded from the back wall, and all items of questionable value were behind the door.

Colin's Heart was the least of what Tad Law had stolen from the innocents lured into his cove. Pearls flowed from one chest, rubies, emeralds, and diamonds were lumped together in another larger chest like semi-precious stones you bag for two dollars.

I have no idea how long I had gone without breathing. I only know that when I did breathe, I reeled from the oxygen.

A piece of paper, folded twice, rested on top of a chest overflowing with necklaces. Lloyd unfolded it while I shined my light on him. He held the note so that I could read it: *I, Colin Law, have on this day 09/23/46 borrowed one bright blue heart-shaped pendant.*

In response to the question in Lloyd's eyes, I answered, "Colin gave it to Sophie. She called it Colin's Heart. Whitelaw and I found it yesterday. John took the diamond from Sophie's cabin. Whitelaw tried to get it back, I guess. They must have thought Danny was there to stop them from their real objective, looting Colin's stash." I squeezed Lloyd's hand. "You called Whitelaw your brother?"

"Lacy didn't raise him alone. It was a joint effort."

"Amanda!"

"Amanda. Danny's more my brother than Aaron ever was. I couldn't have survived what he did. Imagine..." We stared at each other trying. Lloyd gave me a quick hug. "I want Danny to have this place Liv. He's born to it."

I gave Lloyd a peck on the cheek.

"Where's Feron?"

"Dave was...oh, Lloyd!" There was only one door left, the right-hand tunnel, after that we would have to scour the beach for his body.

We closed the inner door, locking it behind us. Then crawled out and let the tunnel door swing shut. The sharp shush of a bolt let us know it was latched. We walked single file to the antechamber. The right shaft descended slightly, ending at a door held closed by a board through iron hoops.

Lloyd opened the door. His whistle echoed off the limestone walls. I stepped around him. Muskets, musket balls, cannon balls, and kegs of black powder lined the walls, including newer wooden boxes dating from the Civil War. All the munitions that one pirate or his descendant would ever need for defense or for mooncussing.

And Feron.

Feron was tied to the iron handle on a chest of musket balls. Blood crusted his right temple, his eye nearly swollen shut. He looked at us through pained eyes over the gag jammed in his mouth. His shirt was open. A nasty bruise blued his ribs.

Lloyd untied him then helped him to his rocky feet. Feron gasped as I slid my shoulder under his left arm. Lloyd closed the armory door behind us. He closed the antechamber door, as well. With me to the front and

Lloyd to his back, we balanced Feron up the narrow stairs then supported him to a chair in the entry.

I shut the door to the keeps and slid the rock star back into place, patting each star in the cross before turning to the men.

Lloyd and I supported Feron to the gold chaise in the Great Hall in front of Estella. Lloyd went in search of Dr. Smythe. I lifted Feron's legs onto the chaise. When he gasped and grabbed for his ribs, I saw the damage Dave had done. I raised Feron's head and stuffed a pillow beneath it.

"What were you doing!" I screamed at him.

He shut his eyes at the noise. I fingered one bloody curl. "Protecting you, I thought. Dan told me about Colin's Heart. I got to Topper, who eventually coughed up the location of Colin's stash, something to do with bats. I tried to find Dan. I couldn't. So, I followed you. I saw Dave grab you. Then..." He closed his left eye, the right was now a pulpy purple mess looking more like an engorged leech than an eyelid.

"What did you do to Topper?" I asked, not sure I wanted to know.

"Scared him. Topper's pretty malleable when it comes to his fingers."

"He's a musician!" I slapped Feron's left arm. He squinched his good eye and whimpered. "I can't believe you would....no wonder Dave kept kicking when he had you down."

"Liv, from the minute you showed they've been bollixing up the works. The first person you confide in—the first—is Dave White!"

I took a deep breath. "How did you get to the chamber?"

Feron blushed, I think, his face was so bruised it was hard to tell. "Collier gave his sister, Best, a copy of the Lady's key. Lacy had an impression of Tad's key made before you reclaimed your purse."

"Where are the keys now?"

"Dave took them, must have. When I came around, they were gone. I've screwed this up royally."

I brushed a curl from his forehead. "Look at you, you want a good scrubbing."

"Whitelaw?"

"Topper shot him. Whitelaw saved me. Then I saved us. Well, not alone. Lloyd came to the rescue."

"Should have been me. You shouldn't have been hurt."

I played with his wavy hair where it brushed his ears.

"They took it, didn't they? We've lost her, haven't we?" he asked.

When I didn't answer, Feron opened his left eye. I waggled my eyebrows.

A great, happy grin spread across his face. He winced then gave a huge sigh.

"Oh, sigh," I mocked.

Dr. Smythe appeared through the French doors with Lloyd hot on his tail. The doctor took one look at Feron and pulled a small flashlight from his bag. Satisfied with Feron's eyes, he checked mine.

"One concussion, none for the girl," Dr. Smythe said, "But, girl, you need a bath to warm up, be sure to soak in it and follow up with liquids. I suggest you get to it before you get any colder."

The men stared at my drying bra. I blushed.

"She keeps giving her shirts to the needy," Feron quipped, even that hurt him.

"And, you, young man, need a night's rest and your ribs wrapped, at a glance." Dr. Smythe and I helped Feron to his feet. The moment we gained the balcony, Lloyd took over for me. Amanda ushered me directly to my bathroom where Peggy had drawn a hot bubble bath. The bubbles soon enveloped me. I slept my head against the iron tub, only to wake with a scream.

Lloyd rushed in. I covered myself as best I could with bubbles. He sat on the edge of the tub and washed my hair. Satisfied that my mop was clean, he toweled my wet hair dry until it curled then kissed the top of my head. I grabbed his wrist. "Del has the keys. They stole the copies off Feron.

He hugged me, "They don't fit together, I'm sure of it. Lacy made the impression of only one side. I saw the keys made from the impressions. No channels. They would never lock together."

"But the key Crispin had made to get into the well!"

"The old pirate lied. Crispin had a locksmith out who was able to pick the lock, but no key made. My guess is that you and Peggy are the only ones who knew there were truly three keys."

"Topper?"

"Danny always warned me about him...tutted over me like an old hen." Lloyd gave a rueful smile. "Lacy called for you. Your father's gone. A woman arranged for his transport. Lacy seemed relieved to be rid of them."

I began to obsess over Gail. Had it been Gail I saw in the crowd, had it been she at the window? She had Del's *jus' in case papers* at the bank in Bakersfield. Del's couriered note: *by now you and Gail*. The image of Gail swiping at the reflected light of the diamond on the bank's wall with her talons splayed haunted me. The only thing missing had been a cackle. *You're not the only game in town, Sonny*. What had he promised her?

Lloyd held a towel out for me. "According to Lacy, she is small and mean."

I stood in the bathtub. Lloyd wrapped the towel tight around me then gave me a rough rub down. Finally warm, he ushered me into my room where he left me to dress. I dressed in Whitelaw's linen trousers and my camp shirt. I didn't bother with shoes. I was going nowhere else tonight.

Lloyd waited on the balcony leaning on the railing surveying the vast emptiness of the ocean. When I joined him, he covered my hand with his.

"Where were you in all this?" I asked.

"I heard you go down the balcony stairs. It was nearly a parade. Feron rattled down the keep stairs after you just as Crispin deBanco came into the Great Hall with the local coppers and a warrant for Whitelaw's arrest. I slammed the door behind Feron while Amanda distracted Crispin. Crispin claimed Danny was complicit in grounding the White Lady and in Aaron's death. Amanda was at her fluffy mommy best, swearing at Crispin for sinking so low. Quite the row! She kept signaling for me to leave. I did. I couldn't very well follow you down, so I came round."

"But..."

"I went to the south dock first to get the cruiser, damn near ran into Topper. Watched them load their take on the cabin cruiser for a bit. After, I went to the north landing. Got a skiff. Ran into a bit of a chop coming around the headlands. Found a crusty, bloody gag, some frayed ropes, and broken branches. Searched the whirlpool for you. Puttered around checking every pod of flotsam. Came back. There you were with Peggy's medical bag in your hand."

"It wasn't their take, it was Colin's stash, all of it, all the white bricks, three boatloads. The drugs will be on the market by tomorrow. In a matter of hours, the Whites will have what they need to pay her debts. They can buy her outright for the taxes," I whined.

"They want the freedom they think the money will buy. The Whites don't want Perfidia; they just don't want us to have her either," Lloyd responded.

"Are you sure? What if Del is in it with them?"

Lloyd took my hand. A stiff wind had risen, the French doors whistled in A flat. As we passed Feron's door, Dr. Smythe was still taping his ribs. Amanda met us outside Whitelaw's room with a finger to her lips and a .45 tucked into the waistband of her silk slacks. Reassured it was us, she stepped aside.

I knelt by the bed. Whitelaw held his right hand out for mine. I took it.

Leaning close, I whispered, "We found Tad's cache. And, we found this."

I held the IOU open so Whitelaw could read his father's words. At his sweet smile, I couldn't help myself, I kissed his forehead. Danny closed his eyes. When he slept, I left. I glanced back through the doors. Amanda was brushing Danny's hair off his forehead with her lacquered fingertips. She adjusted her chair to be closer then took his hand in hers, her third son, the boy she had mothered since he was eight. How had I missed that?

Unable to sleep, I sat on the balcony staring at the Southern Cross until it set. Del had gone missing, with a woman—Gail for lack of a better name. She would be no more than an accomplice though she wouldn't know it. I knew my father; I'd heard his threat. Perfidia was at greater risk not less, no matter what Lloyd chose to believe.

I couldn't stay at Perfidia. I didn't belong to her. I was as guilty as Del. It was only by chance that Whitelaw and Feron hadn't died tonight saving me. I didn't deserve them. With one last wistful look at the starry horizon, I went to bed.

In my dreams, I sailed on a square-rigger into a small bay. A sandbar tore at my hull. The ship rocked to one side, flames shot through the sails. I jumped overboard in layers of petticoats.

I guess I died.

Summer's End

AMANDA STAYED WITH WHITELAW the night. As I entered, she ratcheted herself out of a rattan chair by Whitelaw's bed, smiled, touched my shoulder and left. I sat where she had been; Whitelaw's eyes fluttered open. His right hand lay on top of the sheet that covered him. I held his hand. It was hot. I placed the back of my other hand on his brow. He sighed.

"Thank you," he said, giving my hand a weak squeeze, "For saving me, saving us."

"Hardly. The Whites have your father's cache, the spare keys to Tad's treasure, thanks to Feron, and Colin's Heart because of me. Del has gone missing, leaving a Voodoo-like curse that Perfidia is in more danger not less." I kissed Danny's hot forehead. "I'm going home. The litany of Del's transgressions is too long for any of you to either forget or forgive. Leaving is the only thing that makes any sense."

Whitelaw's gray eyes, dull from pain and fever, never left my face. "I would argue otherwise," he whispered.

"If I don't go, I won't have a shred of self-respect left. It was fun to be pursued, to be romanced even if it was for my shares of Bajan White. But, I'm not a pirate's maiden, I'm not Tad's Beth or Best deBanco, I teach school."

"Again, I would argue otherwise. You've been splendid."

"Peggy told me Feron's sister, Felicia, is gorgeous, very Latin, that Amanda handpicked her for you. If you marry her, Crispin gets a piece of Perfidia. It's one way to restore the balance."

His eyes slid away from my face. No argument this time, but it was okay. I squeezed his hand, kissed him one more time then walked out of the room, managing not to look back or cry.

Feron was sitting in one of the balcony chairs in loose slacks and a light shirt. The shirt was unbuttoned displaying yellow above and below his wrapped ribs. His right eye was a swollen, spongy, black mess, his open left eye dull. His hair was a tangled mop. He hadn't shaved.

He patted the arm of his chair. I sat. He put a hand on my butt. "I've screwed it up royally. And, I lost the keys."

"You didn't see Dave coming?"

"Just you."

I kissed the top of Feron's head. "Only three of us know the tunnel's final secret—the keys don't matter. It's just the centuries of trust broken."

"I should be fired."

"You should cut yourself some slack. Tomorrow, when the bruises start to heal, you'll be your old goofy, rakish self. I have to go now, but if you showed up in Bakersfield some day for a dance, I wouldn't say no."

Feron's eyes shifted to the horizon. "We'll get this cleaned up then I'll come for my dance. Practice, will you?"

I left my proxy vote for the heir with Amanda. Voting was easy. Leaving the heir was not.

Lloyd drove me to the airport where he kissed me goodbye, sweetly, intently and lovingly, my dear friend. I cried as I boarded my flight. I was still crying when it landed in Puerto Rico

The next day, I cried from Los Angeles, over the Grapevine until I saw Bakersfield shimmering in the valley heat. Lloyd called the house four hours to the minute after my flight landed in Los Angeles to tell me how much I was missed. I asked after Whitelaw; Lloyd assured me he was strong enough to sit up, ask for me and slurp soup. I asked after Feron; Crispin had disinherited him.

I unpacked, changed into a man's tee-shirt and crawled into the comfy old sheets on my bed overcome by the chaos I'd created. It was 4:00 in the afternoon. The telephone in my office rang. The brrrrg-brrrg induced me to turn over. In that in-between state, Whitelaw's voice incanted: *She began to cry. It put me to sleep. Can you imagine?*

I woke at 8:00 a.m. on the first Friday of September, knowing I'd had two offers of marriage. One proposal came from a man unsure of his sexuality and one from a man too sure of his. It *had* been nice. But, I wasn't the prize from some raid. I was me, Olivia Lassiter, found at the four corners.

For all my braggadocio, the moment I pulled on a pair of my soft, broken-in Levi 501s, I broke into tears. It was a good thing they buttoned all the way otherwise I would have been incapacitated for the day. My red and white striped blouse did nothing to brighten the detour in my mood. Every time I thought of Feron, I saw his sad eyes as I left. He had lost everything for me. And, Danny would lose everything again because of me.

At the airport, Lloyd had requested that I return the ruby and pearl necklace from Del's safe deposit box, so my trusty Gremlin and I poked our way down H Street to the bank. I showed the safe deposit teller my ID. She called the manager. He was very patient with me as he explained that my father's lawyer had emptied the safe deposit box shortly after the DEA had left. The box had been reassigned since. The manager walked off, leaving me staring at a mural of a stagecoach roaring across the plains a cloud of dust blooming in its wake.

I detoured by Gail's office to pick up my mail. Her secretary handed it to me then informed me that Gail was on a long-planned vacation. They did have a number where they could reach her, but it was for the use of the law firm's partners only. No matter how I cajoled, the secretary refused me the number.

I sat in the car sorting through the mail. I needn't have bothered. It was all mine. The absence of Del's mail and the empty safe deposit box led me to the inevitable. Gail was Del's lawyer, had been Del's lawyer. Del's warning rang in my ear. Indeed, I wasn't the only game in town. Gail had been his fall back plan from the beginning. Now, they'd gone missing.

But, what could they do? I was the prize, I held the shares, I controlled the vote.

As I carried the groceries into the house, the telephone rang. It was Marge Jones, the principal of my school. Marge asked me to drop by around 3:00. I promised to be there, eager to gossip about my new class of eight-year-olds with the young teacher who had substituted for me. My teaching juices flowed. I looked forward to the busy days of projects, papers, and joy. I would forget my father and the damage he had done. I would try to renew my relationship with the Taddys, one built on trust, maybe I could be part of a family after all.

Putting away the groceries, I began to worry about what else Gail had taken. A walk-through of the house revealed Del's empty closets and his missing giant-size suitcase. Cardboard boxes stacked against one wall were labeled in Gail's hand. A picture of Del and I leaned forgotten on his dresser.

The lid of his roll top office desk was closed and locked. The key, kept in the lock, was missing. The painting of Perfidia, flames trees draped across the hip roof, was on its hinges exposing the open and empty safe. Everything missing was Del's, his by rights. Knowing he had vacated lightened my mood. I didn't want to see him again. Ever! I repeated the incantation out loud. The words boomeranged back to me.

At 3:00, I drove down A Street to Roosevelt Elementary School. I walked into the low-slung blond brick building, dressed in one of my shirt-waist teacher dresses and matching flats. Marge Jones was waiting for me in the conference room, as was the Superintendent of Bakersfield City Schools, the school secretary, and a teacher's union representative armed with a tape recorder. Marge ushered me to the chair at the head of the conference table, a cup of coffee, a white pad of lined paper, a pen, and a box of tissues awaited me.

Marge wore her happy, principal dress of multi-colored flowers, the one she wore to brighten her difficult days when some principal duty went against her principles. Marge sat next to the Superintendent, looking as though she would prefer to be in her office disciplining children. The Superintendent cleared his throat. The union rep twiddled his pencil. The secretary wiped tears from her eyes.

"What is this about?" I asked to get whatever was to come done.

Marge slid my application towards me. I read it.

"We have been informed that the birth certificate you provided for identification is a forgery. As a consequence, all other documentation given to the school district is as well. In lieu, of a valid birth certificate, social security number, and teaching credentials, we have no choice but to let you go."

"My father kidnaped me when I was six. They are the only documents I have."

"We were warned that you would claim something similar." Marge clasped her fingers so tightly that her knuckles turned white. "We have done our due diligence. We acknowledge that your teaching certificate is valid, but issued under a false name. Further, all documents, except the birth certificate, post-date your majority. We had to inform the police. I've been asked to obtain your driver's license and passport."

"I don't have my passport with me. It's at my home."

Marge grimaced. "I'll have to ask the police to drive you home. You can give the officer your passport at that time."

"I'll have no way to get around or even shop."

"You'll have to use a taxi until you can clear this up." Marge reached for my hand, "I'm sure you can, probably in a matter of days."

"Will I get my job back when I do?" Four sets of eyes hit the table hard enough to bounce.

Police Officer Driscoll escorted me to my car and drove me home. His partner followed in their police cruiser. Driscoll parked my Gremlin in the garage, staying with it until I produced my passport and my license. He closed the garage door as he left.

Bakersfield sprawls, miles in either direction. The closest grocery store is three miles away, the airport ten and the mall six. Without a car, I could starve to death in the middle of town. Without identification, I couldn't cash a check or withdraw money from my account. As cruel as it was, I couldn't see how Gail's actions in Del's interest related to obtaining Perfidia or to ruining the family. But, I knew it did.

I needed legal advice, so, though it was late in Barbados, I picked up the telephone in my office and called Parradine and Whitelaw. When Lacy answered, I couldn't find words but must have made some small noise.

In his soft burr, Lacy asked, "Olivia? Is that you? Don't hang up. Please, lass."

I opened my mouth, and my troubles tumbled out.

"Oh, lass, oh my dear." It was in the gentleness of his words that I realized the depths of my dilemma. "Not to add to your misery, but we traced your father and his woman friend to Cartagena. No one here thinks that's good. He has contacts, you know."

"Did he call this woman Gail?" I asked.

"Small dark-haired woman, quite beautiful, she could wear Amanda's clothes—that small. She seems capable. Had transport set up, arranged a hospital in Venezuela, that sort of thing. Have you any funds, at all?"

"I do."

I hung up and called a taxi. The ride to my bank took my last ten dollars. I converted the $360 BWI left from the money that Feron had given me at Sam Lord's Castle a lifetime ago. It came to $171.00. When I tried to supplement it with cash from my credit card, I was told my card had been revoked.

I felt the small safety net of dollars in my pocket as I walked the four miles home rather than spend another ten on a taxi.

P

WHEN THE WATERING SYSTEM thumped on at 4:30 a.m., I ran to the door. No one was there. When the mail was dropped through the mail slot and slid across the wooden floor, I ran to the front door. No one was there. When Del's telephone rang, I galloped down the hall to answer it.

Gail's voice tumbled over the line. She didn't bother with hello, or how does it feel to be raped with your clothes on, or aren't you in a pickle. She just said, "Your father and I are in Cartagena. It's beautiful here."

"He's a murderer. You do know that?"

"We've been seeing each other for nine years. He put me through law school. I incorporated his production house. I have his signing authority. Seriously? You expect me to believe he's a murderer."

Anger gorged up my throat. I managed only an uncivilized response. "Del murdered his best friend. He killed my cousin. He stole from his family. He is a rapist."

The line pulsed in the silence.

"I called as a courtesy to let you know that we are married. Del has a new will. He's left me his business and his plantation, Vent Amer, in trust for our child who will inherit at 32 years, plus six which I believe is in keeping with the Code. By now you know the safe deposit box was released. The bearer bonds are cashed and deposited into an off-shore account. Our child and any subsequent children are now the beneficiaries of your trust. He did leave you his house."

"And Bajan White."

"Vent Amer is no longer entailed to you. According to the Code, you cannot own Bajan White stock. You are disowned. As a requirement of the corporate by-laws, you must cede your shares. A document will be delivered by courier today. Once you sign, as you must, your shares will become mine, and I will administer Vent Amer and vote my shares as Del directs me until the entailment ends."

"I keep the stock. I block any takeover attempts. Tell your new husband that."

"Del thought you might react this way. He instructed me to inform you that he ordered the sale of the house you now live in if you do not sign."

"My father told you to sell our house out from under me? You would do that to me?"

"I have a contract with a realtor in my briefcase at this moment."

"He hates me that much!"

"He gave you everything for twenty-seven years. You gave him nothing in return. He feels you deserve nothing, as well."

"Gail, he is the worst kind of evil. He has no compass. Why do you think you're different? Why?" This was the person I had thought was my best friend, I had to attempt to make her understand what she had chosen when she allied herself with Del.

"I'm a lawyer. I drew up the papers. As long as I'm alive, I own Vent Amer. You get nothing and Bakersfield." Greed flowed over the telephone line there was no other interpretation for the tone of her voice. I saw her talons grasping for the diamond's light at the bank, ten days and a lifetime ago.

"You won't win, Gail. You won't." The line went dead.

It was Saturday, Barclay's would be closed. I would have to wait to confirm that I had been replaced as the beneficiary of my trust until Monday though I was certain it was true.

Gail had everything; I had nothing.

I stared at the painting of Perfidia. I felt the rain in the tower, the coals between my feet and the roar of a signal fire. The Southern Cross was invisible in the scudding clouds of a wind-tossed night where mooncussers and pirates ruled reason. I had been lured in and shipwrecked.

A piece of white paper on Del's desk called to me. I practiced writing Stella Harris until the S was fully developed and flowed though I had no desire to be a Harris of Vent Amer about whom words like fence, thief, mooncusser, and murderer were invoked. I had loved Del, adored him, thought him the best father in the world.

I was his plan for revenge. I had left Perfidia in a shamble of damaged heirs, found treasure, lost diamonds, disputed shares, liens and loans and mortgages. No good had come of my adventures.

With a knock on the door, the courier came and went. A thick manila envelope addressed to Stella Harris lay unopened on the kitchen counter. I had no intention of opening or signing my shares away. Del and Gail would have to come for me.

I fell asleep in the folds of the overstuffed chair in the jungle room. When I woke, I made a dinner of macaroni and cheese from the box enhanced by a hot dog, frozen the previous Fourth of July.

When dinner didn't come back up on me, I took an evening walk to the nearest liquor store. I bought a gallon bottle of Gallo Paisano hoping to make it home before drinking it out of the brown paper bag. If planter's punches gave me a commanding rum drunk, I could only imagine the damage cheap, tasty red wine could do.

With any luck, I would pass out cold and wake up on Monday when I would clear up this mess with the organizations that identify you as you. Monday seemed years away. I searched the night sky for any old friend.

Orion hung hip up in the early autumn heavens. My eyes followed the stars of his belt. I joined them with a belt of my own, one finger crooked in the glass finger-hold on the jug.

My head hurt. My teeth felt like a bad velvet painting, crusty lumps and all. My eyes were pasted shut. I stared at the ceiling in my bedroom listening to the watering system. Hours later, the carillon at the

Catholic Church, three blocks up and over, rang at 8:00 a.m., then 10:00. I considered getting up and cleaned up, despite post-wine complaints from my stomach. Instead, I watched a spider, about the size of a quarter, stroll across the ceiling. I waited for the spider to fall on me, wrap me in its silk then eat me bite by bite.

When the church bells rang noon, I rolled out of bed, pulled on my sweat pants, stuck my feet in a pair of furry slippers and slumped into the kitchen. The refrigerator was jammed with healthy food. I turned to a box of cinnamon rolls with frosting drizzled over them. Four cups of coffee and a six-pack of rolls later, I built up the reserve to get the newspaper off the front porch.

A photograph of Colin's Heart dominated the area above the fold. The headline blared *Jewel Surfaces after Centuries*. Collectors had pooled to purchase it off the black-market hoping to donate it to a museum, or so they said. The slot machine rolled three Del's. After two centuries, Colin's Heart, worse Colin's promise, was lost to Perfidia. My own heart ached.

Next thing I knew, I was walking toward the pale blue house with brick trim and a navy blue double door where Gail's parents still lived. After three knocks, Gail's father opened the door. He looked at me like I was selling encyclopedias.

I gave a small wave of goodbye and turned back through their picket fence. He called after me, "We're so pleased for her. We look forward to being grandparents."

I kept walking down the sidewalk, down the next street until I came to the fence designed to keep people from drowning in the Kern River. I wiggled my way through a hole cut in the chain-link fence that had been there since Gail and I had played on the banks of the river as children then as teenagers. The Kern can be fierce. In the spring, it eats people lured in by the soft, flowing surface. Like most things in life, the undercurrent was all that mattered.

I took off my shoes, sat on the shore and dug my toes into the sand of the empty river bank. The sun wrapped its arms around me. Gail was pregnant. Like Topper, I was jetsam.

I sailed rocks into the middle of the river bed. I made goose calls by wetting the leaves of a long, thin-leafed bush. I built a dodgy castle of sand and stone that likely would stand until spring. It had a tower on one side. I broke twigs then laid a tiny fire at the highest point in the castle. Dusk came and with it the breath of the setting sun. With a light breeze to my back, I headed home.

My neighborhood hadn't changed. Couples walked hand-in-hand in the evening. Kids rode their bikes, families grilled in the backyards of their custom built homes with pristine yards and matching thirty-foot ash trees. Reaching Del's house, I picked up some stray leaves from the unmown lawn and dumped them in the trash can before entering through the unlocked front door. Why lock, everything of value was gone?

I flicked on the television. Telly Savalas was stuffing a sucker in his mouth. Crimes were solved first by Kojak then by Mannix. Tires squealed through parking structures, bodies were found, perpetrators arrested, ends tidied. It was clear that the writers had never met the Taddys.

My empty bottle of Paisano rested on the end table, residue from the fermentation littered the bottom of my red wine glass. I thought of getting out of the chair. Instead, drunk, depressed and dour, I slept where I was.

I WOKE MONDAY TO the realization that Gail had my birth certificate. Without it, my plan to regain my identity was sunk. A pot of coffee later, I called Barclays. Del aided and abetted by Gail had, in fact, left me penniless. My wine extravaganza had left me $166.00; I would have to take care if I was to make it last. I had no idea until when?

The telephone rang. It was Amanda. She wanted me to know that an emergency meeting of Bajan White had just ended. "Del's lawyer requested reassignment of your shares in Bajan White as required by Code given that you hold no land. The action was blocked by three votes."

"Thank everyone for me will you."

As patiently as Amanda could, given it was she, she said, "We can't hold them off for long. Your father can't own stock. With Vent Amer now entailed through his pregnant wife, you can't own stock. It would take a consensus vote and a rewrite of the corporation and family by-laws for you to be able to keep and vote your shares."

When the other end of the line jittered too long, I asked, "And?"

"There will be a re-vote on the heir. Del transferred Vent Amer to his wife before the vote. Which means your vote doesn't count. Brendan will lose this time."

"Del's won hasn't he? I don't even exist anymore."

"Enough of that!" A huff only Amanda could produce followed. "As for Del, he has retained Vent Amer through his wife and will manage his shares through her as well. He took a cut for fencing Colin's stash and a larger one for the diamond from what we hear. But, he murdered Colin. We have that in our back pocket."

She meant the Taddys, the people who belonged to de lady, not me.

Gail was right, I got Bakersfield.

After hanging up, I went to the door for the newspaper. It was a gorgeous fall day. The temperature was a perfect 79 degrees. The trees were just beginning to consider fall, in anticipation of the change, yellow tipped the ash tree on the front lawn.

The unmown grass had started to seed.

In my blue short, shorts and yellow tee-shirt, I rolled out the lawn-mower. Grass clung to my reel mower as it tore the long grass. It would take several swipes to get the lawn neat. My next door neighbor waved as she drove by on her way to work. One of the kids down the block called *hey* as he peddled by on his way to school.

Whitelaw once said that twenty-four years was a long time and that he was afraid he was filled with anger, turns out twenty-seven years of lies was devastating.

I leaned on the mower handles to scratch my ankle. A man skillfully parked a bright red rental car at the curb. The fact that the car was red and not gray was a good sign. The moment the driver's head cleared the door, my eyes lit. Feron, in a business suit, carrying an exquisite hand-tooled valise, took one look at the wet grass and chose the driveway.

"Came for my dance," he grinned, smelling as always like freshly printed money.

He motioned me to the drive with his head. When I reached him, he ran a finger along the edge of my shorts. He saw the glint in my eyes and gave me his goofy grin. He had stitches in his right temple, but his eye was open, and his shiner was fading from black to yellow.

"Sorry, it took me so long. I stopped in Louisiana. Celia was waiting with a notarized birth certificate, some photos, and a notarized letter." He dropped his valise to the driveway and reached into the pocket of his suit coat, removing an envelope that he handed to me. "I suggest you change into something acceptable to meet whoever we need to meet with to get you back what we can."

"Lloyd told me Crispin disinherited you over my debacle."

"He'll recant. There's just Felicia and me. My sister has her eye on Michael LeChance. Crispin and Amanda always planned she would marry Danny. See how neat that is? But that's a hard sell for both parties involved. Felicia doesn't want to marry Danny and vice versa. It would be an awful match. So, Felicia will marry Mike and Maison Vol, which will put me back in good standing."

I put my hands on his chest. He took me in his arms, my sweaty face plastered against his bright white shirt. I felt his wrapped ribs beneath my cheek.

"On the bright side, I'm still employed. Lloyd forgives me my inability to keep anything secure at all. And, as my boss, it's his call. Though, between you and me, I think it's a sympathy vote."

Feron put a hand under my chin and raised my face to his. He kissed me until my knees weakened. Satisfied, he checked me over, his eyes suddenly sunny. "Girl, you want a good scrubbing."

I scampered to the house. He followed me in through the open front door, his valise in his right hand. He made himself at home in Del's room while I showered. When I emerged, he was on the phone in Del's office. After a moment of listening, he answered, "I'll do my best."

"Who was that?"

"Danny." He scanned my body. By his rakish grin, he was apparently pleased with what he saw. I wore a flowered dress that hit me mid-thigh and the black Mary-Janes I had worn to Aaron's funeral.

"How is Whitelaw?"

"Better. If we can weather this, Danny will get Perfidia. The Whites will officially be part of the family. Too bad John and his couldn't wait."

"What's being done?"

"John and Dave have an offer in on Sam Lord's Castle. Dave's got the experience. I've put some pressure on my new hotelier friends to push the sale. Topper is considering his options. He's leaning toward the music industry. Everyone is doing something positive with their third."

"So, everyone but Del has profited from his drug running."

"You sound like you think that's wrong." He narrowed his eyes as though trying to conjure my thoughts, adding, "Dan wanted to charge Topper with Aaron's murder and attempting to murder him. I reminded Danny that it would be hard to prove Topper intended to kill him, Whitelaw was a threat and Topper shot. Topper could have tracked Danny and finished him, but he didn't. Though, he probably hoped Danny would drown, but prove that! Frankly, I still think Del killed Aaron. Motive and opportunity, every time."

When my eyes shot to the carpet, he lifted my face to his smile. "First things first, Social Security or passport? I'm voting for a passport."

Four hours later, we parked back at the house. I had a temporary driver's license, my passport application in and my social security number back. Feron was magic. The women behind the counters swooned, the men kowtowed to him. He kept my hand in his and paid for everything. From time to time, I'd catch him glancing at me, his eyes withdrawn and his lips pursed.

"Smile, girl, will you? Please. You're breaking my heart."

I tried. I was someone again. But, I wasn't Olivia. Olivia had been a teacher, someone's best friend, someone's beloved daughter, me for twenty-seven years. I felt the arms of Dondé LeChance holding me, whispering her love, waving as we left in the rickety old car. Del had taken more from me than I could ever measure.

"Would it help if I told you my bruised ribs hurt and that I see stars in peripheral vision?" Feron kissed my cheek. "Marry me."

I tucked the top of my head on his chest and had the first real laugh I'd had since the last one we shared. "Why? Why would I do that? You slapped me. You threw me off a cliff...okay onto a ledge. You locked me in at least once."

"Did not."

"Did, too.

With a sheepish grin, he said, "You wouldn't stay in one place long enough for me to succeed at my job. You made me crazy."

"Lloyd told me that I made him want to roll on the lawn."

"You make me want to settle down, father children, build an empire and give you everything you ever wanted. Marry me." The earnest avowal caught me off-guard. But not so far that I forgot that if I married him, my shares would be attached to Pendu, providing the deBancos the power they sought and the oomph Feron needed to get back in Crispin's good graces. And, there was the other, I would always wonder when next his eyes would go stormy, and his hand would draw back for the blow.

"I can't. But, I can do this!" I rammed my fingers in his hair and mussed up every single tiny bit of it until the waves stood near on end.

"And this!" I reached into his suit coat and pulled his shirt from his slacks so that the tail hung out on one side.

"And this." With the sole of my Mary-Janes, I scuffed one shiny shoe.

His laughter echoed through the old neighborhood until doors began to open. I dragged him by the hand into the house and poured him a drink from Del's liquor cabinet. He leaned on the counter while I made two crab salads. He watched me, his eyes questioning and gentle. I was struck by how handsome he was with his hair in disarray and his eyes on me.

The telephone rang. At my nod, he answered it.

His eyes went three shades darker, his jaw tightened, he didn't take his eyes off me as I moved around the kitchen.

When he slammed the phone receiver into the cradle, I jumped.

"Olivia, damn it, I'll not hurt you. Ever!" With two long strides, he had me by my upper arms. The kiss was quick and hard. "There."

Feron turned down the hall. Next moment, he was back valise in hand, his blue eyes like sheet ice. His shirt tucked in, his hair combed, his shoes buffed. I didn't dare ask. He put the valise on the floor then pulled his money clip from his front pocket. He placed the bills in my hands and folded my fingers around them.

"I'd hoped to stay, can't. When I return, I'll ask again, and you'll say yes."

He took long strides across the lawn, shoeshine be damned, his suit coat flapping. He waved as he pulled away in his red rental car. I watched until he turned from my sight.

EVERYONE HAD ASSURED FERON on Monday that all of the new documents, except my expedited passport, would arrive the following week. Tuesday, I made plans. As soon as my teacher's certificate came with my new name on it, I would take it and my birth certificate to Marge. We'd talked off the record. The substitute, it turned out was no substitute for me. Marge promised to support my attempt to get my job back with the District.

Just after noon, a realtor parked out front and pounded a For Sale sign into the front lawn. I crossed my sweat pant clad legs and flipped to the rental section of the newspaper hoping to find the house of my dreams. Feron's latest loan was still fanned out on the kitchen counter. He had peeled off a thousand dollars. Now my kitchen smelled like Feron.

The telephone rang. The minute I lifted the receiver, Gail snapped, "Bitch!"

The line went dead.

I was staring at the phone when someone knocked on the front door. I frumped to the door in my sweat pants, ragged tee-shirt, and bare feet. Concerned who it might be after Gail's hang-up, I peered through the peephole. No one was there. I went to the kitchen window for a different angle. A second more demanding knock rattled the bolt.

I stretched over the sink to the kitchen window to get a view of the front door. The For Sale sign was in the gutter, crumpled under the tires of a newly parked car. The metal stand lay on the lawn, its rods bent. Two divots of grass showed where the stand had been.

A third knock brought me to the door. Through the peephole, I saw the back of a man's head. His dark wavy hair in tangles, his shoulders set as if he wasn't through with the mangled sign. When he turned to face the door, I yanked it open. His left arm was in a sling. The right pocket of his poplin sailing jacket bulged. His right hand was fisted ready to knock. I watched fury wash from Whitelaw's gray eyes the moment they met mine.

I led him by the hand to the dining room. Whitelaw struggled to pull the lump out of the pocket of his jacket. I held the corner of the jacket down to help him. He handed me a small ring box with a dime store ribbon stuck on top. We sat opposite each other. I put the box on the table between us. He wound his fingers in mine and nodded for me to open it. I fingered the lip of the lid, fearing what it was, unsure of his intent.

"Feron said you seemed awash, that he felt inadequate. He never feels inadequate. He's a most adequate man. Unlike me, I'm at sea most of the time. I struggle to do right."

"My phone rang Thursday night, was it you?"

"Peggy came in waggling her finger at me. I had to hang up. I've been worried about you since."

"I didn't answer the call. I was, as Feron, says awash." He ran his fingers down my arm then tapped the box. I shook my head. I wasn't ready.

"Your father's dead." Brendan Whitelaw heard those words when he was eight, they brought him sorrow, changed his life in ways he couldn't have imagined. I suppose the relief he saw in my eyes caught him off guard, his eyes widened but for only a moment.

"Where did he wash up?"

"Belize. The coppers called yesterday. Feron's on his way down."

"Are either of you responsible?"

"Not intentionally." A small smile tipped the corners of Whitelaw's lips.

"Is that like taking the Fifth in the U.S?"

"John admitted asking Del to fence Colin's Heart. Unknowingly, both Feron and I sent someone after Del. One a fake buyer, the other a fake copper."

"Why Belize?"

"He made the sale in Cartagena then tripped to Belize. He and his lady were spending like drunken sailors. When our people converged, there was a bit of a bruggadown. They called for orders. Feron told the copper to leave Del where he found him. I told the buyer to get the money. So, they got the money and left him where they found him. I think Feron's forever at my mercy." He pushed the box toward me.

"I need to know if this is for me, not for my prize. I need to know if you and Feron flipped for me again."

Whitelaw grasped my hand, holding tight as though if he let go, I'd run. He gathered his words carefully, "Whatever Feron said he meant. Of course, your shares likely played a part. Crispin is raging. I'd be suspicious of me as well. With you, I keep the prize, without you I lose. Come November, I may be nothing but a beat up mooncusser with a squandered law practice and a two-bedroom apartment over Lacy's."

He rested his left arm on his right to take the pressure off his shoulder. Small lines webbed the edges of his eyes. I studied their slight almond shape accented by long black lashes. I pulled the box toward me. A smile radiated from his eyes emerging in the curl of his broad mouth.

Danny covered the ring box with his right hand. "Before you open this, you should know that Collier kept all of the properties his brothers bought, but Pendu. Best owned that. Pendu has always been the only plantation, other than Perfidia, able to control both Perfidia and Bajan White. Feron and I agree that no matter who wins the vote, the entailment of Vent Amer to the Harris family is revoked, and ownership returned to Perfidia in payment of back leases. The documents condoning this are in the inheritance box that would still be missing had you not interfered."

Whitelaw cocked his head. "The fate of Perfidia rests on your shoulders, girl. Whoever you choose, you'll be landed again. The stock will remain yours to vote. Feron or me?"

He raised my hand to his lips and kissed each fingertip. When he finished, I lifted the lid off the box, pulled the tissue paper apart. I expected a ring; I got Colin's Heart. The bold blue diamond flared in the beams of the overhead light. I folded the tissue paper over it, dousing its light, put the lid on then slid the box back to him. Of course, I knew what it meant. It was his promise to me. Had he bought it back or freed it? He was capable of either.

He studied me. I saw the small boy seated on his father's arm, his father holding his mother. The best of both of them played across his handsome face, as he spoke, "I've wanted you since that first night when I saw you entranced by the windmill sweeping away the stars. We're the same. I live with old pain, you with new. I need you. Feron doesn't."

"He said he'd come back for me."

"You'll be mine by then."

With either man, Perfidia would be mine. With one I would have joy but always wonder, with the other I would have the wind at my sails.

Whitelaw ran his finger down my cheek. His eyes under his dark arching eyebrows were the lightest blue imaginable, the gray had so softened. His chair screeched on the tile floor. He rounded the table. I stood. He wound me in his arms as he had on the verge then kissed me as though he could lose me in a minute.

He wouldn't.

Perfidia would be ours. Controlling interest in Bajan White would remain mine. There would be two boys and a girl, ten grandchildren, and our two dear friends; Lloyd, who was ever my best friend, and Feron, who was right. All was forgiven when Feron married one of the radiant Winslow daughters of Apolima. Our children, theirs and ours, would spend each summer as a tribe. Both Lloyd and Feron would profess their love to me regularly, much to my husband's adoring chagrin. Together, my three young pirates would ensure that the sun never set on Bajan White.

Of course, I didn't know any of that then only that I could reef my sails whenever the Southern Cross hung low on the horizon.

Acknowledgements

This is a novel. It is true to the spirit and history of Barbados. Perfidia and the characters occupying it are imaginary. Sam Lord's Castle burned to the ground in 2010, a new resort is built on the site. The pirate legends live on. Drax Hall remains open to the public.

I would like to offer my thanks to my parents who gave me the best high school graduation present of all time—a summer in Barbados and to the wonderful Bajans who spoiled us and told us stories of their country.

This book resulted. I hope you enjoyed it. If you did, please let others know either via word of mouth or by posting a review online. If you're shy, consider buying a copy of my next book, *Dead Legend,* the first book of the Cooper Quartet. In 1955, legendary Navy ace, Mac Cooper, leaves a legacy of suicide and scandal. Twelve years later, with Vietnam in full-throttle, his sons, a Marine Sergeant and a Navy attack pilot, must resolve the past even if the truth about Mac's death destroys them.

About The Author

D. Z. Church has lived in the Eastern, Mid-Western and Western United States. Church served in the U.S. Navy as a Division, Security, and Public Affairs Officer and has worked since as an award-winning advertising Creative Director, and in educational assessment operations, sales, and proposal management.

Made in the USA
San Bernardino, CA
09 July 2020